Siren

HAZEL GRACE

 PLAYLIST

Lovely: BILLIE EILISH FEAT KHALID

There's No Way: LAUV FEAT JULIA MICHAELS

I Found: AMBER RUN

Ocean Eyes: BILLIE EILISH

The Ghost of You: MY CHEMICAL ROMANCE

Saferwaters: CHEVELLE

Dedication

FOR SHEEP, MOO MOO, BONASHA AND BAE

PROLOGUE

Davina

The piercing blow of a horn jolts through the night air and under the star-filled sky that partners up with the full-lit moon. It illuminates the danger we're in, the bad decision of coming here so soon after their treasure was dropped off because they're back again.

But they usually don't come back until weeks later.

Three pirates surround my two sisters and I as my father's words repeat sternly in my head, forbidding us to come here. Alluding to the peril of what could happen to us in the warmer water that meant we're heading too far south and into territory that doesn't welcome my kind.

They shouldn't have seen us.

The crystal blue water must've glimmered just right for them to see the glitch of our tails because the hollers of men have yet to cease.

Especially when my sister, Rohana, was taken first.

Thick netting wraps around her body as they hoist her up the tall wooden ship. My sister, Kali, hasn't stopped screaming in terror with each staggered lift that leads Rohana closer to the deck. The blood-curdling wails and the shouts of men are the only two things I hear until Kali takes a staggered breath next to me followed by a loud creak of something behind us, whining against the waves.

"There's another ship," Kali stammers in the water alongside me, bumping into my side. "They're going to throw their nets."

I glance over my shoulder at the ship with a mermaid silhouette decorating the front of it, catching my next inhale and sending a tremor down my spine.

These aren't just any kind of pirates—they're Hunters.

Men who take my people and sell them for profit. Who, according to my eldest sister, do the most unimaginable things to us.

We're called beautiful, toxic, a fantasy in the sea with the voices of death. These men, they forget the other parts of what makes up a Siren—power. And it's fueled by the ocean, which they are currently sitting on right now.

"Make them turn the boat," I tell my sister. "I'm going to make a jump for Rohana."

"You can't," she screeches. "They'll take you too."

I fix her with a glare because we don't have the time to argue like we always do. I didn't want her to come in the first place, but for once, I'm glad she did because I'm not good at singing.

"We'll all be taken if you don't sing," I retort, watching the ship sail closer toward us. Their nets are already prepped along their starboard side and ready to drop around us if we don't make a move to stop them.

Kali hesitates for only a second before nosediving beneath the chilly water. I do the same, going straight to the ocean floor before flipping back around and barrelling through the crest of waves. The moment I breach them, my body is in the air, arms outstretched to clasp the web of ropes that holds my other sister.

Rohana's hand covers mine instantly the moment my fingers wrap around fibers. "Let go!"

I don't respond, too focused on securing myself and taking the risk of letting go with one hand so I can reach into my bag that's wrapped around my body.

"Hold on to me," I order, looking into her lavender eyes. "Don't let me go."

She nods, and I release my hold, dipping into my pouch filled with trinkets I took from Sunset Cove and searching for the knife I always carry with me. Metal and gems clash against my flesh as I shuffle around the numerous relics.

"Please just let go," Rohana frets louder. "Please."

I ignore her again, I'm good at that. But the listening to my father part could use some work. With six older sisters, I'm used to being picked on and told what to do. I've adapted to disregarding their thoughts when I don't agree with them because they don't see the world as I do. They don't share the same fascination of there being more to life than the ocean. My books show me that, the castles and the piers, the fields of green grass and sand nestled up close to the ocean's border called a beach.

I want to see more, to know more.

My index finger touches the familiar feel of the handle I am looking for, and I clasp my hand around it. But it's not before I hear the shouts of deep male voices sounding uncomfortably close.

"Get her over the deck," one bellows.

"There's two!" another one yells. Rohana's grip tightens around mine, and my blood sprints through my body and straight to my heart that's barely able to continue beating.

I will never let my sister go, not now or ever. And not to a bunch of Hunters who will either butcher or peddle her off.

The net suddenly jerks closer to the ship, along with my attention, and lands on a young boy holding a stick that's looped within the mesh of the net.

He looks around my age, sandy brown hair and dark eyes. Our faces practically align with each other less than two arm's length away.

Too close.

Alarm sounds in my head mixed with the instincts that I always try to nudge and propel away from me. His eyes widen, fastened on me as I do the same, in a stand-still moment where nothing moves and all sounds mute around us.

Opening his mouth, no words come out, and I can't help the shutter that shoots through my frame. I've never been this close to a human before, and he seems to share the sentiment because he's frozen along the railing of the ship.

Suddenly, I hear the hollers of men around us, breaking the hypnotic state I'm in, and it appears to do the same for him because he finally makes a move.

Reaching for something at his hip, I don't wait to see what it is —I just swing.

Cutting through the crisp air that dries my skin, I catch the side of his face with my blade. He drops his stick that keeps us close to the ship, his hands immediately going to the place where I sliced him while the net swings away.

"Get them overboard boy!"

"Swing the net," I tell my sister.

"What?"

"Swing the net," I repeat. "They won't be able to bring us around easily." Rohana uses her body weight, leaning forward and backward while still holding on to my hand.

As carefully as I can so I don't accidentally cut myself, I begin my attempt to sever some of the rope. In the process, the unpredictable net goes in every single direction possible, pumping my adrenaline through my eardrums and increasing the burn coursing through the pads of my fingers.

Then my knife breaks through a piece of binding.

Trying to study the progress while being thrashed through the air, our reality slaps me in the face. With the number of men on this ship and just the two of us, we're never getting out of this.

One small piece and it's not enough to free her.

"Davina." It's a demand to pay attention, to accept the inevitable that I know has transpired between Rohana and I.

We're the closest in age, the two sisters who like similar things, share our wildest dreams late at night, and delve into all the stupid things I want to do.

And coming this far south is by far the most brainless of them all.

I'm going to lose my sister tonight. Lose her over a stupid excursion because I wanted to add more to my collection of trinkets and dodads. Rohana wanted to come, she always does. This time around, Kali caught us, so that's how she ended up here, but it was Rohana that never left my side. She was my other half, my confidant and best friend.

And I just gave her life up for an old, forgotten cove of riches.

"You have to let go now," my sister digresses. "It's okay." Her voice sounds so sure and not scared anymore, it's more accepting than anything.

It rings my gut inside out, a sharp pain hitting the pit of it as she rubs my fingers with hers in a soothing rhythm.

I violently shake my head. "Let me try some more."

Her now dehydrated hand tightens around mine. "It's no use," she says calmly. "You won't be able to in time."

My head shoots up to her. How does she think I'd ever be able to let her go? I'd die for all six of my sisters in a moment's time before I'd let anything happen to them.

I feel my fingers being pried away from the net. One at a time as she starts to loosen my hold on her prison.

"Rohana," I snap, trying to close my fingers tightly back around the rope. "Stop."

I see a tear trail down her cheek as she stays focused on my white-knuckled hand, staring at the only piece of my body that links me to her.

I won't leave her.

I. Will. Not. Leave. Her.

"Davina—" She breaks into a sob. "—please."

My brows furrow as tears burn the back of my eyes. "I won't leave you behind."

"You have to, Sister. You have to save Kali."

"She's fine," I retort, still squeezing my fingers as hard as I can over the rope. Tucking my blade back into my bag, I grasp the net with my other hand.

"Tell Papa I love him," she recites through bated breath. "I love you, too."

"You're not going anywhere," I seethe. "We're going to get out of this."

She shakes her head, halting her work on my fingers. "I'm not, but you are. You must. I will find my way back home."

You won't—it's at the tip of my tongue. No Siren who has ever been caught escaped from the clutches of humans, especially with Hunters.

I glance over at the ship's deck, men are running amok and shouting orders, but my gaze falls back to that boy who I cut moments ago. His eyes are still locked on me, standing by a tall wooden pillar in the center of the ship.

My arms strain and tremble from my own weight as I demand my strength to stay put. I will never let go of this rope while my sister still lays in this man-made prison.

The boy holds his hand out to me, in a silent greeting I think, then pulls out his long sword with the other. Another moment passes before he moves again, he's too far away for me to read his eyes, but his face speaks of grief and sadness.

Then he swings.

I don't know at what, I don't see it. All I see is myself falling toward the water and into the darkness of the shadows that are cast over by the ship.

Dagen

CHAPTER ONE
DΛGEᴎ

My skull is slammed into a wall, followed by a stiff jab to my rib cage. A sharp grunt escapes my lips, but I don't feel much of anything other than the adrenaline fleeting through every nerve in my body. A large hand grips the base of my scalp, yanking my head back by the strands of my long hair.

That I feel.

My booted foot recoils and propels backward into my captor's shin. The other man is already prepared, bashing into the back of my shoulder with both of his fists. Without the use of my hands, that are currently bound by rope, my knees give out slightly until I'm hit a second time, bringing me to the pristine white floors.

My face immediately jolts to the side, backhanded by the man I've just kicked. The taste of metal hits my tongue, and I feel the slow trickle of blood start to stream down my face.

I spit, glancing up at the blond-haired man who just hit me like a woman. Weather-beaten skin, middle-aged, and dark brown eyes that try to intimidate me with a glower. The brawny lads on either side of me don't have the desired intimidating effect.

I've faced worse.

Worse than these two fools that believe dragging and smacking me around is going to induce any fear within me.

I've faced a battlefield full of hundreds of men—two aren't going to do it.

Especially knowing what I was possibly walking into the moment I volunteered to carry on my father's mission.

Or so I thought.

I've never been up close to one, only heard Father's stories of how alluring and dangerous *they* were.

Calculated and vicious things.

Men sang songs about the beautiful creatures that lured a man to his death by a ballad, or even a look. How you felt like a passenger in your own body with the power they wielded over it.

I'm having a hard time thinking it's going to be easy walking out of here alive though.

First of all, these men are strong. I jabbed one in the neck, where his gills were opening and closing, and was almost drowned after being battered with a rock. It only confirmed the stories because they had tails when they knocked me off my small boat and now they have legs.

That was my welcome here.

Now I'm inside a room that isn't like any sort of prison I've ever been held in, on my knees.

Everything is bright, colorful, and picturesque. Something of dreams and paintings that I've seen. The walls are turquoise glass rimming pearl white floors with gold etched into the tiles. There is no ceiling, the sunlight freely beaming down its rays into the room I'm in.

Wherever I look, every item is from the sea, as though we're there. Coral makes up the legs of the chairs, what looks to be a large sand dollar is a table.

It's the cleanest room I've ever seen in my life, not a speck of dirt but myself and my spoiled clothing dawns the room. Along with the salt water dripping off my clothes, making a small puddle around me.

The men at my sides stand abruptly to attention, faces turned toward the door of the room. A glint of white hits my peripheral as I glance over at a beautiful woman with blinding white hair in the doorway.

The top of her shoulders glint from pearl-colored scales that adorn her skin. An ivory crown made of seashells rests on top of her head as she strides deeper into the room, her sole focus locked on me.

My heart kicks up in unison to her steps as I study her in return. She looks like nothing I've ever seen in my life. All her features—eyes, brows, skin, and hair are a shade of perfect white.

Like an angel.

Only I know it's not going to feel like being in heaven based on the greeting I received before my ass even stepped foot on this island.

I watch her chin lift in defiance, telling me that she's someone important—though I already got that with the crown. With such a small gesture, she conveys that anything I try to do in this room will not frighten her, but there will be consequences.

Too bad I don't take any personal interest in fear because I'm too busy invoking it in other people. Filling people with dread seems to be second nature for me, so when she moves closer, nothing but annoyance filters through my body.

Another body enters the room, this time the color blue filling in the features of hair, eyes, and shiny scales, not on her shoulders but forearms. A cerulean jewel hangs off of her shelled crown, hovering slightly over her forehead.

Twins, they are identical save for their different hued appearances.

I inhale a deep breath just for it to be sucked right from my lungs, because two more females march through the door. Not twins this time but just as unique as the first two.

The taller one with pink characteristics and the other all black.

"What the fuck," I mutter to myself, reaching up to rub one of my temples, but I'm restrained by the plant-like rope pulling my wrists back.

All alluring women.

All women my men would love to sink their dicks into.

Pure. Clean. Angelic.

But since I know better, the last couldn't be further from the truth. They are masked with beautiful features but have the hearts and minds of merciless killers.

I'm yanked to my feet as they all stand united in front of me, viewing me like an animal that just ate half their cattle.

It only makes me straighten my spine, ready for whatever plans or actions they may inflict on me.

"Intruder," the white-haired woman proclaims, taking one step closer. The longer she stares, the more her milky brows furrow.

I continue to stay silent because, well, she never asked me a question.

Another steps to her side, the woman with black hair and even darker eyes. The contrast between the two, the light and the dark, isn't lost on me.

Neither is their curiosity because our people have had very limited, if any, interactions with each other. We don't roam this part of the sea much, keeping to the northern lands to take what we want. But my father wanted what was here, hence why I'm standing in front of four women who look bemused, wicked, and hungry.

"He's part of a colony," the pink vixen announces with rose-colored eyes and tan skin. She moves, rounding her two fellow friends, and continues toward me. "A warrior."

"What else?" the white-haired woman asks.

"He came with many men."

"To kill us all," snaps the blue featured female, clutching her hands into fists at her side.

"Silence," White commands, holding up a single hand to seize any further chatter. "What else do you see, Isolde?"

"He has a woman," she continues, her attention slowly falling down the length of my body, and I stiffen my spine. Then she wrinkles her dainty nose. "Who dresses like a man."

My eyes narrow. Edda wasn't unattractive, but she wasn't like the creatures standing before me either. She was an amazing woman, would make a good mother and wife to any man lucky enough to have her.

Which was what my father wanted Edda to be for me. I just wasn't fully sold on the idea yet.

"He's too big," the blue one drones, and as soon as she speaks the words, a sudden rush of fury sprints through my body.

It sends a wave of exhilaration rippling along after it, and I can't stop it before my feet are pounding the slated floor, right for the woman in white.

My irises aim in on her petite frame as my right hand goes to my hip to grab my blade, but I'm still tied.

I don't need it—my head will do just fine.

I'm at least four steps away before the rage is sucked out of me. Calmness replaces my animosity as I stand dazed and breathless from the intensity of it.

What the fuck...

"Stop playing with him, Nesrine," my target decrees, still staring at me. I glimpse over to the woman highlighted in black, breaking from her companion and strutting toward me with confidence announcing every move of her hips.

"A woman dressed as a man?" she repeats, beginning a slow circle around me. "How does that work exactly?"

"She's dirty," the noisy and all-too-knowing woman, Isolde, continues. "Tall but skinny."

"Skinnier than you?"

She shakes her head, a piece of pink hair falling over one of her eyes. "No, but she's pretty."

The soft graze of fingertips brush my lower back, and I fight the urge to flinch and snap at the dark, alluring Siren that's circling me like prey. Taunting me with the caress of her skin along the fabric of my shirt.

"Pretty, you say?" Nesrine wonders then drops her voice. "I'd like to see what that looks like. I can't *imagine* these strong arms grasping on to a woman who isn't more than dazzling."

"He doesn't like it when you talk about her," Isolde bleats again, brushing her bottom lip with her tongue. A satisfied quirk playing off her mouth.

"I wouldn't want to talk about her either," Nesrine digresses. "Such a beautiful man to drop down before a woman who isn't just as lovely." She stops in front of me, her dark eyes leveling with my chest as she peers up, shards of silver now glimmering in them like the stars that twinkle in the sky.

Lifting her chin, her lips twist into a smile. "But maybe that's your problem. You lay with humans."

I grit my teeth, remaining silent because I won't be giving answers to any of their feeble-minded questions. Nor will I play into whatever little mind game she's attempting to act out.

"He isn't going to answer any of our questions," Isolde rattles off matter-of-factly.

"What do you do read *minds*?" I snap, my eyes boring into her.

So much for that.

I can't help the incapcitated feeling of being surrounded by women who have some sort of mental advantage over me because I can't fight that. I can't stop them unless my hands can be wrapped around their throats to *get* them to cease prying into my brain for their own personal use.

Isolde looks unaffected, giving a slight shrug of her shoulders. "Something like that."

I glare at her. "Then read *this* one, you little—"

"I knew he'd be positively delicious," Nesrine beams, rising and falling on her toes like a small child. "He looks like too much man to be easily intimidated."

"Let's just kill him and get it over with," the snow-colored one suggests.

"We don't make any decisions without all of us here," her twin voices. "You *know* that."

"And I also know that this is a waste of time," she hisses. "He's a *Viking*, they don't speak."

"Relax, Atarah," Nesrine exhorts, taking her own liberties and touching my forearm. "There are *always* ways of making a man talk."

I jerk away. "Don't touch me."

"How about shutting him up?" Atarah croons, raking her hand through her colorless hair. "We've wasted enough—"

"Not until we're all here," repeats the blue woman.

"I heard you, Brylee. Do we need to take a vote now on clamping his mouth shut?"

Nesrine grips my shirt and yanks me forward, my chest knocking into hers. But she doesn't budge from the impact, standing still as a stone wall.

"We could have a little fun while we wait," she offers, tone dripping with ideas I'm sure I'm unwilling to participate in.

Looking back down at her, raven hair cups her face twinned by eyes that are bottomless pools of darkness. Her ample breasts are barely covered in an equally dark-colored top that cuts down between the valley of them.

She is every man's fantasy that would quickly turn into a nightmare. The gorgeous she-devil in disguise that could lure any weak-minded man into bed, which would ultimately result in his death—the last fucking thing you see.

Nesrine bites her lower lip, her irises softening as she looks deeper into mine. "What do you say, Viking? How about I—" Her head suddenly snaps in the direction of the doorway.

Actually, all of theirs do.

Striding through the room now are two more women, one an exotic shade of orange and the other purple. But it's not until a third walks in that demands all of my attention.

In fact, she sucks it from me.

Long hair, the color of blood, cascades past her slim shoulders, reminding me of the bright shade of a flesh wound. It's a hue I wear frequently in battle that coats my face and clothing as I slice and thrust my sword into my enemies.

Her brilliant green eyes slam right into my chest before they roam up and lock onto my blues. A gold bustier covers her breasts with a string of pearls that dips down to her torso. A teal, see-through skirt shows off the curve of her hips, down her thighs to the floor. Each footprint exposes a piece of her legs as she comes to stand in front of me with the others.

"Glad you could join us," Nesrine muses, still next to me. "You almost missed all the fun." Red doesn't speak, just stops next to Atarah and moves her attention to the woman still in front of me.

Nesrine scoffs loudly. "*Why?*"

I look around the room for a statement I must have missed because silence still permeates through the space. Except for the humming my body is experiencing in response to the latest newcomer in the room.

I clench my teeth, aggravated all to hell, reminding myself that I have control over my being all the time. Careful not to lose my temper too much, not to make rash decisions, but it seeped from my bones the moment *she* walked into the room.

And I'm torn between wrapping my hands around her throat or ripping the rest of her skirt off her hips.

It's the Siren devilry. Nothing more or less.

I may have never met a Siren before, seen one in real life, but it does *nothing* to my rationality of being a warrior except keeping placid, on guard, and ready to fight.

"Just do what she says," Atarah conveys, rubbing one of her temples.

To my surprise, Nesrine moves and steps in line with the redhead who just entered the room.

Seven—fucking hell.

The seven points of the sea.

The seven temptresses of Lacuna standing in front of me as a united presence, and the undercurrent of the room just changed the moment the new one walked in.

The seven daughters of King Triton.

My mind fuddles around as my eyes ping pong off each of them.

All different.

All dangerous.

All going to make my life a living purgatory.

I'm at a disadvantage because my people don't know much about these creatures, just folklore that has been passed down through the centuries. I've heard how they use their voices to sing men to their deaths. How pirates purposely ward off these waters. My clansmen don't listen to legends and myths from raiders who are already dishonest in the first place, with their manipulative nature. However, walking onto this island, I only expected to face *some* trouble.

Not seven women who obviously possess powers that I've

never experienced and no known defense to protect myself from.

Storm blue hair flips over Brylee's shoulders as she says defiantly, "We're not going to leave you alone."

"We're in this together," adds the creature with golden burnt eyes that are currently burrowing into me.

My own zero in on the new visitor.

It's then that I realize *she's* the leader. The moment they all stood alongside her, showed their loyalty and support, I knew she'd be the one I'd speak to about where we go from here.

"Who are you?" I ask her, clenching my hands that are tied behind me into fists.

Silence—from all of them.

It leaves an eerie and unsteady prickle whisping up my spine. The unknown, that's what I've just walked into. I've always been familiar with my enemies, learned their weaknesses and strengths to protect my men in the throngs of battle.

But they are beings I know nothing about bringing to their knees so I can escape from here.

I never thought I'd die in stillness. Always thought it'd be in the ruptures of combat with men screaming and howling on a grassy valley surrounded by mountains.

Not in a place that looks like paradise with women who aren't really the definition of what I'm used to.

"Now that she walked into the room you all don't know how to speak?" I challenge, looking down the line of them.

"Keep your mouth shut," Brylee snaps.

"We'll decide later what to do with you," Atarah announces. "But first, we have questions."

"I don't have any answers," I reply.

"You do, and we *will* know them." I glance at the new arrival, but she stays quiet.

"Can't help you," I deadpan. Atarah's shoulders tense before she flexes her slim fingers.

At my defiance, the late arrival steps forward. Her head cocks to the side as her leaf green eyes fixate on me. They don't match her hair like the rest of her sisters, her skin is fair in contrast to the different shades of the others.

My knees start to tingle as her scrutiny draws up the length of my legs, hitting my abdomen then my chest again.

I'm not scared, I wasn't when I walked in here, but my breathing quickens suddenly as sweat starts to form on my forehead and palms. I can feel the graze of her irises swift over my broad shoulders, then I feel a jolt from my hips.

Instantly, one of the hidden blades from my pants is in her small hands while she holds it up in front of her face, studying the engravings that Edda had done for me, to keep me safe.

So much for that...

She turns her head over her shoulder, listening to something, but no sound emits through the room. Then her eyes abruptly land back on mine.

I perk a brow. "Don't know how to talk to a man, wench?" She remains emotionless, passive. Maybe she doesn't understand what I'm saying.

Her index finger brushes the tip of my blade, and I'm hoping it draws blood, but it doesn't. A few of the women giggle behind her, but I'm too centered on the woman in front of me.

I don't trust her next move.

I don't know what kind of role she plays with all of them, but she's something different from the rest. They obviously all speak, but she doesn't need to apparently.

Shorter than the rest, more beautiful, but more miserable. I can see it, hiding behind the tints of all those greens in her eyes. Yet, she stands firmly in front of me, alluding no fear as I tower over her.

"He's Dagen the Blood Axe," Isolde announces. "The son of their leader."

"Really?" Nesrine marvels. "I thought he was just a myth."

"He will be soon," another one says. My concentration doesn't break from the she-devil in front of me, twisting my weapon around as she gapes at it like it's a treasure of some kind.

"Know how to use it, Princess?" I taunt, leaning down a tad closer. "Because I don't have all day if you're going to kill me."

She flicks her gaze back to me, unamused, with a speck of rebelliousness glinting in it.

No, she's different—something doesn't feel right about her.

"We have somewhere to be," another one of them speaks up, but the red Siren doesn't move, still gawking at me.

"*Davina*," adds another. I smirk, now knowing her name. Perhaps I can coax her to my side so she'll set me free.

The tip of my blade suddenly appears, pressed into the side of my face, near my left eye.

Blood, that's what I'll call her.

After all, she wants mine, changed her mind that quickly from being the mute bystander to holding my own weapon against my skin.

Slowly, my blade creeps downward, creating a dull pain from the steel etching into my flesh.

"Don't mess his face up too badly," Nesrine muses, her voice already one I recognize from her big-ass mouth. "We don't want *his* blood staining our floors."

She doesn't stop, transfixed on my face; looking for distress, to see how *human* I am. I ball my hands into fists to keep from headbutting her pretty little face. Any sign of violence on my end and it will quicken my death.

"Enjoying yourself?" I provoke, feeling my skin ripping open.

Nothing.

Not a flicker of amusement or even a slight smirk to announce her contentment. It's only then that it slowly starts to sink in, this isn't a normal capture.

I won't be held a prisoner for information about who I am and what I can do for them.

I'm here to quench their thirst for humans.

CHAPTER TWO

Davina

"He has to die," my eldest sister, Atarah, decides, pacing in front of the long table in our dining room. "He's too much of a liability."

Nesrine scoffs, flipping her raven hair over her shoulder. "Liability to whom?"

"To *us*," Atarah snaps. "To *her*." She points at me, almost convicting. Almost forgetting that I'm more powerful than her and all my sisters combined.

What doesn't work in my favor is being the youngest of seven daughters, and being treated as such while I'm the one who's given up the most for them.

"Davina can take care of herself," Nesrine counters. "We need to know how he got through the veil."

"There's only one way," Isolde decrees, strumming her fingers on the polished wood table. All eyes fall on her as she pushes her black-rimmed glasses over the bridge of her nose. "He's a siren."

Some of my sisters laugh, one of them scoffs, to me—she's right.

The spell that was cast down around this island was so only our people could walk on it freely without restraints of water. A protective veil which made the island invisible to anyone that wasn't a siren.

"Unless *someone* forgot to put the veil back up," Brylee

alludes, leisurely bringing her attention to Kali. "Someone has been forgetful as of late."

"I have not," Kali snaps, her amber eyes turning into slits. "And even if I did, Davina always covers for me." Now I'm under six pairs of eyes, and I narrow mine.

I double-check the veil over two dozen times a day, and it hasn't needed *covering* in days.

Unless the Viking has been here for days.

I try to think back on when I last had to secure Kali's inattentiveness, but it's hard when the days blend together. Each day on Merindah, our island, seems like a lifetime, and it was never supposed to be or feel like this.

It was presumed to be heaven, an escape from being under the sea. To experience what it felt like to have the sand under our feet and the sun beaming on our faces.

That's how it started until we learned the price we had to pay for it.

"Regardless," Atarah counters. "He's a waste of time and space. A waste of food, which we are limited to in the first place."

"*Regardless*," Nesrine opposes back. "We need information, to know for sure how he got past the veil and to make sure no one else does. *Especially* since Davina is here alone."

"We can take turns staying with her," Brylee offers. "I mean, we kinda do anyway."

"*No.*" I don't say the words out loud, but they hear them. They hear them because I chose for them to.

One of the sacrifices I've made to allow my sisters to be free from this island.

"Davina," Atarah soothes gently like a motherly figure, a position she's taken up since ours was murdered. "It's too dangerous with him here. He's a *Viking*."

Nesrine begins to fan herself with a smirk. "And holy mother of the sea, he's handsome."

"I'm fine." I counter.

"But—"

"She's not going to let you kill the man," Nesrine voices, with a slice of her hand through the air. "I'm sure she has ideas of her own." She peers over her shoulder at me, the corners of her lips curving into a devious smirk.

"I'm sure it's not what you're thinking," I rebuke.

Nesrine shrugs. "You're loss, little one."

"Do you have a plan?" Brylee asks as the sea breeze blows through the window and picks up her blue hair, wrapping it around her forehead.

There's only one that I have in mind, and I prefer to do it when my sisters leave the island, but knowing them, one will stay.

"I'd like to question him," I convey. *"He might have some—"*

"He isn't going to speak," Atarah retorts.

"You don't know that," I quip.

Actually, I do.

The man looks like he'd rather be tortured to death than respond to anything I'd want to ask him.

I don't mind having my sisters tear into him. In fact, it may give him a reality check of the dangers he ensued when he brought it upon himself to come here. And my fear is that I know *why* he came.

"Your Majesties." We turn to look at one of our enforcers, Sullivan, standing a few feet back. "Captain Tobias Nathaniel is here to see you."

He's bombarded with simultaneous demands, ordering him to make him leave, to bring him inside the castle, what did he bring this time—the same sort of chaos that always brews when you have seven women trying to make a decision and never agreeing on one thing.

Except once—when we all decided to go to the sea witch, Taysa, and obtain this island as our own.

Sullivan looks at me, knowing I'll end up having the final say anyway. I've already upset half my sisters today by not wanting to make any rash decisions on getting rid of the Viking, so I let them hash it up amongst themselves.

I shrug at him, my sisters still arguing over my friend that keeps coming back to the island to either barter off things he brings with him or try to win over Atarah, who hates him with every fiber of her being.

When in actuality, it's a front.

He's just here to spend time with me, and he's the exemption to our rule—well mine under severe feuding with most of my sisters. Rohana and Kali don't mind him because he saved us that night from the Hunters. The rest of my relations are a mix of irritation, concern, and laid-back.

We don't let pirates near Merindah, they don't get that far before we kill them. Or as Nesrine likes to call it, "play with them."

But Tobias Nathaniel is different—he's fearless, stupid, and my *best* friend.

Which leads to an ongoing issue with Atarah and Brylee because he too can pass through the veil with no understanding of why. And the not knowing leaves us all a little restless.

He's not a siren, Brylee practically drowned him one year to see if it'd spark any traits or tendencies within him. Other than him coughing up water for a few minutes and almost dying in the process, he failed the test.

And if the Viking isn't a siren either, what other kinds of creatures could get past the veil?

It leaves so many posing questions amongst us, ones we need to ask Taysa because something is wrong with the spell.

"Let him in," Nesrine bellows, chuckling at my sister's scowls. "I know Davina wants to know what he brought."

Sullivan bows his head before leaving while my sisters

start in on my third eldest sister and her chancy bias of my friend.

"Ladies," a male voice greets cheerily as Nesrine looks over her shoulder and gives me a wink. She steps aside, letting me take in Tobias as he enters with a small chest in his hands. "How are you today?"

"Inconvenienced," Atarah pipes in, crossing her ivory arms along her chest. "I thought I told you to stop coming here or there would be consequences to your defiance."

Tobias might like to mock the reality of what we could do to him, but I'd never let it get that far, no matter how many times Atarah threatens his life. She always seems to forget the simple, yet complicated fact that he released Rohana from the net she was held captive in and the reason why she's not three sisters short.

I watch him smile, his boyish good looks could melt any normal woman's demeanor down, if he was around any normal *human* women. My sisters are unaffected by his humor and charm but a quarter of us like him—myself, Rohana, and Nesrine.

Kali is torn between paranoid and gratefulness. Skeptical because her voice should have impaired his and the crew's ears that day, but he was unaffected. The moment my head broke over the waves, he was peering over the rail, looking down at us when he should've been dazed, confused, and possibly ready to step over the side.

As much as my impulse tells me I shouldn't care about a human, let alone a boy that was on a Hunters' ship of all things, but I'm glad he's here—*most* of the time.

"Ah, yes," Tobias falters. "But you forget that I'm *used* to living in the face of danger, my little snowflake."

Atarah steps in his direction, her eyes turning the frosty white that they do when she is on the verge of losing her temper. "Don't call me by your *nicknames* like it's going to soothe my ongoing irritation with you, Tobias. You're riding on my last nerve."

Tobias gently places the chest on the floor and holds out his hands. "No disrespect, Your Majesty." He looks over at me. "But your little sister seems to like what I bring, and, well, I have quite the collection today."

"I'm assuming you didn't bring any of your human friends on the island as well," Nesrine exhorts.

Tobias glances at her. "No, they're all too scared to venture past the mist. They think it's haunted."

"You're a fool," Atarah spouts, balling her hands into fists. "You bring your men close to our home to capture us and—" That's when Tobias's attention snaps back to her.

He hates when he's accused of bringing people to hurt us. That he'd betray me in any way, shape, or form.

And I believe him.

He's never steered me wrong. Never did he treat my sisters with disrespect, if anything he tried to force his charm on each one of them in hopes that they'd all welcome him with open arms.

Let's just say he had his work cut out for him.

"Amongst other things, I'm a fool, yes," he leers. "But a traitor, not in this lifetime, snow bunny."

Atarah takes another step forward, but Nesrine moves in front of her. "And what do you want in return for these items that you keep bringing?" she asks.

His brown eyes fall on me. "To see your sister smile for once." I roll mine, which gets him to chuckle.

"Did you bring something for me?" Rohana asks him, hands clasped together to keep her excitement in check.

Tobias reaches into his long brown leather coat and pulls out something but keeps it hidden in his palm. My sister skips to him, stopping when she's a foot away, impatiently waiting for him to reveal what he's brought.

19

Extending his palm, a soft gasp leaves my sister's lips before she snatches it.

"Oh, Davina!" She twirls on her heels, holding up what looks to be a gold chain with a large purple gem hanging off it. "It matches."

I crack a grin. *"It's beautiful."*

Nesrine walks in Tobias's direction and bumps his shoulder purposely while stating, "Good luck with that."

Striding from the room, the rest of my sisters follow her but not before Atarah gets to make her final comment, of course.

"The next time you step foot on this island, *pirate*, make sure you bring someone for my sisters and I to play with. We don't like it when someone plays favorites."

She bumps his other shoulder then sends me a warning look before withdrawing from the room.

Rohana ignores Atarah's hostility, clearly in her own state of euphoria, because her lavender hair wraps around Tobias's shoulder as she gives him a hug. Mumbling a quick thank-you, she scurries out, following the rest of my siblings.

Tobias sighs, adjusting his brown coat, and brings his attention to me. "I swear, one day she's going to kill me."

"She'll have to go through Rohana first." The left side of his mouth quirks as he picks up his chest and rests it on the dining room table, rust sprinkling onto the surface.

"I'm sorry that it's taken me so long to come back with things, got caught up in Port Thetis but..." Tobias cracks the lip of the chest as it whines in protest, expressing its age and the amount of time it hasn't been opened. "I brought you this, Princess."

Gems of different colors; reds, blues, and greens along with long strings of pearls fill most of the bottom—but it's the small dagger on the top that gets my full attention.

One like the Viking's.

It's beautiful, no special encrusted gems or engravings embellish the weapon except for the etched lines down the middle of the knife. The handle is black and gold while the blade makes a sharp descent into a fine point.

How many stories this weapon must have—the bloodshed, the crusades it could've sailed or marched on. Every object has a story, and that's one of the best curiosities and wonders I have about each thing Tobias brings me.

"Of all things, you pick the blade," Tobias chortles with a shake of his head. "I bring you rare jewels, you choose the most dangerous thing out of the chest."

I ignore him, turning it in my hands and examining any hidden clue of its past or journey.

"I'll keep the rest of it here for you in case you change your mind. Give some to your sisters," he voices. "There's enough for you there. And speaking of, I better leave before your sister makes good on her word."

I don't respond, still studying the new item to add to my assembly.

"I might not see you for a few weeks, I have to go make good on my own word with another pirate who stole something from me." I can feel his eyes on me. "So take care of yourself."

I hear him walk away, all the things around his waist clacking and clicking together.

"Don't you dare come in here giving me gifts then tell me you're going to go fight your stupid human battles." I hear him halt. *"What did they take from you?"*

"It's more like whom—they have my brother."

My head jerks up to him with plummeted brows. *"I thought you said he was dead."*

"I thought he was."

"Then how do you know otherwise?"

"I've been searching for him."

"Tobias," I say softly. *"Why haven't you told me?"*

He gives me a feeble grin. "Didn't want to get your hopes up."

He means *his* hopes up.

Tobias's younger brother, Lorne, disappeared when they were children and, for about five years now, Tobias had exhausted all reports of him. No leads of a young man with a scar in the middle of his forehead that he followed were successful, and it only grew his ongoing irritation. To the point where Tobias suddenly stopped searching because each time cracked his heart more and more.

"Do you know if he'll be there when you arrive?" He shakes his head, averting his gaze from mine. I turn over the dagger in my hand. *"Take this, I want you to be safe."*

Tobias looks up to the blue sky. We don't have ceilings in the castle because it never rains, and I like the sun on my skin. "I have swords, little one."

I gesture toward it with my head. *"You humans can never have too many weapons. Take it."*

He reaches out his palm, and I gently place it there. "Thank you." I bow my head in acknowledgment. "I'll miss you."

I glance back up at him but don't say a thing.

"I miss us when we were children. Time has changed a lot of things."

"We grew up."

"But did we have to grow apart?"

No, we didn't. I've just been pushing him away because I didn't want Father to find him here. It wasn't safe, he'd kill Tobias, and there wouldn't be anything I could do about it.

My sisters, I could stop—the King of Lacuna, also son of Poseidon, there wouldn't be enough words for him to listen to make him decide to keep a human alive that's trespassed onto our island.

Everything got worse when I submitted myself to Merindah, my father became more on his guard, more weary of the sea. He has my sisters checking my every move, and the moment one of them leaks that a Viking is here—he'll die too.

His fingertips graze my cheek, and my body relaxes at his touch. "I think about you all the time."

"*I don't sing*," I retort. *"You're not sired to me in any way."*

"No, you just looked at me that night with challenge and fear in your eyes, and I knew that I'd never be the same after meeting you." I glance at the small scar on his left cheekbone from my knife that fateful night.

I owe Tobias everything, and in return, I'm saving his future by attempting to keep him away from this island—it hasn't been working very well.

I just never have the heart to make good on my word to hurt him the next time he comes to visit. It could also be because I'm selfish.

I enjoy the outside world coming into mine or the vexatious feeling of how much I care about him. Tobias was that breath of fresh air, the person who never made me feel like there wasn't a limit to what I could do.

"*You should go.*" The longer he stays, the more risk.

"But you don't want me to. I can see it in your green eyes."

"*I'm not a map, Tobias,*" I counter.

He grins. "No, you're just the X on mine."

Fixing him with an exasperated look, I never wanted him to be more than the boy on the boat. Never thought I'd see him again, until I did back at Coral Cove. He waited for me there, he said, for two weeks.

I should've let him starve to death.

But apparently I have a conscience, and he did the unthinkable going against his shipmates.

Which doesn't explain half of the things that's wrong with Tobias.

Things that can't be overlooked, but somehow I do because he's more than the boy who rescued us.

He's the man who may have stolen some of my heart.

"Thank you again," Tobias finally says when my silence has stretched to more than he can bear. "I'll bring you more things when I—"

"You might not want to come back," I cut in, not wanting to entertain the idea or excitement. *"My sisters are getting leerier. You don't belong here."*

Tobias smiles. "Do any of us belong?"

"Answering my question with another question won't get lost on me, Captain."

He lifts his shoulder with a half-shrug. "I tend to live on the dangerous side of life, Princess. No offense, but your sisters don't scare me. I might be a fool, but I'd travel around the sea twice to see your eyes light up at something small like a blade."

I fix my jaw, trying my best to look annoyed. *"You are a fool like Atarah says you are."*

He chuckles, tucking his chin into his chest. "Maybe I am. Regardless though—" He looks up at me. "I'll take my chances."

"You don't understand. There is a—"

"There isn't anything you're going to *say* to make me change my mind," Tobias alludes with a stern tone to his voice. "You're the only thing that makes my life—see you in a few days with some news." He turns on his heels, evading my effort to keep him free from harm.

And I'm not the only one in denial about what this is. How our friendship is a dangerous game we're playing and neither of us wants to fully stop.

"Tobias, please. You don't—"

"Why do you keep pushing me away?" he snaps, twirling back to face me. "What did I do?"

I open my mouth like old times. That's how they feel when we're together. When we were younger and wilder, more free and reckless.

I wish a thousand moons I could go back because I'd be able to talk to him out loud instead of in his head. For him to *hear* my anger and worry when I tell him that this is for the best.

Because it is, and I can't bear the thought of losing him. It'd be like losing my right arm, loss of function and ease.

"I've loved you forever," he censures. "But you weren't an option for me. I can't live *in* the sea and you couldn't live out of it. And now you're walking on an island, with legs and lungs that can withstand the air, but you don't want anything to do with me." He inches closer. "We used to dream about it, remember? You told me that we'd hold hands on the sand and let the waves sink our toes into the beach. You said you'd —" He stops, locking his jaw while his nostrils flare.

Tobias is an easygoing man, and it breaks my spirit to see him upset.

And to know that I'm the cause for it.

"It's not that I don't want you here," I mutter. *"It's how you're here."*

"I told you, Davina, I don't know how I can get by the veil. There's something wrong with it."

"There can't be anything wrong with it because you and—"

"Me and what?"

I straighten my spine. *"No human has been able to get through it before nor can they see it."*

"I only know about it because of you. *You* showed me."

"But you're not a siren."

"No, shit, I almost died trying to prove it to you," he practically spits, throwing his hand in the air.

25

"Then how are you here? How is it that—"

"Is it because I'm not trustworthy enough?" I watch him cringe, and it makes me sick to my stomach. "Have I ever stolen anything from you?"

"That's not—"

"Don't say 'point' to me," he berates. "I'd never do anything to you—*ever*. I'd never let anyone find you. I'll never hurt you. You're just too much of a coward to face what we dreamed of. You're worse off here—" he waves his hand in the air. "—than you were in the sea. Maybe *you* don't belong here."

He gives me his back once more, his strides longer and more meaningful in his escape to leave me, so he can get back onto his ship, where he feels more like himself.

"You promised you'd never leave me angry."

He responds with a loud, annoyed sigh but turns back around and stalks toward me again.

Stopping right in my space, he drops his head and gives me a long, stilled kiss to my forehead. His soft lips press into my skin, and I feel his bothered state, how he wishes I could be who I was before.

I can't be her anymore.

"You take care of yourself, Princess," he utters.

Then I let him leave.

I don't know if he'll come back like he said he would or if the days he's away will change his mind.

All I know is that I want him to because I let my selfish side win with him every time.

CHAPTER THREE

Tobias

I can't stand the way she looks at me now—like a stranger. An intruder in her world that shouldn't be there, and yet, I am.

The first time I laid eyes on Davina, we were on different sides of sea level. She was a beautiful creature that lived under the sea, and I was a young lad that ran with my uncle's bunch who trailed and preyed on her kind—Hunters. A growing group of men who either sold, killed, or raped sirens.

Thankfully, my Uncle Declan wasn't very good at it.

Except for *that* night.

When he first spoke about the women who sang men into rocks, off ships, and ripped their heads clean off, I believed his drinking habit had worsened.

That, or his mind went adrift off the deep end because he sailed the Black Sea a million times over and had no concept of the real world on land anymore.

Hunters were just superstitious pirates that liked the quest of something challenging and alive. Sirens were worth quick gold on the market, though, again, I'd never seen one at Port Royal, where I grew up with my Uncle Declan. Half the time when he got word of sightings, he would leave me alone with some money to fend for myself, and while I spent a lot of my time at the fishing docks, no magical creatures ever showed up dead or alive at the pier.

Until the night Davina and her sister, Rohana, hung from that net, I didn't believe they existed.

Then there was the slice on my cheek Davina landed that really set in the reality that they were real.

Looking into her eyes, I felt the fear. She looked around my age, determined and strong while hanging onto the net, attempting to cut through the thick threads of the rope.

It was the evening everything changed for me.

Sirens were real, not a made-up drunken tale my uncle believed, and I wanted to protect them.

I wanted to conserve *her.*

I never would've stayed with my Uncle Declan if Lorne hadn't disappeared. Three years younger than me, my uncle fed me a line of bullshit that he got up and left me behind, wanting to search for treasure and a new world.

He'd never abandon me.

Lorne disliked my uncle probably more than I did and never in a million years would he leave or desert me.

Someone kidnapped him, I was certain of it. Pirates were always looking for deck boys and forcing young children into their trade. I'm afraid my brother fell victim to it, and I've been following leads for years only to come up short.

He's a grown man now, and I fear with the amount of time that has gone by, I won't recognize him anymore. His face is starting to dim with time inside my head, and I beat myself up with more years that pass. But until the leads dry up, I'll continue to search for him and try to hold on to the thread of hope that still dangles within me.

"We're ready to board when you are, Cap'n." I glance over to my skipper, Ashton, an older gentleman who used to run with my uncle. The gray hairs on his head display all the close encounters of death he's almost succumbed to, while the wrinkles on his face tell stories of how many years he's been at sea.

He's like a father to me, the only other person besides my uncle who remembers my brother. Even though he didn't see him but a few times, his knowing reminds me that I'm not imagining things.

Port Royal is a busy trading town, and this isn't the first time my brother has been mentioned being here. The stories about him range high and low, that he's a merchant, a Hunter, a dirty pirate who's running from the Banishian Navy.

While all of these could be true, they don't bother me as much as thinking that Lorne is no longer alive.

I want him to meet Davina.

I want to know if he's met a woman and if he's happy.

If he even remembers me.

As every wish and fantasy starts to build in my mind, the moment I step off the ship they crash just as quickly.

The minute the informant tells me that this alleged Lorne lookalike left last night on a ship heading south, my heart falls for over the hundredth time, igniting the repetition of anger and frustration.

I'm tired of coming to this port, where everyone knows his name. Not because he's famous around the sea but because I come here practically once every three months searching for him.

"One day, lad," Ashton conveys, the moment he recognizes my obviously fallen face.

He slaps me on the back as I make my way into my corridors, knowing the repetitious drill when I come back empty-handed—leave port as quickly as possible and don't fucking ask me where we're going until I come back out on the deck.

My bottle of whiskey is the first thing I reach for the moment my door closes. It's enough to know that he's gone, but with every glimmer of promise to find him, I'd rather stop looking altogether because it only ends in one conclusion—self-loathing.

How can someone like me find Davina every time on an invisible island that no other man can see, but can't find his own brother. I have men all over the southern hemisphere under my command, but Lorne escapes me every time.

Just like Davina is trying to do—avoiding and evading our friendship.

Her defenses are up, she doesn't trust anyone, and she's scared, while there is a limit to what I can do about it. I can't give her the answers she needs on how I'm able to step foot on Merindah let alone locate it.

It was naive of me to think her being in my world would change the dynamic of what we are. How I've lived in a fairy-tale of wanting to make her my wife one day and have children of our own.

I don't need the sea as much as I need and want her, but Davina is a siren, the sea is within her and what makes her who she is.

And I can't compete with it.

CHAPTER FOUR
DAGEN

I 've lost track of how long I've been here, chained to the floor of the room I was brought into. My shackles are long enough for me to stand and walk a small circle, but it strengthens my frustration at being padlocked in this space.

Rubbing my forehead, I think about my crew, more than likely coming up with a plan. I don't think they fully understand what they'll be walking into—*I* didn't know what the hell I was roaming into.

I was told by my father that this was practically an uninhabited island, in the middle of nowhere, where only a few people may reside. It didn't make any sense, but I did as I was told, giving myself a change of scenery from the mountains and valleys of Lothbrok.

Now I'm locked up in a paradise of hell with bitter women running the show.

The faint sound of footsteps patter along the tiles, and I jerk my attention to the door as it opens.

Rose-colored hair peeks from behind it, then steps into the room, leaving it open for the next body to walk in behind her.

Davina.

The little bloodthirsty siren who left the room the other day without uttering a single word.

"I'm Isolde," the other announces like we haven't met before as she stands a safe distance from me. "You will eat."

I don't respond, just continue sitting on the hard floor.

"He doesn't look harmful," she suddenly states, tossing a loaf of bread at me. I scoff loudly for them to hear, not bothering to catch the item she threw at me. Obviously they haven't heard all of the alleged *myths* about me then.

My name is written and spread off the lips of people everywhere from where I'm from. I didn't earn Dagen the Blood Axe just because I could hold one.

I've butchered hundreds of men to protect my people. Loyalty and pride flow through my veins just as my blood does freely.

So harmful wouldn't be lost on a conversation about me.

"He's haughty and ignorant," Isolde professes then jerks her attention to her sister. "Absolutely not."

Davina fixes her with an insistent look, not backing down from whatever the hell it was that Isolde answered "no" to.

"Out of the question," she digresses, adjusting the spectacles on her nose. Davina narrows her eyes.

"I won't bite," I offer as both of their eyes fall on me. "Hard, I mean."

Davina stares at me while Isolde looks back at her.

"Atarah will—" She stops then rolls her eyes. "*Five* minutes." She turns on her heels and begins to leave the room. "And I *won't* knock."

Slamming the door behind her, she leaves me to bask in the one siren who captivates every inch of my body.

This is what they are all about.

Seduction.

Beauty.

A fatal monster.

I perk a brow. "Still don't speak, eh?" She continues to

stand there, giving me the full view of her body under very little clothing.

Today she's wearing a pink bandeau covered in pearls and seashells, her naked torso of ivory glistening in the sun overhead, with a white skirt of meshed material that gives me more of a regard of her toned legs.

But what's different is the crown, the one made of not just seashells, but old pendants and chains. They drape over the shells of different shapes and colors, professing her rank.

"If you're going to stare me to death, please, just take my knife and stab me a few times in the chest."

Silence.

"What do you want?"

More silence.

I sigh, rubbing one of my temples with a chained hand. "Well if you're going to mute me to death, it's working."

I think I see a smirk, but it disappears just as quickly as I thought I saw it.

"What do you want?" I repeat. "Because I'm not going to tell you anything." She steps forward, which jolts me back a little.

Standing to have a better position on her, I watch her continue her trail toward me—a dangerous one.

One she should think twice about because if I have a mind to, my chains have enough slack to crush the little thing to death.

"You might want to keep your distance, Blood," I warn. "It's not a smart idea for you to get too close to me."

She doesn't listen.

The stupid little girl takes no heed in what the hell I just said as she traipses closer with her bare feet. Either brave or stupid, I'm going to take my opportunity if it presents itself.

A foot away, she halts, peering up at me with those stunning greens, and I can't help but explore her face. Two freckles on the left and three on the right side of her high-boned cheeks, long eyelashes, and a button nose. Her plush lips are pink and impeccable.

And the fucking enemy.

"You don't know how to speak?"

She blinks.

"I'm going to take that as a 'yes'."

She stares.

"I'm not going to say a thing about—you're wasting your time."

Another blink.

"This only works to my advantage, Blood. I've never killed a young woman before that wasn't armed."

With a sword or ax.

Davina has a whole other arsenal that I don't know about, I'm sure, and unfortunately, I'm going to find out the hard fucking way.

My chains rattle as my hands quickly seize her neck, pressing the tips of my thumbs into her windpipe.

Yanking her toward me, I wait for widened eyes to fill with anguish, for her lips to part in shock, but she remains unfazed.

Unaffected.

Calm.

Until a surge of scorching heat burns the pads of my fingers, immediately getting me to release her. I fling myself back at the pain coursing through my hand.

I can smell the odor of burnt flesh, my instant need is cool water which, of course, there's none near.

"The *fuck*," I bellow, shaking my hand in the air to try and ease the discomfort.

Nothing—*again.*

Looking down at my fingers, they're red but the skin is still there.

I jerk my eyes to her. "You magical piece of—" She perks a brow, ceasing my next words.

She understands *everything*.

She's not stupid or ignorant. She's as cunning and smart as the rest of them.

"This no talking shit works both ways, Blood," I snap. She gives me a once-over, sizing me up, because to her right now I'm nothing.

I'm no threat.

I'm not a worry in her mind.

I'm a prisoner on her island, and I'm not getting out of here unless I tell her what I've come for. But I think she has a pretty damn good idea of what that certain something is.

"You can't keep me here forever, sweetheart," I sneer, jerking on the chains that still bind me to the floor. "You better make up your mind on what you're going to do with me."

I'm not built to be a prisoner of war nor will I stay one. She either kills me or lets me go. And if she does neither, I'll take my chances and find my way out.

Davina abruptly turns on her heels and walks away. She and I are not done yet.

That's all her expression said.

CHAPTER FIVE

Davina

I shouldn't be here alone, but I am—again. This time without one of my sisters. This time without a plan. And knowing deep down that this second visit is going to be as worthless as the last one.

I'm not scared of him, the Viking—Dagen the Blood Axe.

It's just a name. Question is, how much truth lies behind it? How much blood has he spilled like my sisters state that Vikings do?

Besides his cocky, self-assured attitude, he's just another human to me. I wouldn't classify him with Tobias, but he does have that fearless and half-witted air about him.

Intrigued to know more, I found a book on them in my library. They're known for their brute force and loyalty, allegedly fearless and large in stature. Known to mercilessly conquer cities and villages, killing anything in their path.

It was the chapter about taking over land that really alarmed me. And the more that it sunk in, the more the idea of sending him back out of the veil floating facedown seemed more favorable. His people could then pick up, whatever was left of him, after my sea creatures nibbled off him.

Sitting on the floor, the Viking's knees are brought up to his chest, looking like a small child instead of the brawny man that tried to strangle me last night.

He doesn't notice me silently walk in, looking outside the french door at the moon as I contemplate my next move. It only lasts for a split second before furrowed brows and ocean blue eyes bore into me.

His long brown hair cups his face, giving him a barbaric look along with his facial hair and beard. And the longer I stare back at him, the more his brows deepen like I've done something to *him*.

It's quite the opposite, and he should know that. I'm sure he wouldn't let strangers march all over his land. But here I stand, a few yards from the agitated man that is now my prisoner, and I should be thinking of ways to get rid of him.

Not curious.

"Miss me already?" he grumbles, looking back at where he was looking before I walked in.

I answer by stepping deeper into the room, aware that I'm more powerful than him and not fearful of the muscles that bulge from his shirt. Or the thighs that could stomp me into dust. I was afraid of what his plans were and what else was going to happen due to his being here.

It was self-righteous suicide. Which made no sense because he doesn't seem like an idiot.

"Still not speaking, are we?" he asks, still staring outside.

Pretty much, yes.

He doesn't deserve for me to speak to him, but I'll have to at some point. And as much as he doesn't frighten me, I sense no fear in him either, which does nothing for me because dread makes people do stupid things.

"Did we move on to boring me to death now?" I thrust back a chuckle, no wonder Nesrine likes him, he's sarcastic and crass like her. "You can leave, Blood. I'm not in the mood for a staring contest."

I do something risky, something my body warns me

profusely not to do, but I force it to anyways—I sit in front of him.

Crossing my legs, I straighten my back, hoping that the innocent look in my eyes gets him to speak.

"What now?"

I tuck a piece of hair behind my ear.

Purity, that's what Father says I am. A sweet shell in a bottomless ocean that he wanted to protect from the evils of this world.

But he'd never be able to do that.

Even undersea, threats were imminent. They were everywhere. Not just from the creatures that lived under the ocean, but the Hunters who chased and captured my species for sport.

"That pretty little face isn't going to fool me, Blood."

The warm breeze picks up in the room, encompassing me, but it sends a cool shiver down my spine. I don't know if it's warning me or that I'm anxious being in this room with him again. Or it's that I'll have to have him killed because he's too hard-headed, which means I'll receive no answers.

"You haven't decided yet," he claims. "To kill me or get whatever you can out of me first. You're curious about me just as much as I'm curious about you because your people don't come up to Scotland and Norway, and we rarely come down here—" He looks at me. "—and you want to know why."

I nod.

"Does it matter?"

I nod again.

He leans toward me, inhaling a deep breath as though he's smelling me. "Too bad."

My jaw locks as I notice a faint scar above his brow. The straight nose that falls to perfect lips. And the movement of his fingers around a bulky ring.

He twists it on his index finger—an animal of some kind that I know I've seen before in one of my books marks the top. It's gold and gaudy, something Tobias would bring home to me.

"Never seen a ring?" he asks, snagging my attention back up to his face. In my silence, he takes it off and holds it out for me to take.

Extending my palm, he drops it, letting me feel the warmness of the metal on my cool hands. I clasp it then go to slide it down my finger but stop.

This isn't mine, and I don't know what it does if I put it on.

"Go ahead," he urges.

I glance back up at him. He reveals no emotion or intentions of any kind, but I don't trust him. I hold up his trinket for him to take back, and he does the same, extending his palm for me to drop it in.

"It's a family ring, been in my family for years."

I clasp my hands together and wait for more, any small pieces of information that he wants to tell me so I can build a rapport with him.

"Do you have things like that?"

I shake my head.

"Do you know how to speak?"

I shake my head again.

"Interesting."

I cock my head to the side.

"I mean, that's unfortunate."

My brows furrow.

"I'm sure you'd have a lot to say, especially since you can't say it."

I crack a grin, something like that. And I bet sometimes my sisters wished I was mute altogether.

"I figured. Are you the leader? You don't seem like the oldest one of the bunch. They're your sisters, aren't they?"

I look at him straight-faced.

"You're the youngest. The white-haired woman is the oldest. She's bossy, like me. I'm the oldest."

I bob my head, letting him obtain something of me so he continues to talk. If he wants to chitchat like Tobias does, maybe this is a way in. Maybe it's a human thing.

"You must get the brunt of a lot of things."

I rub my shoulder, feeling the repetitive dryness of my skin. It starts to itch if I'm out of the lagoon too long. Unfortunately, with the agreement for the desired spell Taysa cast on the island, the sea water actually burns my skin. The lagoon is the only place I can ease the itching and abrading feeling of my body.

"Are you hurt?" he asks me, laced with what sounds to be concern.

I rip my hand away from my skin, not realizing that my face gave anything away.

"You don't belong out of the water. How is it that you're able to be on land?"

Too many questions.

I begin to push myself off the tiles to stand, which elicits an immediate reaction out of him.

Yanking my foot from underneath my butt, his grip promptly gets me to react, jabbing my free one into his chest.

It does nothing.

Before I can hit him again, my body is underneath his, hovering over me like an animal. He has the hairy bit down, and his beard and hair makes him look like a beast toying with his prey—that being me.

"I'm sorry it had to be you," he recites in my face, his breath hot on my skin. "But I have to go."

His hand comes up to my throat again, and he squeezes,

harder than I remember the first time. My mind is still muddled from being taken by him so quickly, but my siren tendencies—I'm trying to keep them at bay because I'll hurt him.

He's a caged animal, and I got too close, so this is half my fault.

The air gets more difficult to inhale as he squeezes hard. My eyes meet his, so ocean blue and crystal-like. They are a perfect contrast to his dark features. They're sad, almost remorseful, as I hear myself choke at him trying to kill me.

Kill me.

How ignorant he must be to think I'm so helpless, seeing how I burnt him once already. But the knowledge of what I can do doesn't seem to cast any sense in this man. He wants to learn the hard way.

And he's going to *feel* it the hard way too.

My palms find his broad chest, his muscles flexing underneath my skin, and I push—hard.

His body leaves my space, flying backward in the air as my lungs take in a deep breath. But I don't wait for it to settle into my body or for me to take another, I'm up on my feet, watching Dagen slide along the floor as his chains halt him from going any further, jerking at his wrists.

I hear him grunt and suck in a gasp as I wait to see how much time it takes for him to recover.

I don't know why he's so fascinating, but he's proven to be the most dangerous thing I've ever been this close to. And he proved it by making a second attempt to try and hurt me while I've been trying to stay civil with him.

"You forgot to mention you have the strength of ten men," he mumbles on his knees. His hands are positioned in front of him as he hunches over, blood trickling on the pristine white floors from his wrists.

I grunt inwardly, he's already been warned.

He peers up at me, the corners of his lips curved into a smile. "That's all you got though?"

I snort, letting him hear that.

Actually, it's not.

CHAPTER SIX
DAGEN

I haven't seen her in three days, counting the moons to keep track of the time. I'm brought three meals, all different, all delicious, but I'm passed the point of being able to stay in this room any longer. My wrists are bloody and chafed from the metal digging and rubbing into my flesh, but it doesn't stop me from trying to escape every day.

I know I'm in some sort of denial about being able to leave here, not wanting to accept the fact that my fate lies in the wish of a woman.

Or women.

Attacking Davina was a risk, the only option I had. I was hoping she'd have a key on her for my chains or that I'd piss her sisters off enough that they'd just put me out of my misery.

Since that didn't work, I've been looting my time with worthless ideas and brooding over the circumstances that I'm currently in.

Watching the sunrise in the sky, I know that lunch will be here soon. Another man sliding a plate to me and a cup of some sweet drink while not uttering a single word seems to be the routine as of late. No amount of taunting and none of my attempts to anger them have gotten me a reaction in any kind of way.

They're as personable as a damn rock.

A few moments later, the door to the room opens, and I don't bother to look over at it.

I'm tired, my body feeling weak from lack of movement. My mind is battered with hopelessness, and I'm wondering when my father is going to come.

He may not.

If the risk is too great, he won't put our men in peril to rescue one man. Even if that one man is his eldest son.

"You look lonely," coos a feminine voice, lofting into the emptiness that is my prison.

Glancing over my shoulder, I take in Nesrine striding through my prison with assurance in every sway of her hips. Her breasts are covered in a black fabric that coordinates with her tan skin that curves into wide hips and legs of a goddess.

It's her black eyes that give me pause.

Mischievous and untrustworthy—they glide over me easily, and I know this isn't a social call.

Standing from the floor, I feel better having at least the height on her as she pauses a few feet from me. Shifty eyes still take me in, and I keep mine closely monitoring her next move because something about her reeks of conniving.

"So they sent in the next one to see if you can get me to talk?" I inquire with a lifted brow. "I hope I didn't hurt the little one too much?"

"On the contrary," Nesrine states, hiking her gaze to my face. "Was checking to see how *you* are."

"I'm fine."

"Says the blood caked around your wrists."

"The art of a prisoner trying to escape." I give her a quick once-over. "I'm sure you would do the same."

"Not exactly because I wouldn't have done what you did."

"Mindless me." Nesrine hoists a shoulder, one that reveals black and silvery scales that are forming there.

Interesting.

Maybe I can keep one of them hostage and from the water. Not sure how I'd keep the rest of them from attacking me but—

"We all make mistakes," Nesrine replies, yanking me out of my daily contemplation of impulsive ideas. "It's how you rectify them that'll be your test, Viking."

"Give it your best shot," I taunt. "You won't get much farther than your little sister."

She smirks, taking another step closer to me. "I think we'll give it a try, huh."

Her black eyes cast over in a glossy hue, tantalizing and mesmerizing, drawing me deeper into them. I start to relax as I feel every nerve ending in my body begin to tingle in response.

It's the first sign to tell me something is wrong.

Coercing myself with all my will power, I yank my eyes away.

"Why did you come here?" she asks me. "You're far from home." My body buzzes to the sound of her voice, soft and almost lullaby-like.

It wants more, to feel a sense of relaxation because I've been tense and uneasy for days. It's a comfort of some sort, soothing me into a decompressed state.

I almost want to sit back down and just let it take me over. Let myself bask in some sort of peace for a little while because the thoughts scattered through my brain have brought nothing but chaos and frustration.

These chains have not only secured my body in one place but increased the reality that if I don't betray my father, I'm not getting out of here alive.

"You must miss it," Nesrine mutters softly. "Being in a

foreign land with people you don't know can cause a sense of panic."

As soon as she says the words, I start to feel it—worry and alarm.

My heart begins to race in my chest, thumping in arhythmic beats. Sweat begins to form on my brow, and I peer around the room, just to see it's exactly the same—nothing's changed.

"I want to help," she issues gently. "Let me help you go home."

Her words—they hit my gut.

That's what I want. To go home to my hut, eat the food I'm accustomed to in a place where I feel safe. To be around people that know me, respect me. To expand our colony for the growing families that reside there. My mission was to keep them all safe and well, not wanting for anything because I'll be their leader when my father passes on.

Hands touch my chest, making me flinch in response. Peering down, Nesrine looks up at me, nothing but sincerity and kindness illuminates off her face.

She's beautiful, it's almost unreal. I've never seen a woman with flawless features and skin before. One that carries so much confidence and authority in her curvy frame.

"I'm sorry," she offers. "You're just so...different." Her fingers slowly descend down my chest until they hit the top of my abdomen. Imploring eyes still look at me, imprinted with vulnerability. As though she needs someone like me to protect her.

"Are there many like you?"

I exhale a staggered breath as the trail of her fingers descend. "Yes."

She bites her lower lip, her gaze falling to mine as my cock stirs for the first time in—I can't remember when.

Rising on her toes, I can smell the sea. The fresh air and some scent of sweet nectar or fruit. The aroma wafts around me, sinking me deeper into this woman's trance that has offered to help me.

Maybe it's because I'm tired of fighting. Or the fact that my restlessness has weakened me into a subdued state. Regardless, it feels good.

It almost feels right.

Nesrine keeps her dark eyes locked onto my blues, and I don't want her to look away. A sense of calm continues to circle around me the more she studies my face—intriguing and speculating.

She doesn't wait, letting herself go in this odd transfixion that she and I have. Her lips press into mine, gentle and velvety, coaxing me to follow.

And I do—I can't help it.

My lips widen, slowly taking her deeper. My cock stirring in my britches, hard and aroused, a wave of lust hitting my gut like a swift punch. The tip of her tongue traces mine, and that's when my hands grip her hips, pulling her delicate body into mine.

My body is on a high, rubbing my hardness into her stomach, a soft moan escaping her lips as she lets me devour her mouth.

I'm lost in this sensation of starvation for a woman. One who doesn't exist in my world. One who possibly doesn't know how beautiful she is under my taut exterior.

Grabbing her ass, I lift her, her long legs automatically wrapping around my hips. My dick rubs against her pussy, letting us both get a taste of the friction of what it would and could be like to sink myself deep inside her exquisite body. Her fingertips press into my shoulder blades, silently urging me for more as we battle with our lips and tongue.

And more is what I'm more than willing to do.

Every swallow of her moans.

Every delicate sweep of her lips compels me to give into my hanker for a woman. To let myself live in this moment of pure ecstasy with a female that I will never encounter again.

Her softness mirrors off my hard chest, her lips mesh in line with mine, begging me to take her.

It taunts me, picks at my body to just lay her down on this floor and drive myself deep and hard into her enticing body.

"We need to stop," I tell her between licks and strains of our mouths. She responds by gripping me tighter, her breasts rubbing along the fabric of my shirt.

"We should," she replies. "But it doesn't mean I will." She bites my lower lip, releasing it before taking my mouth again.

If this is hell, I'd gladly lounge in it—it'd be worth the trip.

"You don't know what you're getting yourself into," I mutter. "I don't fuck nice."

"Exactly how I wish you wouldn't be."

She feels like a feather in my hands, light and easy to maneuver. Accessible for me to even fuck her like this without having to lay her on the hard tiles. I'm drunk out of my mind on an eagerness I've never felt this strong before.

Not since I was a young lad.

Not since I knew fucking was a way to release built-up tension and stress, besides killing men, and the adrenaline rush it produced.

"How did you come to be here?" she inquires through another kiss. "How is it that we've never met before?"

"Different worlds," I reply. "But I'm glad we haven't."

"Oh?"

I grip her ass tighter. "I'd have to kill a lot of men to keep their hands off a woman like you."

She chuckles softly. "Don't worry, I can kill them too."

It crashes down—everything.

The lust.

The desire.

The relaxed state my mind was just in.

The fact that I'm a prisoner here.

I immediately drop her, not giving a shit if she falls on her ass, and step back to regain myself.

I don't know what happened, how I just indulged in a fantasy where nothing was wrong to realizing that I'm in a shit load of trouble.

A wicked smirk plays across her face, all-knowing and telling that I was tricked into letting my guard down.

She didn't accomplish anything, just the stiffness of my cock, but I still feel used. I was reduced to a pawn in whatever little game she was playing, and we both know what that fucking was.

"What's the matter?" she hedges, her lips red and beaten with my kisses. Normally, a man would feel some sort of pride in that.

Me, I want to wring her neck.

"You think controlling the way I feel is going to get you what you want," I rasp, grasping at my nerves to get back in line with my head.

I feel drugged, disoriented, and battered, mentally and physically after her little witch spell.

"Was worth a shot," she surmises. "Besides—" her smirk turns into a full-blown smile. "—it was nice, wasn't it?"

"It wasn't *real.*"

She glances down at my cock still hard in my pants. "You sure?" I take a step toward her, hearing the chains for the first time in minutes announcing where I am, how I got here and what I am compared to the creature in front of me.

"Keep your magic to your damn self," I sneer. "Because if you didn't have it, we'd be on different sides right now."

"Which only further confirms that I'm *better* than you, Viking. Don't forget it." She takes a step of her own toward me. "And if you touch my sister again, I'll make it so much worse. That was *nothing*."

"Then tell your sister to stop poking the bear," I retort.

She wrinkles her nose. "The what?"

"Stay the fuck away from me. *Kill* me or release me, there isn't any other way this is going to go."

Nesrine raises her eyebrows. "Oh, there's another way. We'll just see how strong you are to fight it, Viking."

"I'm already suited up, witch."

"I'm not a *witch*," she snaps then releases a heavy, indifferent sigh. "They're vile creatures."

"And you're not?"

Her eyelashes flutter. "Did it feel like I was moments ago?" I snap my mouth shut. "I knew you'd be a fun little toy. Keep your heart guarded, brute, you'll need the extra defense."

I narrow my eyes. "That won't be a problem."

Her mouth curves into a smile. "Sure it will."

And just like everyone else that walks into this room, she walks out, leaving me alone to ponder my own thoughts.

I'm fucked, but not when it comes to my heart.

It's because my life is in jeopardy to the wants and desires of seven devious women who want something that they can't get from me.

I'd kill one of them first.

CHAPTER SEVEN

Davina

Laying on my plush settee in my small library, I try to devour words about love. I read about a young girl who learns that not all men are what they seem. That's how I felt about the Viking, as my fingertips brush the nape of my neck where he wrapped his hands and pressed his thumbs into my throat.

I didn't think he wasn't dangerous, just his stature alone screamed unstable, fierce, and strong. His arms were the size of my thighs, his length towered over all my sisters, and his piercing blue eyes bore into each and every single one of us. As much as we don't trust him, he shares the sentiment, and I can't say I blame him.

Problem is, he trespassed on my land, my *home*, and that isn't something I'm going to take lightly.

But for what and how?

Merindah was supposed to be concealed from the outside world. Unseen by any human or being that sailed or swam by it to keep my sisters and I safe. A stupid idea that we all had, sick of the water and the monotonous sea. Filled with dreams from my mother's diaries of another world, where humans walked on land and laid in the sun. How they didn't dry up when out of the water but could go into it whenever they chose.

She spoke about an island with palm trees and shade.

Fruit that hung from plants and animals that lived there. It started a revolution for my sisters and I, including Atarah, to seek out the only person that could possibly make it happen —Taysa the sea witch.

While she hated the term "witch," she healed the sick and injured creatures of the blue with her magic, helped build cities, and protected my sisters and I from danger.

She saved Brylee once from a herd of sharks.

She mended Kali when she was stung by a bloom of jelly-fish, turning her skin pink for a few days, which clashed with her orange features. Isolde loved how she matched her pink hair and eyes, walking around for days calling Kali her twin, which only irked my sister more.

Taysa was Atarah's sounding board when she got her heart broken by a siren named Bran. He crushed her spirit to pursue another Siren, and instead of using Nesrine's abilities to make him feel miserable for all eternity, Taysa told her not to let anyone have that sort of power over you.

Not only was Taysa an overseer but Mother's best friend. Always around for birthdays and celebrations, spoiling us with gifts and filling our minds with stories of creatures who once roamed the sea. I was certain she'd give us everything in her power the moment we asked until we approached her about an island of our own.

That she flatly refused before it left the tip of Atarah's tongue.

Taysa didn't like using desired spells because it was dabbling with fate and everything comes with a price—one that she didn't know and couldn't control.

My sisters and I, being the stubborn and persistent crea-tures that we are, pestered her for weeks. Composing lists and reasons on why we should have an island of our own, that Mother would've wanted us to have it—our own piece of paradise.

Taysa warned us, numerous times, and I can't blame my current predicament on anyone but myself. She finally gave in after numerous attempts of breaking her down. The price, though, wasn't one my sisters and I took seriously. We weren't allowed off the island afterward, stuck to stay on land permanently. The friendly salt water we swam and were born into burnt our skin, which devastated Taysa. She ran to our father with the news, distressed and frightened.

So I made another deal on my own and behind my sisters' backs.

For my sisters' freedom to go back into the sea and be with our father, I gave up my liberty—to stay on the island for their release. However, not only was I stuck on this island, but the second desired spell also took my voice.

Taysa understood why I did it, knew that my father having at least six of us would be better than having none. And to this day, she comes to visit me by the shore to give me updates on finding a way to get me off the island and get my voice back.

It's a double-edged slice to me though.

On land, I can stand next to Tobias, but that's all we do. Nothing of what I dreamt of I've done with him, knowing one day I'll return to the sea, and I can't break his heart.

Even though I knew it would happen anyway.

Ridding myself of my current thoughts, I decide to stay away from the Viking to think about my next move, which is the most pressing matter. Obviously keeping him locked up was doing more harm than good. I learned that pride is the most important thing a man possesses, I just wasn't privy to letting him roam the island, where my father could find him and make things worse.

A wave of black catches my attention, and I don't have to look up to know what it is.

"*Nesrine*," I call out, not lifting my eyes from my book. She creeps around like the shadows, hiding when she doesn't want to be bothered, which I can sense is right now.

I hear a small groan then her footsteps entering into the modest library.

"Hello Davina," she greets with a fake chipper tone. "What are you doing?"

"Reading, what were you doing?"

She swings her arms at her sides. "Oh, just visiting our Viking."

I peer over the pages of my book. *"And?"*

"Tight-lipped man."

"Uh-huh." I drop my book into my lap. *"Why is your skirt all twisted?"*

Nesrine looks down at it nonchalantly. "Too big."

"Did big hands land on it?" I watch my sister's brows furrow then relax. She knows I can read her, she's not that stealthy when it comes to hiding things.

"I was just trying to help," she offers with a shrug.

"At least you didn't get strangled. He can't stand me. The nice approach isn't working."

"I beg to differ." Nesrine scoots my crossed ankles over so she can take a seat. "You just come off timid."

"I drew blood," I counter. *"I ran a blade down his face."*

"That's child's play to a man like that."

"I flung him off me yesterday."

She crosses her slim legs. "It probably felt like a shove."

"Whose side are you on?"

She pats my calf. "Yours, of course, I was just trying to help, as I said." I open my book back up and stare at the pages.

"When is father coming by to visit?"

Nesrine picks at her skirt. "He hasn't said, been busy with the advisors on how to move forward with the folklore."

"The folklore don't come over here."

"No, but we're being blamed for a lot of their killings."

I tsk. *"Who cares?"*

"Father, apparently." She lets out a sigh. "He doesn't want us to come off as barbaric."

"We lure men into the ocean by song, can you think of a better way to die? Besides we only do it when they come around our territory."

Nesrine shrugs. "Not if your singing is coming within my ears." I give her a small kick to her hip, which gets her to chuckle.

"Have you told him about the Viking?"

"No. It'd just cause more of a mess, besides we have this."

"Atarah isn't on board."

"Atarah is one person," my sister retorts. "And there's seven of us."

"She'll get Brylee on her side for sure. Maybe Isolde and—"

Nesrine's head snaps to me, brows furrowed. "Why are you worrying about this so much?"

"Because he's in my home," I stress. *"Where did he come from, why is he here?"*

"It's obvious, isn't it? Mother's cuff."

I shake my head. *"No, they don't—"*

"Why wouldn't they? Men talk, legends and myths are born. Vikings are land-hungry people, why wouldn't they want it *and* Merindah?"

"Because it's mine—I mean, ours."

"You need off," my sister conveys. "You've been here too long." Her words are soft, but they're hard against my chest.

I'm changing, I can feel it. My siren tendencies are dimming; the more time I spend on land, the more my body forgets.

Mind you, I've adapted a new superpower, if you will. Instead of being able to sing my victims into a daze, I can burn them. My skin ignites into a blaze, which was what the Blood Axe experienced the other day.

"We've already spoken about this," I claim, pulling my knees to my chest. *"There isn't any—"*

"And we'll speak about it as many times as I feel fit."

I send a glare in her direction. *"There is no other way than to ask Taysa to take another thing from us. We're not going to do that anymore."*

"There is another way."

"Which is?"

"Kill her."

"Are you mad?" I fully sit up, tossing my book to the side. *"She's been like a mother to us."*

"We'll kill her," she continues cooly. "And bottle her energy so the island remains ours."

"You can't kill someone who has helped us."

"She's not ignorant, Davina, she knows what she's doing."

"We all knew what we were doing," I defend. *"She warned us, we spent months driving her crazy with giving us a safe place to walk and run on."*

"I'm not fully convinced that she didn't know what would happen."

"You're just upset that I'm still here."

"I am, but why can't a witch find another way?"

I lift a shoulder. *"I don't know. Maybe there is no other way."*

"Keep your guard up," Nesrine goes on, pulling her raven hair off one of her shoulders. "It's the best advice I could ever give you."

"I will, but you can't blame Taysa for what I asked her to do."

"Working on it," she replies with a weak grin. A brief silence develops between us, and I know she thinks she should've been the one to offer up something else to let the rest of us go free and back into the ocean.

I've just always been faster than her.

"What do you think we should do with the Viking?"

She looks over the room. "He's nothing we can't handle. But we truly need to find out why he's here. If his people know about the cuff, more of them could come. And we need to know how he got through the veil."

"Like Isolde said, maybe he's a siren."

Nesrine gives me a look. "He's no siren. He isn't built like one, he doesn't feel like one. I would know, I've been the closest to him."

I open my mouth to ask her what in the world she did but refrain. *"A spell maybe?"*

"Possibly."

I draw my brows together. *"You don't think Taysa would let someone on our island."*

"Not if she wants to live."

"We wouldn't know either way," I counter.

"Not unless we find a way to get the Viking to talk."

"Is his boat gone?"

"Been gone for over two days, they may come back."

"I read Vikings are loyal, I would think they would."

"Remember it's only in a book," Nesrine warns. "Not everything you read is true."

CHAPTER EIGHT
DAGEN

"Make a move," Brylee warns. "And we'll slit your throat right here." Easy to say when her twin sister already has a blade positioned there.

Removing the metal from my skin, Atarah steps away from me, rounding my body to stand along with her sister.

With a large bowl of water, Brylee hunches to the floor and spills it over the white tiles, letting it puddle out in whatever way it wants.

"Sit," Atarah orders. I mimic her glare but decide to abide by her request.

The women sit on the other side of the puddle, knees touching each other, while I look back and forth between them. If it wasn't for their different colored hair and eyes, I'd never be able to tell the difference between the two.

Deep-set eyes, creamy skin, and a slightly pushed-up nose, each of them wear their little crowns on their heads as to remind me of where I am and who they are.

Like I need the reminder.

Atarah peers down at the puddle of water, her white-rimmed eyes turning brighter and more vibrant.

"Take your time," Brylee states calmly.

"What the hell are you doing?" I snap. They ignore me, as Brylee focuses on Atarah gawking at the water.

"Sorry," bellows another voice in the room. "I couldn't get past Nesrine." I glance up to see Isolde walk into the room.

"You haven't missed anything," Byrlee offers. "Take a seat."

I roll my eyes, now having three of them in the room like this is going to do a fucking thing to make me speak.

"He's irritated that he's here," Brylee suddenly states. "He didn't think he'd be captured so he came alone."

"So, he is stupid," Isolde conveys, pulling her pink hair into a bun of some sort as she takes a seat on the floor.

I don't even get the opportunity to send her a glare because Brylee shakes her head. "That's not possible."

Isolde looks at her. "What isn't?"

"He didn't think we'd be here. He didn't believe we existed."

Fuck.

More superpowers that I can't compete with. This keeps me in a dangerous spot because my secrets need to remain just that. If they find out more about why I'm here, I have a feeling that tonight is going to be my last night on this island.

"His facial expression states he's in shock," Isolde mutters.

"Wouldn't you be?" I retort.

She presses her lips together. "No."

I roll my eyes.

"A mission," Brylee frets softly. "In front of a group of men who all wear the same clothing as him. Furs wrapped around their shoulders, burly men."

Her words take me back to my village, where my father publicly announced that I was coming here. Where my men roared with excitement and hope that we'd obtain the item I came here for and be protected against any further invasions from the Highlands.

Atarah and Brylee are reading all of my thoughts from today. Which would mean they'd learn about my mission.

"Didn't you mention a woman?" Brylee asks.

And I was thinking about Edda today too.

I try to think of more things other than the most important. What I had for breakfast today, how I missed my
people, how I wanted to go home and fuck a beautiful lass
that resembles—

A hand slams against my cheek, sending my head to the
side.

"*Watch* your thoughts," Brylee fumes. "You won't be getting
your dirty hands on our sister." I neglect the sting tingling my
flesh because it's working. The harder I think about something, the more it muddles my thoughts from earlier.

"I was afraid that was going to happen," Isolde whispers.
"He's in love with Davina."

I chuckle deep within my chest. "I wouldn't call it that,
darling."

Brylee's eyes still bore into my head, but there isn't shit
she can do about what I'm thinking. It's the one thing they
can't control, which feeds my cockiness.

"He isn't scared of us," Brylee bristles. "But he doesn't like
being held by women."

I point a finger in her direction. "True."

"Your women not strong enough, Viking?" Isolde taunts.

"Wanna let one come on this island and see?" I counter.
She grins, amused that I think any human can take her on.

If Davina can throw me across a room, well...

Brylee's brow perks, and I know she saw, heard, or whatever the hell she and Atarah are doing, that Davina hurled me
a few feet.

"Wish I could've seen that," Brylee conveys.

"I'm sure," I deadpan.

"What did Atarah see?" Isolde asks.

"Davina throwing the Viking across the room."

Isolde's eyes fall on me. "*Really?*"

Atarah's breathing starts to become labored and loud, her hand suddenly clutching Brylee's arm. Her whole frame starts to convulse while her eyes are still clenched shut.

"Take it easy," Brylee coos. "You're trying too hard."

I don't know which entertains me the most—the difficulty of them trying to read my inner thoughts or the struggle that Atarah is experiencing to push and shove away the useless nonsense and find the things she's seeking the most.

Serves her right for acting like a bitch.

"*Stop*," Brylee snaps, her hand going to her forehead.

Isolde grabs on to her other arm. "What's wrong?"

Brylee shakes her head, pressing her lips together to stifle back what looks to be pain. "This isn't right."

"What isn't?"

Brylee's crystal blue eyes zero in on me. And so does her arm, seizing my shirt and yanking me in her direction.

"Why are you here?" she snarls. "What did your father *want* from here?"

I don't flinch, keeping my face emotionless. "Rich soil."

"There are forests and sand here," Isolde retorts. "Your father is either a fool or you're a liar."

I look over at her. "Prove it." My back hits the hard tiled floors, followed by my skull, with Brylee's full weight on top of me.

Sitting on my stomach with both of her legs on either side of my waist, she leans over to get in my face.

"The truth will spill from your lips," she leers. "If you think our not being able to read you is all that we have, you're mistaken."

"Looks like you're having a hard time," I mock. Brylee lifts my body, bringing my back off the floor, then slams my head right back into it.

"We might have to beat you stupid then. Don't think my little sister will stop us from—"

"We have to go," Isolde alludes suddenly. Brylee doesn't move, ready to rip my throat out. "*Help* me with Atarah."

That gets her sister to move. Climbing off me, Brylee and Isolde help a dazed Atarah off the ground.

Nothing else is said as they guide her out of the room, leaving the small puddle of water in their midst. It won't be the last time they'll try to get my truths to spill from me.

Either they'll kill me or the little one with red hair will. And I'd rather look at Blood when she makes me take my last breath.

At least some of this would've been worth it.

CHAPTER NINE

Davina

I've read somewhere that the third time's the charm. I don't really know if that's completely true, but since I learn from my books as of late, I try it.

Stepping into the room where Dagen is kept, I peek around the heavy door to see what kind of man I'm going to face today. The manipulative one or the one who straight out wants to try and strangle me again.

Instead, I'm met with something I wasn't expecting to see.

Dagen the Blood Axe—shirtless.

His muscles are a work of art, like a sculpture made of stone, painted with faint red lines—scars. One starts on his bicep, moving down to his forearm, and another runs down his back, starting from his shoulder and trailing underneath his pants. Water trails down his frame like a river, flowing through little crevices in his stomach muscles as he uses a sponge to wash himself clean.

He's what Nesrine would call an idol.

Atarah would say he was Hades.

I would say he's a man of many faces. Ones I'd love to peel back and learn, but he's taught me enough already about what the definition of a Viking is, and I don't want to kill him this time.

The traitorous door squeaks as I push it open more, which has Dagen already looking in my direction.

"Back again?" he snides, continuing to wash his body without shame.

I mean, he shouldn't be, he's beautiful. But I came here for an entirely different reason, and I was going to follow through with it.

The moment I walk further into the room, he smirks, his presumptuous attitude getting the best of *him*. I see broad and tawny chests all the time, but it's his facial hair that has me intrigued, to know what kind of scars he carries under it.

"Figured you'd come back sooner or later," he continues.

I roll my eyes. He doesn't see it, but regardless he's a bother. I'm hoping my plan of letting him free to roam the castle works. He might open up to me more, form a bond or trust me, although, I don't think he does that very often. He appears to be a man of honor, and the enemy is anyone who isn't like him.

A warrior.

A Viking,

A human.

Standing a few feet away, I'm already on the defense waiting for him to make a sudden, misguided move to attack me again. His chains rhythmically rattle as he moves his hands around his body to bathe, but his eyes stay locked on me.

Showing me he's just as suspicious of me as I am of him.

"What do you want now, Blood? I told you I'm not going to talk."

Hesitantly, I reach for his wrist, and surprisingly, he lets me take it. His skin is raw, caked in blood while the rest washes away with the water.

"Are you going to try and seduce me, too? What are you, sixteen?"

My eyes dart up to his and narrow. I'm a Princess of

Lacuna, and he's going to respect me if I have to make him bow just to be petty.

"Seventeen?"

I lock my jaw, my temper starting to rise.

"I think we're pushing it with eighteen, Princess," he admits.

This...I bite my tongue, holding off the next words that want to filter into my head.

His insults aren't going to get me to break. A prideful man who likes to tease and berate women isn't the worst thing I've dealt with in my life.

Reaching up into my hair, I find one of my small barrettes. He watches me intently as I place it inside the small lock of his chains.

"That isn't going to do anything," he contests. "You need a key."

I ignore him. He doesn't know anything.

About me.

About what I'm capable of.

About what I need to know to protect myself and my family.

We're becoming a rare species, many of us have died due to lack of food from the fishermen and pirates excessive fishing.

"Why are you helping me?" he gripes, sounding ungrateful.

Surprising.

I bet if someone offered him a meal while he was starving, he'd reject it because he didn't hunt it himself. I'm amazed he's been eating here, but it's more than likely to keep his strength up to escape.

Back to ignoring him, I continue to work the lock, looking for the pressure point to be able to twist and open it.

His hand clasps my chin, and I flinch backward. "Hey."

65

His fingers still grip my face. My defense starts to build, heat starts rising from inside my body as his flesh fuels that energy.

He's going to try to hurt me again.

"Why are you helping me?" he repeats, softer this time. "Traitors never end up safe in the end, Blood. They'll kill you."

I perk a brow. If he's speaking about my sisters, they can get upset, but there is no way he's getting off this island alive. I have soldiers everywhere, courtesy of my father and sisters, and my sea friends, AKA sharks, surround the island as we speak.

He won't make it one league before he becomes shark bait.

He releases me, taking a step back as his height looms over me. "You better think long and hard about this."

I have—thought about it for a whole five minutes, made sure the ocean was secure, and that he had a room for himself with a bed.

One step and I'm inches away from him again, taking his wrist and starting all over with the lock. He remains silent for the first time in my presence, which I'm betting is a rare occurrence.

The clads of one of his chains fall, thudding in a heap to the tiles.

This is my last chance to turn away, my conscience states. However, I'm left with no choice but the obvious.

He won't speak like this.

He won't address the issue of how he got through the veil if he's locked up like a prisoner. My people, we don't let intruders walk or swim freely, you're tortured until you speak. You starve unless you open your mouth. You become pieces of the sea afterward.

Maybe he'll see that we've evolved over the centuries to

be less murderous and more peaceful. I can't say that we don't still sing men off boats to their deaths and drown them in the ocean because Sirens still do that. We need to keep fear instilled in humans because they are getting too courageous in their ways.

Hence the man standing in front of me.

"Blood," he mutters. "The moment this last chain falls, I'm running out of here."

I continue at the lock.

"You heard what I said, right?"

I look up at him from under my lashes to confirm I have and back down to the clamp around his wrist.

"You're a stubborn thing," he comments. "Something we have in common, I guess."

We have *nothing* in common.

He's a brute, I'm a killer when need be.

He's a human, I'm a creature of the sea.

He's cocky, I like to think I'm logical—most of the time. This one doesn't seem like it could fully work out in my favor.

I hear the lock click, the steel opening and dropping to the ground. I expect him to do what he said he's going to do—run.

But like a stone wall, he stands there.

We both know how this is going to work, he's going to try and escape, swim off the island, possibly get himself killed, but it won't answer the questions I have floating in my head.

He might come back with more men next time if he makes it to his ship. It's possible they can get past the veil just like he did, which is another inquiry. That might be the most important question of all. Getting through our defenses and arriving here.

The choice is his if he wants to live or die.

I glance up at him, his rugged face studying me. Probably

wondering why, after everything he did to me, would I let him go.

Again, he doesn't know me. It's how I keep humans and creatures on their toes.

Turning on my heels, I let him decide his fate and the path he wants to choose. My sisters and I will find out how he arrived here.

Even if I have to go back to our old ways.

CHAPTER TEN
DAGEN

She's delusional. Utterly and crazily insane. The little vixen just unchained me and, pretty much through facial expressions, said she didn't care.

I don't know how long I've been here, I've lost count of how many moons and suns have cast and fallen altogether, but I do know it's been over a few of them. The little hellcat must not understand that, to get information, you need to make your prisoner weak—mentally and physically.

I wasn't quite there yet.

Achy, yes, but about to have a mental breakdown—not even close.

She glides out of the room, and I cautiously follow, waiting for one of her brutes to attack me the moment I leave.

Instead, they're standing outside the door, looking straight ahead as though this didn't just happen.

The teal mesh of fabric that she's wearing sweeps over the continuing white tiled floors as it opens up into a large foyer with a large double-wide staircase of gold and the recurring white. The ceiling is all glass in here too, letting the sun beam down and light the room in all its cleanliness.

I've never seen a place so pristine. So majestic and beautifully built. Double doors appear to my left, alluding to the outside, where it continues to be bright.

"Blood," I call, regretting the neediness in my voice. We both know I'm not getting out of here alive or at all.

I can't swim back home. There are sharks in these waters, and I'm going to guess there isn't going to be a boat ready for me to leave. So that still leaves me at a standstill.

Davina turns around, the sunlight protruding off her angelic face and high cheekbones, green eyes locking onto me.

"What do you expect me to do?" I ask.

She shrugs.

Shrugs.

And turns on her heels to continue out of the room. I march in her direction, grasping her arm and spinning her around. Immediately, I'm sliding across the floor on my ass because the little hellraiser is strong as fuck and apparently doesn't like to be touched.

"Do you have a boat ready for me?" The two men outside my previous room stand on either side of me, but I keep my attention on her.

She shakes her head then looks to both the men on my left and right. Grubby hands grip underneath my armpits and lift me to my feet, but they don't let go. I thrash to get out of their hold, but I get nowhere.

This feeling of helplessness, it only propels my anger for being here. Why my father sent me on a suicide mission over a wrist cuff that allegedly was one of our ancestors' I may never know.

"Are you going to kill me now?" I seethe.

She sends me an exasperated look over her shoulder and continues walking as the guards make me follow.

I've seen castles, taken over a few in my time, but nothing compared to this.

While most of the places I've been were supported by wooden beams with dark paints and wallpapers, this palace is in different shades of blues. Every wall has a window to let in the light, even the ceilings. There are no gaudy pictures of gods and goddesses, but coral reefs make up some of the wall structure, and shells of all shapes and sizes hang from them.

The place is cheery and bright, mirroring the sea with all its design and hues of color.

After two turns and a set of stairs, Davina stops at a room and twists the door knob, stepping aside to let me walk inside to a bedroom of royal blue and gold. The bed is large with white sheets and pillows, a large desk sits on one side of the wall, while a large hutch resides on the other.

The room is magnificent, but it seems to be another prison.

I turn to Davina, who still stands in the doorway, her two men behind her.

"Another prison?"

She shakes her head.

"Then what?"

"You're a visitor in Her Majesty's house, Dagen the Blood Axe," one of her men state. "Make yourself at home."

My gaze falls back on the young siren in front of me. "This won't be my home, Blood."

She hits me with a glare. I don't know what she was expecting—to adopt me? I might act like an animal at times, but I'm not looking to be anyone's pet.

"Dinner is at six," the other man instructs.

"I won't be hungry," I allude.

"Then she'll drag you there."

I perk a brow. "Really?" She smirks, and I cross my arms over my chest. "I'd love to see that."

She sizes me up while I do the same, and damn, there's a lot to admire about the little temptress who hasn't tried a quarter of the things her older sister did.

Which was a lot.

Just the idea of fucking has been on my mind since it happened. My cock has been wanting to sink deep inside a woman for days, my imagination running wild with scenarios and positions.

None of them including Edda.

She isn't my wife, I'm not ready to build a family. I'm meant to save our people, it's what I'm good at. But seeing these woman, barely clothed, the most beautiful of the opposite sex I have ever seen, my fantasies just don't end with a fully clothed Edda.

Instead with green eyes and red hair. Her hand wrapped around my cock and lips pressed around the tip. My fingers through the strands of her hair and—

My new bedroom door slams shut, leaving me alone once more.

Giving the room another look over, it's better than sleeping in the middle of the hard tiled floor. Next dilemma is waiting on the little broad to see if she thinks she's going to drag me out of this room to eat dinner with her.

The little Siren isn't going to get what she wants.

—

She drug me to the elongated dining room table with a knife to my ribs. I guess she didn't specify how she was going to get me into this room. I was hoping for her little hands to try and wrap about my wrists again while she attempted to pull me from my new place of residence, but my dreams have been more vibrant and outrageous lately.

Seated at one side of the table, Davina sits across from me while her enticing sister, Nesrine, sits to my right.

"Now this will be fun," she mutters, her hand gliding across the back of my chair as she plops down beside me.

The others file into the room slowly, while I ignore her, each taking a seat and passing stares mixed with glances of blended emotions, murder, and curiosity. Davina remains unaffected while Atarah glares at her from the head of the table.

Fucking wonderful.

Pinned between the woman who kissed the living fuck out of me and the older one who wants my head on a spike, this is going to prove to be the most interesting dinner I've ever had.

"I heard you have your own room now," Nesrine coos on my right. I don't answer because I'm done playing her little mind games.

"Well," states the tangerine-colored sister that I haven't met. "We hope you enjoy your...stay."

My brows furrow because she's just as insane as the little blood temptress who likes knives and shoving people across rooms.

Nesrine leans closer to me. "If you're...lonely at night, Viking, I don't mind—"

"I *mind*," I snap. I can feel her smile—literally, her presence exceeds everyone else in the room except the hellion sitting across from me.

"Of course you do," she replies in a low whisper. "You already have your eyes set on the little one who can heave you across the room, make you bleed, and haul you against your will."

I turn my attention to her. Black hair braided and tied on top of her head, a pink flower that I've never seen before embeds itself in her locks.

"The only *sight* I have," I gripe, "Is getting the hell out of here."

She winks. "Absolutely."

"Do your people eat fish?" I glance around the table, landing on the Siren with purple hair and matching eyes. Sitting next to Davina, her eyes glimmer in curiosity as she blatantly stares at me like I'm a foreign object to her.

I guess I am.

"Yes," I reply.

"Did you know that your population is dwindling one percent every year?"

"What?"

"Your people," she repeats. "You're becoming a rare species like us."

My brows narrow. "Where did you—we're not dwindling."

"I've never seen anyone like you before," the orange-haired woman states. "Do you all have broad shoulders and hair on your face?"

"No."

"Do you eat hor—orce—" The purple siren looks at Davina. "What are they called again?"

Davina doesn't look up from the table, but the purple siren snaps her head back to me.

"Horses," she states, snapping her fingers.

I open my mouth, but Nesrine starts laughing and leans into me. "You'll have to excuse our sisters." She points at the woman with orange hair. "That's Kali." Then the purple one. "And Rohana."

"That's rude, we didn't introduce ourselves," Rohana conveys, covering her mouth. "But do you really eat horses?"

"No, we don't—"

"Enough," Atarah orders. "Remember your manners at the table, ladies." Rohana rolls her eyes, and Kali shifts in her chair.

"Davina," Atarah quips, which prompts her to finally look up. "Make sure next time...you mention that you'll have guests."

Blood's eyes turn into slits.

"I just said *next* time."

Alright, so they can hear or communicate amongst each other through some sort of mind magic. And I want to know the reason.

"Why doesn't she speak?" I ask, settling back on Davina. I feel seven pairs of eyes do the same to me.

"She doesn't like strangers," Rohana informs.

I quirk a brow. "Really? So, she can?"

"No," Isolde retorts, deepening her coral-hued brows.

"Why?"

Nesrine bumps me with her elbow. "Stop asking questions, Viking, when you know you won't get the answer."

True, but still not going to stop me.

"I don't believe she's scared for a moment." Davina's forehead creases. "So there's something you all are hiding."

"Which would be?" Atarah drones.

"It's linked to how you all are on this island," I state.

"A real spy," Nesrine remarks. "Doesn't take a head full of brains to know that."

"You'd know if your people were from here," Isolde alleges, leaning her elbows onto the table. "It's not a secret."

I shrug. "Then tell me."

"Oh, I'm sorry—" Isolde smiles. "—that's *if* you were family."

I gnash my teeth. Every single one of these females are a pain in my balls.

Now I'm about to eat dinner with seven little vagrants who kill men at sea just because they can. My father might think he is ready to storm the island, but I'm hoping he thinks twice. Because I have a feeling these women are suited up and waiting for my men to show up for me.

And they're not scared at all.

CHAPTER ELEVEN

Davina

"Why do I always find you alone?" a male voice asks, amusement laced in each word, and it only means one person—Tobias.

Standing from my hunched position, I turn from my small tide pool of starfish to face him.

"I brought you something," he offers before I can speak a word, digging into the pockets of his brown pants, striding toward me.

A foot away, he stops, opening his palm and revealing a white rock. When he shifts his hand from side to side, it illuminates shades of orange and green, fading and reappearing again with each angle.

"It's called a fire opal," he conveys. "It reminded me of you."

Extending his arm, he waits for me to do the same so he can drop it in my hand. I do, letting him place the stone in my palm, brushing the smooth rock with my fingertips before throwing my arms around his neck in a hug.

He chuckles, wrapping his arms around me in return, and nestles his face into the crook of my neck. "Did you miss me?"

"*Hardly*," I jeer, giving him a squeeze before releasing him. Looking back down at the rock, I tilt it in different angles again, playing with the colors. "*It's magic.*"

"I guess so," Tobias replies. "I found it in Port Royal."

He doesn't go on, which means he didn't find Lorne. I can see the disappointment that marks his face. The sadness in his dark brown eyes that he tries to hide from me. That's the good part about knowing someone for so long, they can't hide from you.

"It's beautiful, thank you."

"I'll bring you some of that cheese I was telling you about next time," he conveys. "I just didn't have the chance to this time around."

"I'm hoping it won't be for awhile," I concede.

"Why?"

I shrug. *"Just lonely when you're not here."*

"But you tried to get me to stay away last time."

I peer up at him. *"You know why."*

"Sometimes I think you want to either get me killed or you really do care for me, I'm not sure which yet."

"How could you say such a thing?" I rebuff. *"I'd never let anyone hurt you."*

He shrugs. "Nor I, Princess, but—"

"There are no 'buts'. I'm protecting you from my father, who doesn't care if you're my friend or saved my life."

"Which he doesn't even know about."

"Tobias," I warn. *"Why are you trying to pick a fight with me?"*

He averts his gaze. "I'm not."

"You are because you're upset with me. Because I'm—because you know I'm still adjusting to—"

"Another prisoner, eh?" My body stiffens immediately. I didn't hear *him* coming, normally his large boots give him away against the tiled floors.

Which makes me wonder if he purposely snuck around because he heard someone speaking.

"Who the hell is this?" Tobias whispers, well, more like

seethes. I inhale a deep breath because I'll need one to deal with the nosy Viking and now an agitated friend.

"We'll talk about it when he's—"

"We'll talk about it now," he counters. "Who and why is—"

"You keep pirates in your company," Dagen announces. "Can't say that's surprising with the—"

"Who are you?" Tobias carps, looking over my shoulder.

I turn on my heels to find Dagen leaning against the door panel, looking in on Tobias with his burly arms crossed over his chest. Like he's looking in on something bad that I'm doing, as though he just caught me.

Dagen nods toward me. "I'm her prisoner."

"Oh, Davina," Tobias murmurs with concern laced in his tone. "You didn't."

"I did," I tell him. *"Because he trespassed on my island."*

"He's a Viking, Princess," Tobias warns. "He's not an injured sea creature you *picked* off the ocean floor."

"He'll be free when I find out how he got past the veil."

Tobias's head snaps to me. "He got past the—" I stop him when my head whips in his direction to give him a glare. "How? There's no possible way that he could—"

"You can hear her?" Dagan chimes in, staying grounded to his spot. I knock into Tobias gently, warning him to watch his next words.

"I can hear her," Tobias claims, which is immediately followed by my pinching him. *"Ouch."*

"Shut your mouth," I seethe. *"The less he knows about me the better."*

"Why?" he asks, rubbing his bicep. "It's not like he can do anything."

I mean, he's right, he can't, but I don't want him passing along the information to his people.

"Do you walk around telling all your pirate friends about how you're able to come here? That you come here at all?"

"I don't have—"

"Why is it that I don't hear you, Blood?" Dagen digresses, apprehending my attention again. "Are you scared of me?"

I scoff while Tobias chuckles next to me.

"I wouldn't push her, mate," Tobias offers. "She's not as fragile as she looks."

"Trust me—" Dagen pushes himself off the panel. "—I know."

I watch him stride toward us, dressed in brown slacks that I was able to get for him from one of our enforcers and a white shirt that stretches tight over his chest. His hair pulled back and his facial hair, now longer over the course of the week, still not hiding the overconfident quirk of his lips.

Dagen's focus stops at Tobias. "Who are you?"

"Tobias Nathaniel, the Prince of—"

"The Black Sea," he finishes for him. "I've heard of you."

Tobias stands taller. All of a sudden pleased that his dumb name has been passed around while quickly forgetting that he's talking to my prisoner not a friend. "Yeah? I didn't know my name went up that far north."

"It does," Dagen states. "But nothing that you should brag about. Might want to leave that off your introduction next time."

"What? Now, why?"

"It doesn't matter why," I snap. *"Who cares what men like him think about you?"*

Tobias shifts his weight. "I care because I'm not a cut-throat asshole who goes and steals ships and—"

"Rapes women," Dagen fills in. "Steals from other sailors who carry aid for villages and—"

"I *don't* rape women."

"That's not what's spoken about you when I'm—"

"What's raping women?" I ask Tobias. He looks down at me with furrowed brows, looking upset and angry. My head

snaps to Dagen, and I step forward, extending my arm for him to leave.

He upset my best friend, and I've had enough of him already.

Dagen gives me an amused look. "You can't just *tell* me to go?"

My brows deepen further.

"Did I make your *friend* mad?"

Another step from me.

"What are you going to do, Blood?" he taunts. "Throw me across the room again?"

I reach around my waist and pull out his blade, which does nothing to his straight-laced face.

"Killing a man with his own knife," he marvels. "Classic barbian right there."

I close the distance between us, stopping when our chests brush. My eyes barely meet his shoulders when I peer up at him. His blue eyes entertained as our gazes lock.

"Question is," Dagen continues. "Do you have the gall to do it?"

I believe gall means courage, and if that's the case, I'm surprised the Viking doesn't recognize that I do.

Then again, I read that Vikings were stubborn creatures who were tunnel-visioned and tenacious.

"Pretty little thing like you doesn't like hurting—"

"*Watch* it," Tobias seethes behind me. "I don't know how y'all treat women at home but you won't be talking to her like that."

Dagen doesn't look at him. He doesn't even blink at the anger lacing through Tobias's tone. What he does do is lean forward, coercing me to smell the leather that always trails off him.

"You don't need a bodyguard," he mutters, holding my agitated stare. "Especially a pirate who'll rob you blind and

—" The sound of boots echo behind me, and I know it's Tobias stomping toward him.

"*That's enough,*" I order Tobias. "*Stay where you stand.*"

"Two minutes and I've already had enough of this man," he shouts. "You should've—"

"*You don't have to live on this island day in and out,*" I counter. "*And I need information out of this man. I need to know how he got by the veil. How do you get by the veil? He's the second man from another civilization that has come here without my permission.*"

"We've been through this," Tobias replies. "All I know is that it's just me." I want to press him further, but we've been back and forth on this subject. He claims he doesn't know, and I've accepted it, but with a watchful eye.

"*You're a man of power,*" I tell my best friend as Dagen glances down at my lips. "*Your body exceeds it. Something about you makes no sense, you don't remember your father or mother but you weren't affected by Kali's singing that day when Rohana was taken. You must come from—something.*"

He must be something unearthly because there is no way he should be here. But Tobias fails to believe it while I know he's in denial. He doesn't like to speak about his past, doesn't remember much, he claims, and Isolde has a hard time reading him when she shouldn't.

"A man that's about to be attacked doesn't just stand around for it to happen," Dagen exceeds through our conversation. "I'll finish my half of our conversation later."

He leaves the room, his boots now making a reverberating sound off the pristine tiles so I know he was eavesdropping before.

"I don't know how I'm able to cross through," Tobias mutters. "I'm sorry, Davina, I know it leaves you unsettled."

I turn to face him, his chin tucked into his chest that is decorated with a long gold chain that I gave him years ago. A ruby pendant hangs off of it, the color of my hair to remind him of me whenever he has to go back off to the sea.

"*We'll figure it out,*" I convey, not believing for a second that we will.

There is only one person who might be able to help, and even then I'm hesitant about learning the truth that she'll discover. Taysa is nothing but honest, brutally so, that it's hard to swallow. I'm afraid that whatever Tobias is, it won't be something I can deal with.

"I'd never hurt you," he proceeds. "*Ever.*" His hands cup my face while his thumbs gently brush my skin. "You need to get into the water, you're getting dry."

I attempt to pull my face away. "*I'm tired of swimming in a tidepool of water when the sea is not far from me.*"

"We'll find a way for you to go back," he promises, keeping me within his grasp.

That hope he tries to fill my head with, I gave up on it a long time ago. Without going to Taysa and giving up Zeus knows what, I've abandoned my hope of feeling the salt water soak into my skin again. The morning swims with the orcas and fish.

"I won't fail you," he whispers. "I promise."

I glimpse back at him, those chestnut-brown eyes have always looked at me the same way he is now—optimistic.

My nose is nestled into Tobias' shoulder, my whole world turned upside down within seconds. Ones I still wouldn't change if given the opportunity.

"It's going to be okay," he coos, brushing my hair with his hands. "We'll find a way."

A wrecked sob is his answer as he holds me snug against his body. He's always been a cushion of comfort, someone I can rely on because he saved Rohana and me that night. And my gift back to him was a scar along the left side of his face.

"I promise," he continues. "I've never broken one. I'll protect you from anything."

My voice never comes. It doesn't because it can't. I earned my sisters' freedom off the island by giving up something that made me who I am—my voice.

"Just nod if you understand." I do, while inhaling a deep breath. "We'll tell your father that—" My head jerks up.

He can't.

My father would be furious if he found out that I befriended a young pirate, let alone one that ran with Hunters.

Furiously, I shake my head, strands of hair slapping me in the face.

Tobias latches on to my cheeks. "Stop."

I bite my lower lip to keep myself from going into a nervous fit.

"Then I won't," he alludes. "I won't if it's going to upset you."

A harsh wave of oxygen leaves my lips. I'm relieved that he listens to me. That he always listens to me. He's the only one in the world that I confide everything to, but it shouldn't be this way. He shouldn't be my rock.

He shouldn't be anything.

CHAPTER TWELVE

Tobias

I t hurts, but it makes sense, I wouldn't fully believe me either. But honestly, I don't know how I'm able to pass the veil. Davina says it's magic, that no one but a Siren can pass through, and I'm neither a Siren nor any sort of magical creature. If I was, I would've found my brother already.

We've already proven that I'm not a living creature that can breathe under the sea. Nor can I sing, been told that several times from my men on the ship that it sounds like a dying whale the moment I try to belt a note.

Regardless, I'd do anything to make her believe me. When she turned into a walking being on this island, everything changed.

The way she looked at me.

The way she laughed.

She doesn't do much of that anymore, and I blame some of that on myself. All I used to talk about was her being able to sit with me on the beach and how I could hold her close. Now that she has those capabilities, I don't think she knows how to deal with being something other than a Siren in water.

"*I know you promised,*" Davina finally says. "*And I believe you.*"

I shake my head. "You don't. Everything...everything is different now."

"*We're just older now,*" she replies with a shrug. "*It happens to—*"

"I think you loved me before and now you don't."

Her brows furrow. "*I do love you.*" I shift my weight.

It's my fault—we're two different species of beings. I have more emotions than her, and we just don't mesh. I fell in love with a sorceress who never cast a spell or song on me, and I should've known better. I should've fought with everything I had to keep her away from my heart.

"*You didn't find your brother.*" I shake my head because I can't say the words out loud. It's too much and too hard to swallow every single time I come back empty-handed.

"*You will find him,*" she pledges. I almost scoff, look who's being naive now. The world is too big, and I'm only one person with a crew of fucking idiots that can't keep Lorne in one place for enough time so I can catch up to him.

"*I'll help you.*"

"How?" I leer. "You can't step foot off this island."

"*I know someone,*" she says carefully. "*Someone who can help us find—*"

"You're *not* going to go back to Taysa and ask her for another desired spell," I snap. "Are you out of your fucking mind?"

"*She might be able to—*"

"*No,*" I digress. "No more spells. No more magic. No more lies. No more—" I wave my hand in between us. "*This.*"

"*What's this?*"

"The stupid little illusion that we're friends when clearly we've just become—"

"*Don't say another word that you'll regret later,*" she warns. "*I'm protecting you.*"

I take a step toward her. "From whom exactly? When is the last time your father visited you?"

"Thankfully, not for a while," she replies, crossing her arms. *"He makes everyone nervous. He walks around judging and complaining about how nothing is good enough. He issues out—"*

"This island *isn't* good enough for you," I vouch. "You don't belong here."

Her eyes slit at me. *"Are you saying you don't want—"*

"Don't say another word *you'll* regret later," I counter. "I wish for more than you could ever imagine."

"But you're scared."

I perk a brow. "Of?

"What you men call rejection."

I look heavenward. "You read too many books."

"You bring me the books."

"Going to have to start looking at what I'm bringing you next time."

"I think you do," she notes. *"I've learned more from what you've brought me than anything I could've under the sea."*

"But?"

"You don't act like any of the men in those books."

"How?" My eyes widen a little when I think I see her cheeks flush a soft shade of red.

I've never seen Davina blush, she's too impassive most of the time, and the rest of the time she's either teasing or chastising me for something.

"They hold a woman in their arms and—" My arms think before my brain registers her body pressed into mine, my hands gripping above her hips.

"Like this?" She nods, looking into my chest. "What else?"

"You know what else," she mutters as she slowly pulls her gaze to meet mine.

"I'm not going to kiss you, Davina," I whisper. "You remember the last time I tried."

She blinks.

She remembers.

I was on my ship, standing on one of the wooden planks over the hull. The closest place to the water where we could talk without yelling at each other. She would sit with me for a few minutes before her skin would start to dry out, and I went for it. The sun was setting, making shades of pinks, oranges, and purples color the sky. It illuminated her skin and the green shades of her eyes.

It ended with me getting a mouthful of salt water and wet clothes.

She apologized, saying she wasn't used to people like me being so close to her. So I kept my hands to myself.

Until now.

Now I wanted to see how far she'd let me go, but I wasn't about to get flung from the room like she did with her bed one time when I told her that I didn't like how she went and made a private deal with Taysa that took her voice.

It wasn't that I didn't like her on land, I do, it just makes her extremely unhappy.

"Are you not a man?" she asks me innocently. I clench my teeth because, even though she doesn't know it, she's pushing me.

"In flesh and blood, Princess."

"Then why won't you—"

"Didn't you hear what I just said?"

"Doesn't mean I'll do it again."

"Do you want me to try and kiss you again?"

"I think you ruined the moment," she hedges. *"I've read that it's immediate and, sometimes unexpected."*

"Next time," I allude, releasing her from my hold and taking a step back. "You're just curious, and you need to get rid of the Viking."

"I need to know how he got through the veil first."

"He isn't going to speak, Davina. You think I'm stubborn, those men are downright fearless. It doesn't matter what you've done to him, he won't pierce a word from his lips."

"I haven't tried everything yet," she retorts.

"Which is?"

"I don't know."

"You think your father will get upset seeing me here, imagine if he finds *him* here."

"He isn't expected to come until—"

"If that Viking gets his hands on you unexpectedly then it'll—"

"He already has, and I took care of—" She doesn't finish her words because I'm already on my way out of the room in the direction he came from.

He's dead—plain and simple.

The brute thinks he can just touch my Davina while getting to walk freely around the island to do Hades knows what.

Not on my time.

Definitely not when I'm around. And he sure as fuck is going to learn to respect the living hell out of the woman that one day may open her heart to me, instead of using me as a teacher of things I know she doesn't want from me.

My body spins around to face Davina again to unload another wrath of words on her, but she speaks instead.

"You will not see him."

"Already did," I reply. "And yes, I will."

"Tobias."

"Davina."

She lifts a brow. *"He is larger than you."*

"He's *stupider* than me too."

"Please." Her face falls into a frown, one that would usually get me to do anything for her, except it falls short from hitting my rationality.

89

This time, I'll get to kill something that actually deserves it. That touched something that I hold dear to my heart.

"No," I deadpan.

"For me."

"That won't work." I take a step toward her. "You see, I don't handle a woman being touched or—"

"I handled it."

"It shouldn't be something you have to handle. Let me just kill the fucker so you'll be safe, and we'll look for how he got through the veil elsewhere."

"We need information now."

"How many times do I have to explain to you that he won't speak? They are loyal to their people."

"If he wants to live the rest of his days back home with them, he will speak."

I lean forward. "You think trying to get him to be your *friend* is going to make him address all your concerns? Well I can testify firsthand that—"

"You've never been around a Viking," she counters.

"I've been around killers and Hunters, Davina. I've seen men die before speaking. And that Viking in there is worse than all of them combined. Your sweet little face isn't going to do shit."

"My face has nothing to do with—"

"What do your sisters say?"

"It doesn't—"

"I know Atarah doesn't like it."

Her eyes immediately turn into slits. *"Are you speaking to her without my knowledge?"*

"No, but she hates me, so I know she'll despise him. I've been a pain in her ass for a few years now, so at least she knows who I am."

"And she tries to get me to kill you off every other time you are here."

I shrug. "You have a soft spot for me, darling, what can I say?"

"I need to try. I need to know if there is anything he knows that maybe you don't."

"The only thing we have in common is that we're men," I profess.

"You're killers."

"Most men are."

She locks her jaw. *"Not my people. Women are the killers."*

"We're both humans."

"That could be something, but your men can't see the island."

"I'm out of options."

Davina remains silent for a moment before stating, *"Maybe you can speak to him."*

"He won't speak to me. You'd have better luck with him telling you to fuck off than I would. He'd flat out try to obliterate me with his fists."

"Then let me handle it."

"You're pushing it, Davina."

"I normally do, according to you, but this is serious."

My nostrils flare. All of this is crucial to her well-being and her home, but she's taking it too lightly. Handling something that she knows nothing about.

The Viking and I might be men, but he's a different sort of male, and Davina has never been around a human other than me. He'd have no conscious of hurting her.

I'd kill for her.

But trying to get through her thick skull about it is like convincing my men to wear dresses.

"I promised I would protect you," I rebuke. "I put my life on it."

"And you do."

I gesture toward the door. "I can't when I'm searching for Lorne and you have a brute walking around your home."

"*He can't hurt me,*" she chimes.

I peer over my shoulder, back at where he left. "He won't have a chance to."

"*I promise, I'll be careful.*" She touches my forearm to regain my attention. "*I promise.*"

"You can't control everything, Princess."

"*Like you can't control the sea, Prince of the Black Sea.*"

"That's fate."

She straightens her spine like a little warrior about to go fight a giant. "*And I'm his.*"

A heavy sigh escapes my lips. "There seriously is no arguing with you is there?"

She smirks. "*You're finally starting to realize it.*"

"How will I know you're safe?"

She places a hand over my heart. "*Here.*"

CHAPTER THIRTEEN
DAGEN

The first mistake the little Siren made was obvious—she let me walk freely through the island with no guards hovering or watching my every move. The second mistake was showing me how much the pirate meant to her. She was protective, angry, expressed it through her eyes—which speak volumes.

And I've never seen eyes so green in my life.

At another time, maybe in another place, I would've claimed that woman. I wouldn't have wanted any of my fellow clansmen to touch her. I'd probably even fight to keep her because her skin was kissed by the sun, nothing like the ivory-color I'm accustomed to. The sun doesn't stay for long in Lothbrok, and if it does, it's shaded by clouds.

Davina glimmers in the rays of the bright sun, and I can't help but examine her when we're in the same room.

But the pirate, he makes no secret about being in love with her. While her eyes read her emotions, his are covered all over his face like war paint. It's in his tone, the touchy mood swings that he just presented, and now I know I can use him as a pawn.

He's tall, almost my height, but definitely not my size. He's not a scrawny man by any means, but he's nothing that would scare me on the battlefield. He's slender in build, his forearms show some muscles displayed by his rolled-up sleeves. His light brown hair is also affected by the sun because I've never seen that shade either.

But the long sword that is hoisted on his hip, I want to know if the boy can use it. The irony of using it on *him* isn't lost on me, and it surely would make the little Siren lose her mind, however I need a means to leave after I obtain what I've come for.

After they argue, which I don't hear all of, but his voice carries like a bird, Davina walks casually out of the room they were in and toward the double adjacent doors that lead outside.

I follow from afar, learning her hobbies, her everyday things that she does. She's a woman, and women like talking. Though, I'm at a disadvantage because these aren't just women but creatures who prey on men. However, I need to make every effort to obtain some of her trust and get back to my ship, which, hopefully, is still waiting for me.

Outside, the sun is extremely bright as she strides on a stone path surrounded by flowers of many colors, tall and bundled together. The route curves to the right, where a large pond lays in the middle of the grass and rocks.

She stands at the edge of the water, stretching her arms over her head while tilting her head to one side, showing off the slenderness of her neck. Her red hair beckons out against all the green of trees that don't look native here but at home. Some are palm trees but others are pine and oak surrounding the lagoon, which presents as odd to me.

A small splash and Davina's body is gone, the rippling of water the only thing making any movement that she was here and not in my head. Everything seems like a distorted and blurred dream here, each thing more bright and vibrant. Nothing I've ever seen or imagined possible in my head, and it all lays forth in front of me.

Davina's head suddenly pops up from the water as she

brushes back her hair and swims away from me, dipping back down into the reservoir. I inch closer, not bothering about hiding my presence anymore. If we're stuck together on this island, might as well make the best of it and obtain what's needed for me to leave.

Her head pierces through the water again, and the moment it does, I make her jump with my words.

"So are you and the pirate coupled together?"

She twirls in the water so quickly it takes me back a second at how she can move so fluidly. Her eyes glower at me as I step closer.

"He's a strapping lad, I guess, if you like thieves."

I'm still met with narrowed brows.

I shrug. "You don't have to talk to me about it." I smirk. "Wait, you don't speak to me at all."

She rolls her eyes and starts swimming away from me again.

"How did he get past the veil?"

She freezes then slowly brings herself to face me again.

"I heard your little fight."

That gets her to swim toward me. Her eyes slam into my body, and she looks predatory.

Seductive.

A woman that needs to be fucked into submission because her whiny little pirate isn't going to do it.

The look in her eyes discloses that she wants to kill me for eavesdropping, but from the conversation that I half-heard, she won't get to venture down that path—yet. The little she-devil needs information from me after all.

I gesture to the water. "No, please, I'll do the talking. You continue to enjoy your swim."

My body is suddenly hit with a huge wave of water, shoving me backward until my back hits the ground.

Evil little wench.

Pushing myself up into a sitting position, my clothes stick to my skin as I shove my now disheveled hair back from my face. Only her eyes and nose appear above the water, and I know she's hiding a damn smirk on her face.

"Sensitive subject?" I jeer.

She ignores me and continues to swim around in a small circle.

"You're right to keep him away from me," I proceed. "I'll use him to my advantage."

She doesn't stop, my words ineffective to her ears. She must think I'll concede to her wishes because I'm free and don't want to be chained back to a floor.

"You underestimate me, Blood," I announce. "I'm not like your pirate."

I've killed men like him before breakfast when I was a wee lad.

Learning how to fight at a young age was normal in Lothbrok. For centuries our clan has been thrown in the throngs of chaos when we were at war with the Highlands. It was ruthless and merciless, women and children were murdered just as often as men. Our homes were burned to the ground, sometimes entire villages, and the strike of their warriors was always imminent—always coming.

When I turned seven, my father's worst fears came to fruition when my siblings and mother were killed. I don't remember them, maybe because I tried to lock out any sort of animosity that proved to be a weakness. It was best not to be emotionally attached to another human being. But loyalty ran deep within my veins, and that's how I always stayed with my people and my father.

He never remarried, I watched his heart break plenty of times over the years when I was a child and families would gather together in the square. When siblings would play in the village and I stayed home alone to work. He never pushed me to be social, just a leader.

And that's what I am.

Which is why I'll use whatever she cares about to her disadvantage. When you don't have a weapon, the other option is knowledge; the strengths and weaknesses of your opponents. And since I couldn't take out a group of Sirens with my bare hands, clues would work just as well.

We might not know each other, never crossed paths before, but I'm going to be something that goes down as a nightmare in her history.

—

Sitting in the room where I'm held hostage, it's the only spot that holds any sort of comfort. I've already scouted the small island, it's just a few huts surrounding the castle with no boats or anything large enough for me to float on. Not that I expected to find anything where all these beings swim as transportation, but I thought I'd try my luck.

The door behind me creaks open, but I don't turn around from the window, already smelling the familiar scent of sea salt wafting through the air.

"I'm not in the mood for the staring contest, Blood," I allude, too busy pondering the thoughts that plague every second and minute here.

"Who are you?" The voice is deep and gravelly, and I snap my head in the direction of it.

Standing before me is a gray-haired man holding a trident in one hand and glowering at me like I just stepped into a place where I shouldn't be—which technically I have. I know how it feels when said stranger walks onto any land I own in Lothbrok.

I kill them with no questions asked.

My eyes fall on his shining crown, and I stifle back a groan. When I thought it couldn't get any worse, I think it just may have.

Shirtless, the man, if you'd want to call him that, cautiously walks over to me, his long hair stopping above his ribs as he slams the bottom of his weapon on the floor.

"Who are you?" I counter.

"This is *my* island," he retorts. "And you will answer *my* question."

His island, meaning he's linked to the girls, which makes him the mythical King Triton.

"I'm Dagen the Blood Axe."

The man's brows furrow as he continues toward me again. "Who brought you here?"

"I came here on my own."

"Impossible," he snaps. "*How?*"

"I just told you, but you haven't told me who you are."

"I'm King Triton," he proclaims, confirming my fear. "And you will answer me with respect and the truth."

"Again," I convey. "I trespassed on my own."

He doesn't waste a moment, positioning his weapon to shove in my direction. It catches my right arm, grazing my flesh, creating a biting pain, and I know there's blood because it's sharp as fuck.

Taking a step back, I instantly have to duck because the king already has his trident flying horizontally to take off my head. The moment it passes, I charge him.

Our bodies collide together until his swiftly halts from moving. His hand finds my hair as he tries to pull me off him, but I answer his move with a punch to the ribs. A muffled grunt leaves his lips, and I'm thrown off him, landing on my back.

His weapon thrusts down, but I dodge the hit, hearing it

break the tiles next to my torso. My foot hurdles in his direction, hitting him in the thigh to gain a bit of time to shove myself back up.

It buys me no time though because he's already stabbing his spear at me again, barely missing my head.

The ground underneath me starts to rumble, disturbing the limited furniture in this room. I stumble to get back up as he swings his weapon at me again, this time slamming into my shoulder. Numbness radiates through my whole arm as I slide to the side to get away from him, awaiting another hit.

It never comes.

I jerk my attention to him, distracted with whatever is behind him. His body is so wide that I can't see what it is but hear the pattering footsteps approach deeper into the room.

Then I see her—the woman who drips beauty and strength standing beside him with a frown.

Davina's green eyes study me, inspecting me from head to toe, which gets me to furrow my brows.

Is she worried about me?

"How long has he been here?" the old man leers. "And *why* didn't I know this?"

She must communicate with him because he speaks again.

"How?" He returns his glare to me, so I'm not sure who he's speaking to. "*You*," he roars. "How did you get past the veil?"

"I didn't know about this veil," I reply. "I knew where I had to go, and I came here."

"From whom?"

"My father."

The king perks a brow. "Who is he?"

"Oryn the Great."

"Great at *what*?" he asks.

My eyes bore into him. "Killing. He's a great leader."

"That sends his son to do what, exactly?" I look over at Davina, who's engaged in what I'm saying.

She wanted this, to know why I'm here and how. I honestly didn't know about this veil that they keep speaking of because I could see the island clearly.

"I'm here for my own reasons, not to harm your people," I recite. Which is true, I don't plan on assassinating or harming anyone that doesn't try to hurt me.

King Triton looks over at his daughter. "Did he hurt you?" She shakes her head, which earns her a glare from me.

I did try to hurt her, *several* times. So why she's trying to save me only alludes to one thing—she wants to know more.

"I don't believe you," he responds, looking back to me. "You're a Viking. Your people are barbaric and land hungry."

"You're speaking of the *Highlanders*," I retort. "We only take what—"

"I'm not interested in your history," he transmits. "What is your reason for being here?"

"To explore this land and any—"

"This land is not within your realm, boy. We're extremely south from you—"

"I can't convince you why I'm here then," I seize. "I just told you."

"And since I don't believe you," he claims. "You'll die."

Davina seizes his large bicep.

"I've said my peace," he fumes, keeping his attention averted from her. "You're naive to think you can convince this man to tell you the real reason he's here."

Her hands rip away from him as she takes a step back.

"Stand up." It's a feminine voice, sweet but stern that just filled into my head. Her stare is still pinned on the king, but I do what it tells me to do and get to my feet.

"Do not defy me," the king berates. "He will not—" He halts, which makes me believe she spoke again. Meanwhile,

I'm still reeling over how I may have heard her speak to me and how odd it is that it wasn't said out loud.

"The real reason," the king continues bringing his attention to me. "If you don't tell my daughter by the end of the *week*, I'll be back to finish the job, boy."

I open my mouth to tell him that everything I said is all he's going to get out of me, but he turns on his heels and leaves the room.

Davina stays put, watching him stride out, her shoulders sagging in defeat because she knows there isn't anything my adamant ass is going to expose.

"You spoke to me," I blurt, needing to state the obvious.

Slowly, she brings her eyes to me. *"Don't get used to it."*

I smile, I can't help it. I knew she'd be a fucking smart ass with a mouth that fit her fire red hair.

"Too late," I reply. "Already did." She scoffs, peering back at the door that is wide open but leaves behind her father's words. "Why did you save me?"

She shakes her head, inhaling and exhaling a loud breath. *"I should've let him kill you, but I still have questions."*

"I'm not sure what more I can—" She snaps her head to me.

"Your line of lies isn't convincing, Viking. You're here for another reason."

I perk a brow. "And what reason would that be?"

Davina positions herself so that she's facing me straight on. Chests aligned, eyes perfectly centered on me, a small lift appearing at the corner of her lips.

"I'm not so naive, as my father so perfectly pointed out."

"I don't doubt it," I voice. "But I don't know about this veil that keeps being mentioned. I saw the island clear as day."

"Which only means one thing."

"Which is?"

"You're a Siren."

I chuckle. "I can definitely tell you that I'm not. You do not want to hear me sing."

"Then you're something else. A merman, maybe?"

I shake my head. "Not one of those either."

"Well, you're not just a Viking."

"I promise you, Blood, that I am. Through and through and full-blooded. Whomever put up this veil messed something up."

She wrinkles her nose. *"That's impossible."*

"And why is that?"

"Because," she deadpans.

"I have nothing else for you," I tell her with a weak shrug. "All I want to do is go home."

She perks a brow. *"And bring the rest of your army here?"*

"This island is too small to do anything with—" I give her a dismissive wave of my hand. "—and I can't farm on it."

"Farming is growing food, correct?" I nod. *"Doesn't sound like a Viking to me."*

"And what does sound like one?" The corners of my eyes crinkle. "Since you know my people so well."

"I've read about your people," she scowls. *"You kill people for land. You extend your territory with blood and killing."*

"That's the Highlanders," I retort. "And we only kill if—"

"So you don't march on others' land?"

"We do but—" She crosses her arms along her chest, that determination I get to experience firsthand.

"Is it your land?"

"No, but—"

"That's enough for me to know. Which is exactly what you're doing here."

"I don't *want* your land, Blood."

"Stop calling me that."

"That's what you like though, isn't it?" My eyes tighten on her. The glittery bodice of purple, the way it dips and gathers up her breasts so that I can see the mounds that tease to be touched. "You want to kill me so bad, but you're holding back, why?"

"You don't know a thing about me," she seethes.

"Nor do you know me."

"I know that you're here without my permission."

"And that's it."

"We'll see," she chants. *"Think about the week I bought you and how much you want to tell me."*

"And if I make it up?"

"I have ways of making good on your truths, Viking." She takes a step toward the door and peers over her shoulder. *"Dinner is at sunset. I'll make sure you're not sitting next to my father."*

CHAPTER FOURTEEN

Tobias

"The Mistress is coming up on our starboard, Cap'n," Asher announces over the chatter and rustle of my crew.

Glancing over to the right, I see the massive ship glide its way toward us. It's intimidating if you didn't know who it was. The massive masts and sails colored in red to make the ship look sinister and blood-thirsty. Its cannons stationed along the sides, ready to fight at any moment—which always sets me on edge.

I don't trust my Uncle Declan.

As the years have gone by, he's become more bizarre and leaning toward the bow of mad. His hunger, almost obsession, over hunting Sirens is all he thinks and speaks about. When I was a child, it was the pursuit of treasure and gold. The prospect of chasing down the riches and glory that came with it. But if my uncle spent more time hunting treasure than he did Sirens, he'd own half the world by now.

Instead, he's adamant about hunting down the species that I'm now trying to protect, mainly Davina, and the betrayal I have to keep ensuing to make sure she's safe.

"Bring the girl out," I tell Asher, stepping down from the Captain's deck.

My men stop working, shifting nervously and keeping their heads down the moment they see the Executioner board our side. My uncle elicits a fear that lingers inside them, and I let him keep it. It keeps them doing what I need them to do—which is to keep their mouths shut.

"You all know the drill," I grumble as I walk in front of my men, who have positioned themselves in a straight line. "Keep quiet, your heads down. You speak to *no* one but me."

I get words of agreement and nods as I wait for my uncle to finish docking down next to my ship, Deliah. The moment the ship is safely secured, my uncle's voice booms over the crashing waves.

"Tobias," he greets in a slur, hopping over the banister of my vessel and landing unsteadily onto his feet.

He almost falls, but I don't make an attempt to catch him. He's already made my life complicated enough. Especially when I wanted to break out from underneath him and go off on my own, making a point to tell me that I wouldn't be anything. That I'd never amount to the name I was given because I was too stupid to do any better than what he taught me.

Now I run my own ship, a faithful crew, and have kept the biggest fucking secret known to man away from the man who calls himself the Tyrant of the Water.

"I see she's still floating," he quips, looking around the deck.

"It would seem so," I deadpan. He slaps my shoulder with his chunky hand and rounds me, inspecting for whatever dumb shit he thinks he's going to find.

"I heard you were south," he alludes, more like snoops because I know he has other ships reporting back to him on my whereabouts. We can add paranoid to the list of characteristics that make up my uncle.

"I was."

"Did you find anything?" The moment he asks, the doors to my corridor open and a loud squeal permeates the air.

My men cover their ears along with my uncle, and imitating them, I do too—even though I don't have to. The voice of a Siren has never bothered me, never made me feel a certain way, or compel me to jump off my ship to my death.

It's how I was able to save Davina and Rohanna that fateful night when Kali sang and screamed at the other ships to steer them away.

Another high-pitched scream, and I don't have to look over to know what it is—I caught it. I hunted it down because it would show my uncle what I wanted him to see. And that was me following in his footsteps while leaving me the fuck alone for small periods of time.

"Holy—" My uncle doesn't finish his words because he's already striding toward the creature that now holds all of his attention.

A Siren.

She's probably one of the most beautiful ones that I've caught. Her coral-colored hair matches her tail and scales. Her flawless skin glistens in the sunlight countered by sharp nails and a nasty cut to her brow from thrashing around the tub I had her in.

"Where did you find this one?" my uncle asks, stunned and in awe like he's never seen one before in his life.

Too close to where Davina is.

"Southwest," I respond instead. In the opposite direction of Merindah.

"How?"

I glance in his direction, watching him stand over the Siren that is straining to get out of her ties. It makes me avert my attention because I feel the guilt that starts to stab at my conscience every time this shit happens.

"Saw her on some rocks along the shore of Cabitha," I profess. "We lured her in by letting her think she was going to get us to crash into the rocks and dropped the lines when she got too close."

My uncle spins on his heels to face me. "How were you not affected by her song?"

I smirk. "Can't tell you all my secrets now, can I?"

He frowns, his peppered gray brows descend down his haggard face. The man hasn't seen sleep in years, too focused and hell-bent on his next capture and kill mission.

The moment he doesn't see me budge, he cracks a grin.

"Alright, lad," he claims with a chuckle. "Fair enough. Are you going to sell her?"

"She's yours." Bile begins to rise from my stomach to my throat as I shove the words from my lips.

His brows furrow. "Mine?"

"It was your birthday last week, wasn't it?" I clasp my hands behind my back to keep them from plowing into his skull. He doesn't deserve shit from me, but this is a sacrifice that has to be made to keep him away from Davina.

And I hate him with my entire fucking being.

His blue eyes widen like a little child's. "You remembered." He marches toward me and clasps me into his bulky arms. "She's a beaut and a fine piece for my collection."

"Collection?"

He releases me. "I've begun collecting them."

I frown. "I don't understand."

"We skin 'em, like fish." He makes a hand movement of slicing something with a filet knife. "I have them hanging in my corridors as decoration, and soon I'll have enough to decorate my ship with."

You stupid son of a bitch.

I force back my cringe, my body weakening at the thought of Davina or one of her sisters being peeled and abraded then thrown up like an ornament.

"Would you like to come take a—"

"I'm on my way to Saint Bernards to look for Lorne," I profess quickly. "He's been sighted on—"

"You're still looking for him?" His brows snap together.

"I am."

His face softens. "Boy, he's grown up now. How would you even know it's him?"

"I'll know."

And slightly in denial.

"You've been chasing him around for years," my uncle professes, waving his hand around in the air. "How do you know he's even still ali—"

"Call it a personal pursuit," I recite. "Besides I'm on my way over there anyway."

My uncle stares at me a second longer then bows his head. "Alright. Will you be in Port Royal for the Founder's celebration?"

"I didn't plan on it but—"

"Come," he orders. "You look like you've been on the sea for too long and you need a woman. You're looking a little pale."

I set my jaw and give him a brief nod. I need more than that.

Ordering his men to take my captive to his ship, my uncle hollers at my crew to stay true to their captain, like they need the reminder.

Setting his attention back on me, he slaps my shoulder again. "You take care of yourself out there," he says. "I'll see you in a few weeks."

"See you then."

With one last smile that exhibits a gold tooth, he leaves my ship. The tension in the air going off with him.

I do have to go to Saint Bernards to find Lorne. Then, I need to go back to Davina and tell her to keep her sisters within her realm. The moment any of them set off, I can't protect them from my own kind, and I swore to keep them protected. The price of keeping her safe and the role I have to play to keep my uncle away from her home is large.

And it's the only fucking way I know how. Because if I can get past the veil as well as the Viking, who knows who else can.

CHAPTER FIVETEEN

Davina

Inner would've been delicious if I could focus on it. If my father wasn't glaring at Dagen then diverting it to me as if I was some smitten girl around a handsome, dangerous man that I planned on keeping forever at my side.

I didn't plan on keeping him.

I decided on using and disposing of him in two different scenarios, depending on how all this went. I'd either give him to my sisters or let him go free. The latter was going to subject me to a lot of yelling, chastising, and bickering, but I wasn't as blood starved as my siblings. Nor did I like the cleanup afterward.

But with my father here, things were going to escalate, and Dagen's presence means he might stay longer.

Don't get me wrong, I love when he's here. He reminds me of home, the only living parent I have left, and he loves me dearly, even though his eyes speak of wanting to beat the stupid out of me right now. It is foolish, letting a giant man roam the island to do hell knows what, but I have to try. I have to try to see if he'll speak to me. If he's here for a heinous reason or for just what he had said—to learn the land for his people to take. He never had to say that, it sounded bad enough, but he did.

And I can't help but want to believe him on that part.

Which poses more questions on what would he do if I did let him go. Would my sisters be safe here? When I woke up one morning, would there be ships surrounding the island to overtake it?

Each scenario, the same fear resided in each—my sisters, father, my people, and I would be at the mercy of humans.

Dagen excused himself early, and I followed shortly after but not after him, quite the opposite. I came to the small little place on the island that is completely mine.

My secluded little cove.

Where I keep and collect all my treasures along with Mother's diaries and the item that she left behind.

Her golden cuffs.

Well, one of them anyway. The second hasn't been found, which worries my father and sisters more than anything because it holds the power of the sea, the queen's side of the kingdom. With it in the wrong hands, it would shift the elements. It would mean my father would have to defend his kingdom from the one who holds the missing cuff in order to protect what was ours. And he wasn't as young as he used to be.

Stepping into the darkened cove made of hollowed rock, I follow the light that sparks from my torch. Nothing but silence and my footsteps greet me as I walk deeper into the cool space. The place where everything that means anything is, for the most part.

The moment I make another turn inside, the moon lights up the room from a small hole in the ceiling overhead. I light the stationed torches that I already have here, watching my golden trinkets glimmer. The mountains of books that haven't made it to my bookshelf in the castle stacked up all over along with the human items that Tobias brings back for me are all put in a specific place.

No one comes here but me.

No one is allowed or even knows about it. It's the only spot in the world that completely and utterly belongs to me.

"Nice place you have." I jolt, my hand immediately going for the first thing I can reach as I spin around to throw the item at my intruder.

Dagen blocks the trinket and continues to stand there like he has any right to be in my space right now.

"What are you doing here?" I snap. *"Get out."*

He ignores me, admiring everything cluttered and organized throughout the space. He makes it feel smaller with his considerable frame as he scrutinizes the area.

"That means get out."

"I will," he alludes slowly. "I just wanted to see where you disappeared to."

"It doesn't matter where I go. This is my home."

"Unfortunately, I know that too." He takes another step forward. "This is all...beautiful."

"I don't want you here," I chide. He looks at me then, soft and curious, almost normal.

But him and I are far from common.

He's a warrior of the land while I'm a killer of the sea. Mind you, I don't go off hunting like my sisters anymore because I can't, but once in a while, I dream about it.

It's in my blood, my nature. Killing those who hunt us down for sport runs deep within who I am. The stories and myths made us the bad species, luring men to their deaths by getting them close to the rocks or using our voices to tip sailors overboard. Decade-old Sirens used that trick for sport and entertainment, but now we have more accomplished and well-deserved prey—Hunters.

While we've always been a condemned species, Father said that we became who we are when Persephone was abducted by Hades. She seems to be doing just fine since she married him and rules the underworld.

Taysa's story is that we came about by mermaids, two sisters challenging each other for a crown, and one turned into an evil monster to lure all her lovers to their deaths. Folklore, fairy tales, myths, and legends, I just think we were meant to be like everyone else.

We hunt.

We want to conquer.

We crave our own power.

"How long have you collected all of these things?" he asks, looking toward the ceiling, where I have chiseled the stone wall to make shelves. "My sister would've loved this."

"You have a sister?"

"And a brother."

"You must miss them," I reply softly, taking advantage of his opening up to me.

"I do, every day."

"Well, if you tell me how you passed the veil, I'll let you go home to them."

He looks down at me. "They're dead. And I still don't know." He breaks his attention from me again and turns around to look at what's behind him.

Never turn your back on your enemy.

It automatically echoes in my head. Tobias lives by that rule, so I'm surprised when Dagen does it. But it gives me the opportunity to study him further without him knowing that I'm gaping at him like that smitten girl I was talking about earlier.

His dark hair is pulled back in a bun, hiding the length that used to cascade down his shoulder blades that bulge through his shirt. The brown fabric displays a flat torso, which I've already seen, slimming down to his waist and thick thighs in olive pants.

"Then how did your father know about this place?" I inquire as he brushes the wall with his fingertips.

113

"Honestly, I'm not sure," he voices. "I thought this was just a normal place to locate. He told me that the lands were rich in soil for farming, but it's just covered in sand and tall grass. You don't really question my father."

"You know that makes zero sense to me, right?"

He turns around to look at me and then nods. "I know. I wouldn't believe me either, Blood."

"Then how would you find out if someone was telling the truth?" I cross my arms along my chest, genuinely curious.

He perks a brow then slowly walks toward me. "You really want to know?"

"I do."

"I'd torture them until they spoke."

"And if a woman trespassed?"

His lips quirk. "Would that woman be you?" I bow my head. "You don't want to know the answer to that question."

"I asked, didn't I?"

He releases a mirthless laugh. "You're a woman, that's different."

"I'm stronger than you," I retort with furrowed brows.

He rounds me and leans down a bit. "But your emotions aren't."

"I'm not one of your females in your village," I grumble then twirl on my heels to face him. *"We're more fierce together."*

"I've noticed that," he deadpans.

"So what would you do if one of my people trespasses? How would you get them to spill the truth?"

"If it were one of your sisters, I would've killed them or given them to my men to play with."

"Play with?"

"If it were you," he continues gradually, like he's thinking about it. "I'd seduce you."

"You're not my type," I blurt because I have nothing to say besides that.

I don't even know if I have one. Besides Tobias, no other man has been interesting to me until the new man standing in front of me. And even then I think it's more curiosity than anything.

"I'm a man, Blood," he asserts. "I *am* your type." With his back still to me, it takes everything in my power to not shove him forward.

"That's where you're mistaken."

He turns on his heels and looks at me with a raised brow. "Oh? And how's that?"

"You know nothing about me."

"Because you're spoken for?"

"I'm not spoken for. No one will own me."

"Then you might want to tell your pirate friend that," he advises with a twist of his lips.

"Don't worry about him," I carp. *"You'd have to come up with another plan to get me to speak."*

"The same goes for you. You letting me roam free on your island isn't doing anything except upsetting your sisters and now your father. Now what?"

I shrug. *"You have your week. After that, you're out of my hands."*

"Then you better use me to any advantage you have in your little head because I'm going to die."

I don't know why, but the truth in his voice pierces my chest. I don't like him, but I respect him. I don't believe him, but he's loyal to whatever cause he's serving, and I'm trying not to fault him for that. I might have even been a little more forgiving if it wasn't for him scouting my land and getting past my veil.

"Then pray to your gods," I reply calmly. *"And you can leave now."*

He simpers with amusement in his features and makes his way toward the entrance of the cove but not before leaning a little closer to me.

"You'd be mine, Blood," he mutters in a deep octave, his breath tickling my shoulder. "Underneath me, over me, and with me inside you. I'd *never* let you go."

His words waft around me filled with promise and something else that heats my already warmed blood. His declaration, it's just the chitchat of a man that is desperate to leave freely.

But if he doesn't talk, I won't be able to give him that.

CHAPTER SIXTEEN
DAGEN

The sound of music muffles behind my bedroom door, which has me out exploring the scene. There isn't anything else to do, Davina won't hold a conversation with me longer than five minutes to build any sort of trust, and her sisters look at me like they want to murder me for fun.

So for hours, I've stayed in my room plotting because I found what I came here for.

The cuff.

A plain gold band that sat behind colored glass on one of Davina's shelves between a chandelier and small chest. It glinted off a mirror, catching the end of the cuff that almost didn't catch my eye. My father said it wouldn't be flashy, no gem stones or engravings would decorate the piece.

And that's exactly what it was—plain.

It belonged to our people and was stolen, holding more power than it portrayed from its humble appearance. More promise than I could ever hope for to keep our lands safe and secure against the impending Highlands.

The cuff was magic.

Magic that would bring back the creatures I've heard so many stories about and made my father so addicted to appropriating its return.

Dragons.

As a child, I believed those stories. I was enchanted by the fact that these large beasts flew and roamed our lands within our control. But when I grew up, I started to think my father fed me that line of bullshit to keep my faith when times were hard.

Until he came to me weeks ago with information to seize this relic, only entrusting me to bring it back home. The only thing I knew was that it was golden, plain, "might look like a piece of junk," as my father put it, but I knew of nothing else.

No veil.

No realm of princess killers.

No trying to get myself out of this mess I was currently in.

The moment I'm down the hall, the music gets louder and draws me deeper into the castle toward the large dining room we eat in, like I'm one of theirs. Like they own me and I'm their little puppet.

I'll play the part if it gets me closer to Blood's curiosity.

When I make the last turn inside, there are people everywhere. Men and women dressed, actually scantily dressed, in seaweed, shells, pearls, and leather. I notice King Triton immediately, standing above other men with his broad chest puffed out. He's speaking to them casually until his hard eyes fall on me. His mouth moves a moment longer then he turns his back on them, which sends them in my direction.

Three of them march toward me nonchalantly, and the reason is apparent. The King wants me to know I'm not welcome here, that his daughter isn't here to save me, and that I'm fucked.

I was fully aware of that.

I study the men like I'm trained to do. Each bare-chested, holding large rods with a sizable shell on the top. It makes me wonder how often they've used them, if they know how, and if they've killed more people than me—I doubt it.

The moment they reach me, I'm immediately surrounded and herded outside like a sheep. We're not far from the garden with the large pond that Davina swam in, a perfect and secluded spot for them to try and batter me up, possibly kill me. But without a blade, I don't expect them to get very far, unless they have the strength of the girls, which means I'm worse off than I thought.

With the men following close behind me, I glance around the reclusive surroundings for a weapon of my own. The only things around me are ferns and various flowers. Nothing like oak or pine trees from home to break off a branch and try to gain some sort of advantage on them.

Suddenly, my foot is caught and yanked from behind, taking me to my knees and palms. A sharp pain hits my right kidney, but I force back the thoughts of experiencing or registering it fully.

Instead, I stand back on my feet and twirl around to punch the closest one to me. My knuckles slam into the side of one's face, and I quickly block another blow from the man to his left with my forearm.

The third man moves forward from behind him, trying to spear me in the stomach. Twisting out of his range to the side, I grip his pole and realize it's covered in barnacles.

I can feel my flesh rip at the sharp edges of the little rock-looking creatures as I let go, when my face is knocked to the side by a hard hit.

Immediately, I'm yanked forward and lifted in the air. Fisting my hands, I slam them down on my enemy's shoulders twice before getting him to release me to my feet. Rather than wait on the other two's next move, I snatch the man to my right by his neck and clobber my fist into his ribs. A grunt escapes his lips, and I catch movement behind me as I peer over my shoulder. My elbow catches another in his chest as I swing my head back to connect with another's face —hopefully, a nose.

I feel a collision to my chest, but my adrenaline blinds me from anything else except killing these fools. This isn't my first time being outnumbered and weaponless. Not my first ordeal where the odds were against me.

A strangled gurgle sounds behind me, but I don't turn to look. I'm too busy hauling my fists in calculated movements between the two men in front of me. It's not until one of them gets behind me that things start to take another turn.

Positioning his rod against my neck, he pulls back, attempting to choke me out while the barnacles dig and twist into my skin. Gripping the rod with one hand, trying to ignore the cuts on my palms, I thrust my free elbow back, trying to make contact with his body. Until I'm sucker punched in the stomach by one of his associates. My hold on the rod slips, allowing my enemy less tension to cave in my windpipe.

A flash of red appears in front of me followed by a pair of green eyes that are slitted and narrowed. The rod is suddenly ripped away from my throat, letting a faltered exhale leaves me lips.

"*Duck.*" I do as directed, leaning over to place my palms on my knees as I try to catch my breath as quickly as possible.

I hear rustling and grunts as I peer up to see that the man in front of me is holding Davina in his grasp up in the air.

I barrel toward them, kicking the man at the knee to cause him to loosen his grip so I can rip her out of his clutches. She comes out of his hold as I yank her behind me. As soon as she's safely positioned, I'm on him, punch after punch until I can't feel my knuckles anymore. Not until I feel small hands on my shoulder blades, silently telling me to stop.

It's immediate, my reaction to her. I can still feel the blood pounding through my head, my lungs straining to trudge in air, but my brain, it doesn't remember the fucker I was just beating to a pulp. It's zeroed in on her, and being mixed with relief and pissed that she stepped in.

On my knees, straddling over one of her father's guards, I stand to confront the female who thinks it's her place to step into fights. However, the moment I peer down at her, I'm speechless at how innocent she looks. How easy it was for her to transform into a guiltless beauty when she just over-powered a man trying to kill me. Staring up at me like I am someone she wants to spare from a fate worse than death.

"You're hurt," she acknowledges, her gaze on my neck. *"I'll get someone—"*

"What do you think you're doing?" I snap, taking a step toward her. "You don't step into a man's brawl."

"It was my brawl," she retorts with a raised chin.

I point behind me. "I was the one in between three men. You just strolled by."

"These are my men."

"They're your *father's* men."

"I think you mean 'thank you'," she offers.

I inch closer. "Listen, Blood. I don't need saving. I don't need your help. I don't need your pretty little eyelashes blinking at me like this was just a normal day, doing normal ass things. Stay *out* of my way."

I begin to turn on my heels to head back to my room until her hand grasps my forearm.

"You need to be looked at," she drones softly. *"You're bleeding."*

The corner of my lips quirk. "You like to see me bleed, sweetheart. Besides I'm used to it."

Her brows furrow. *"Only by my hand, Viking."*

"Are you saying you're going to tend me?" I lean forward

and cross my arms. "Because I'll have to admit, I'd look forward to that."

"I'm sure you would."

"Is that a 'yes', Blood?"

"No."

I shake my head. "You need to learn hospitality."

"You need to learn manners."

I straighten my spine with a smirk. "You're probably right. My mama wasn't able to teach me any."

"She died," she deadpans.

My jaw tightens. "Do you read minds too, Blood?"

She shakes her head, keeping her eyes locked on my blues. *"Isolde doesn't read minds, she just sees the past."*

"How?"

She shrugs. *"She just does."*

"And what can you do, Blood?"

"How did your mother die?" she counters. I fix her with an exasperated look then avert my attention.

I don't talk about my family, I don't have one anymore. The closest thing I have besides my father are the people that rely on us to keep them safe. To do that, I need to procure the cuff that was stolen from my people. I don't know why Davina has it, and I don't have the opportunity to ask her either. The objective is clear, the mission has to be successful —I need to get back home.

"She was killed by an enemy clan," I tell her. "Along with my brother and sister."

I expect her face to fall, to look at me with sorrow and sympathy, but she just blinks, something I can't say that I don't appreciate.

"Did you kill them?"

I drag my attention to her. "What?"

"The people that killed your family," she offers. *"Did you kill them?"*

"I think I've met my match with you, woman."

That gets a smile from her. *"There's a speck of smarts in you after all, Viking."*

"If I was smart at all," I allude. "I wouldn't want to hear your voice over you in my head."

She lifts a shoulder. *"I can't do anything about that."*

"Has it always been like that?" She shakes her head. "How did it happen?"

"A spell."

"A spell?" She tears her eyes from mine. "What did you do?"

"It's what I asked for," she offers.

"Why would you do something like that?" She doesn't respond, which pricks my curiosity. She's headstrong and stubborn, which doesn't make sense, I can't imagine her discarding her pride to have someone do something for her.

"I understand you not wanting to speak about it," I allude. "We're enemies after all."

She peers back up at me. *"Are we?"*

I shrug. "Seems like it, I guess."

"Depends on why you are here to determine if you are truly the enemy."

"I already told you and your father."

"But is it the truth?"

I sigh. "How can I prove it to you?" I don't like how her brow lifts and her eyes glimmer with insight.

"I know a way."

CHAPTER SEVENTEEN
DAGEN

It's the only way. The direction of earning her trust and possibly getting me off this island. Sitting on a hard bench made from rock of some sort, I stare into a pair of rose-colored eyes that have been staring at me intently with zero emotion dilating in them. Not to mention the other six of them surrounding her and me like we're some sort of sideshow.

I've never seen someone so focused in my whole life. To the point where it's slightly uncomfortable, but I guess this is how she can really "delve into my past," as Davina puts it.

I don't know what she can see or how far back, fully aware that all of this can bite me in the ass if she sees the conversation of my father and I talking about the golden cuff. I won't walk out of this alive, definitely clear on that.

"Well," Atarah carps. "What do you see?"

I keep my eyes still, fearless. Praying to gods I haven't prayed to in forever that my secrets remain just that.

"He's experienced loss," Isolde conveys slowly. "A deep emptiness while he was a child."

My jaw locks as she pries into memories I don't want to hear. Those times were rough, dealing with a father who didn't know a thing about raising a child on his own. How I didn't know how to grieve my mother and siblings because I had no emotional backup or anyone to tell me it was okay to cry.

Until Edda.

Her hard exterior growing up with five brothers gave her an intimidating demeanor, but inside, she was kind and sweet. Opening up a side of her that not many people saw.

"We don't care about that," Atarah chides through my thoughts. "We want the important—"

"You know that's not how it works," Nesrine retorts. "She sees what she sees."

I see a shape of white start to pace the room, obviously irritated that she doesn't know how long this is going to take. Atarah and I have that in common.

"He doesn't know love," Isolde offers. My brows furrow immediately. It was an odd thing to see, but she's not wrong.

I don't think I'm capable nor do I want to experience it. It's a worthless emotion really, the point of marriage was loyalty and commitment while producing offspring to keep your legacy alive. Everything else was nonsense.

"No, he's not married," Isolde voices. I didn't hear anyone ask her a question, so I pull my eyes away for the first time and find Davina standing behind her, in between two of her sisters.

"If you wanted to know more personal details, Blood," I state with a smirk, "you could've asked me yourself."

She fixes me with slitted eyes when I look back at her sister, Isolde.

"Blood, there is a lot of it," she announces to the room. I almost scoff, in a room of another set of beings it might give someone pause, but not these she-devils.

"Is that why you call me Blood?"

I shake my head. "It's because of your hair."

"What?" Isolde asks.

"I wasn't speaking to you."

"Are you speaking to him?" Brylee asks out loud. She must answer 'yes' because she continues. "Why? He doesn't need to—" She stops, and it frustrates me that I can't hear Davina unless she wants me to.

"He's a warrior," Isolde digresses. "He's fought in many battles, been injured."

"*How many times?*" Davina asks. I glance at her again with an exasperated look, but she ignores me and fixes her attention at the back of her sister's head.

"Well over a dozen."

"Nineteen," I answer.

"He was tended to by that woman in the furs." Davina cuts her eyes to me.

"Edda," I tell her, looking for any sort of jealousy to spark in her pupils—none.

"He's supposed to marry her," Isolde falters. "His father wants and speaks of it several times."

"That's such a disappointment," Nesrine mutters next to my right ear. Davina's eyes follow her sister, whose hand brushes my shoulder and glides across to the other.

Isolde looks at Nesrine. "He isn't sold on the idea."

Nesrine shows up on the other side of my face. "Now *that* is interesting. Tell me, Viking, how will you ever go home to boring-looking women when you've seen the best there is to offer here?"

Again, another fact. All of the sisters are exotic beauties, each with their own different features and shades, but the only one I've been slightly fascinated with is the one who doesn't speak out loud.

I try to keep reminding myself that their powers are something that might be addictive. I have no clue if it's my thinking or if they are doing something purposely to keep my guard lower than it should be. But the more time I'm here, the more I find myself opening to them—especially *her*.

"He'll be the leader of his people," Isolde quips, her brows slowly starting to descend. "But he doesn't know if he wants the power."

"Of course, I want it," I retort. "I'm the eldest son of Oryn the Great. It's my duty to—"

"Relax on the honor," Nesrine mumbles on the side of my face. "We wouldn't blame you if you wanted to stay here."

I pull myself away from her and turn my head in her direction. "I don't *want* to stay here."

Her black eyes glimmer in amusement. "Of course you do. What man wouldn't—" She stops her next words, head slowly turning in the directions of her sisters, which I can only guess on the one. "You need to stop coddling him."

Silence fills the room, and Nesrine straightens her back seconds later, leaving my space.

"Don't leave me in suspense," I announce, pulling my head to Davina. "What do you want to do with me, Blood?"

"You already know what I want from you." She meets my stare, bold and exquisite. Her crystal-green eyes collide with her hair, already making her stand out.

And I hate how much I notice it.

"Can you read my mind if I whisper something to you?" I ask.

Davina's brows snap together. *"No."*

My lips lift. "Then I'll say it out loud. I'm hoping what your wanting to do with me involves your plush lips and my hands meshed in your hair while I—" My long strands are yanked back as I stare up at Atarah's pearl-colored eyes glowering down at me.

"Watch your dirty mouth," she seethes. "I'm growing tired of you and the words that leave it."

"I can't read him when he isn't looking at me," Isolde chides. Atarah lets me go with a shove, but I'm more disappointed that I didn't get to see Davina's face while I finished my remark.

I'm met yet again with Isolde as she continues her strange ogling of me.

"His father sent him here," she immediately states, sending my body rigid. The girls suddenly move closer, encompassing me in their circle, and I can feel their anticipation seeping into my skin.

"What else?" one of them asks impatiently.

"He was asked to come here," Isolde continues, her brows drawing together again in concentration while I meet her eyes with defiance in my head. I will lose every ounce of trust with Davina and all my work will go to shit if Isolde spills the truth.

"For what?" Nesrine prods from behind me. Then her voice is closer. "You better hope it's for adventure, Viking, because my eldest sister has been wanting to rip into you since laying eyes on you."

I'm not afraid of death, not fully, dying in paradise at the hands of seven women might be a feat for some men, but me, I'd rather die on the battlefield with my pride still intact— which might be in a few minutes from now.

"To observe the land," Isolde recites. "To see if this island held any good soil for farming." I stare at her, listening to the words that leave her mouth. I repeat them once because it's what I wanted them to believe so how good are these so-called powers that this Siren has?

My mind begins to slowly reel at my luck, how she didn't just out me in a room full of beings that want me dead.

"You told the truth." My concentration is broken the moment Davina speaks, my eyes immediately falling on her. She gawks at me, appearing taken back that I spoke the truth. I can't say that I blame her because I'd never believe me either, I would've been buried in the ground somewhere.

"That's absurd," I hear Atarah upbraid. "We're on an

island. Why would he make a trip back and forth such a long ways for farming? It makes no sense."

"It doesn't," Isolde replies calmly. "But—" Atarah rounds the stone slab I'm sitting on and stands in front of me, blocking my view of Isolde.

"Can you be wrong?"

"I never have before," Isolde states. "It's what I saw and heard."

"But it makes no sense," Atarah argues, clenching her hands into fists.

"Give it up," Nesrine asserts. "You just want to kill him."

"Because he's not supposed to be *here.*"

Nesrine shrugs. "Something is wrong with the veil then."

"I'll have to summon Taysa," Isolde chimes. "There has to be a reason."

"What did you girls find out?" a male voice booms through the room, changing the air and adding some testosterone.

They all remain silent for the first time, heads bowed and averted from telling him exactly what happened here.

Except Davina.

She's still studying me with confusion and relief plastered on her face, while I feel a small twinge of remorse that she isn't rallying with her sisters and believing it.

"Well?" King Triton persists, stepping deeper into the room.

"He's telling the truth," Davina voices with a small smirk to her lips.

"The truth?" I feel his hesitation land on me, and I tear myself away from his daughter to him. "What are you?"

I perk a brow. "What?"

Shirtless with gray chest hair and his trident in hand, King Triton strides toward me as his daughters step away to allow him room.

129

"You have something special about you," he stresses through deepened brows. "You're not just a Viking."

"I can assure you I am."

His beefy hand lands on Isolde's shoulder, who is still sitting in front of me. "Go rest."

She instantly does as he asks, striding out of the room while taking a few of her sisters with her. The king takes her place and swallows the chair with his compact body. Davina takes a step toward him, followed by Atarah, remaining silent behind him.

"You know this changes nothing," he tells me. "I don't trust you, and letting you go free is out of the question."

"So even though I'm innocent of the crimes you've accused me of committing, you're still going to kill me?"

"I'm a just man but not a stupid one."

"Then where do we go from here?"

Atarah crosses her arms. "He won't be missed. His ship won't be able to wait around forever."

"Is it still there?" her father asks.

"It arrived yet again the other day."

"How many men did you bring with you?" he asks me.

"I'm not going to give away my men," I deadpan.

"Then you'll give your life."

"Father, he's just proven that—"

"You can leave, Davina," he orders. "I'm going to speak man to man with this Viking." She opens her mouth, but Atarah links her arm with her sister's and escorts her out of the room.

King Triton lets a few moments pass before he speaks again. "I respect a man who'll protect his people, but you'll also have to respect mine."

"Your killing me is going to do nothing but upset your daughter and cause the slaughter of more innocent men."

"My daughter?" he repeats as he leans forward. "Why would my daughter care about you?"

"Because I'm like a damn pet, apparently." He doesn't seem amused, but I was hoping he'd play into the daughter line I laid down. If he is the man I think he might be, he may think twice about hurting his youngest daughter. I heard fathers had a soft spot for the most part for their little girls. Mine always referred to my sister as his little lass with stunning dark hair and ocean blue eyes.

"Why didn't you bring other men with you onto the island?" he asks, quickly recovering.

Good question.

"Most of my men came down with scurvy from the long voyage," I lie. "And I didn't want anyone to slow me down nor did I want to carry around a dead body."

"So you kept *all* of your men aboard a ship?"

"Thought it'd be easier coming in and out."

He elevates a brow. "Alone?"

"Alone," I repeat.

"Sounds awfully foolish in case you got hurt."

"I planned to be in and out." He seems to like that failed outcome because a small quirk plays off his lips.

"You're a prince to your people?"

I shake my head. "No, we don't have hierarchy of that nature where I'm from."

"So you won't be missed then." I stand from my chair, already tired of his attempt to make me feel intimidated. Seeing Davina relieved at my alleged telling of the truth spoke volumes. I have his daughter in my back pocket, and it's up to him if he wants to play the devil in this conclusion of events.

"I'll be more than missed," I address confidently. "I'm the Blood Axe. The fiercest warrior of my clan. Get rid of me and you'll have more than just my men surrounding this magical island you call home. My father won't rest until I'm home safe."

"Small words coming from a big man," he replies stoically.

"Truths, Your Majesty," I mock. "Give it a shot and try your chances. Because my people will burn this island to the ground."

CHAPTER EIGHTEEN

Davina

"Why do you keep trying to keep me alive?" His voice doesn't startle me anymore with the annoyance always laced in his tone. I've become accustomed to the way his pride always leads him, and he hates being helped.

"Why do you always keep asking boring questions?" I retort as I keep walking along the shoreline.

"Curious," he alludes. "You seem to be the only one who fights for it."

A wave crashes higher up the beach, and I jolt away so that it doesn't touch my skin. The once calming sea is not only harmful to sailors when they cross our borders but now me as well. It burns like acid, reminding me of the choice I made to let my sisters go freely off this island while I remain a prisoner.

"Scared of the water?" Dagen asks me, walking in line with my every step.

"Hardly. I just can't touch it anymore."

"Why?"

"Again with your questions," I sigh, keeping my eyes straight ahead for the line of forests that I want to hide away in.

So much for that idea.

"Only fair since I was interrogated."

"You're a prisoner here."

"And you're bored here."

I halt midstep in the sand. *"What do you want?"*

Dagen stops with me, aligning his tall body with mine. "I think I already answered that question earlier."

I'm hoping what you are wanting to do with me involves your plush lips and my hands meshed in your hair.

I stare at him not because I have nothing to say but because my mind is playing out that scenario. Dagen is broad and strong, his blue eyes stand out over his dark features, giving him a kind demeanor when he isn't scowling.

"Thinking about it?" he inquires confidently while his mouth twists.

"Give it a try, Viking."

He lifts a brow. "I'm afraid I'll fly across this beach if I do."

"Smart man."

"How can you swim in your little basin of water out back if you can't touch the ocean?"

I shrug and begin walking again. *"No idea."*

"How long can you stay out of the water?"

"Few hours, my body has adapted, and I can be without it longer."

"How long have you been like this?"

The pit of my stomach starts to ache at the reminder. *"Almost three years."*

"How old are you?"

I snap my attention to him. *"How old are you?"*

"I've seen thirty years."

"And you're not married?"

He keeps his eyes on the sandy beach ahead. "No."

"I'd ask why but I'd obtain your broody answers."

"More than likely."

"Edda not good enough for the infamous Blood Axe?"

"She's a good woman," he offers. "Strong, kind, she's loyal to the clan."

"But?" He remains silent, insinuating that there is more to the story than he wants to talk about. I can't say that I'm not curious. If he was a man of my world, he'd have Sirens fighting to have him, to keep him. It'd be an interesting sight to see how he'd handle that.

We breech the woodland edge, the light dimming the moment we pass the brush. Birds sing and tweet a lovely melody, welcoming me to the unobscured outside, where all my problems lie. Dagen follows close behind me, and the instant the trees open up a bit, he jerks me back. My back collides with his chest as his arm wraps around my middle and beneath my breasts.

"Stop," he demands, tightening his hold on me.

My eyes narrow. *"For what?"*

"What the hell is that?"

I glance around. *"What?"*

"Those." His arm extends in front of me, pointing straight ahead to nothing. There is nothing dangerous on this island but my sisters.

"Need you to be more specific."

"The things flying around." He begins to pull me backward, and then it hits me when I understand what he's talking about. Ahead are blue specks of light, floating around the sky in beautiful spots and patterns, softly lighting the forest.

"Those are noctiluca," I tell him, resting my hand on his forearm. *"They won't hurt you. I promise."*

His grip loosens as I break from him, proceeding to walk deeper into greenwood that reminds me why I wanted a place of our own in the first place. The air is different in here, fragrant and refreshing. A small little place for me to trample through to clear my head. The aqua-colored tones swirl around me, welcoming me back. I consider the little creatures my friends, they guide me through the woods and illuminate my way.

"Davina." I arrest my next step and turn around to face him. Dagen stands still in the place that I left him, brows furrowed in response. His shoulders are tense, in a stance ready to fight.

"Trust me, Viking," I tell him, extending my hand for him. *"I've saved you how many times? I'm not going to kill you now."*

He surveys the area once more before moving forward and, surprisingly, takes my hand. I guide him deeper into the coppice of trees and bushes, streams of the sun breaking through the tops. It's peaceful here, nothing but nature surrounding us to keep all the bad things out. All the battling thoughts in my head about Tobias and how I led him down this path when I should've kept him away from the island. My disappearance may have hurt him, but he was strong enough to endure it.

It was just that I couldn't.

I release Dagen's hand, but he still stays fastened to mine, following me to the small opening where I always sit on a fallen log. Orange and red leaves path out my trail, and when I place a foot in the crevice, Dagen gives me a small yank.

"You're either brave or stupid, Blood," he professes. I revolve on my heel to face him.

"It's safe here," I oppose. *"This is my home now."*

Slowly, he shakes his head. "You don't belong here." His words hit me like a slap to the face. I'm about to pull my hand from his until he continues. "You don't belong anywhere."

"I don't understand what you—" His free hand comes up to my face, cupping my cheek and chin.

"Are you an angel or a devil?" he proceeds as his thumb grazes my warm skin. "Because something like you shouldn't exist to mankind. We can't handle it."

"I'm the daughter of King Triton," I vouch with furrowed brows. *"Son of Poseidon."*

"So you are unearthly," he hedges softly as his blue eyes float from my lips to my green irises. "How is a man not supposed to want you? To fuddle plans that have already been made and make them question their whole future."

"You're speaking of you," I state, feeling his warm breath touch the tip of my nose. *"You want me."*

He blinks then releases a stuttered exhale, straightening his spine. "What idiot wouldn't want a beautiful woman? It's just the strong ones that can resist it."

"Are you that strong, Viking?"

He abruptly drops his hand from my face. "Yes."

CHAPTER NINETEEN

Davina

It's been two days, but I can still feel his hand on the side of my face. Still feel his warm palm seeping into my bloodstream. I've avoided him because Atarah is right, it's dangerous and short-sighted to get attached to anything that isn't safe. We don't have the luxury of being open when the world hunts us down for sport. Where my sisters have to worry about being scooped from the water, never to be seen again.

And then there's father.

He left this morning after a swift lecture about how *all* my sisters will be taking up shifts to protect me and my ill-advised decisions regarding Dagen. We argued, mostly about his fate that is solely based on the limited information we know about him. Mine is the same, but it doesn't mean he has to die.

Actually, I honestly don't know what to do with Dagen. All I know is that my conscience is pleading for me to keep him safe. That he's like Tobias, and I'd kill anyone who tried to harm him. Maybe it is that he's human. That he's shown civility and a twinge of kindness. He did try to protect me from the noctiluca the other day, so he must not want to see me harmed either. It would've been easier to let me get hurt so that he could make his escape.

Or it could be the fact that he's manipulating me to gain more of my trust so he can betray me.

"Surprising that I'd find you here," I hear my sister, Rohana, jeer as she steps inside the library.

I glance up from my book, grinning at her as she strides through the room. Her purple hair is braided back, lavender eyes looking at me in amusement because she knows what I'm doing. I'm dodging the sullen Viking and all his muscles.

"You've always known me the best," I quip, resting my novel on my lap.

"Because you're the less boring one," she chuckles, sitting alongside me. "Coast is clear of Father."

I nod, tucking my chin into my chest. *"I know. We fought."*

"You always fight."

"Not like this. He's going to kill him, Ro."

She places a hand on my thigh. "We'll think of something. We always do, don't we?"

"Remember, Sister, my ideas aren't always the best."

"But they always work out." I want to tell her she's insane because I almost got her killed and in plenty of trouble with Father, but refrain. Instead, I release a heavy sigh and clutch the leather corner of my novel.

"Sometimes I feel like maybe it would've been easier to let Atarah put him out of his misery right away."

"She's afraid of things she doesn't know," Rohana divulges. "And she feels like she has to protect us all."

"She's not Mother," I oppose. *"And not every human is a monster."*

"But she can't see past the ones who killed Mother."

A violent chill rips up my spine, causing goosebumps to protrude through my arms. How could I forget? I found her first, lying face down as each wave crashed into her body. Her beautiful yellow hair floating aimlessly around her.

She was speared through the heart, the lance still embedded in her body. I remember the blood-curdling scream that left my body, the sea creatures that scattered off at the agony in my tone.

"Pondering does nothing but bring those memories back," Rohana chimes beside me. "It's best to leave them be." Easy for her to say since I wouldn't let her near our mother until the spear was removed, even though I preferred and ordered it that way.

"Are you on babysitting duty today?" I ask her with a smirk.

She chuckles. "They know better than to leave me alone with you. I'd let you do whatever you wanted."

"Who's still here?"

"Atarah was brooding in the garden earlier. Brylee is probably in her room, writing in her diary about how she wishes she could have the courage to stand against Atarah one day. And I believe Isolde is resting."

"Do you think she saw everything?" I ask.

"With the Viking?" I nod. "I think so, she's never been wrong before."

"It just doesn't make sense why his father would send him here, to an island, to look for good farming."

"Maybe they are running out of good land."

"But aren't we leagues away from them?"

"I honestly don't know, they could've moved more south. It would be a nice place for people to settle."

"Yes, but how did they know about it?"

My sister lifts a shoulder. "Could be word of mouth."

"Another Siren?"

She gives me an exasperated look. "Females have large mouths."

"It just makes no sense how he found the island and got past the veil."

"I honestly think something is wrong with the spell,"

Rohana notes. "Because the same goes for Tobias. He's human, how does he freely come and go?"

"*The mystery that eats me alive,*" I recite. "*I'm surprised Atarah hasn't squealed a word to Father.*"

"She knows he saved our lives, so I'm assuming she cuts him slack."

"*Hardly looks like it.*"

"You know Atarah tries to keep a hard front, when in reality, she's as soft as you are."

I fix her with furrowed brows. "*Her and I are night and day.*"

"But the same. Both hard-headed and strong. *Stubborn.*"

"*I'm more merciful than—*" My body shudders involuntarily, shaking my entire core right down to my bones.

Rohana's hand squeezes my thigh. "Are you okay?"

I push myself off the settee. "*Something is wrong.*"

"Wrong? What happened?"

I don't answer because I'm already out of the library and in the foyer of the castle. The hairs on my arms are standing on end, my breathing shallow at something that doesn't feel right.

Striding and listening, I hear water splashing from the garden. I pick up my pace, passing guards and flowers in glass vases that Isolde likes to decorate the house with. Busting through the double standing doors, I make my way down the path, still hearing splattering of water and female voices.

Meeting my small lagoon, I see Brylee and Atarah in the water, standing next to each other without making a move. It's not until I see a large forearm break through the water that I know what they're doing.

Which is exactly what I told all my sisters *not* to do.

"*Atarah.*" My voice is deathly, sharp. I never thought I'd want to kill one of my own sisters, until now.

Both of my sisters' heads dart to me, but they don't let go of him. They don't release his head from underneath the water as they see me standing here as a warning. One that will only last for a second longer.

"Go inside," Atarah demands, toneless.

It's all I need, I delve into the water and make my way to them. I see blue start toward me, Brylee, in her attempt to stop me. You see, the problem with being the youngest is my sisters think I'm weak, stupid. That I can't handle my own when I'm the one who has handled everything thus far to keep them safe.

A hand grasps my forearm, and I force all the anger to surrender from my body. The moment her fingers tighten around my flesh, my whole body burns, getting her to immediately let go and cry out in pain.

I don't waste time that I don't have, I swing my hand back and hit her in the jaw while my eyes are locked on my eldest sister, who thinks she can take it upon herself to kill my prisoner.

Atarah pushes Dagen's head deeper into the water before I lunge for her. My fingers attach to her throat, shoving her into the element that will only give her more power. A loud gasp of breath sounds behind me, and I know that Dagen has come up for air finally—alive but still not safe. There's still Brylee behind me, probably ready to finish what I know Atarah started.

I'm pulled underneath the crest of the lagoon, immediately slapped in the face from my sister to get me to release her—I don't. My fury is feeding the Siren part of me that she forgot still resides in me. Sometimes I think she forgets that just because I can't transform back into my original self that I'm not like her anymore.

When I don't let go of her throat, she mocks my action, careful not to put a lot of pressure on my windpipe, which makes me believe she's not taking me seriously. So I do exactly that, squeezing as hard as I can to give her a taste of what she just gave Dagen.

My body is suddenly ripped from hers, large hands wrap around my naked torso as I'm pulled through the water. My head pops over the water, and I already know there's only one person who warms my skin the way *he* does.

Spinning around to face him, I'm about to yell at him to release me until I see the blue tint in his face from lack of oxygen. His chest heaves violently, begging for more air to fill his lungs that are probably filled with water.

My head is yanked back, almost taking my whole body with it, but with Dagen's hold on me, it stays there. Bringing my arm in, I propel it back, connecting with the side of Atarah's face. I shove Dagen back, hoping that he stays afloat on his own for a moment longer.

I twirl around to see my sister's eyes as white as the clouds in the sky, furious with betrayal locked in them. Except, she was disloyal to me when I clearly stated that nothing would happen to the Viking.

"He has to die, Davina," she seethes. "He's a danger to us all."

"*He didn't kill our mother,*" I return. "*You went against me.*"

"To *save* you. All of us."

I point an index finger at her. "*Don't follow me or I'll kill you. Don't forget who wields more power here.*"

"You won't land a—"

"*Won't I?*" I rally. "*You defied my words and took it upon your-self to take action. This isn't your island anymore, your home. It's mine. Don't step foot on it again until I tell you it's okay to do so.*" I inch closer to her. "*And if you betray me on the other issue at hand, Atarah, I will rip your throat out.*"

I'm referring to Tobias, and she knows, deep down, that if

she ever uttered a word about him, not one person in this world would be able to stop the wrath I'd rain down on her.

Not waiting for her to respond, I tuck myself under Dagen's arm and help him to shore. Brylee intelligently stands aside, letting me get him inside and into his room. Once I lay him on his bed, wet and cold, I make my way to his small dresser until his hand jolts out to grab me.

Without thinking, my skin immediately warms in warning. But I settle myself down, trying to contain my fury that is literally burning from the inside out.

"How many more times are you going to save me, Blood?" he proclaims weakly.

I don't know how to answer that. Don't understand why it's so important to keep him breathing and defy my family. Again, it must be because of Tobias.

"*As many times as it takes,*" I offer, pulling my arm from his hold. Quickly, I gather up some dry clothes and sit along the side of his bed. "*You have to sit up for a moment.*"

He does what I request, and I help him position himself so I can pull his wet shirt over his head. I demand my eyes to not linger down the length of his body, down to the muscled torso and chest that I've seen once before when he was chained to the floor and bathing himself with a cloth.

I toss the shirt to the floor before retrieving the dry one and pull it over his head. He puts his arms through, wet hair dripping onto it as I gather another shirt to dry his hair.

"You don't have to do this," he tells me. "I've been through worse."

"*You're lucky I came just in time,*" I disclose. "*Another minute and you'd be dead.*"

"How did you know where to find me?" I can feel his eyes on me, going up and down my body like he's studying his prey.

Like he's going to learn something.

"Not sure."

Lies. I felt it.

"I was thinking about you," he replies. "How I was about to die without feeling what your lips felt like. How you'd feel underneath me as I kiss every inch of you—" I start from the bed and back away from it.

He shouldn't think of me that way. I shouldn't want to save him. We shouldn't even be around each other, but he trespassed into my home, and here I am saving him from death.

"Watch yourself," I caution. *"I told you to trust me, not tell me all your emotions."*

He lays back on the bed and looks up at the ceiling. "I never thought I would either. I guess I've never been so close to dying before."

"You said you've been injured many times before."

"I have, but not drowned, Blood."

"Were you scared?"

He's silent for a moment before he says, "Just scared of the things I haven't done yet."

I nod, not that he sees it, but I can understand that. I felt fear in my own blood when Rohana and I were hanging close to the deck of Tobias's uncle's ship that night.

"I'm going to have some guards stay by your door," I tell him. *"And I—"*

"You don't have to do that." I open the door, ignoring his request because he's not going to tell me what to do and not to do either. He'll have what I give him.

And that's my protection.

145

CHAPTER TWENTY
DAGEN

"*C*ome with me," Davina whispers from my sleep. Her voice is soft and velvety, caressing my body, which responds immediately by hardening my cock.

This wouldn't be the first night I've dreamt of her red hair laced in between my fingers or her soft flesh pressed into my hard chest. I've just never heard her so vividly before.

Until she shakes my body, alluding that this is far from a dream.

I crack an eyelid open to see her hovering over me, her green eyes meeting my blues. It's not until I see the urgency in them that gets me to slowly sit up.

"What's wrong, Blood?" I ask her as her fingers graze down my bicep, wrapping around it to tug me off the bed.

"*You have to come with me*," she repeats with a stronger yank. Standing on my feet, I follow her from the room.

When she reaches the doorway, she stops, peering out to look both ways before guiding me through. I want to ask her where she's taking me, but since it looks like we're on a secret mission, I remain quiet, listening to the soft patter of her feet on the tiles.

Davina leads me outside and along the shoreline to the cove that I invited myself into last week. Secluded and dark, my cock stirs at the thought of my second chance at life and how I'd like to pursue my daydreams of kissing those beautiful lips of hers.

It must be the rescue attempts, the way she defended me against her eldest sisters and the ferociousness that left her body that turned me on. Edda was nothing compared to the shit I saw Davina do yesterday. If she was on my side, in my clan, within my grasp—she'd be mine.

We come to the small entrance of the cove when Davina turns to face me. *"You have to go."*

My brows descend. "What?"

"You have to leave this island, now." Her words, they hit me in the gut. They were the last thing I expected her to say. I was thinking she wanted to show me something or warn me away from her sisters. But this…

"There is a boat in here," she points behind her inside the small niche. *"You can sail to your ship."*

"I—you can't—is it still there?"

She nods. *"Yes, Rohana told me that it still waits for you there."* Davina gives me her back. *"Follow me."*

I do, dazed as her words sink into my brain.

You have to go.

I quickly scold myself because that was always the plan. The cuff and sailing back home to protect my clan from the highlands. It was always the mission.

Davina stops and waits for me to get closer to her. *"Stay here, I have some provisions that I need to grab for you."*

"Blood," I begin. "You can't just—"

"Stay right here," she repeats then hurries off into the moonlit beach.

My conscience ticks at me, demanding I move and follow through with my quest. Turning around, I look at all the trinkets Davina has scattered around the room and shelved on rock walls. My vision focuses in on my right, two shelves up where the gold cuff lies in between a small wooden chest and a chandelier.

I demand my feet to move before she gets back, telling myself that she'll never notice. Stepping on a large boulder, I yank it off the rock shelf and tuck it in the back of my slacks. Quickly, I get down, just in time for her to show back up with a small sack of things.

"Food and a blanket," she announces. *"No one will harm you when you set back to your vessel."*

"You're going to get in trouble for this, Blood," I advise. "Are you sure you want to deal with the—"

"I'm sure," she deadpans. *"You need to be off this island before my sisters wake up. Leave immediately once you set foot on your ship."* She won't look at me, just waiting for me to nudge past her and do exactly what she's told me to do because I know I'll never get another chance.

Except my boots are frozen to the ground because I'll never see her again. I won't be coming back to see her without the threat of her sisters and father. Without possibly getting past the veil again.

"Hurry," she urges. *"You don't have much time, Viking."*

My hand comes up to her cheek again, and she flinches this time. "I've already lost count of the times you've saved me."

"Just don't come back here again," she counters then peers up at me. *"You won't get lucky a second time."*

I'll miss you, it's at the tip of my lips, but I hold them back. There's no point in expressing my emotions, they wouldn't change anything. Besides, I've always had a hard time conveying what I wanted.

And that is to have Davina pressed up into these rocks so she could experience how she made me feel being near her.

"Viking," she stresses. *"Please."*

My thumb brushes her cheek. "You take care of yourself, Blood." She nods, fixating on my chest.

With all my strength, I move, swiping up the small satchel she brought and brushing against her body to exit the cave. I don't look back, letting my boots sink into the sand as I see a small boat crashing softly along the shoreline from the waves. It looks ancient, the boards cracked and fractured, but it's the only way off the island, I'm sure.

Throwing the bag into the small dinghy, I push it deeper into the ocean, stepping inside to row in the direction of my ship. I can feel Davina's gaze on me, the silent goodbye that both of us want to voice, but our pride keeps us from doing so.

I'll never see her again.

Never will I experience such beauty and strength. Going back home to face Edda is something that my brain isn't looking forward to, and I hate myself for it. We weren't betrothed to be married yet, but Isolde was right, my father has been pressing it. Stating that I need to protect our bloodline and produce many heirs to secure our lands and legacy.

And he isn't wrong.

With power comes sacrifice, doing things we don't want to do and making decisions that will never flee our minds.

Mine will always be the red Siren on the island.

The way that I can't touch her or bring her back with me. How I'll never know how it'd be to lay next to her or hear her say my real name.

Why does that matter?

I'm a prisoner of hers that she mercifully let free, something that I can't say that I have much of. If the tables were turned, I'd never let her go, regardless of what she said or the truths she spilled. Time would work against me, her beauty and allurement would sink into my soul, and it would seal her fate all on its own.

The small boat fights against the waves, rocking fiercely up and down. Reaching behind me, I grab the gold cuff, making sure it's still with me. I fear that it'll go overboard with each jolt of the unforgiving sea.

After what seems like forever, I see my ship sitting patiently for my arrival. It's eerie in a way that there are no loud sounds of the crew sauntering over the waves. They're probably all too drunk and sleeping off their spirits since there is nothing else better to do than wait for me to come back.

Arriving at the side of the ship, I use the old rope to tie myself to it. Tossing the bag of things Davina packed me over my shoulder and the gold cuff still in my hand, I climb the side, careful not to slip and fall with the limited use of my hands. The closer I get, the more I hear male voices overhead.

After today, I fear that everything about me will change.

Geezus fuck, it shouldn't. I was held against my damn will, chained to a floor, almost drowned, and had my ass practically kicked. There wasn't anything that I should miss from that Zeus-forsaken island.

Except I did.

Glancing back, for the last time, the island is hidden by the mysterious veil that Davina and her sisters spoke about all the time. When I get into my cabin, I'm ripping up the map that holds the location of this place. She protected me, so I'm going to do the same. Even if it means never coming back on an impulse to see her and experience her green eyes peering up at me again.

I make it to the railing, heaving my satchel over the side and pulling myself up over it. We'd need to make a quick job with departing, as Davina said, so her sisters don't get the opportunity at killing us all.

Pulling myself up to stand, I freeze in horror at the scene

that awaits me. The air from my lungs is sucked away, leaving me breathless at the gore and blood. You'd think I'd be used to seeing it, after all the many battles I've participated in, this is a normal day for me. But after being in a paradise-like state for well over two weeks, I feel like that piece of me is hidden behind my psyche.

Puddles of blood cover the wood floorboards of the deck with my men scattered around, laying face down with their arms spread on either side. The ship sways back and forth in place, emitting the squeaks and eerie whines of the ship.

A soft moan pulls at my attention as the color of bright blue catches my periphery.

Brylee.

And when she's there, Atarah isn't far away. Scanning the area, I don't see either of them, but I do see *her.*

Davina stands still to my right, marked with burn marks and blood over her stomach and arms. Her face is marred too like she just walked through fire to get here.

Because she'd have to, the sea burns her flesh, she told me.

Narrowed eyes pin me to my spot, angry and almost violent, but they're not the stunning green that they always are—they're red.

Blazing red, the color of her hair, appearing demonic and misguided with lies.

My lies.

How she finally found out the truth, I don't know, but I do know that there would be no talking her into letting me go now.

"Blood," I digress, trying to keep my voice calm and collected. "What are you doing here?" Her hands clench to her sides at my question. That I had the audacity to even ask or ponder on shit I already know about.

"I'm here to take what you stole from me," she fumes softly.

My eyes fall all around her, surrounded by my men all battered up and bloody. And like a princess of death, she stands proudly in the middle of them.

Unafraid.

Unfazed.

But harmed. That's the only thing that still rings out to me, that Davina is still human after this. It didn't take me long to get to the ship, so the fact that she beat me here and paid a price for it, hits my gut.

Her crimson eyes fall on the gold cuff still gripped in my hand. *"I trusted you."*

"I didn't tell you to," I deadpan. Her scrutiny jerks to my face, and then I see it—the hurt.

"No," she replies slowly. *"You didn't."*

"I have to take this, Blood," I reason. "My clan needs it."

"For what?"

I shake my head. "I can't tell you."

Davina takes a step over a man's dead body but keeps her gaze locked on me. Even with the burn marks, she's still beautiful.

With the blood, she's seductive.

And with her power, she's dangerous.

"The cuff is mine," she quips. *"And it'll stay with me."*

I counter her step with one of my own. "My people are at risk."

"And so are mine."

I quirk a brow. "How? This is an old piece of junk."

Her nostrils flare when a loud cry breaks through the silent air. Looking to the left is Brylee, standing behind one of my crew members on his knees with his head in her hands.

"Give her the cuff," she orders. *"Now."*

"Blood," I drone. "I wouldn't have taken this if I didn't

need it." I peer back at her. "But my people will die if I don't take this home with me."

"You must've not heard what I said the first time," she seethes. *"It's mine."*

I open my mouth but nothing comes out. I silently promised myself to keep her safe, but I need to keep my own clan unharmed as well.

"Do I need to fight you for it?" she challenges. *"Is that what it's going to take?"* She doesn't wait for me to respond, not even think. Her hand is on my throat as she squeezes, cutting off my oxygen supply as she bores her eyes into me.

The woman that captivated me, she isn't standing in front of me. It's the Siren that men in my village spoke about— cunning, vile, and fatal.

The last one holds true because she stares at me like I'm her worst enemy and not the man she's saved a handful of times.

And maybe I am.

I betrayed her trust, made her believe something that wasn't true because I had things of my own I had to accomplish. Things may have changed, I may have grown to like her, but everything surrounding us remained the same.

"I was going to let you go," she leers. *"You didn't deserve to die. I couldn't watch what my father would've done to you, what my sisters whispered about because there is a piece of me that is my mother—kind and gentle. But that's what got her killed. You see, she was trying to save a sailor from drowning during a storm—"* she leans in closer to me. *"—and do you know what they did?"*

I already know, her face says it all. Her mother was murdered, and that's why her sisters hate me and her father wants to feed me to some sea creature, I'm sure.

"A spear," she continues. *"Right through the heart. And I found her there. What you're holding is hers. The Queen of*

Merindah cuff, the only thing that holds any value to me. And you took it."

"I didn't know," I tell her. "I was told that—"

"You should've asked," she drones, looking uninterested in what I have to say. *"But now it's too late."*

I nod under the tightness of her hold. "Alright, Blood. Go ahead and do it. I understand why."

She cocks her head to the side. *"Do what, exactly?"*

"Kill me."

A slow pull at her lips appears. *"Kill you?"* She shakes her head. *"I'm not going to kill you, Viking."* Then she shoves me over the rail, the blue sky becoming more distant as I fall backwards toward the sea.

And see black.

CHAPTER TWENTY ONE
Davina

Never again.

Never again will I be sucked in by Dagen's lies, or see the kindness that he tries to coax me with.

Everything was a lie.

His decency.

His words.

His give-a-shit-about-me approach.

I fought my eldest sisters over him. Left marks and tension between us. And I'm too proud to apologize for it now. I'm too embarrassed that I let a man come between my sisters and I.

A man that wasn't even one of us.

I read about his kind, how incredibly cruel they are. How fearless, which I found foolish because it could lead them into dangerous predicaments. The brute force they could oppose on a people for their own personal gain.

The last was what I was most afraid of.

But since the quarter of his men that my sisters didn't kill were here, that would leave no one to wait for him beside his father in whatever faraway land he's in.

Isolde had the ship burned down while Rohana and Nesrine helped me get to shore as quickly as possible. My skin, red and blotchy, stings and tingles from the salt water—a reminder that I trusted the wrong person.

The men were held together, chained to the floor in a different room than Dagen. He would get to stay alone as to not come up with any additional planning to get free. Unless he wanted to swim home, there was no other way for him to leave the island.

A soft knock sounds on my bedroom door, and I call out for the person to enter. Looking into the mirror, I watch my sisters Brylee and Isolde enter quietly.

"We came to see how you were fairing," Isolde greets, taking the lead inside. But my attention is on my other sibling, who's wearing a red mark across her cheek from my hitting her.

Remorse batters me again, right into the pit of my stomach. I'm a fool for letting him into my world, for trusting him.

"*I'm alright,*" I lie, tucking my chin into my chest before turning around to face them.

"We'll have your dinner brought to your room tonight," Brylee professes, her blue eyes full of attrition.

I stand and slowly make my way to her. "*Bry, I'm—*" I reach for her face but pull my hand away. "*I'm sorry.*"

She gives me a weak smile. "Don't be, it's been awhile since we fought."

"*It was uncalled for.*"

Isolde clutches my hand. "You didn't know."

"*But I should've known,*" I retort. "*He's a...*" I trail off because memories of Mother flood me. Finding her floating there with her eyes open, her mouth agape from the shock of being pierced by a spear.

"Atarah is scared to come in here," Brylee leads on, sitting on the edge of my bed. She wiggles her brows. "Who's the brave one now?"

Isolde squeezes my hand before releasing it, plopping

down on the bed next to her. "How many times did I have to convince *you* to come in here?"

Brylee runs her fingers through her cerulean blue hair. "You didn't feel how hard she hit me."

I open my mouth to apologize again, but Isolde beats me to it. "You deserved it."

Both Brylee and my eyes widen.

"*What?*"

Brylee squeals. "For what?"

"For attempting to kill the man when Davina told you 'no.'"

"*It doesn't—*" I start, but I'm immediately cut off by Brylee.

"He's trouble. Davina has too good of a heart to make any hard decisions."

"*I'm right here,*" I chide, crossing my arms.

Isolde rolls her eyes. "So you and Atarah think you can just *make* everyone's mind up that you don't agree with and do it anyways. Like the time I wanted to let Nalolen court me, but you thought he was too scrawny, and Atarah believed he had a brain the size of a pebble."

"He was an idiot," Brylee counters. "We saved you a lot of—"

"*You both can take your fight outside my room, I'm not in the mood.*"

Isolde stands from my bed and adjusts her glasses. "Right, I'm sorry. Taysa is making up an ointment for your burns, she'll be here tomorrow to deliver it."

"And we can ask her about the veil as well," Brylee adds. "We have a lot of questions."

"*That sounds great,*" I force from my lips. "*Thank you.*" They both give me smiles, careful not to touch me as they give me an air hug. After they leave me, I get comfortable inside the silence of my own room.

I have plans for the Viking.

Ones that won't stop pacing and tramping into my brain. It's as though he flipped a switch inside me, fueling a rage and being that I never matured before.

He may want death by the time this is over—mercy, even. But it won't be by my hands. There are worse ideas more than death that I have planned for the Blood Axe.

CHAPTER TWENTY TWO
DAGEN

I t's probably one of the most helpless feelings in the world. The most sickening and forlorn experience that still hits my gut when I know the men it's happening to. I've done it before, so the visual is something I can see.

Another loud shout of agony sounds through the walls, and it keeps the hairs on my arms on end. It twists my gut into knot after knot to the point where I don't think it'll ever untie itself.

"Davina!" I shout at the top of my lungs for the hundredth time. I know she's out there somewhere. That she's doing all of this as a show to weaken my defenses and fess up to more information.

Thing is, this time I don't have any more. Her declaration of the cuff being her mother's makes everything worse. It composes more questions, ones I don't have the answers to because I was told something completely different.

Maybe my father was misinformed. And maybe he wasn't. I'm having a hard time swallowing the idea that he'd send me on a suicide mission for something that truly wasn't what he said it was. Davina confirmed that the cuff meant something, but it sounded more sentimental than anything. Another mystery to the many I have stacked on my plate right now.

Despite them, the real problem is that I have no ally here anymore. Davina is solely against me, her sisters have been there, and it'll just fuel the fire of their resolution to kill me because I'm more than a threat now.

I'm a fucking thief.

The reality of it hits my pride. I did it for the good of my people, that's what taking it meant. And while they still stood out there, opposing the Highlands, everything still remained the same.

I needed the cuff and off this island.

The door to the room where I was held the first time opens, and my heart races in double time to see Davina. Except it's not her. It's an older woman with unique features and a stout body. From her nose to her forehead, a hue of green covers her skin. She's dressed in all black, a gown that covers most of her neck, down to the floor.

Her eyes crinkle at the sight of me, curious and a little alarmed. Standing from my seated position, I face her, ready for anything at this point because nothing is what it seems here.

"Are you Dagen the Blood Axe?" she asks me in a scratchy tone.

I give her a curt nod. "I am."

Her dark eyes follow down the length of me. "But you're just a boy."

"I'm not—"

"Don't get upset." She holds both of her hands up in defense. "You're just not what I expected is all."

I watch her walk deeper into the room, hands clasped together as if she's pondering something. Besides King Triton, she's the only other middle-aged adult I've seen here on the island.

And she irks me.

The air feels thicker in her midst, different. As though something else walked in with her that wasn't human.

"You're in a heap of trouble, son," she conveys. "How did you pass the veil?"

A heavy sigh escapes my lips because I'm tired of being asked the same question. "I have no clue."

"Did you feel anything the closer you got to the island?"

I shake my head. "No."

"I'm sure you know by now that no one besides a Siren and myself can get passed the veil."

"And what are you?" I prod.

She gives a weak lift of her shoulders. "They call me the sea witch because, just like the girls, I'm not understood so easily."

"Then what would you call yourself?"

"I am a sea witch," she alludes softly. "But I'm also a Selkie."

I blink at her. "A what?" She chuckles, a light and easeful sound throughout the room as she bows her head into her chest.

"We're an endangered species. A Selkie is a shapeshifter, who have been torn about through legends, just like Vikings. You're known to be violent creatures. I'm known to be malevolent and cruel."

I perk a brow. "Are you?"

"Only when it comes to the girls." A small quirk of her lips tells me they mean something to her. "I've helped raise them since their mother was murdered, fought quite a bit with them too. I never had children of my own because when the Hunters came into existence, I never wanted to bring another being into danger."

"If you have magical powers, why don't you just annihilate them?" I challenge.

"Because not all bad things need to be killed," she offers. "Just their minds altered. If I believed everything that was said about your people, I'd let the girls rip your heart out of your chest."

I furrow my brows. "But you're not? And why should I believe you?"

Pulling up a small stool from the corner of the room, she keeps a safe distance from me and sits down.

"It's what I just said," she replies. "Altered minds. There's more to you than meets the eye. I can feel it."

I fix her with a skeptical look. "I'm just a warrior on a mission."

"That passed the veil that I personally put up."

I express half a shrug. "Didn't do a very good job."

She chuckles again. "Apparently something is wrong. And I intend to find out what. Which brings me to why I am here instead of Davina."

Her name captures my attention. "What do you want to know?"

"Davina stated that you mentioned your father needing the cuff for your people, do you know what for?"

I weigh my options, telling her would possibly put my clan at risk. The magic that my father stated that lied in the cuff would bring creatures from it to protect us. If this sea witch knew about it, she may want it too.

"I don't question my father," I vouch. "I just do as I'm told."

She bobs her head. "Fair enough, I imagine. Have you ever had any sort of extraordinary things happen to you that were unexplainable?"

"I'm not an enchanting creature," I chide. "I'm a man who kills his enemies and protects his people. Nothing more or less."

The sea witch/Selkie stands from her chair. "I'm trying to help you, so help yourself. If I don't have any explanation as to why you're here then your men that you wanted to protect so much are going to die. I raised these Sirens, but when they are pushed into a corner or threatened, not even I can get through to them. And with Davina—" she sighs. "—you don't know what you're getting yourself into, boy."

"Looks like I'll have to take my chances," I quip, keeping her gaze.

"Then you're in a whole world of pain," she consents delicately. "She'll kill them. Your men, she hasn't—"

"I don't know anything else than what I told you," I allude. "I can't make something up to appease her."

The woman takes a deep breath. "Good luck." Turning on her heel, she leaves the room and me with my thoughts.

I'm going to need more than luck.

I'll need a fucking miracle to get me out of here alive.

CHAPTER TWENTY THREE
Davina

The moment I enter the room, Dagen gets on his feet and brushes his palms on his thighs. We haven't seen each other in four days, each one of them filling my head with ways to make him speak. Actions to make him break down and crumble to his knees so that I finally get the truth. He'll be stubborn at first, more than likely had an idea in his head that he would rather die than spill his secrets.

It's what I'm hoping for. It'll just make his not dying so much sweeter.

Death will be an easy way for him to escape consequences, and I want the exact opposite. I crave to watch the years go by and his pride be stripped away. His hope diminished and crushed under my bare feet so that it'll always send a reminder of what he tried to take from me.

"Blood," he mutters, as I step closer to him. His eyes fall all over me, studying and remembering what I look like as though it's been that long.

It hasn't been long enough.

Every ounce of betrayal that I've felt for this man has only fueled my inner rage and beast. Just the sight of him and his words of seduction and kindness prompts the revival of how my sisters were right. And I was wrong, naive even, to believe that the Viking could be someone like Tobias.

Someone with a heart and conscience because, in the end, we are all just trying to live.

However, Dagen was here to take.

So I would reap everything he held dear to him. His men, his pride, his stubbornness, and, eventually, his soul.

"Why aren't you healing quickly?" he prods, noticing the redness of my skin and the scabs that still remain from my burns.

Dumb fool, I might be a special creature but healing quickly isn't one of them.

Stopping a few arms' lengths in front of him, I call out to my sister, Kali, ignoring his question because it's time to start the end of Dagen's world.

The shuffling of boots enters in from behind me, followed by pleas of life. Dagen's eyes lock on to one of his men, an older one with a long beard and aged wrinkles all over his face.

"Priamos," he croaks, taking a step forward but is halted by his chains.

"My mother's cuff," I recite. *"Why do you need it?"*

Dagen hesitantly pulls his focus from his man and puts it on me. "My father sent me here to obtain it."

"Why?"

His blue eyes fall back on the man he calls Priamos. "I don't know."

"Do you not speak to one another?" I snap, clenching my hands into fists. I knew this wasn't going to be a simple feat, that it'd be like physically pulling the truths from his head. Something that Atarah and Brylee tried to do, but somehow, he blocked them.

And they'd try again.

Being twins, their energy is combined between the two. They aren't able to read and focus without the other, and right now, Atarah is still healing from the intense headaches she's been experiencing. Which further proves my point that there is something hidden about him.

"I do what my father requests," Dagen tells me. "I'm loyal to him, so there was no need to question."

My eyes narrow. *"You're a stubborn being, Viking. You weren't the least bit curious about the reason? Your father spoke to your clan about your trip here, he had to have given a reason on what you were expected to bring back the cuff for."*

"Dagen," Priamos urges. "The key to loyalty is a man's strength."

"Inside safety and danger," they both chime together.

I roll my eyes, motioning for Isolde, who snuck in moments after Kali to bring him closer to me. Shoving Priamos to his knees, I step behind him.

"Blood," Dagen warns. "I already told you what I know."

I look up at him from underneath my lashes. *"But I don't believe you."*

"How can I—"

"Prove it to me?" I interrupt. *"Tell me why Isolde couldn't read your eyes."*

He looks over at her. "I don't know."

"There isn't anyone in this world that I'm not able to see inside their past," Isolde informs him. "But you've hidden truths."

"How would I do that?" he challenges.

"Because you're more than a Viking," I accuse. *"You're not just a man."*

"Then what is that pirate you have visiting here?" he counters. "He got through the veil."

"But I can read him," Isolde argues. "And I can't you."

Dagen shrugs. "I'm not anyone special but a warrior on the field."

He's lying to me. Right to my face and trying to use the

manipulative gleam in his eyes to sway me back into believing him.

I meet his gaze, letting him see that his lies mean nothing to me. *"You're a liar."*

My hands clutch the sides of Priamos's face, and I snap his head, hearing the loud crack that follows after it. Dagen's eyes widen as Priamos's body falls lifeless to the white-tiled floors, just like his dishonesty.

"Grab another one," I tell Isolde.

Dagen's eyes fall on me, filled with something new—fury. "You're dead."

"I thought you'd make me yours," I taunt with a cock of my head. *"With you deep inside me."*

"That was before you just snapped my man's neck," he fumes, straining on his chains.

"We've only just begun." Hearing another man's footsteps, I turn to the younger lad whose eyes are wide and frightened.

Giving him a sweet smile, I make my way to him.

"Whatever you're planning to do," Dagen sneers behind me. "I'll make it worse on you."

I cup the man's face, letting my fingertips slide over the few days' growth protruding off his cheek, and he flinches violently.

"You'd have to get to me first," I provoke toward Dagen, giving his man before me a gentle smile. *"I'm not going to hurt you."*

"Please," he quakes. "I have a family at home."

"I'm sure you do," I reply, patting his chest. *"You're here to keep your friend company."* I peer over my shoulder. *"You want a friend, don't you, Viking?"*

He just glares at me, so I turn back to his friend.

"What's your name?"

"Tybalt."

"How old are you?" He tries to look over my shoulder at his leader, but I press my palm into his chest to answer me.

"I've seen twenty-two intervals."

"You'll stay here with him, okay?" He nods then Isolde takes him to the other side of the room, a good distance away from Dagen, and chains him to the floor.

"Blood," Dagen gripes. Slowly, I turn around to see his shoulders squared up, his brows so deep between his eyes that wrinkles form. "You *are* mine, remember that."

A soft scoff leaves my lips before I withdraw from the room.

If he thought watching his comrade get his neck snapped was bad, wait until he finds out what's going to happen to poor Tybalt.

CHAPTER TWENTY FOUR
DAGEN

Tybalt leans against the wall by his shoulder, picking at a string on his pants and softly humming a stupid song like nothing is wrong.

Every fucking thing is wrong.

I'm starting to think the kid has gone stupid because only two days ago Priamos was killed, and he sits there as if we're being taken care of like welcomed guests and not prisoners.

"Eat your food," I order, taking another bite of my fish.

Tybalt glances over at me and gives a slight lift of his shoulders. "Not hungry right now."

"You haven't eaten in two days," I snap. "*Eat.*"

"Maybe I'll—" I throw my plate at him, and it clinks against the glass wall before falling onto the floor.

"Do what I say. You need to keep your strength up."

"For what?" he asks with a glint of amusement in his tone, not at all affected that I just propelled something in his direction. "She said she wasn't going to hurt me."

"Did you not see what happened to Priamos?" I rant. "He's dead now. And we will be too if we don't get out of here."

Tybalt stares back at his pants. "How you expecting we do that?"

Fuck, I don't know. It's the question of the last few weeks. I've never had the problem of being surrounded by water with no way of getting off unless I swam the hell home.

"Just eat," I say instead as the door to the room opens.

In walks Davina, dressed in a mesh robe of mint green and a brassiere of white material and shells. She looks glorious, well-rested, and a fucking bane to my existence right now.

I meant what I said. When I get my hands on her, she'll never get free of me. She might be able to toss me around the room, but there has to be a weakness to her. A deficiency to her strength that I can protrude through.

"*Sleeping well?*" she asks Tybalt as she hunches down next to him. She blocks my view, but I think I actually see the lad blush.

Zeus and everything glorious and holy on this Earth.

This kid is going to be as worthless to me as these chains clad to my wrists.

"Very well," he replies. I see her hand rise to caress his head then she stands and turns her attention to me.

"*How are we doing, Viking? Ready to talk?*" When she's a safe two feet away from me, she stops, giving me a small glimpse of the apex in between her legs.

I hit her with a scowl. "Already did."

"*How is it that your men know nothing about why you're here? Or are they sworn to secrecy?*"

I hold back my look of shock because *everyone* was there when my father announced the gold cuff. My fear has been that someone would've already spoken about the dragon through ways of torture and fear but, apparently, they haven't.

"Because there are no secrets to tell," I rebuke.

She smirks then looks over her shoulder at Tybalt. "*He hasn't been eating.*" She would know that because I'm sure people are reporting back to her about us. Her men come in here to take us to relieve ourselves then bring us right back into this room.

"*Pity how he doesn't know.*"

"Know what?"

"That he's starving himself to death," she mutters.

It hits me upside the head the moment the words sink into my brain. She's making him do this, and he has no idea. No fear or consciousness of what he's doing. Davina said she wouldn't hurt him, and she kept her word, making him do it all on his own.

"What did you do?" I growl.

She squats in front of me, still keeping a clear distance of my reach. *"I'm giving you something. A little piece of what's to come. The days and weeks you'll spend here watching your men die one by one."*

"When I told you I'd torture people that trespassed on my land, I didn't mean for you to do it slowly."

She smiles. *"Where's the fun in that?"*

I push myself onto my knees so that my height towers over her. "Remember what I said, Blood, you won't like it when I'm in charge."

"You keep dreaming about that." She straightens her spine. *"Don't worry, I have something planned for you later. Wouldn't want you to think I was playing favorites."*

"Can't wait," I reply through my clenched teeth.

—

The jingling of chains emits through the night, reminding me that Tybalt is in the room with me. That he still hasn't eaten and is still in good spirits as he continues to sit in his corner. I've run out of ways to threaten him to take one fucking bite of food, that it'd make me satisfied as his commander for him to do so.

Nothing.

A soft moan exhales through the air, but I keep my eyes closed, needing my rest for whatever Davina has planned for me. If it involves more stares and my having to look into one of her sister's eyes again, I'm going to lose my shit.

"Fuck," mutters a voice within the room. Cracking my eyelids open, I look over to the corner, where Tybalt crawled into a ball and fell asleep.

Except he's not the only one in the corner.

Red hair illuminates from the moonlight that seeps into the room. Her head falling back as her body rocks back and forth.

I close my eyes and reopen them.

This is a dream.

It has to be because I've thought and fantasized about it too many times. However, it was me underneath her as she rode my cock, not Tybalt.

"Holy mother of Athena," Tybalt groans. "You feel amazing. Is this real?" He's answered with a delicate chuckle.

"*It's real,*" she whispers loud enough for me to hear. "*So fuck me like it's the last thing you're going to do.*"

I hear his grunt and see his knees bend as he pounds into her. Into the woman who drove her nails inside my skin to the point where I wanted to strangle her with my bare hands and do exactly what the lad is doing right now. My resentment has passed its peak, surpassing the level of being able to stay calm.

Yanking on my chains in frustration, I set myself to stand, all while seeing Davina's head turn in my direction.

"*Didn't mean to wake you,*" she coos, letting Tybalt continue to drive his dick inside her. She looks down at him, her hair cascading over her shoulders. "*Don't stop.*"

"*Stop,*" I deadpan, my eyes boring into his body.

But he doesn't, my words mean nothing. It's her that

possesses him, body and soul, and she's trying to get into my fucking head.

She's already there.

She's been there. Now she's using her little antics and tricks to drive me fucking crazy. To the point where my fingers are itching to clasp around my own man's neck.

I can't see Davina's eyes when she turns in my direction, but I can make out the look on her face—defiance.

"*Go back to sleep,*" she croons then lets out a harsh exhale, dropping her chin to her chest. "*Yes, Tybalt, like that.*"

"Yeah?" he utters, suddenly confident. "You like that, beauty?"

"*Yes,*" she breathes. "*Mhm, you're so good at this.*"

I jerk at my chains, forgetting for a split second that I'm bound. She wants this reaction out of me, the rage and thwarting, which will pose a problem for her in the long run. The moment the opportunity presents itself she is going to wish she never did this. Wish she'd thought harder about keeping me here.

Regardless of the cuff, she took this too far the moment she snapped Priamos's neck. She should've just killed me and got it over with.

"*The big, bad beast is up,*" Davina mutters. "*Show him how you fuck a woman properly, and with respect.*"

"I'm going to," Tybalt says eagerly, clasping her hips. "My God, you're so tight."

"*Blood,*" I seethe. "Your game isn't going to make this *thing* between us be over."

"*Keep talking,*" she voices on a shaky breath. "*Your deep voice is going to make me come.*"

"You'd like that, wouldn't you?" I rally. "My cock inside you instead of his."

A mirthless laugh leaves her lips. "*I don't know. Tybalt is doing a really good job, aren't you?*" Leaning forward, she places a chaste kiss to his lips. His cock slowing as he relishes in their moment that I'm firsthand witness to.

That I don't want to *be* in.

"I'm going to come," he stresses urgently, pumping himself faster. Davina lets him continue a moment longer before she pries herself from him.

Standing, she straddles him between her legs, watching him pump his cock and freeing his seed over his stomach.

She rakes her hand through her hair and leans forward. *"Wasn't that worth dying for?"*

Tybalt chortles, pushing himself up on his elbows. "The best way to die."

"Good." A skin-prickling crack jolts through the room as Tybalt's body lifelessly slumps to the floor. Davina disregards him just as quickly as she snapped his neck, steps over his body, and strides in my direction. I'm blind with rage and remorse. These men will all suffer for my getting caught, and Davina will make sure I see every single one of them die.

"That was for you," she jabs, stopping in front of me. *"My sisters won't be so kind tomorrow."*

Then she disappears out the door, leaving me with a dead shipmate and my dick semi fucking hard.

CHAPTER TWENTY FIVE

Tobias

My ship rocks to the left as a cannonball hits the hull. Men skid along the deck, holding on to each other and any object they can to keep from falling while I'm staring at the fucker on the other ship, tipping his large black hat at me. On the Captain's deck, he's above everyone, in perfect view and as cocky and stupid as ever.

Delilah was built to be the strongest vessel in the Black Sea. With the most cannons, the strength to carry the largest amount of gunpowder and men. Whoever this lout thought he was, he is going to be pondering it beneath the waves of my ship.

He thought he was someone, I've never seen his ship before, but he flew a red Hunter flag and has been trying to ram us for the last five minutes to get some of their men on board. Some have attempted to, swinging off lines to land onto our decks just to delve right into the ocean.

However, the main problem was how far south he is. How close he is to Davina's home and that no Hunter has ever come this far because Sirens are known to like the cooler water. So, immediately, something tips me off that this isn't a coincidence because it has my Uncle Declan written all over it.

"Fire," I bellow to my crew, already used to the sound of the twelve cannons going off almost simultaneously.

The ship rocks back a little from the force as I peer over at Asher, who has taken the wheel.

"Damage report," I order.

"Few more hits, Capt'n," he yells back. "Should be able to disable 'em."

I turn back to my crew. "Load up." They follow instructions, packing the cannons and waiting for my next order.

"Theon," I shout over the whines of the ship, hitting the larger than normal waves that's causing the damage it's taken thus far. He appears at my side within seconds, silently waiting for me to speak. "I want the best men on the ship suited up to fight. The next round of cannons should incapacitate them."

"Aye, aye, Capt'n," he replies then scurries away.

"Men, get ready," I charge. "The next pass they make, I'll give the order to fire."

The anticipation makes it feel like a lifetime. Impatiently I watch my men stand along the rail to receive my direction, adrenaline sprinting and heaving throughout my whole frame.

It feels like forever for their ship to turn around and make another drag along our vessel. The wind picks up around us, reminding me of Davina's red hair and how she loves to sit along the ocean's edge. How I left her with a dangerous Viking to find my brother, who's still missing.

"They're along our starport side, Captain," one of my men exclaims. My eyes fall on their bow, sailing alongside our edge.

They are going to try and jump our ship.

"Start firing the left side," I bark, pulling out the small blade Davina gave me as I stride toward the banister.

The first shot goes off, busting into the close proximity of the enemy's ship. Snatching up a rope that has a pronged-hook at the end, I toss it over their railing and catch the wood banister of the enemy's ship.

"Fire the center guns and watch for the splintering wood," I yell. The roar of more shots go off, making wood fly in every direction as I pull back from the debris. "Anchor the ship and tie it off. I want them close."

Shouts and chaos sounds on the other side to their ship. Metal clanking together as I get ready to board. Peering behind me, over a dozen of my men are armed with their weapons. Knives, swords, and pistols decorate their attire as I jerk my head to the side for them to board.

That's when everything happens in a blur.

My jumping onto the ship, my dagger inserting into a man's neck as the splatter of warm blood hits my hand, the cries of men in the throngs of battle while my main focus lands on the fool who decided it'd be a fantastic idea to attack us.

Climbing the stairs to the Captain's deck, I don't get but two steps before a blood-curdling scream rings through the air. It's not the scream that gives me pause but the sex *of* the scream that just penetrated the air.

It's a woman's.

Turning on my heels, I look around the deck for anything in a dress but see nothing. I blink at the reality that I'm in. A woman on this ship would be close to impossible since pirates are so superstitious of them being on board, let alone look at it. Plus, the crush of men fighting doesn't leave much room for me to see anything else.

"Please," wails the same voice. "Don't do this."

Glancing over my right shoulder toward the sound, the door to the Captain's corridors is open slightly. Cautiously, I make my way toward it, pulling out the pistol at my side in case I need to blast it into some lad's face that might be awaiting me.

Peering around the door's entrance stands a burly man, violently shaking something in front of him. The soft gasps and sobs of weeping illuminates that I did in fact hear a woman that is now in the hands of a pirate, rattling her around like a doll. With my non-existing patience already being inconvenienced by being bombarded by a random group of assholes, I'm at the man's back, driving my blade into his shoulder.

Crying out in pain, he hunches over slightly, giving me the perfect opportunity to pull back and jab it into his neck. He falls into a heavy thud on the floorboards and leaves me to stare at the woman in distress that just became another mission I didn't sign up for today.

And all I *can* do is stare.

Wavy, raven locks make up her hair, plush pink lips tremble in fear as she gapes back at me with dread filling her features. But that's not what gives me pause or makes my body lock up in shock.

It's her eyes, so clear-cut and vivid. That glimmer in hues of greens and a twinge of brown. They are almost identical to Davina's. So close in fact, that, for a moment, I believe it to be her with darker hair.

"Please don't hurt me," she begs with her hands extended before me. "I just want to go home."

Pocketing my knife and pistol, I take a step back. "I'm not here to hurt you. I'm from the other ship." It doesn't take the terror out of her eyes as she begins to cower away from me, backing deeper into the room.

"Listen, Miss, I know you have no reason to trust me, but I need to get off this ship. If you want to stay here, you're welcome to but I'd advise against it. I'll take you home."

"I—you don't—I don't know," she quakes.

"I'm Tobias Nathaniel," I offer. "I don't hurt women or auction them off. I can—"

"You're the Prince of the Black Sea."

I nod, feeling the rumbling of the ship. "I am, and we have to get off this vessel because my ship is about to sink it."

That gets her to move in my direction. I give her my hand, which she takes immediately, following me outside and toward Delilah. A man abruptly stands in our way, and I waste no time, pulling out my pistol and aiming it at his forehead. Gunpowder wafts in my nose as I step over his body, but I'm halted by the woman in my clutches.

Peering over my shoulder, she's frozen, glancing down at the man I've just stabbed. I forget she's a woman who doesn't deal with this bullshit on a daily basis, so I round the fallen man, getting her to follow another path to safety as I get her onto my ship.

"Get her something warm and some food," I tell one of the first men I come across. "She'll sleep in my bed."

"I can't," she retorts. "I mean—thank you but—" I nod anyways, and he immediately guides her away without further questioning as she still complains and frets over my order.

"A few men are still alive on the other ship, Cap'n," Ashton informs me while approaching my side. "Do you want prisoners?"

Readjusting my coat, I try to brush off how beautiful the woman I just saved is, how, even though we are surrounded by a thicket of danger, she still argues with my instructions.

Something Davina would do.

It's been over a month since I've seen her. Every night I look up at the stars, wondering if she's looking at the same ones. If she thinks about how different our lives are now that we're older and everything has changed. I didn't want them to, but she forced it.

"Kill them all," I convey. "It'll send a message to good 'ole Uncle Declan."

CHAPTER TWENTY SIX

Davina

"He's losing his mind in there," Nesrine frets across the dining room table from me as I continue eating. "We need to do something before he harms himself."

I scoff. *"He won't kill himself."*

"He might pull an arm off with the way he's pulling on his chains." I finally look up at her from my plate of fish and seaweed to fix her with a glare.

"What would you have me do, let him roam the island free again?"

She shrugs. "It's not as though he can go anywhere."

"No."

"Davina," she argues softly. "If he really injures himself, you'll get no answers."

I stab my dead fish with my fork. *"Won't get any anyways. He won't speak, I know it. And we are running out of his men to persuade him."*

Almost all the prisoners we've brought onto this island are dying and not by our hands. Within hours of them being locked away, all of them became extremely ill. Some regurgitating their food, others coughing so loudly it echoed down the halls.

Each day, one or two of them die, and one by one, I've lost some of my leverage to make Dagen speak.

"Then what's the point of his being alive?" Nesrine asks, leaning back in her chair and crossing her slim arms over her chest.

"There isn't one," I reply. *"Other than the idea and pleasure of having him suffer for years to come."*

"Without his men, you have no leverage."

"Then I guess we'll never know, will we?" I deadpan.

Nesrine reaches over the table, extending her arm across it for me to take her hand. "This isn't you. You don't do vengeance."

"Why wouldn't I?" I snap. *"Is it because I'm stuck on this island and banned from the sea that I'm not like you anymore?"*

Her brows deepen. "I'm not saying that at all. It's just that—"

"Are you done talking about this," I sigh while dropping my fork. *"Because I am, and you just ruined my meal with talks about the Viking and misplaced sympathy."*

Nesrine removes her arm and straightens her back. I know that I'm taking my anger out on my sister, but at the moment, I don't care.

"I understand you being upset that he betrayed your trust, Davina, but we can't find any reason why he isn't telling the truth."

"He stole from us. He wanted the cuff to take the sea, sounds pretty self-explanatory to me."

"Let Isolde try again," she imparts. "He's not in his right mind now, she might be able to dig deeper."

"I don't want to hear any more about his village or his clan. I don't care if he—"

"Are my girls fighting?" The sing-song voice immediately gets me to cringe and ignites more irritation. All I want to do is eat in peace. Which is becoming a rare commodity as of late because my sisters won't leave the damn island.

The taps of Taysa's shoes saunters through the large

dining room as I send one last glare in Nesrine's direction before she gets closer to us. The last thing I want to do is upset Taysa because that's all that happens when we argue. Another thing to add to the growing list of issues I'm facing.

"Just disagreeing," I answer, finally looking over to find her with a perked brow as she pulls the chair next to me from the table and sits.

"You're fighting over the Viking," she alludes.

"We were just talking about what else to do," Nesrine conveys. "Just family business." It's a cheap shot. My sister is upset that all this has happened when it shouldn't have because of the veil. How Dagan should've never been able to grab the cuff, how Tobias shouldn't be allowed to come and go as he pleases. It's been something she's bottled up and now is finally releasing after all this time.

"I come with news," Taysa informs cheerfully, ignoring Nesrine's comment. "About the veil."

"What is it?"

"It's broken," she states. "The desired spell must've not considered just Sirens but other magical creatures or we're in the midst of Sirens ourselves that can walk on land permanently like you."

"So you didn't do it right," Nesrine sneers with slitted black eyes.

Taysa glances in her direction. "I did it right, someone may have toyed with it."

"What?" That coming from both me and my sister.

"That's impossible," I continue. *"How? They'd have to know of the spell, first and foremost. Then they'd have to—"*

"I'm not the only witch in this world, my dear," Taysa replies while giving me a light tap to my hand. "Spells can be manipulated. We were made by gods, we aren't supposed to exist. Spells can be altered if the right witch knows how to do so through dark magic."

182

"*But how would they even know of this place?*" I ask. "*To the world, we only live in the sea.*"

"People talk about things they shouldn't."

"*No—*" I shake my head. "*—Tobias wouldn't breathe a word about us and this island.*"

"It's not just him," Taysa continues. "There are traitors in every faction of people. Not all Sirens are as secretive and loyal as you'd like them to be. It's possible that the Vikings have some sort of person within their clan that could've put a small defect through the veil. You were able to bring his men on the island but most of them are dead because of the magic. They don't belong here."

"Which means there's something up with Tobias and Dagen, Davina," Nesrine relays. "We already know Dagen isn't who he says he is, but Tobias might be—"

"*It doesn't matter if Tobias is something else,*" I snap. "*He'd never hurt us.*" I don't miss Nesrine sending Taysa a pleading look nor the faint sigh from Taysa. I may have been naive with Dagen but not Tobias. I know him better than *anyone* at this table. I've heard his fears and dreams, his hope of finding Lorne and the things he wanted to do in his life. His loyalty ran so deep within his veins that it'd be impossible for him to betray us.

To betray me.

"We've already tried to drown Tobias," Nesrine reports. "To see if he was a siren, but he didn't show any sign of—"

"But you stopped it from fully happening, didn't you?" Taysa inquires. "That boy didn't die, and he would need to so his true being would revive."

"*And he won't,*" I gripe. "*No one is laying a hand on him or they will answer to me. And trust me when I say—*"

"Can you...bring him back to life?" Nesrine interjects. "If he does die."

I slam my palm on the table. *"Didn't you just hear me? We are not taking that chance."*

"I can't," Taysa replies. "Not even dark magic that I know of would bring him back to life. Only a god."

"Our father is the son of Poseidon, could he do it?"

"Nesrine," I warn.

Taysa sighs. "I honestly don't know, my child. If Davina feels so strongly about him, I wouldn't chance it. Is the Viking affected by any of your powers?"

"Some," Nesrine conveys. "But we feel like there is a barrier of some sort."

"A barrier?" Taysa asks. "Like some things come through but others are out of focus or disoriented?"

"Not so much for me, but Atarah had a splitting headache for days after her and Brylee tried to dig into his thoughts. We were hoping that, when we captured him the second time, he would be thinking about his plans and why he stole the cuff."

"Sounds like Norse magic."

"What's that?"

"The oldest kind of witch, they are called seeresses. They are feared by many and hated by religious groups because of their evil practices. They require sacrifices, mainly humans, to offer a need or want by said people or persons. For the desired spell I casted, it took away something from you, that was the consequence. For a seeress's magic, they demand a life, something to show how worthy and serious they are."

"So, you're saying that this seeress could influence the desired spell?" I press. *"That it could be altered?"*

Taysa bows her head. "I'm sorry to say that they are more powerful than I am or ever have been. A seeress can tweak a spell but not fully get rid of one that is set in place."

"So there's like a hole in the veil?" Nesrine inquires.

"Where whomever needed or wanted to be here would be able to get through?"

"That's correct."

"So can you close this hole? Fix it?"

Taysa nods. "I can, it's going to take some work. I'm not as young as I used to be."

"What else would we have to give?" My sister's next question sets an alarm off in my head. With every action causes a reaction and consequence with sorcery.

"With the veil still being partly up," Taysa replies. "I don't think anything. I just need to place a patch, if you will."

"And how quickly can you make that happen?" Nesrine asks.

"I'm going to go home right now and start working on it. I need to eat and gather my strength." She stands from her chair and pets my hair. "Keep the Viking alive until I get back, child. I might be able to make something for him to drink that will spill all his truths."

Nesrine rises as well. "We'll keep him safe. I'll tell Atarah and Brylee to diminish whatever plans that I know they have cooking in their heads."

"Good, I'll be back in a few days. Send for me if more trouble brews." Making her way from the room, she doesn't stop before saying, "And keep the pirate here too if he comes this way again. We'll have to do the same, Davina."

I nod, it's all I can do. Two outsiders can come onto the island, both unknowns of how they are able to get passed the veil. And if I have to keep my best friend in the dark to protect my family, it'll have to come to pass.

Because even though they are the bane of my sanity, my sisters are all I have left of my mother.

CHAPTER TWENTY SEVEN
DAGEN

"I'm tired of looking at you," I snap at Isolde as she gawks at me for the last ten minutes. "You're not going to find anything that I haven't told you already."

"Shut up," Brylee snaps back, sitting next to Atarah, who is gawking at another puddle of water again.

They're trying to team up on me, Isolde reading my past memories, the twins doing some weird thing with reading my current thoughts. Kali is staring at me with her arms crossed ready to do something I guess, and Nesrine hasn't stopped smirking. All while Rohana and Davina stand along the wall toward the back of the room.

Thing is I can still see the red she-devil.

And so fucking help me when I get free of my chains I'm going to make that girl never forget the look in my eyes when I do ungodly shit to her because I already have them all planned out in my brain.

Splashing seawater at her skin to watch it burn her flesh.

Having *her* chained to the floor for a couple of days.

Fucking her out of my system over and over again to shove Tybalt out of her brain and anyone else for that matter.

Brylee snaps her fingers in front of my face, ridding my thoughts that have plagued my head for days. My focus narrows in on her, blue strands of her hair swept across her forehead. Those intense indigo eyes burning animosity into my face.

"One more fucking thought about *touching* my sister," she seethes in a whisper. "And I'll rip your throat out."

"Too messy," Kali retorts. A knife appears out of nowhere. "Stab him."

"I'm fucking tired of these little magical rounds," I spit out. "If you weren't all high and mighty, we'd be in different —" A loud, piercing shrill fills my ears as my immediate reaction is to cover them—but I can't.

Chains are still bound along my bloody wrists as an intense pain fills my head, my temples throb immeasurably to the point where I believe I'm about to collapse on this hard floor and pass the fuck out.

Another second and it suddenly stops, my lungs heaving in short gasps of air as Kali makes a movement that has me looking over at her adjusting her jaw.

"Did you fucking do that?" I snap.

She cocks her head from side to side like she's stretching to go to battle. "I did. And if you're good, I'll sing you a lullaby that'll make you go to sleep."

"I'm going to make you fall asleep *permanently*."

"Hatred," Isolde says, squinting her eyes through her glasses. "A people called the Highlands are his enemy."

A wave of vulnerability hits me to the point where I feel overly helpless and vanquished of myself. They couldn't just kill me and let me salvage my pride, instead, they had to meddle and prod the truth from me, which makes me worthless, not an emotion I'm privy of feeling.

I've been fighting my chains for days, my muscles ache, my wrists numb from trying to squeeze through the metal to free myself. My back is stiff from lying on the hard floor, and now with this headache, I'm just about ready to accept my fate of being here forever and never seeing any of my clansmen again.

But a piece of me begs to hold on for just a little bit

longer. That maybe they'll never be able to discover what the cuff means to the future of my people.

However, I'm playing off the conscious of the girls, killing a man who grabbed an item that his father ordered him to obtain—I don't think so. I'm in a hell made from hopes and dreams of safety, where my death will be the end result.

"There are a lot of late-night talks," Isolde notes. "Between a group of men, maybe elders?" My father's council, his most trusted men to help plan out our next move with the Highlanders.

"They're important," Brylee adds. "He knows these men. They are vital to his people to keep them safe."

"Stay the fuck out of my—" The high-pitched shriek sounds in my head again, and I buckle over.

The strain against my eardrums and temples is unbearable. Like being slammed in the head repeatedly with clubs on every inch of my skull.

I can't focus on my breathing—only the pain.

Again, it ceases, leaving me in a worse battered state than before. Another burden of catching my breath, the same violent pulsating of my temples, then everything crashes at once in my brain like a stampede of horses.

Davina.

Her little tyranny of torture is a petty way to get back at me for stealing from her.

When in Lothbrok, if she didn't speak within a few days, her fate would be sealed. She'd become someone's whore, maybe a servant in someone's household. I wonder if I'd still want to fuck her knowing what I know now. Even though the roles would be turned, it'd be—

A swift twinge of pain hits my body, but it's against my bicep this time, a stream of blood drifting down it. I lock my jaw as I flash my attention to Brylee, who grips the knife in her hand that Kali gave her.

"I told you," she leers through slitted eyes. "My *sister*."

Unexpectedly, Atarah gasps loudly, straightening her back like she just came out of a nightmare with eyes widened in shock.

Brylee immediately comes to her aid, holding on to her arm. "You did too much," she coos. "We did it for too long this time."

"You can't drift from me," Atarah croons, her chest heaving in and out with large intakes of air. "Every time you speak to him, you break off from me."

Brylee huddles closer to her. "I'm sorry."

"I think it's time for Rohana to give it a shot," Nesrine announces.

"No," Davina snaps.

"He's weak," Isolde adds. "It'd be the perfect time."

I lean in her direction. "Go fuck yourself, Pink." She rolls her eyes and removes her glasses, taking her leave from the chair in front of me.

It allows an impeccable view of Davina.

Her skin is a tad bit darker than I remember, her red hair braided back from her scalp to display the structure of her face.

Her eyes meet mine, worried and anxious, and I don't know what Rohana has to do with any of those things. But I've seen a similar reaction out of her when King Triton introduced himself to me with his trident and a few thrusts following that.

"I can do it," Rohana announces, raising her chin while striding in my direction.

Davina grabs her arm and twirls her around. *"This isn't a good idea."*

"I can handle it."

Davina catches my gaze again and shifts her weight to one leg. *"It isn't going to be fun."*

Her sister touches her forearm. "It'll be fine, you all are with me." Turning on her heels, she continues to make her way to me. A soft smile playing off her face, which would be alarming except Rohana seems to be the most mellow and carefree of the seven.

Standing behind me, she places both of her palms on my shoulders. "This isn't going to hurt. You might feel a tingle though."

"How about we pretend we already did whatever it is you're going to do?" I carp, just wanting to be left the fuck alone so I can let my headache subside.

She gives me a small squeeze. "Just relax."

"I'm not *relaxed.*" She doesn't respond, and that prickling sensation hits my flesh from underneath my clothes.

It moves aimlessly down my arms and chest, making its way to my toes. And the moment my whole body feels odd and weak, Rohana tightens her hold on me.

"Things would be different," she sneers, "if you didn't have powers."

Davina creeps closer, her focus on her sister behind me. *"I have a reason to keep you here. You stole from me."*

"You don't understand," she retorts. "My people need safety. The Highlanders are growing in numbers by the month."

My brows furrow.

Fucking Zeus, she's revealing everything I'm feeling.

"You'll need to find another way," Davina deadpans as my gaze falls back on her. She squares her shoulders as Rohana stands in front of her. They're about the same height, staring at each other like they are about to fight or tear each other's hair out.

I couldn't give a shit at this point as long as they take it outside this room and away from me.

"I could've told you all that," I grumble, leaning back in my chair.

They both ignore me—shocking, the only thing I think they'd shut up for is if I told them exactly what they want to know.

"You're going to suffer at my hands," Rohana fumes, clenching her hands at her sides.

Davina looks over at her sisters huddled together, possibly searching for what to do, when Rohana's hand suddenly seizes her neck. Swinging a leg around Davina's legs, Rohana knocks her down to her knees.

The sisters rush to her aid, but Rohana is already expecting it, raising her free hand to start a sudden gust of wind in the room. The puddle on the floor rises from the ground, mixing with the strong whirlpool of air to block the sisters from impeding on her hold of Davina.

Everything happens so quickly, with so many bodies, that it's hard to watch every detail, but my gaze always lands back on Davina. She's already punched Rohana in the gut, weakening the spiral of wind to let Kali through the barrier.

Kali yanks Rohana away from Davina but receives a backhand to the side of her face. Davina tries to ram her, but the vortex picks her feet off the ground and whips her around. A flash of white and black hair meshes within the mess, a bunch of shouts and grunts fill the air.

Then Davina's body is thrown across the room, skidding to my feet. Her arm is outstretched above her body as she slowly pushes herself to sit. Then an animalistic roar releases through the room, and my attention jerks to Rohana, holding off her sisters with the strong vortex of wind, but it's what she's holding that gets my heart to drop into my stomach—the knife.

Davina is already on her two feet, hands on her knees to

catch her balance, and when Rohana's eyes narrow in on her sister, I've seen it all too many times.

Standing from my chair, I heave my body in front of Davina and give my back to her sister. It doesn't take long for the knife to intrude into my shoulder. For the abrupt ache of pain to start penetrating through my back. Followed by a sharp exhale of air on Davina's face as she peers up at me with expanded green eyes.

My rage—it's gone. As though Rohana sucked it out of me and drew it into herself. But it doesn't change the fact that I stand here in chains with a knife in my back that was meant for her or that she wants to make me a pet to torture mentally and physically.

"You shouldn't have done that," she whispers.

I wince when I move to lean closer to her. "I told you that you're mine. And I'll be the one to punish you."

"This is going to hurt," Nesrine warns, suddenly at my flank, then tugs the knife from my back.

"Fuck," I bellow, making Davina flinch.

"Put pressure on his back," Isolde chides, before doing just that and sending another wave of pain down my spine. "Or he'll bleed to death."

"Geezus fuck," I seize. "Stop *touching* me."

"Oh my goodness. Did I do that?" It's Rohana, her voice timid and upset. Now I know why Davina didn't want her to use her powers. Every emotion I felt, Rohana acted it out, and if it wasn't for Davina's sisters, she would've been fucked.

"It's fine," Nesrine replies nonchalantly. "He's a big man."

"That's a lot of blood," Rohana conveys.

"How deep did you go?" Isolde asks. Then I feel something insert inside my wound, a gut-wrenching twist in my stomach before blackness takes over my whole body and takes me to some peace and quiet.

CHAPTER TWENTY EIGHT

Davina

S tanding in front of a large fireplace, I can feel the heat dry my already dehydrated skin. But the flames remind me of the pain and mental suffering I've endured over the last few years. The sacrifices I've made to keep my sisters and father safe, as well as our kingdom from the Hunters, and the desired spell that wanted to cease their freedom.

Our people used to come to this island freely, able to roam the land, but after so much time had passed, I envied their being able to go home. So I banished the amount of Sirens that could come here.

I'm the lost princess of Lacuna that they never see anymore, and I miss my friends. I miss the creatures I adopted and the underwater cove that holds all the things I found in shipwrecks. I endured the loss of the sea for so long that it feels like I don't belong anywhere anymore. A restless and lost being who roams a piece of space with no purpose or use of anything.

The patter of footsteps softly echo off the hall outside the study, allotting to my sisters' presence. They were going to see if they could drag anything out of Dagen while he was in and out of consciousness. Isolde tells me he's sweating profusely, that it's called a fever and some humans don't make it afterwards.

I guess I won't fully get my revenge after all.

That's what I keep telling myself anyway. All the things that happened to him were his own fault, and he had no one else to blame. Nothing on this island belonged to him.

"You need to step away from the fire," Atarah mutters softly, her hand wrapping around my arm to gently pull me away. "You'll burn your pretty skin."

She knows it won't. I can burn myself alive and nothing would happen. Somehow I can pull from the sun's heat and radiate it from myself. Dagen was the first one I've ever tested it on, still didn't get him to talk so, again, the worthless part sinks in a little deeper.

"We have some news," Kali offers as all my sisters find seats to take in the sitting area. I glance at her to begin, but her amber eyes fall onto Atarah.

"Go on with it," I urge, sitting in between the twins.

"He came to for a few minutes," Kali states, twisting her orange hair around her finger. "Atarah and Brylee were able to seep into his thoughts to see if he was contemplating anything."

"And what did you find?"

"Confusion," Brylee mutters. "He was trying to remember what happened before he fainted onto the floor."

"Then you," Atarah resumes.

My brows furrow. *"Me?"*

"He remembers looking down at you and into your eyes," Brylee sets forth. "How he wished the tables were turned. And how his coming here was a mistake."

"It was a mistake."

"Things are getting worse," Isolde pipes in, clasping her hands into her lap. "He's starting to care for you."

"He hates me. Lusts for me, yes, but isn't that what men do?"

Brylee places a hand on my knee. "It's not just that. He

wondered how you were doing. Then his concentration went to the cuff."

Of course it did.

"It's to summon something. And we don't know what that something is."

"We think it's magic," Rohana voices. "Since the cuff already holds half the power of the sea next to Father's, it could only be used for something like that."

"Remember when Taysa mentioned Norse magic?" Nesrine asks across from me. "We looked it up in one of your books. It's sorcery from the north. The Viking is from there."

I look around the room at my sisters' full attention on me. They know I have some sort of connection with him. That I let him go because I didn't want him to die. I despise my poor judgment and weakness, which could've caused the death of everyone I love.

But never again.

The only person outside my sisters that I fully trusted was Tobias, and that was the way it would *always* stay. Not some burly man with a lewd mouth and secrets that he won't reveal.

"So, we have a plan," Isolde recites, her coral-colored eyes glancing between Atarah and Brylee but not me, which sparks caution. "Seduce the Viking."

I begin to leap from the lounge. *"Are you out—"* Atarah's hand shoots out to sit me back down.

"He cares for you," she says with a squeeze to my thigh. "And as much as I *loathe* the idea of him touching you, we aren't able to delve any deeper into his head. We thought with him being weak right now it would make it easy but something is blocking us."

"The Norse magic," Brylee adds. "He got through the veil. He knew where to find us. The seeress would have enough magic to pinpoint us, possibly a locator spell."

"*But what would Vikings want with the sea?*" I challenge. "*I've read that they are warriors and farmers. They don't sail around like Tobias does. What would be the reason?*"

"We don't know," Atarah states. "Maybe they made a deal for protection. We've seen these Highlanders mentioned in his head over a dozen times. They *are* a real threat to his people in his mind."

"We know it's not something you want to do," Rohana utters softly. "We all don't want you to submit to someone who has betrayed you."

"I'd do it," Nesrine claims with a smirk. "But he already knows all my tricks."

I mean, what choice do I have?

"*I'll do it.*" I receive a bunch of voices at one time, asking me if I'm sure and I don't have to do it if I don't feel comfortable, but I ignore them. "*I'll get the information.*"

Then he dies.

CHAPTER TWENTY NINE
DAGEN

The sound of soft snoring pulls me out of my deep sleep, followed by the thudding in my skull. I'm assuming the girls let me fall lifeless to the floor because I feel a large bump on the back of my head.

Slowly, I perch my weight on my right elbow, the moonlight streaming into the room to slightly illuminate it. The wheezing still continues, and I glance through the room only for my eyes to fall on a body laying on the floor with a pillow under their head. Slim legs, the hump of a curvy hip and flat torso, it describes all the sisters, but I'd know this one anywhere.

Davina sleeps peacefully a few feet away, and I blink a few times to make sure I'm not seeing things.

She's still there.

My movement toward her rattles my chains, alluding to the fact that even though I was stabbed and possibly have a head injury, they still have me bound.

But she's in my midst, and I've been waiting for this moment for weeks.

As slowly as I can and without gasping in pain from my shoulder, I crawl in her direction. The tile digs into my knees, but the light in the room guides me to her easily. I half-expect her to jerk to attention at my closeness, but she lays still, arm thrown over her midsection as her chest heaves in small breaths of air.

Reaching for her hair, I gradually and carefully pull out one of her bobby pins to work at my lock like she had prior. A few twists, loud cuss words in my head, and it pops open. The loud release stirs her, and since I know I don't have a lot of time, I seize my opportunity.

Tucking my arm under her lower back, I tug her toward me. A sharp gasp leaves her lips, but she's already underneath me, my knees on either side of her while my palms rest on the sides of her head.

"Hi, Blood," I greet with a lift of my lips. She smells like the sea and looks so small beneath me that my cock stirs in my pants.

I've dreamt of having her like this, to have her surrender to me. For us not to be surrounded by everyone on this island.

Without her glaring at me with hatred and disgust in her eyes.

"What are you doing?" she scolds as I lower my body closer to her.

For the first time since arriving here, I feel powerful, like *myself*. Like I have some sort of control of this situation, even though I'm fully aware that she can turn against me at any minute.

"I told you that I couldn't wait to have my hands on you," I mutter.

She releases a soft scoff. *"What are you going to do? Attempt to kill me?"*

My hand finds her smooth neck as I clasp my fingers around it. "I think you'd deserve it, don't you?"

"I don't know," she claims. *"Is that why you stepped in front of that knife for me? Would've saved you the trouble if you hadn't."*

I clench my teeth together. She's right, it'd save me a world full of agitation but not from all six of her sisters.

In their sadness, I'd be dead, and that'd be the end of my

story. Though the looming question that she asks is something I don't have the answer to. Without me stepping in front of her and taking a blade to the back, it would have torn the sisters apart if Rohana had taken my anger and killed her sister with it.

Would've solved my problem, but my death might be a little more painful after that event.

My fingertips graze the hollows of her neck. "I like to handle my own issues. And you, Blood, are the bane of my existence."

"Feeling's mutual." Her palms find my chest, but she doesn't shove me away like I think she's going to do.

Instead, she keeps them there like she's trying to feel what I'm feeling. To gain all the conflicted feelings I'm undergoing right now because I *am* conflicted. I'm torn between crushing this woman's windpipe and ravishing the lips I've been wanting to touch since I first laid eyes on her.

"Did you think I was teasing?"

She shakes her head. *"No. You've tried already, failed, and now you're going to attempt to do it again. Can't say that I blame you, I did kill some of your men in front of you."*

"Which means revenge in my book, Blood."

She gives a light shrug. *"It's called gaining information in mine. From a man who stole from me and thought it'd be okay to step foot here in the first place."*

"You killed innocent men."

"And you put my entire family at risk."

"Which means you have to *fuck* someone in front of me?"

"Just something I learned from Nesrine."

"It was a cheap fuck," I tell her, curling my hand that lies on the tiles. "He didn't get to warm you up, did he? Make you burn inside to the point where you were begging for it."

She remains silent underneath me.

Too much pride—I can relate—she'll never admit how she

feels the slight tension between us. The tug and pull, like two magnetic forces of the Earth.

"Too bad I'm not going to either," I mutter, tucking my face into the crook of her neck. "I've been waiting for this for too long."

Her fingers clasp around my shirt. *"You need to get back."*

"You might as well kill me then," I retort. "Because you're not getting out from underneath me until you can hear my voice speaking to you when you come. Until you feel me filling you up to erase Tybalt and the pirate that comes to visit you." I lay a soft kiss onto her flesh that immediately relaxes her body and the fingers clutching my shirt. "How many times has he fucked you?"

Now, she nudges me back, but not hard enough for my frame to give us any space.

"None, huh?" I chuckle deeply. "Too bad he won't be able to now."

Davina scoffs. *"You have a mighty large amount of confidence, Viking, to think that you'll be able to do anything to my mind."*

"You've never experienced someone like me before." Another kiss. "And you won't again."

"So, what, you think you're going to rape me and then kill me? Sounds very Viking of you."

I pull my head from her neck to look down at her. "I don't *rape* women."

"But I'm underneath you and not by my will."

I scoff. "We all know you have the strength of ten men, Blood. I'd be across this room, like I have been before, if you didn't want me here."

Davina leans up until she's inches from my face. *"Just so we're clear, no one will ever own me."*

"I want to." I start laying kisses on her cheek. "I want to

hear you scream my name, but what's unfortunate is that I'll only hear that in my head, won't I?"

She turns her head to the side, but I clasp my fingers around her chin, turning her back to me.

"It doesn't make you less of anything. The best warriors have flaws. The most honorable leader has a weakness."

She lays back down on the hard floor. *"What's yours?"*

"You're already my enemy, Blood, how much more do you want me to give you?"

"Everything," she bleaks. *"Why did you take the cuff? It means something more than what you're telling us."*

My hand roams up to rest on her cheek. "I told you, it'll help my people."

"How?"

I roll my eyes. "You have a sturdy man on top of you and all you want to do is ask questions."

"It's imperative that I know."

"I can't tell you." I exhale a heavy breath. "If I could, I'd tell you everything. But it means too much to my clan for it to get into the hands of the wrong people."

"And I'm the wrong people?"

"I'm trying to convince myself that you are, but you have a soft spot for me."

"Do I? I already know that you have one for me." She brushes a piece of stray hair away from my face and tugs it behind my ear. *"You saved me from that fight with Atarah and Brylee."*

"It was two against one," I gripe. "Bad shit can happen."

The tips of her fingers skim my cheek. *"And the knife. You could've been killed or worse."*

I chuckle. "What's worse than death, Blood?"

"Not taking chances."

"I already took a chance, and it ended me here chained to a floor with a wound that more than likely needs to be sewn up."

"It's closed," she replies, her index finger yanking softly down on my lower lip. *"Rohana felt guilty enough so she stitched it for you."*

I clasp her hand before it falls away to her side. "I'll have to thank her for that." Pressing a kiss to her palm, I feel a faint shutter leave her body. I continue up her wrist, using my tongue to lick a trail to her bare shoulder.

"You're beautiful but too dangerous, Blood. So if you don't want me, you better push me away because when I get going, I'm not going to stop."

Her hand comes up to my cheek and brushes away some of the strands of hair that stray onto my face.

"Do you understand what I'm saying?"

She nods.

"And what?"

"Don't be soft with me," she whispers.

"I don't fuck soft," I inform, releasing her face. "But I'll make sure you come at least twice this time."

"Then show me everything." Her voice is so soft and therapeutic that I don't give her another moment to think about it, clasping her lips between mine and savoring the fantasies that are now a reality.

The nights locked in this room where my mind could freely roam over her. How it'd feel to go balls deep and lose everything that has happened since I've been here.

It's almost too good to be true. That she's allowing me to do this, touch her, let her submit to being underneath me. Letting me fuck her out of my system so that I can feel somewhat myself and in control.

But it's not lost on me that we both need this. That we both need a release, though, I didn't think it'd be with me. And I sure as fuck didn't want it to be her. I didn't like the pull my body did when she was in the room. How fucked up it was that after killing some of my men and fucking one of them right in front of me that I'd still be so attracted to her.

It's the Siren thing.

It has to be.

There is no way in hell that without it I'd keep her alive. That I would've taken a knife for her and not regret doing so.

Except I thought Sirens sang their victims to comply to their will. And she hasn't done that—none of them have.

Davina's hands cup both sides of my face, deepening the kiss with her tongue, and an immediate growl escapes my lips. Keeping all my weight on my left arm, I let my right hand roam down the length of her body, passing her ribs and landing at her hip.

"Lay on your left side," she mutters.

"Not this time, I want you right where you are." Pulling down the bottom half of her garment to her upper thighs, my thumb brushes her clit, releasing a heavy breath from her.

Working her into a frenzy, I bite down on her bottom lip, letting my teeth graze her skin before releasing it. She captures my lips again, wrapping her arms around my neck to pull me closer.

Moving her legs around slowly, she tries to work her undergarment further down her legs. I clasp onto them, ripping it off and letting the fabric dig into her thigh to show her how my not fucking nicely needs to be taken seriously. How my dick is begging to be let out so it can sink into her wetness.

And that's what I do.

Keeping my knees on either side of her legs, I yank down on my slacks, letting my cock spring free.

"Open your legs for me, Blood," I demand. With some rearranging of our bodies, she does as I request. The moon has shifted its light in the room to illuminate off the floors next to us, casting a shadow to the left side of her face but lightening up the right.

"You're the most beautiful creature I have ever seen in my life," I proclaim. "But I'm not so stupid as to know what this is."

"Good," she sighs when my cocks spreads her opening. *"Because you'd be everyone's fool if you fell in love with me."*

I chuckle. "We're safe in saying that I won't." And with that, I plunge into her.

Her tightness, the way she squeezes me inside her, I can barely breathe. I can barely register anything else but this.

Dragging me back to her again, she kisses me softly and languishly. Almost begging me to fall into the depths of everything that is her.

Deadly and alluring, the perfect combination to make a powerful man give up everything, including his secrets, just to please her.

Except I can't.

My clan is at risk with such information. People could die with the power that resides in that cuff, and I can't trust Davina enough to not turn on me.

Just like I did with her.

"You feel like heaven," I mumble against her mouth. "And if the tables were turned, this would change everything."

"But you're in hell," she replies. *"Don't forget it."*

I answer her truth with another thrust, as I keep pounding all my frustration and anxiety about the future into the woman who holds my freedom.

She cared for me before, somewhat I would say. She wouldn't let me go free if she wasn't afraid for my safety. But if I could make her feel like that again, she might give me a second chance.

"Hell seems to be a lot more my speed," I allege, circling

her clit with my thumb again. "Sometimes I think I was born from it."

"Maybe that's why we feel this. Because men say we're the devil."

I kiss her lips again. "You may act like the devil, Blood, but you're a sweet girl who wanted to save a big bad Viking from dying. I think that's borderline saint right there. And whether you'd like to admit it or not, the only one here to protect me."

CHAPTER THIRTY
Davina

I t's hard to sound fierce when Dagen is working me into the break of insanity. His driving into me feels like nirvana—beautiful, endless, on a cloud just waiting for release. The weight of his body, the way he's wanting to pull my wits away, it's nearing impossible to hold on to.

He wants to own me.

I want his report on what the cuff holds for his clansmen.

Unless things change, we'll stay at a stalemate. His pride will stay intact with protecting his people, and my fury will end up torturing him to the point of oblivion.

Except, it's fading with each passing day, and I can't hold on to it much longer.

The respect I have for him, a human that wants to salvage his people but doesn't want to harm myself and my sisters, it's a hard feat to keep hating him.

Besides, all his men are dead from an illness we can't decipher.

"Hell or heaven," Dagen whispers against my cheek. "I'd go through it to be able to do this just one time. Did you sire me to you? Is this why I feel an indescribable haul?"

"No."

"Then what is this?"

I honestly don't know because I feel it too.

I've tried to destroy him and, in turn, free myself from

caring about him. But his eyes bore into me every time with a twinge of high regard, and I can't help but sink deeper.

"We're just two different creatures that are curious about each other," I deadpan.

His tongue laps against my neck, and I release a shuttered exhale. I've never felt this numb and alive at the same time.

"I'm more than curious about you, Davina."

I pull my head away from his to look into his eyes. *"You called me by my name."*

His lips inch closer. "That's your name, isn't it?"

Just the softness of it off his tongue sends me on a new high, one I've never experienced before with anyone.

"You've just never—" He thrusts deeper into me, taking my next words along with him.

"Never what?" There's a cockiness in his tone, which gets me to heave my back off the floor so he can take me deeper. "Fuck."

"Oh my—" His lips seize my next words, using his tongue to make me start to fall apart inch by delicious inch.

"I want you to be mine," he groans. "For just right now." I hear his words, but they don't fully register. I'm so much higher than them right now, drifting deeper into the abyss of the pleasure that he's giving me when he should be wanting to strangle me again.

"Blood," he urges. "Say you're fucking mine...please."

"I'm yours," I hiss through my pleasure. *"And I'm going to—"* I begin to writhe underneath him, rising as my orgasm hits me like a heavy wave, crashing into my body. His mouth takes mine over again, and he growls.

"I'm coming," he grunts, pumping into me faster. I clutch onto his biceps, letting him ride out his high until he collapses on the floor next to me. Our heavy breathing permeates through the air with thoughts of what I just did.

What I let him do.

I told him that I'd never let him own me, and even though it was only for a moment, I still feel vulnerable. Something that feels like a common occurrence with us. But what remains is the truth that I still don't know and the events that follow him.

I either kill him or set him free.

"You're something else," he mutters next to me, still on his back. "I don't think I'll experience anything like you ever again."

He won't, I'm sure of it. No other woman in this world has the weight of her family and kingdom at risk like I do.

Moving my hand to sit up, I feel the metal cuff to his chain hit one of my fingertips. *"Was it that good?"* I ask, giving him something to focus on.

"Not that I want to tell you this, but you were perfect."

Clink.

I clasp the metal cuff around his free wrist and hear the heavy sigh that breaks out from his lips.

"It was good while it lasted," he croons as I push myself to stand. His hand reaches out to clasp my wrist and pull me back toward him. "You're not leaving me until I get one last kiss, Blood."

The muscles of my mouth quirk on their own as I comply with his request, pressing a chaste kiss to his lips. Coaxing mine wider, he slips his tongue in once, my body humming to the feel of him again.

"Good night," he utters against my lips.

Zeus, this man.

I want to take him to bed with me and let him sleep on something more comfortable than the floor.

Getting to my feet, I grab my discarded pillow and slide it under his head.

I should just put him out of his misery because if he

doesn't speak the knowledge I need, he's going to pay with more than what he bargained for.

Straightening my spine again, I'm gripped on to yet again by the Viking who doesn't know when he's pushing it.

"Let me know when you're ready for me again," he muses then allows me to rip my arm from his hold.

Conceited man.

—

I hear my sister's hollering through my bedroom door that Tobias is here, and I can't hide my excitement. Throwing my door open, I rush down the hallway and look through the open pillars at his small boat that he leaves docked on the beach.

Down a small set of stairs and another hallway, I'm outside the castle, my bare feet sinking into the hot sand until I see *them.*

As in Tobias is not alone.

Dark hair sways in the ocean breeze as Tobias breaks from his *guest,* striding in my direction with a giant smile plastered to his face.

I try to smile back, I do, but I know it's fake and is coming off as a scowl.

"Princess," he greets, extending his arms for me to jump into. I would, if *she* wasn't here. And it's puzzling because he's never brought someone along with him before, and why he has now, already has my defenses up.

"What's wrong?" he asks me. "You didn't miss me?" I take the three strides to get to him and wrap my arms around his torso, receiving a small squeeze in response and a kiss to my forehead.

"Who's she?" I gripe. Tobias doesn't let me go, breathing in my hair and laying another kiss to the top of my head.

"Don't get mad at me, she's injured."

"From what?"

"I saved her from Hunters," he tells me, releasing his hold on me. "She's been through a lot."

"Haven't we all," I object, letting my gaze fall back onto the woman who I'm going to let my sisters play with if Tobias doesn't give me a good answer. *"What am I supposed to do?"*

"I was on my way to see you and was attacked. I found her on the other ship, was hoping she could stay here for a few days to heal up. Her ribs are busted up, and we've been hitting storm after storm. Some land might do her good."

"I don't have time to babysit her, Tobias. I have my hands full already."

His brows snap together. "The Viking is still here?"

"Yes."

"But—"

"You're watching the lass," I retort. *"She's your responsibility. Let me meet her."*

Before I kill her myself and save both of us the trouble of tending to a stranger.

Tobias motions for her to come closer with his hand, and hesitantly, she does—she should.

She's beautiful and lovely, something that promises to be more of a pain than anything in my eyes.

"Davina, this is Vlatka. Vlatka, this is Davina, Princess of Lacuna."

She curtsies, but her eyes stay plastered on the scales forming on my shoulders from lack of water. "It's very nice to meet you. Thank you for letting me—"

"I'm not letting you," I snap. *"You're not allowed to roam the halls only to stay in your room. Your welcome is limited."*

She glances up at Tobias, curious I'm sure as to why she heard me only in her head, and I want to snap her neck. "Of course, regardless, I appreciate it."

I summon one of my men in my head for them to take this little wench to a vacant room. *"Don't make me regret this."*

"I promise—" She extends both of her hands in front of her, green eyes gleaming with innocence. "I'll stay where I'm told."

"Davina is just tired," Tobias offers for me. "She's had a lot going on." I shoot him a glare, but Vlatka nods her head.

"Of course, I can only imagine."

My jaw locks in place as she bats her long eyelashes at Tobias. Before I can compel another snarky comment, Sullivan arrives at my side.

"I want a man at her door at all times." I instruct for only him to hear as the woman gapes at Sullivan's frame.

He nods then clasps her forearm to guide her away to the castle, and no sooner is she out of ear shot, Tobias rounds on me.

"What was that?"

I perk a brow. *"What was what? You bringing someone here when you know that no outsiders are allowed except you."*

"I didn't bring her here purposely," he counters. "She's hurt."

"That's not a problem for either of us. And still you put my sisters and I at risk."

"I'd never let anything hurt you. You know that."

"Do I?" I turn on my heel, letting my question hit him as hard as it's hitting me that he has a woman in my midst, my home, and now another problem I have to deal with.

CHAPTER THIRTY ONE

Tobias

Something happened when I wasn't here, and I had a gut feeling it would when I left her alone with the Viking. As much as Davina doesn't like to think it, she's naive, knows nothing outside the water and this island. Vikings are the core of brutality. He will hurt her, that much I know, just to gain his freedom.

And I'll have to pick up the pieces.

I don't mind having to do so, but if I can stop it, I'm going to. Whether she gets pissed at me or not.

Snatching her upper arm, I turn her around to face me. "You're not allowed to leave upset, remember?"

Her green eyes burrow into my browns and remain there. *"But I am upset. You just put us at more of a risk."*

"I'll keep an eye on her," I retort. "And I *will* be keeping my eyes on the Viking while I'm here too."

"That's under control."

"How?"

"Seven sirens versus one Viking, who do you think is going to win?"

"But who is going to protect your heart, Princess?" She blinks, didn't expect me to call out what I think is already happening, which she just confirmed. "Something happened, I know it did. I should've never left you."

"You have to find Lorne." Slowly, she pulls herself out of my grasp. *"That's important."*

"I don't think I'll ever find him," I allude with a shake of my head. "He's starting to fade from my memory. Every year that passes makes it more blurry. I think I should just let him go."

Her brows furrow. *"You can't. He's out there, I can feel it."*

"Can you?" I try to smile but fall short with a quirk of my lips. "I don't know, Princess. He escapes me every time. Maybe he doesn't want to be found."

"Maybe he's scared."

I shrug. "Don't know."

"Tobias—" Her palm comes up to my chest. *"Don't lose hope."*

"It's gone, slipping further away each day he still remains missing." I place my hand over hers. "I'll be okay."

"So you've decided to pick up damsels in distress instead? You can't give up on Lorne."

"I already told you," I seethe. "She was hurt."

"Then take her to the next port."

"I was already halfway here."

"She needs to go."

"Davina," I warn. "I promise you that—"

"I don't want your promises." Her brows furrow in frustration. *"I want you to keep this island safe. Now she'll know about us and speak about how there are Sirens here that can walk and talk to her."*

"She won't know you're—"

"That's if we can keep her locked up in a room." She looks over to her left. *"Which I should go do right now."*

"Davina, I'll—"

"You have to choose," she snaps. *"Me or her."*

"What?"

"Me or her. She has to go."

"So you don't trust me anymore? What happened when I was gone?"

She pulls her hand from mine. *"You have until tomorrow."* She begins to stomp away, but I grab her again.

"What's wrong? Tell me. You used to tell me everything."

"It's best you don't know a thing, Tobias. I've been trying to tell you that for years. The more you know, the more of a liability you'll be. The more I can't protect you. It'd kill me to see you die over something you shouldn't know."

"Your sisters should know me by now," I defend. "You've always been someone I'd protect."

"But you just betrayed it. You brought some pretty raven-haired woman here and—"

"Is that what this is about? Another woman?"

"No," she retorts quickly. *"It's about protecting my family."*

I brush back a piece of her hair with my index finger. "You are my family. You're everything to me." I cup her cheek. "Everything."

"I think you should leave," she mutters, tucking her chin into her chest. *"It's not a safe time for you to be here."*

"Davina—" I tuck my hand under her jaw and lift it to meet my face. "—I'd never leave you when your world is crumbling."

Quickly, she wraps her arms around my body in a hug, squeezing me for dear life, admitting my fears that there is so much more to the story than what she wants to tell me.

"You will fall victim to this if you don't leave me," she utters into my chest. *"And the only way I can preserve you is if you never come back."*

My next intake of air seizes in my lungs.

Just the thought of never seeing Davina again stabs at my chest. It sends me into a state of anxiety and heartbreak because I'd die for this woman in a heartbeat with no questions asked.

"How can I leave you when I love you?" I assert in a low

whisper. "It's like taking my next breath and never giving it back."

"It's because I'll watch you take that last breath and I'd die right along with you." She peers up at me. *"Please don't put me through that."*

I lower my head. Shit, I've been doing it for years with coming here and the possibility of running into her father, who would smite me down as quickly as I blinked.

My lips gingerly brush against hers, and fuck it, I want more.

More of what she can't give me.

More of what I can't have.

And knowing it makes everything about this so much worse than it should be.

CHAPTER THIRTY TWO

Davina

W hile my world has been flipped upside down the moment Dagen stepped foot onto this island, it just proved to get worse. Not only do I have a dark-haired woman who calls herself Vlatka locked in a room in my home but another woman has dared stepped foot on my sandy beaches with a burly group of men that look just like Dagen.

All equipped with swords, axes, and brows descended in anger.

Standing in the middle of my six sisters, we watch them come off the small dingy and disregard it quickly. The pack of men is led by a tall woman dressed in fur and leather, a long sword in her hand as I keep my eyes solely locked on her.

"Edda," Isolde voices to us. "That's the woman I saw in Dagen's head."

My blood begins to boil at her name. She looks fierce, beautiful even, with her blonde hair braided at the scalp and down to her shoulders. Appearing to have cut down a few people in her day with the scowl that hits each and every single one of my sisters and I.

"Dagen the Blood Axe," she bellows, her eyes narrowing. "Where is he?"

"I'm going to kill this wench," Atarah seethes to my left.

"Right now."

"Not yet," I assert. *"We might be able to torture this one for information. But you're more than welcome to the ships."*

There are two of them within an easy eye's distance away. Which means they are through the veil, the one that Taysa confirmed is cracked, putting us in more danger.

The woman points her sword at one of my sisters to the right of me. *"You. Where is Dagen?"*

I take a step forward, breaking from the united front with my sisters because I'm seconds away from snapping this maiden's neck.

Clenching my fury into my hands at my sides, I meet her scowl with one of my own.

"You'll speak with respect," I fume, *"when you speak to us."* Her eyes widen a tad when my lips don't move but she can hear my words.

Looking over her shoulders at her men, who stand stoically behind her, she finds some sort of confidence again because her gaze falls back upon me.

"I don't serve you," she rebukes with a rise of her chin. "I'm here for my leader."

"The Viking that stepped foot on my land, you mean?" She bristles like it means nothing to her. That only her people are allowed to trespass on land and no one else. Arrogance does run deep in that bloodline.

"Is he alive?" she asks.

I nod. *"He is."*

"I need to see him."

"You will see him when I see fit, and you will state your name to me."

"I am Edda, his woman." I didn't realize I was marching in her direction until a soft hand lands on my upper arm to halt me in place.

"Remember," Nesrine says next to me. "Information. She may hold it."

"Destroy the ships," I order. *"We'll show her how much power she really welds around here."*

My sisters speak amongst themselves within our heads so the intruders can't hear while the wind starts to pick up around us, moving the waves of the sea to crash more loudly on the beach. The sun's rays are blockaded by dark clouds, as rain starts to pour down on the ships but the island stays dry.

Each pair of their eyes look over to their comrades on the ship, the ones who are about to drown within my realm of power—the sea. Ironically, the one I can't touch.

A small whirlpool starts to form in between the two docked vessels, as well as more pounding rain against their decks.

"What are you doing?" Edda rants over the noise of the waves.

None of us answer her, she's about to visually see what's going to happen when she so graciously decided to look for her *man* and leader.

I watch the sea start to move the ships along in a circular motion around the edge of the growing vortex of water, the faint yells of men crying out in alarm. A giant crest of a wave slams into one of them, sending it tipping to its side but not enough to plummet into the undertow of the whirlpool.

"Stop," Edda bellows, her eyes burrowing into me. I don't acknowledge her, letting my sisters do what they've wanted to do since the moment they saw the evasive vessels come through our veil.

Another gush of wind hits the second ship, making it pivot from side to side. A loud snapping of wood permeates the air while another influx of water sends it crashing to its side, overcoming the whole vessel, and when it calms and blends back into the sea, both barges are gone, leaving scapes of boards and debris floating on the surface.

A sharp scream hits my eardrums, and my head follows the intrusion to see Kali on her knees with a long spear sticking from her shoulder.

It's all I need to see.

My insides feel like an inferno while my full attention stays locked on the woman who just gave an order to have my sister attacked. Hand on her neck, the scent of burning flesh fills my nostrils. I hear a muffled shriek of pain as I tighten my hold.

She is going to die by my hands.

Not only are my feelings about Tobias staying on the island this morning brewed and littered with relief and frustration that he didn't listen, but now I have to deal with the aftermath of Dagen and his people trying to save him. Not only those things but also the veil that is now more damaged and fleeting of safety for my sisters and I.

Our whole kingdom.

Movement in my peripheral gets me to focus on my surroundings, but it's a surge of water that becomes a wall between myself and the goon of men behind her. Another ear-piercing scream bellows from the air as Edda's men cover their ears to Kali's wail of pain.

"You just sealed your fate to something more awful," I snarl into her face, yanking one of her hands away from her head. *"And you just killed all your men too. Congratulations, Edda. You're all dead."*

CHAPTER THIRTY THREE
DΛGEN

A nother squeeze to the man's neck I'm fastened onto and he falls to a lump at my feet. Moving quickly, as to not alert anyone else that I'm missing, I creep up the short stack steps to Davina's room.

It's a risk, that I'm damn sure of. But I can't resist the urge to see her. To smell the sea salt off her skin and brush my fingers through her long tresses.

Last night was unbelievable, and I'm addicted to this woman. If I'm here, against my will, I'm going to enjoy every moment I can with this Siren who captivates and starves me for more.

Reaching her door, I'm certain to get attacked the moment I step foot into her bedchamber. Ready for her to throw me against the door and question why the fuck I'm here. But the eeriness of the silence infuses the air to an almost deafening sound.

I eye her bed, seeing a small frame lying underneath the white sheet that is highlighted by the moon.

Taking a step toward her, I'm careful not to alarm or scare her, which I will because, fuck, I'm creeping into her room in the middle of the night.

"Take another step, Viking, and I'll put you through the wall."

My lips twist into a smile. "That'd be different." She stays in bed, not moving, but I can tell her back is to me.

"Would it be? Was that something you did with Edda?" The

mention of her name makes me jolt back a little. A sudden rush of memories of home and the comfort of being there surge through me like a bolt of lightning.

"Why would you mention something like that?" I censure through descended brows.

Davina turns herself to face me on her side and, fuck, I wish I could see her face that is now casted with shadows.

"Because she's here," she mutters. *"Badly injured, by the way."*

I'm two steps closer. "She's here?"

"Don't sound so excited," Davina snaps, sitting up on the edge of her bed. *"She threw a spear through my sister's shoulder."*

I'm suddenly on my knees in front of her. I know how much her sisters mean to her, and the evidence that I care more about Davina's well-being and state of mind than my own clansman and potential wife shows me that my loyalty is starting to veer off in a direction that screams traitor.

While my brain barks at me to stand up and demand to know what happened to Edda, my heart pleads to find out if *she's* okay.

"Who's hurt?" I ask. "I might be able to help."

"You helped enough," she sneers, averting her eyes from me. *"By you being detained here, it brought your people to my island to try and save you."*

"Which sister?" I repeat.

"Kali."

"Is she alright?"

"She'll survive." She pulls her eyes to me again. *"But your Edda won't."*

A sharp stabbing pain hits my gut. I should be more worried than I am even though I don't want her to die. I don't know how many men she has with her, how many ships. How many of my clansmen will fall victim to her small hands.

My father should've never made us come here. Over a

legend that he was fully convinced was real but I've always had my doubts about it. I've never seen a dragon nor has he, and the longer I am on this island the more I think all this talk of some magical cuff is just a myth.

"Blood," I say softly, pulling her calves closer to my body. "You need to rest." Abruptly, she stands, kneeing me in the chest and almost toppling me over.

"I need you out of my life," she fumes. *"You made everything worse. Everything was fine before you came here with your foolish mission."*

I rise to my feet, towering over her, and I can feel it. The anxiety and sadness controlling her body—my presence being the cause of that and how I wish I could take it away but I can't.

I don't want to be a faded memory because she'd never be that for me. She is a living and breathing light of freedom that I didn't know I needed. Being under my father for so long, I never fully considered myself a servant of the people.

Don't get me wrong, I don't mind it, it's just it was my father's rules, and that was that. I've gotten so used to following him that I never fully made important decisions of my own. Ones that could sway my life forever, and regard-less of the reason my father put me here, I'm glad that he did —and that scares me more than anything.

More than Davina.

More than wanting to succeed on my own.

Wanting more of the Siren in front of me who can't see past the reason I'm here and see me for who I am.

Wrapping one of my arms around her waist, I tug her toward me. "I didn't mean to become a problem, but I don't regret coming here."

She scoffs. *"You are a fool. You've endured enough, don't you think?"*

"I got to meet you, didn't I?"

"I killed your men," she counters, looking back up at me. *"I threw you across a room, clad you back in your chains, burned you, my sisters almost drowned you in the lagoon. I had your whole fleet burned to ashes."*

I let out a heavy sigh. "Yeah, there's all that."

My fellow clansmen just paid the price to save me, but I can't fully be surprised by her reaction. She's warned me, I would've done far worse and quicker than giving me time to admit the truth. They were collateral damage, and I'm holding the woman who ordered their deaths.

Who's more fucked up now?

I hear it ringing in my ears, that what I'm doing is beyond traitorous and insane. That I should continue my plot to get off Merindah and go back home. Killing the girls is impossible, I've already choked on my pride on that account. However, Davina is something that has fully captivated and snatched me from my old self.

"It was your people," she seethes with a weak shove. *"I killed your people."*

"I understand why you did it, and as fucked up as it is, I can't fully fault you for it." She tries to take a step away from me, but I hold her against my chest.

"I think you've gone mad."

A mirthless chuckle escapes me. "May have." My fingers brush up her back. "But I can say you've been an adventure."

"I will kill her." Her eyes turn a darker shade of green, filled with promise and warning.

"You don't have to." That earns a hard jerk out of my grasp.

"She called herself your woman."

"I'm sure she did."

"And you—you laid with me last night."

"I did, and I'd do it again." A hard slap comes across my face followed by a sting on my cheek.

"I'm not a whore you can lay with while saying that you are engaged to another," Davina snarls. I reach up to cup her face again, but she smacks my hand away.

"I'm not *engaged* to Edda, Blood. It's something my father has been persistent on."

"And?"

I shrug. "And it's not something that I want."

"Did you tell her that?"

"I've been a little busy being held captive," I state. "And it wasn't a conversation I was in the mindset of having before I left either. Figured when I got back, if it came up, I'd make my intentions known."

"Which are?"

"Now you with the questions."

"Answer me, Viking."

I can't help the smirk that plays off my face. "You're so stunning when you're mad."

She tilts her head. *"Would you like to go back to being chained up because I can make that happen right now."*

Erasing the space she put between us, I brush a few pieces of her hair back and tuck them behind her ear. "How would I ever be able to go back when I've had the honor of knowing what it feels like to experience Davina, known as Blood to me, but the Princess of Lacuna to most? I think I'm one in a million that has gotten to be this close to you."

"Not the only one."

"Ah, yes," I quip as I cross my arms. "The pirate. Where is the Prince of the Black Sea these days?"

Davina straightens her spine. *"Here."*

"And?"

"And how did you get out of your chains?"

"Your bobby pin."

She rubs her temple. *"I forgot about snatching that back. "*

"I hope you didn't forget anything else," I counter, taking

a step toward her so that the back of her knees are against her bed.

"No," she deadpans.

I lean toward her. "I want to do it again." I kiss her temple. "And again." Another press of my lips to her forehead. "Until you can't think about anything else."

"I can't think of anything else but your whore stomping onto my—" I kiss her nose.

"She's not my whore, I've never slept with her."

"Then why did she—" I lift her into my arms, her legs automatically wrap around my waist.

"How about we speak about you kissing me and what comes after that," I chime in, turning us around so that I can sit on the edge of her bed. Her knees hit the mattress, trapping me with her body—a place I never want to leave.

"I don't want you to get used to this," she mutters.

I stretch myself closer, hovering my mouth over hers. "I'm already used to this, and I'm enraptured by it." My hands grab her ass, letting her thigh feel my already growing cock.

"You don't know what you're saying."

"I definitely know what I'm saying. Question is, do you?"

"You want to..." She lets her next words trail off into the distance.

"Fuck you," I finish for her. "That's exactly what I want to do." I flip her body to my left and lay her on the side. "But first, I want to taste you."

"Wha—" I spread her legs, thanking Zeus that she's naked underneath the mesh material of fabric that she's wearing when my hand roams to the spot I want to discover the most.

"Already wet for me, Blood," I note, positioning myself between her slim limbs. "You don't know what that does to me."

"What does it do?"

"It makes my cock beg to be inside you." I don't let her

respond, not even the opportunity to think of a comeback, because my tongue is already lapsing her clit and, fuck me, she tastes like conjury and heaven all tied into one.

If I had to give up my life after this I'd die a man satisfied. A man who was able to experience a woman like Blood. There wouldn't be anything else in this world that could fascinate me as she does now.

I knew I was drowning in a black hole with her, that coming up from it would be nearly impossible, but my body and half of my head, the lower half, wants to keep coming back for more for as many times as she'll let me.

A soft gasp leaves her lips as my mouth clasps her sex, arching her back so that she can be closer to me. So that she can take more of what I give her.

It only summons more urgency within me to make her come apart in my control and discover what her release tastes like against my tongue.

"Dagen," she mutters off a broken breath. *"Oh my..."*

"Do you want more?" I tease. "Because I could finish just like this, with your delicate moans of pleasure and the way your breathing is hitching from the buildup. I could die right now knowing that I had one moment to worship you. Where you were completely and utterly under my authority for just a few moments."

Her hands clutch the bedsheets at her sides, crippled sighs and exhales of air filling the space between us. Distance that won't be between us for long.

A faint tug at my hair causes me to peer up at her. Davina looks down at me with pure lust and hunger in her eyes that it breaks the rhythm of my breathing.

"I want us to do it together."

"Together," I repeat. "What do you want from me, Blood?"

"I want us to feel the crashing of euphoria together...like the last time." She didn't have to ask me a second time, I'm already

working the button of my pants as she wraps her legs around my hips.

Leaning up on her elbows, she kisses me, her tongue following right after. I'm already drunk off her, but the insistence of her wanting me the same way I want her makes me disarm all of my defenses against her.

Nothing around us matters.

No one here makes me give a damn.

Everything else is a blur and a faded mist of what she is to me right now.

With my cock finally free, I position myself to her entrance, slowly sliding into her depths. Her mouth opens but no words come out, nothing but the feel of us joined together.

"You are remarkable," I recite. "Nothing has ever felt like you."

"You're torturing me," she gripes as I make my way in deeper, harboring onto my biceps.

Bending closer to her, my mouth sweeps hers. "I told you I would."

"I didn't know it'd be like this."

A soft chuckle leaves my chest. "I've considered it." I plant another peck to her lips. "But I didn't know I'd be in excruciating agony myself."

Davina licks my lips as I lazily start to pump inside her. *"Is it that bad?"*

"More than you know."

"The end result is so much sweeter though," she teases.

I fill her to the hilt and release a satisfying groan. "But then it's torture because I want you again."

"I want you too," she replies.

I freeze, mid draw from her pussy as her words spill over me again. "What did you say?"

Davina covers her mouth at the same realization.

Plucking her hand away, I bend in closer.

"Say it again." She shakes her head, a soft whimper slips from her body.

"Blood," I coo softly. "One more time. You can do it —for me."

"I want you too," she repeats, and my heart cuts short on its next beat.

It's her voice, loud and clear. Smooth and sweet, and not a dream.

I just heard her speak.

My hands clasp both sides of her head to keep her linked to me through our eyes. "You spoke." She nods as I see a glistening tear fall down her cheek onto the bed. "Why are you crying?"

"I haven't spoken in so long," she whimpers, her hand trailing up to her throat. "It hurts."

"Because you're using muscles that you haven't used in a long time."

"I can't—"

"Shhh," I console. "Let me pay homage to your body." I sink into her deeper. "You don't have to say anything, sweetheart."

Slowly, I fill her again, praising her body with my cock and lips as I fall deeper into the abyss of her. If it wasn't enough to be in the same room alone with her, it was her words that quickly became my undoing shortly after.

"Come with me, Dagen—my Viking."

The moment Davina releases my name from her lips for the first time right to my ears, I come undone with her.

Chest to chest, breaths mingled into one, Davina kisses my lips and tells me to stay with her.

Thing is, I think I want to forever.

CHAPTER THIRTY FOUR

Davina

I'm welcomed by the calming breeze of the ocean. A serene feeling to the scene that is going to play out before me today. Like animals, I kept the Vikings outside, surrounded by my men and tied up because I didn't want them any closer to my sisters. Nor did I want their ambiance within my home. It was bad enough they were on my island but to have them inside felt worse.

Sullivan meets me a few feet away, impassive and stoic as he speaks. "They are ill, Your Majesty. They have been sweating and coughing all night, we stayed a safe distance away but one man did run into the ocean. He was...disposed of by sharks."

I nod. *"Thank you, Sullivan. Send my well wishes to your wife."*

"Thank you, Your Majesty."

Striding toward my prisoners, I feel my sisters come down the beach. My voice still feels strained by speaking last night, and the reality of it has yet to sink in. If I'm speaking, it means the desired spell is fading quicker than we thought it was and someone being here is making it weaker.

"Davina," I hear Atarah call for me. Patiently, I wait, eyeing Edda who is already staring at me with hatred in her eyes.

Within a few seconds, I feel the slue of my sisters near me.

"We're bringing out the Viking," she alludes quietly. "Maybe it'll release some information to use from either side."

"He wasn't in his room when we found him," Nesrine chats on my other side. "How is the plan moving along?"

"*Fine*," I seethe even though it doesn't feel like one anymore.

I enjoy Dagen near me, I love how he speaks to me in that deep tone that weakens my bones. I believe he's breaking me down as much as I am him, and that's a dangerous thing to do.

"Which one of you would like to speak first?" Atarah asks as the band of them stand in defiance.

"Untie us and we'll speak," Edda orders.

"Not happening."

Edda looks back and forth to her comrades and shakes her head. "We have nothing to say but what we've already told you."

"Maybe torturing your leader will make some words come fleeting to your mind," Atarah retorts.

My body remains calm, but my mind is racing at the thought. I don't want him to be harmed any more than he has.

Nor do I think I can stay idle and let my sisters do Zeus knows what to him just to extract the things we need to know.

Edda smirks. "Good luck with that." Her eyes fleet away from us and widen, the first indication that Dagen isn't far behind.

The way she looks at him, with admiration and relief, makes me want to drive her head into the sea and not let her come up until she's no longer breathing.

Maybe I'll get that opportunity.

"I came for support," Tobias asserts suddenly at my side. A small jump from my body and I'm peering up at him giving me a weak grin.

"You should be babysitting," I assert, glancing back to my prisoners.

"I have that one big guard watching her door. Arwa —Arowan—"

"Arwran," I snort. *"You only see him every time you're here and butcher it while I correct you over a dozen times."*

"Just wanted to see if you remembered is all," he chuckles lightly. I bump into his arm gently as Edda's eyes go to her right.

"Dagen," she mutters loud enough for us to hear. "Are you hurt?"

Slowly, I bring my gaze to him, standing strong and tall, hands tied behind his back with seaweed.

"I'm fine," he deadpans, stealing a look in my direction before landing back to his fellow clansmen.

Brylee steps ahead, her blue hair pulled back to illuminate the perfect bone structure of her face. "Should we start with the lot of you or your leader?"

Silence fills the air, except for the crashing of the waves on the beach. I'm on edge because Dagen's life hangs in the balance, and my sisters and I hadn't fully discussed our hard limits.

"The leader it is," Brylee states, already striding in his direction.

"Watch yourself," I warn her so that only she can hear me. *"No slicing just yet. The woman will speak."*

"I have to at least jab him," she replies back into my head. *"To show them I'm serious."*

I fight the urge to roll my eyes and refrain from further

replying because she's right. A group full of Vikings isn't going to give up information that easily.

"The cuff you came for," Brylee announces to Dagen, who glances down at her. "What is it going to be used for?"

Nothing.

Brylee slams her fist into his torso, and he bows down in pain.

"The cuff," she seethes, yanking him up by his hair. "Why do you want it?"

Another swell of quiet and Brylee backhands him.

Taking a step back, she looks over at his friends. "Anyone else want to speak yet? My twin, Atarah, is a little more ruthless than I am."

"We don't spill our secrets," Edda berates.

"And what secrets would that be?" Nesrine inquires. "We were told your leader came here in search of farmland, but this is an island as you can see."

Edda looks over at Dagen for confirmation and straightens her spin. "That's right."

Atarah scoffs loudly. "Liar."

"Prove it," Edda snaps.

"We will." Atarah makes her way to Dagen, but I halt her with an extension of my arm.

"*Let me do it.*"

"Are you sure?" I don't acknowledge her but march to him, feeling all eyes on me.

His blues land on me, and he uncoils his body to stand, looking at me with softness and care.

Something I wish he didn't have for me right now.

"*You have to speak,*" I tell him only. "*Or they will kill you all.*"

"I know," he whispers.

"*So you'll die for them?*" I snap.

"What do I get if I say what you want to hear?"

My brows furrow. "*What?*"

"What do I get?" he repeats. "Do I get a piece of your heart? Your soul? Because just the memories won't be enough for me."

"*You're acting crazy again,*" I retort, turning away from him.

"Blood," he says sharply. "How far will you go to save my life?"

"*Not right now.*"

"Do not lay a hand on him," Edda barks. "He is Dagen the Blood Axe and you wouldn't dare do what you're thinking about doing if he wasn't tied."

A slow smile breaks my lips. "*I already have.*" My elbow lands in his gut, the escape of air leaving his mouth makes me cringe.

"Geezus fuck," he groans behind me. "I can't wait to fuck the shit out of you, Blood."

His promise warms my entire body, and so does the fact that his little wannabe wife is standing in front of me while he speaks filthy things to me.

"*Answer my question,*" I yell for everyone to hear then speak to him only. "*Tell me the truth and I'll give my entire self to you.*"

"You're serious?"

"*I swear it.*"

"You'll be mine?"

"*Let's see how much I like the answer and how much truth it holds.*"

"The cuff holds the key to—"

"Dagen!" Edda screeches. "Keep silent."

"You will all die if I don't tell them what they want," he counters. "I've already seen enough of my clansmen fall."

"They've beaten you down, haven't they?" she presses with slitted eyes in my direction. "She sirened you to her so that you'll do what she asks."

"I haven't been coaxed by anyone to do anything since

I've been here," Dagen retorts. "Or they'd already know everything."

"But you wouldn't do this," she scolds. "This isn't who you are. You're loyal and steadfast. You're a born leader who—"

"I know what I am," he growls. "And I know what I need to do."

Her face contorts in a look of disgust. "You'd be labeled a traitor."

"By saving my people, Edda?" he challenges. "I have a feeling that what we came for is a lie anyway."

"A lie? It was your own father who sent you here."

"And his own stupidity that may have cost his son his life."

"He would never," she claims. "You're his only son."

Dagen ignores her and positions his body in front of my sisters. "I'm ready to speak," he claims. "But I need the floor, apparently Edda developed a mouth on the voyage over here."

"You will ruin *everything*," she all but snarls. "Your fellow clansmen are more important than these clothless females who have satisfied—" She stops her next words, more than likely embarrassed to speak them.

"Speak," Atarah orders Dagen as she strides closer.

"My people started to believe again in a myth about a decade ago, I was a young lad when I first heard it. A powerful creature that would protect us from the Highlands as they kept attacking our smaller villages and killing everyone who resided in them. Women and children were slaughtered like cattle, and we weren't able to be everywhere at one time.

"My father grew extremely restless, I remember him pacing the floorboards in the middle of the night, trying to come up with a plan until one day he had it."

"Had it?" Atarah repeats.

"My father came home from a trip with it. Stating there was a way to keep us guarded and preserved."

"What kind of creature?" I ask.

He meets my eyes. "One that flies and breathes fire. A creature that could be faithful to us and—"

"Dagen," Edda warns, taking a step forward.

"Davina," Dagen stresses, snatching my attention from Edda. "The cuff was supposed to bring my people dragons."

"You *traitor*!" she screams, her voice penetrating the air around us.

"I was told it was stolen from us centuries ago," he continues. "I don't know how he knew where it would be or what we would have to do to summon this so-called power, but I didn't question. He's my father, and I'm allegiant to him, there was no need for me to doubt him."

My brows furrow. *"Dragons?"*

He nods. "I know, it was my first reaction too, but we're out of options. The battles are more bloody and brutal. Almost daily each party loses more men, and it's as though we're spawning more only to train them to fight at a young age and send them right off to the battlefield to possibly die. We don't want to do that anymore."

"Why would we believe you now?" Atarah challenges. "You've been here for weeks and not uttered a word about these living, fire-breathing things."

"I ignite fire," I tell her. *"It's not impossible. I've seen them in books."*

"But they don't *exist*," Atarah retorts.

"We're not supposed to exist," I carp back over my shoulder. Bringing my attention back to Dagen, I'm about to speak, but he beats me to it.

"I know I'm blocked from Kali's powers," he admits. "And Atarah and Brylee, I don't know why, but what I do know is that they can confirm it."

He nods at his men, who stand perplexed and nervous behind Edda.

"They won't spill a word," Edda counters as she raises her chin. "You are no longer—"

"Your animosity on the matter," Brylee interjects, "makes me believe him." It's then that Edda rushes her, slamming into Brylee and almost knocking her to the ground.

Atarah reaches them first, yanking her off her twin while I'm only inches away. Everything happens in slow motion, but it's my name that thuds in my skull over and over again.

It's Tobias.

He's never seen this side of me—the rage, passed the point of return where the target in my path doesn't have a prayer unless it possesses some sort of magic.

It'll disgust him, he'll never be able to look at me the same. Never understand the stress that has been prickling at my sanity for weeks. How I can speak out loud now and humans can come freely onto the island.

The veil isn't a cover of safety anymore. My sisters and I are wide open to every single enemy on this Earth, and Edda was no exception.

My palm encloses around her neck for the second and last time as I let go of every single ounce of stress, anger, and hopelessness.

Every burst of energy I release through me goes into her. Her screams and pleas at the top of her lungs ring in my ears as my whole body feels engulfed in flames.

With her hands tied behind her back, she can't push me off. She can't try to pry herself from my grasp, but she's trying to drop her weight so I release her.

The longer I hold on, the more I can feel the heat between the two of us. Flames reflect in my eyes as I watch the distortion of Edda's face in pain, the wails that she releases in my face are all muffled now.

My name is called out over and over to let go, but she touched two of my sisters. Called herself Dagen's woman when clearly she's not.

And she tried to save someone I wasn't ready to give up yet.

Edda's skin starts to peel off her face as my head starts to feel airy and cloudy. A sharp gasp hisses behind me as I think I felt someone try to touch me.

The once pretty girl who stood before me looks like a black and red mess. And the strength that boiled through me, fleets from my body.

Edda's body buckles under my fingertips, and I don't remember anything else except the blackness that surrounds me and another shrilling scream filling my ears.

CHAPTER THIRTY FIVE

Davina

My eyes flutter open to blurs of bodies in my range of view. A warmth of blankets over and around me, followed by the movement of a large hand on my lower back.

I blink a few times, letting my perception focus in to find all of my sisters lined up at the bottom of my bed staring at me with amusement, distaste, and irritation.

Shifting to sit up, my palm lands on a hard chest, and I glance to find Dagen sleeping next to me, his breathing calm and faint through the air.

"Good morning," Nesrine greets the moment my eyes fall back to them.

"How long have I been out?" I ask, rubbing my eyes then my forehead.

"Few hours," Brylee replies. I glance out the window to see the moon on full display, illuminating the sky over the trees.

My focus lands next on Kali, whose shoulder is bandaged in white cloth. *"How are you feeling?"*

"Better than the woman you burned alive," she snorts with a chuckle.

My eyes widen. I know I hurt her, but it really didn't register until now. I recall the flames, the smell of burning flesh, the screams—*multiple* screams.

"*I remember another voice,*" I convey. "*Another scream, but I don't think it was that Viking wench.*"

"Taysa," Rohana voices. "She was coming up from the ocean, it was her you heard."

"*Is she alright?*"

My sisters all look at each other for a moment until Atarah says, "She's fine. But there is a problem." I raise a brow for her to continue as she exhales. "The issue is why did she scream the moment you killed the Viking woman?"

"So I did some research," Isolde breaks in, opening a small book she's holding. "A witch can link herself to people."

"*Link herself to…*" I let my words trail off. "*That makes no sense. Why would she tie herself with a Viking? And for what?*"

"The veil is crumbling more and more," Isolde replies. "The men that came with Edda, they aren't as sick as the ones we brought back with Dagen. They are coughing, but they lasted overnight. The older men of Dagen's crew died within hours the last time."

The veil is failing because I have my voice back, though it's hard to use vocal cords that I haven't used in a long time.

"You're right," I allege. "Because I can speak freely again." My sisters gape at me, some covering their mouths while the others gasp and chuckle at the thing that was taken away from me for years.

"It's so beautiful," Rohana beams, eyes brimming with tears.

"And surprisingly still annoying," Atarah remarks on a broken chuckle as I roll my eyes.

"As much as we love to hear your voice again," Brylee states. "It just further proves our point. Taysa put the veil up, she screamed the moment Edda died, and there is still not a fix to it. She has a solution for everything, but the one thing that protects us is diminishing day by day. Hence why the Viking is here, how Tobias can come freely back and forth and neither one of them gets ill, that's another dilemma."

"You think she is linked to them?" I ask, feeling the friction in my throat from speaking out loud.

Isolde tucks her chin into her chest. "We don't know yet, but it's plausible." I shake my head, feeling Dagen suddenly stir next to me.

"Davina," Kali coos. "We have to think of all the possibilities. Every single one of them."

"But you'd say all of this in front of him?" I mutter, jerking my head to the man who's still holding me against his body.

"We're still not scared of the burly man," Nesrine quips. "Regardless, he's still exactly what he was before, *ours*."

"Where is Taysa now?" I ask.

Isolde adjusts her glasses. "Sleeping in her room."

"We'll discuss this more later," Atarah states. She clasps my foot and wiggles it around before Rohana rounds my side of the bed and gives me a hug.

"Welcome back, Sister," she whispers in my ear then kisses my temple.

Together they leave, softly closing the door behind them when a pair of hands wrap around my middle and pulls me back to lay next to him.

"Deep information," he grumbles through his sleep, his eyes still closed.

"You heard everything," I accuse.

"Most of it," he retorts.

"Then why did you pretend to still be asleep?"

He tugs my body closer to his. "I'd rather not deal with your older sisters." He cracks an eye open to look at me and smirks, closing it seconds later. "How are you feeling?"

"Confused."

"About?"

SIREN: A DARK RETELLING

"You."

"I'm not a witch, Blood," he counters. "If I was, I would've already used some powers to escape this island."

"But you didn't get the cuff back."

His blue eyes open and zero in on me. "I don't want the cuff." He reaches out and clasps his hand around my neck, pulling me closer to his face. "I want you though."

His lips are on mine the moment the words leave his mouth, slowly and memorizing. His tongue languidly enters my mouth, a soft groan mingling in between our breaths.

"You're going to be the death of me," he utters between kisses. "And I can't think of a better way to die."

"No one is dying," I breathe.

He breaks from me and throws his legs over the edge of the bed. "Speaking of dying, you need water."

"I don't need any—"

"Where can I get you some food?" he asks, going to a pitcher that sits on a small dresser against the wall. "You need to eat something."

"I'm not hungry," I reply, now sitting on the brink of my bed.

"Need to eat."

"Dagen," I counter as he walks toward me with a small glass of water. "I'm good." I take a sip of the warm liquid to appease him and hand it back.

He places the glass on my bedside table. "Does swimming in the lagoon help you regain your energy?"

"Sometimes."

"We should let you go back there and—"

"Drinking water helps, I'm good until the morning."

"But you need to get your strength back up."

"It's up," I deadpan.

"You might feel that way but—" I stand, shoving him back

a few steps to show him that I am perfectly able to still defend myself and get him to shut up.

For a moment.

Dagen chuckles and shrugs. "Point proven."

"I'm fine," I repeat as he snakes his arm around my waist to pull me closer.

"I hear you, Blood."

"I'm scared," I mutter, holding onto his forearms. "You might be a key to something so much bigger."

"I've met that Taysa woman," he tells me. "And she gave me this eerie sensation."

"You might be linked to her somehow."

"Never seen her before besides the other day."

"Are you sure?"

He lifts me, and my legs automatically wrap around his hips. "I won't let anything happen to you, Blood." His ocean blue eyes state that they won't, but it doesn't soothe the rumbling in my gut.

The warning that there is more to all of this than what we know. And my main fear is that it'll be too late by the time we do.

"Your distrust is written all over your face," Dagen states, staring up at me.

"It's not that I don't want to trust you," I allude softly. "It's the lack of answers that gives me pause."

Dagen's hands squeeze my ass. "I have one answer that I'd like to obtain from you."

"Which is?"

"You said you'd give your entire self to me if I told you about the cuff." He twirls us around and strides toward the door. "How good was my answer?"

I fight back my smirk. "Good enough."

"Good enough?" he repeats with raised brows. My back

hits the wood of my bedroom door, where he slides my body down his to land on my feet.

Spinning my body around, he presses my chest into the hard surface, my head tilted to the side to see him standing close behind me.

"Am I supposed to take that as consent to own you, Blood?" He brushes my long hair away from my neck and leans in to whisper in my ear. "Because normally Vikings don't ask."

I'm buzzing to the sound of his voice, the breath that tickles the sensitive part of my body. He doesn't stop assaulting my senses when his hand starts to pull the mesh bottom of my outfit to the side, exposing my upper thighs and ass to the cool night air.

"I keep to my word," I whisper.

His face nestles into the crook of my neck as he licks my skin and follows it with a kiss. "Forever?"

"Why would that matter, Viking?" I hear him work at his pants, making my legs clutch together in anticipation.

"Because I'm yours forever, Blood." I begin to turn on my heels, but his palm lands on my spine, his words playing off my soul.

I'm yours forever.

They are words I thought I'd never hear come from his lips.

Never did I think I'd want to bottle them up and keep them forever. But his sentiment and with his body so close to mine, I'm so ready to give myself up to a man who thrusted himself into my world without my permission and buried himself in it.

His cock grazes my ass cheeks as he says, "Spread your legs for me, beautiful."

I do what he asks, my fingers resting on the door. More than willing to submit to him and deplete my pride for another moment of bliss with him pounding all his frustration and lust into me.

Slowly, he glides into me, bending down to reach my height. Enclosing his arm around my middle again, he hoists me up, keeping my chest flat against the door.

"Bend your knees back and hook your ankles at my hips." His fingers graze down to my torso and brush my clit while I do what he orders. "Yes, Blood, just like that."

Sinking deeper into me, I let out a moan, palming the door to help keep myself up.

"I won't let you fall," he whispers. "Now tell me how much you're mine." Another thrust as my cheek presses into the wood.

"All yours," I chant.

"All mine." Another heave of his cock inside me, and my next exhale is propelled from my lungs. "Does that feel good?"

"Yes," I gush. "So good."

"You feel amazing against my cock," he groans, picking up his pace. "I love that I can hear your voice." I can hear him start to lose control. His fingertips digging into my skin, his breathing picking up in sporadic discharges of air.

I smile to myself, things that would be so normal for other people aren't so usual for us. How things have shifted from where I was sliding a blade against his face to see what kind of man laid under his flesh just for him to be plunging into me now against my bedroom door.

"Dagen," I whimper, knowing that the sound of his name out loud will help to his downfall. "Harder."

He kisses the back of my shoulder blade. "I don't want to hurt you."

"*Now.*" I cry. "Own me." He doesn't wait for anymore encouragement, picking up speed, our grunts and moans mixing together in the room, and I'm about there.

My lower stomach clenches, listening to him in pleasure as he continues to possess every inch of me.

Until there is a loud knock on the door.

"Davina!"

My eyes widen, my next intake of oxygen—it's gone.

"Fuck," Dagen curses, letting me down gently. He makes sure my skirt is covering my ass before he takes his hands off my waist, and pulls up his pants then lets me open the door.

Tobias stands on the other side with brows knitted together, his white shirt untied at the top to show off his tan chest when the door opens further, and my best friend's eyes fall on the Viking behind me.

"The fuck are you doing here?" he snaps. Out of the corner of my eye, I see Dagen rest his forearm off the door while stepping closer to me.

"Could ask you the same question," he deadpans.

"You belong in a cage," Tobias snarls. "Preying off the kindness of—"

"Tobias," I urge, my heart in my throat. "We can talk outside the room if you'd like."

His eyes broaden. "Did you just—your voice."

I give him a weak smile. "Just happened."

"But, how did—" I gently push him back so I can walk out of my bedroom, just to turn around and face Dagen with a raised brow.

"I'll be—um, back."

"You better," he replies then slowly closes the door. The moment it clicks, Tobias is on me. His body inches from mine, towering over me.

"What is he doing in your room?"

"Well, he was there to make sure—"

"Are you fucking him?" His use of words makes me outwardly flinch along with the harsh tone in his voice.

I can hear it all perfectly, every syllable and feeling that he's adverting—pain, hurt, embarrassment.

"Really?" I snap.

"How are you speaking right now?" he presses onward. "It's been years since I...I remember it like it was yesterday." My hand finds his arm, but he quickly withdraws it from me.

Swallowing my hesitation, I say, "The veil is disappearing and so is the spell."

"And you're—" He looks back at the now closed door. "You're with *him*."

"I'm not with anyone," I retort. "I mean, I don't—there hasn't been any talk about—"

"Did I not hear you groan 'own me'?" I can feel my whole face blanch. The numbness that takes over my entire body because it's not mine anymore.

I've changed over the course of weeks, and the old Davina, the sweet, naive one, she's gone.

Right along with the veil. And Tobias has always waited and served me with every action he's ever made.

"Tobias," I begin. "You know I love you. There isn't—"

"But you love him now," he cuts in. "Isn't that what I just heard?"

"I never said the word 'love'. You're making this—"

"Worse?" He shakes his head and gives out a disgusted scoff. "No, *you* did that."

CHAPTER THIRTY SIX
Tobias

I t's over, but it did begin—a long time ago when she was still a young girl who swam under the ocean and I was a young idiot that was smitten by her beauty.

Everything that is beautiful fades, I just didn't think it'd be because of a stranger who wanted to invade her land and steal something that meant the world to her—something that belonged to her mother. I never thought I'd see Davina get starry-eyed and foolish to the point where she'd put herself and her sisters at risk when I've spent years keeping Hunters off her trail.

It's pathetic really, how I thought things would change. How one day I thought she'd see me again and not past me. And within a span of ten seconds and the gravelly "own me" that slipped through the cracks of her bedroom door, my heart plummeted, hit rock bottom, and shattered into a million pieces.

"Psst." I glance up to the empty hallway to see one of the girl's men standing guard at Vlatka's door and her head peering around the door frame.

"What are you doing up?" I ask, shoving my hands into my pant's pockets.

I'm in need of a drink, my ship, and the open fucking sea to erase Davina out of my mind, almost forgetting about the stowaway I saved that now I needed to rid myself of.

"Couldn't sleep," she whispers loudly as I continue toward her room. "I'm taking it that you couldn't either?"

"Something like that." I stop along the guard's body and give him a curt nod. "I'll take responsibility for the guest."

"Her Majesties have stated I stay around her at all times," he deadpans.

I shrug. "Then follow me down the hall to my room I guess." Jerking my head for Vlatka to follow me, the padding of her feet rhythmically sound through the night air. The ocean's breeze sifts through the stone pillars, the wide-open spaces giving a perfect view of the shoreline below.

When we get to my bedroom, the guard does what he stated he was going to do and plants himself outside of it. Thankfully, I've left enough brandy in my room for special occasions, and this would be one of those I-want-to-burn-every-memory-of-this-place-within-my-head kind of moments.

"Do you want anything to drink?" I ask, making my way to the small hutch.

"Sure," she replies, stepping deeper into the room. It's padded in a deep red, the only room in the house without blues and teals decorating the walls and furniture. Davina had this room done specifically for me. Pine bed frame and chairs with cushions of red velvet. Deep dressers to hold all my clothes and a hutch to store my belongings. A perfect view of the back garden that also allowed a nice breeze to waft through my room.

I need to get out of here.

"Do you often walk around at night?" Vlatka inquires behind me.

"No."

"It must be your sea legs that make land uncomfortable," she continues.

I pour a generous amount of brandy into my chalice.

"Something like that." Finishing off my glass and then hers, I offer the drink to her before downing mine in one gulp.

"Is something wrong?" she asks with perfectly shaped brows that descend in worry.

"Nothing's wrong." I smack my lips together, letting the bitter taste hit my tongue and sink into my empty gut. "We'll be leaving here tomorrow."

She takes a small sip of her liquor, which immediately makes her face twist from the pungency of it. "Okay," she squeaks, then wipes her mouth with the back of her hand. "I haven't been feeling too well here. I think it's the air."

I snort. It's more than that. It's fucking magic that shouldn't be here.

Pouring myself another glass, I turn around to see Vlatka give the drink another try, but she purses her lips again.

I reach for her glass and gently pry it from her fingers. "You don't have to be polite. It's not for everyone."

"Thank you." She starts fidgeting with her fingers as I rid myself of her beverage.

"Are you uncomfortable? Would you like me to walk you back to your room?"

She shakes her head and tucks a piece of her dark hair behind her ear. "No, not at all."

"Then what is it?"

Her green eyes glance up at me from the floor, slamming into my chest because they are almost the exact shade of Davina's.

"I've been having difficult thoughts."

"Difficult thoughts?" I raise a brow, lifting my drink back up to my lips. "About what?"

"You." She bites down on her lower lip, and it's then that I notice how plush and pink they are. How her breast fit snugly in her mint green dress and the curves of her hips.

"Me?"

She nods. "I was wondering how it'd be if I—" She stops immediately, a faint blush creeping up her cheekbones.

I gesture with my brandy for her to continue. "Please, go on."

Taking a timid step toward me, she hauls her eyes back to meet mine—innocent, shy, and completely human.

Maybe that was the problem all along.

Building myself into a fantasy when I knew that they didn't exist in the real world. The island was my getaway to be free from the reality of not being able to find Lorne and how many times I've failed.

"I want you to kiss me," she blurts through my thoughts. I begin to choke on my drink, pounding my fist into my chest to relieve the shock of her words.

She rushes to me, hitting my back softly with her palm like it's going to do anything. My mind replays her declaration again in my head as I clear my throat, hastily downing the rest of my second shot of liquor.

"Are you okay?" she frets, still patting my shoulder.

"Yes," I croak, the moment the liquor hits my head. Turning on my heel, I begin to make my way back to the small hutch that holds all my alcohol, but Vlatka's hand comes up to brush my upper arm.

"I'm sorry," she claims, removing my glass from my hand. "That was inappropriate and—we can just talk. I just needed to get out of that room, I was going crazy."

I wave a dismissive hand in the air. "It's fine."

"How about we get you to bed and the guard can walk me back to—"

"We can just...talk," I offer. "Tell me more about your—"

"I don't want to talk about my husband or the fact that I ran away from home." She tosses my cup on my bed. "I want to talk about new adventures."

"Alright, what do you plan on doing after I drop you off at Port Royale?"

"I was thinking more of right now." She grazes a nimble hand over my chest. "I've never done anything like this before but...adventures, right?"

My cock agrees to it, strains against the button of my pants to lose myself in entirety to the beautiful woman in my room.

But all I can see is red.

Red hair and green eyes. Lush lips and years of memories linked to it.

My eyes flutter back the vision of her. The urgency in her tone within the throes of passion with *him*. I left her here while he worked his way into her bed, and there was no coming back from that. I don't even know if I'd be able to let it go, forgive her, for things to go back to being the—

Lips press into mine, slightly dry and hesitant. I haven't had a woman in so long. I never could get Davina out of my mind when I was off to sea to even delve into someone else.

But now, she picked the Viking over me, and I have to start removing my heart from her small hands.

Opening my lips wider, Vlatka follows my lead, letting me burrow my self-pity into someone else. Her arms wrap around my neck, begging me to keep going, all while I have a civil war within myself to stop and just let me drink myself into oblivion.

A faint moan escapes her lips, and I imagine it being *hers*. My fingertips clutch on to the woman in front of me, pulling her into my chest, like my mind has played a million times in my head.

"Take me to bed," Vlatka encourages. "Erase the bad memories with something worth holding on to."

Guiding her to it, I don't hedge over anything—I can't. I

keep pressing forward until her back hits the mattress and my body collides with hers.

We all experience heartache, pain, but mine started with a dream at sixteen years old when I saved a girl from death, and she just butchered my life into fragments of nothing.

—

Every morning here feels the same—a dream. The sun is always bright, the faint chirps of birds greet the early day, and it's promising. Regardless of the monotonous start, my mood is worse. I left Vlatka asleep in my bed, her legs tangled with mine, and the sentiment irritated me because she shouldn't be here within my sheets with me.

Letting my irritation simper throughout my body, I head to the dining room for any sight of food so that I can get my energy up and leave. I can't argue with Davina when she's set on something, it's like prying food away from a shark and telling them they can only eat plants while wishing them good luck.

She's set in her ways, pulling her stubborn tendencies out each and every time, but *this* time, I'm not settling while sitting back to watch it happen.

I stride into the large room, overlooking the long dining room table only for me to falter in my steps at a woman sitting at the far end of it. Kind eyes and cocoa brown hair with some gray and green streaks line her head, she keeps chewing her food as she stares at me.

The air feels tight and congested, clogging my lungs for my next breath as I study the odd features of her face.

From her nose up, her skin is a shade of green that

slightly sparkles with each movement of her jaw chewing her food. Her eyes are dark as they study me while I gape at her.

"You must be the pirate," she greets, picking up a silver knife and cutting into a stick of butter. "I've heard a lot about you."

"Yes," I manage to force out, but I stay planted close to the entrance of the room. The hairs on my arms stand on end, warning me to watch her and that something is off with her presence.

"You must be hungry—" She nods toward the various fruits and loaves of bread that lay on the table. "—help yourself."

"I just came here to grab and go," I reply. "I have to take off today."

She nods, patting her chin with a maroon napkin. "Of course. Davina said you don't stay for very long."

The mention of her name out loud by someone else hits my gut. I don't want to hear it nor do I want to even think about the shit I discovered yesterday.

"I'm Taysa," she offers.

"The sea witch."

She grimaces at the name but quickly recovers. "I'm called that, yes."

"I apologize. The girls speak highly of you." She smiles at that, looking down at her plate as though she's recalling memories that she's had of raising them.

"I consider them—" She looks up at me, and goosebumps shoot through my whole body. "—special."

Movement catches my peripheral, and I glance up to see the Viking standing in the door frame of the other entrance into the dining room. A sharp "shit" escaping his lips as he tries to quickly exit but stops when my eyes pin him with a glare.

"Ah, the Viking," Taysa beams, peering over her shoulder

to discover the third body in the room. "Take a seat, we have much to discuss."

"I'd rather not," he retorts, mirroring my displeasure of him in this room with a scowl.

"But you need to," Taysa counters. "Both of you."

We share our focus on her, but she ignores it, popping a berry into her mouth as she continues to enjoy her meal.

Dagen doesn't pry from his spot and neither do I, but I know we're both thinking the same thing besides strangling the fuck out of each other.

"Quickly, boys," Taysa urges with her hand. "It'll only take a moment."

Delaying for another minute, Dagen moves, rounding the table but stands a few feet away from me, waiting expectantly on her to speak so that he can flee the room where I'll follow right after him through another exit.

Peering up into my eyes, she glances at Dagen then back to me and smiles. "Tobias, congratulations, you found your brother."

My brows immediately snap together as I watch her chew another berry, casually and collected as though she just told me the sky is blue.

"What?" I snap.

She points an index finger at Dagen. "Your brother. Dagen, meet Gathan, your younger brother."

"He's *not* my brother."

"He is your brother," she defends. "And I would know because I'm the mother to the both of you."

"Are you out of your fucking mind?" Dagen thunders. "My mother is *dead*. I heard her screams."

"You *thought* you heard her screams," Taysa notes with her fork pointed in his direction. "It's amazing what magic can do to make the mind think one thing. Especially a small child's."

He violently shakes his head. "Bullshit. Both of my siblings were taken with her as well."

She nods at me. "That would be him."

"Then where is my sister, Kelaya?"

Taysa averts her gaze, lips pressed together into something I can't put my finger on. "She's dead."

Dagen takes a lofty step forward. "How?" His tone is venom, shaking the tension in the room to new heights while my mind is reeling at her revelation that the man standing beside me is my Lorne.

"She was, in fact, killed by the Highlands while I was trying to get Tobias and Kelaya out of the village."

A harsh silence fills the room, engulfing us together in some odd trance of truths, or lies, and I'm confused. I don't believe her words. Not when there isn't an ounce of authenticity in them.

Dagen the Blood Axe, he's *not* my brother. Mine is lost to the world, and I can't find him.

CHAPTER THIRTY SEVEN
DAGEN

The woman who made me squirm the last time we met was mad. The tall, lanky little shithead that stands next to me is not my brother.

He isn't Gathan.

Everything about him screams stranger. Besides the medium-brown hair and shitty looks we've been giving each other, we have nothing else in common.

I'd know if Gathan was alive, I would feel him. The first moment I laid eyes on the little fool next to me, it would've sent something coursing through my body. If he was my blood, I'd be fully aware that we were linked together—plain and simple. So this kook of a woman sitting in front of me is imagining shit and making up stories.

Except, to my utter frustration, she knows my sister's name.

"Kelaya was killed with my mother and brother. And his name was Gathan," I seize. "You could've gotten any of this information from—" I wave my hand in the air. "—whatever kind of magic you witches do."

She eyes me with exasperation. "Tobias *is* Gathan. I took him to his Uncle Declan, which—" She looks over at Tobias. "—isn't your uncle. Just some fool I paid to keep you safe until you were old enough to take care of yourself."

"What makes you think either of us is going to believe this tall tale," Tobias chides. "This is the dumbest shit I've heard in a minute." He looks over at me. "Beside the fact that a Viking got taken by a bunch of women."

I take a step in his direction. "Says the weak fuck who can't pull his head out of his ass when *clearly* she doesn't want you."

Tobias squares on me. "Yeah? Explain to me how I've been—"

"Besides both of your stubbornness that you get from your father," Taysa cuts in. "I'll explain everything that you need to know because both of your lives are going to change."

"Make it quick," Tobias carps. "I have a tide to catch."

Taysa chuckles and forks a piece of cheese. "You're not going to sail off today, Son."

He tenses. "*Don't* call me that."

"Both of you sit down or this will go a whole different way." Her dark eyes flicker with warning, and I've seen unimaginable things lately so this can play out in so many ways.

Tobias and I look at each other before he moves to pull a chair out. Following his lead, we're both seated in front of her—eager and anxious to hear this bullshit story that'll make no sense.

"You're both aware of this veil that the girls keep talking about, how no other creatures besides a Siren, and myself, can pass it. No one can *find* it. Except for the two of you."

"Davina showed me the island," Tobias voices. "Shit was no surprise or anything I randomly fell upon."

She extends her index finger at him. "But *I* allowed you to get past it. Coursing through your veins right now is my magic. Both of you *are* my sons, spawned from the same father who is Oryn the Great."

"This idiot is no Viking," I carp. "But nice try."

"You're not much of one either, apparently," he retorts

257

back. "Don't you people kill others with branches or anything you can get your hands on? You're failing pretty quickly on that feat."

Taysa's eyes turn into slits. "And you fight like brothers. I needed heirs to succeed me after I die as well as when I'm alive. I knew I should've had more daughters."

I place my palms on the table, about to stand. "Well, amazing story, thanks for that."

"I will summon you to that chair, Dagen—" She pops another piece of cheese into her mouth. "—if you try to move again."

"Then why separate us?" I challenge. "If he is my brother, why did you take him from the village? Makes no damn sense, isolate us just to allegedly make you stronger or whatever."

"Because I needed him to be something different. You're a Viking, Dagen, through and through. Your loyalty proceeds you, but I needed your brother to be something diverse." She looks at him. "The Prince of the Black Sea."

"And?" I press. "Who cares?"

She leans back in her chair. "Two sons who rule the land and the sea."

"It's just a name," Tobias voices. "Men gave it to me."

"Because you've earned their respect. How do you both think you were able to get past the veil? Dagen's men became ill and died on their own because no human is capable of setting foot here due to the spell I cast over the island. With my being able to stride through the veil, so is my bloodline— the both of you, my *sons*."

"So you wanted two sons, with names on land and sea, and so what?" I snap.

"You're familiar with the golden cuff you stole from Davina and her sisters. I sent you here to obtain it for me."

"I've never seen you a day in my life," I retort.

"You didn't need to," she conveys. "You do whatever your father tells you to do, and I told him to send you here. I knew the girls would keep you here while Tobias brought me the other cuff."

My head snaps to him as he says, "I don't have a magical cuff."

"Do you remember the day Davina's mother was killed?" He nods slowly. "You found something on the deck of your ship, randomly, more than likely thinking it was a piece of junk."

He shrugs, raking his hand through his hair. "I remember it, but I don't know where it is."

Taysa removes her hand that is underneath the table and displays a duplicate of the same cuff I stole from Davina's cove.

"This is one of Queen Kiherena's royal cuffs. It holds a quarter of the power of Lacuna. The other one is in Davina's hold. Brought together, they hold half the power of the sea—a goddess."

I glare at him. "How is it that you didn't know about this?"

"Did you just hear what she fucking said?" he seizes. "It randomly showed up on my ship. How the hell was I supposed to know what it was?"

I point at the both of them. "You two are in this together."

"Fuck you," Tobias sneers. "This is the first time I'm ever meeting her, but you said you have already. As well as you trespassing on this island without any—"

"*Enough*," Taysa bellows. "Another reason why I kept you apart. Brothers are either enemies or best friends. It would've been a pain for me to bring you two together if you weren't separated."

"Let me guess," I rebuff, pulling my attention away from

Tobias and directing it at her. "You want to become this goddess."

"You raised these girls," Tobias scolds. "You can't take their right. Besides, you're a witch, it wouldn't just be given to you."

"It *would* be given to me," she fumes, tapping the gold piece of jewelry on the table. "Whoever kills a goddess, *gains* their power. Except I can't have it in the sea, Triton would find it."

"*You* killed the queen?"

"And since I wasn't around to obtain the cuffs, it goes to the closest bloodline of mine." She locks eyes with Tobias. "Which would be you."

Abruptly, he stands, palms underneath the table as though to flip it, but he freezes. Jerking with his strength, the table remains still.

Taysa ignores his temper tantrum and gapes at me. "I told your father that if he sent you to retrieve the cuff and bring it back to me, I'd release the dragons."

"There were dragons?" I ask. "Those weren't just a myth?"

She shakes her head. "Not a myth, but I wasn't going to give them to your father. I was going to give them to you."

My brows deepen. "My father is the leader of—"

"Not anymore. He's an old fool, to say the least."

Now I want to flip this table over.

"Tobias, sit down," she orders. "There is more to this story."

"I think I've heard enough," he seethes.

"Sit down, you idiot, and focus," I berate.

He snaps his head toward me. "*Make* me." I'm about to stand on my feet, but Taysa slams a hand on the table, rattling everything on it.

"*Enough*. Sit down."

Tobias slowly does as she demands while keeping his jaw tightened.

All of this—it's too much. And we've both played pawns in this old bitch's game.

"What's next?" I hiss. "You want us to rule under you when you get these two cuffs together? Because good luck trying to get them from the girls."

The slow smirk that appears on her face is directly aimed at me, I already know what she's hinting at. I haven't paid my price yet for the other cuff. Tried but failed, was tortured and got to fuck the woman of my dreams, but it doesn't mean she's going to get me to do anything unless she threatens Davina.

Which she will.

Her face says it all.

"You'll get it for me," she announces.

"Not going to happen."

"For their safety, you *will*. If I don't receive the second cuff, I will send your clan and every Hunter in the sea for these girls until I have it. They'll think you are the one to blame, and you'll be dead within minutes."

"Still not going to happen."

"This is insane," Tobias roars. "You think you're just going to summon us all of a sudden to do shit for you? You're right, you should've had more daughters."

"I will kill Davina in front of the *both* of you unless I collect what I want. And it won't be a slow death, don't test me in my ability to torture someone."

"Sorry, old lady," I dismiss. "But seven against one, you didn't plan those odds out very well."

"That, and how would we know that you'll stay true to your word?" Tobias asserts. "You're betraying the girls you raised."

"A contract," she says softly. "You rule above the sea—"

She looks at me. "—and you'll rule the land. Beneath the sea is mine while you both rule under me."

Tobias scoffs. "You'll have to go through Triton first."

She waves a dismissive hand. "Let me worry about that. Together, we'll rule the world."

"I think the asshole next to me and I can agree that we're not following you anywhere," I reiterate.

Taysa lands an impassive look onto me. "I heard your cries at night, Son. You missed what was taken away from you but be careful who you trust. Your father knew I was alive, as well as your brother—still living and breathing while he let you believe otherwise. So when I tell you he's weak, he *is*. You've grown up into everything I could've hoped for. Winning over your clan will not be a problem, especially when the dragons are under your power and control. You'll save your people from the Highlanders and become a hero, a legend."

"I won't betray my father," I growl, clutching my hands together to keep from ripping her across the table.

"Even after what he's done to you?"

I shrug. "I don't believe you."

"Which part?"

"*All* of it."

Pressing her lips together, she bows her head. "Your upper left arm, there is a birthmark. It looks like a triangle with a straight line going through it. You were a stubborn child who loved leaving pinecones under the elders' beds and a little blonde girl kissed you at four and told you that she thought you would grow up to be a burly man with no skill as a fighter." She averts her gaze to Tobias. "At least she got the last part right."

I don't shake my head, but I want to.

Everything she says is true. That little girl is married now to one of the fiercest warriors in the clan.

"You, Tobias or Gathan—whatever you want to be called now—you followed Dagen around like a shadow. You broke your right wrist while jumping off a small cliff thinking that you could fly because your *brother* said that you could if you got enough height."

On cue, Tobias and I look at each other—we're brothers.

Both of us know it, those small details would only stem from a mother who knows and tended to us—who was *there*. My father couldn't and didn't give much information about the dragons to the elders because apparently there was more to the story.

He made a deal with a sea witch, and that would've never gone well with the clan. I knew my father was desperate for a solution but not to the point where he'd send me on a suicide mission with the possibility of never coming back.

"Dagen," Taysa digresses carefully. "To keep Davina and her sisters safe, you will obtain that second cuff for me. Betrayal can be looked at from so many different sorts of angles, but there is only one validity to it. Yours will be to save her after I kill her father for the whole sea and take what I've been working for, for over two decades. The cuff or the death of all seven."

CHAPTER THIRTY EIGHT
Tobias

The look on Davina's face is slowly splintering every fragment of my heart.

My body begs to pull her into a hug, but I refrain from touching her. From letting myself fall back into her because I can't for my own sake and because Dagen stands next to me, wearing a stoic expression on his face.

I've always had a soft spot for her. Always put her ahead of myself, and I want to keep doing it, no matter how many times the vital organ that keeps me alive breaks, but there has to be a point to where I stop throwing so much of my heart at her for my own sanity.

We've told her and her sisters everything Taysa told us, down to every last detail. Davina advised that the cuff was in a cave of some sorts, safely hidden, but it was still a dangerous place for it to be in. Especially since the sea witch still resided peacefully on Merindah and even telling the girls is a risk all on its own.

A chance that Dagen and I decided to take because they needed to be prepared rather than blindsided.

And he and I knew what had to be done.

We're linked to a witch that, with her power and spell-bound magic embedded into our bodies, we can't be here anymore. It's why I've always been able to walk freely through the island and come through the veil without a problem. It's also why the asshole next to me can continue to win Davina's heart, and there isn't shit that I can do about it.

Atarah, Kali, and Nesrine surround Davina as she stares at the floor in shock while the other girls are still inside the house, carefully standing watch to make sure Taysa doesn't snoop around keeping tabs on us or what we're doing.

Even though, with her powers, she may already know where we are. She could be listening right now for all I know.

"This can't be true," Davina sputters as Nesrine wraps a comforting arm around her shoulders. She's shaking, but she's trying to keep herself together. If I know the woman at all, it's that she doesn't like to break down in front of anyone. That she feels uncomfortable letting out her fears around anyone.

"It's true," Dagen retorts. "There is no other way, Blood, that me and the pirate are here without being harmed."

"That's why we couldn't read him," Atarah adds. "Why I always felt like there was a wall between him and I. Taysa blocked us from being able to see the true reason he came for the cuff before telling us." She shoots Dagen a scowl at the last bit, which does nothing to the Viking but make him stand his ground.

"We need another witch," Davina alludes. "Someone to break the link."

"We don't know another one," Kali whispers. "There aren't many around."

"The Norse witch," she quips then snaps her head up to Dagen and I. "We can find one."

I meet her green eyes filling with hope. "We don't have time, Princess." Her brows immediately descend, not liking my answer.

"We have to try," she retorts through furrowed brows.

"Why isn't anyone trying to figure out an answer?" She shrugs Nesrine's arm off her shoulders. "We need Isolde."

"She's in the library," Atarah mutters. "She's trying."

Davina's hands ball into fists. "What do we do with Taysa? She can't just roam free with the—she *killed* Mother." Her focus lands on the exit of the cave. "She needs to die."

"She's strong," Kali replies. "We have to plan this out."

"We slit her throat. *I'll* slit her throat."

Dagen chuckles while I roll my eyes. This woman, I swear to Zeus, is going to send us all to the deep end with the antics she comes up with.

"You just can't walk up to her and do that," Nesrine counters.

Davina glances over to her older sister. "*Watch* me."

"Let's be sensible—" Atarah places her hand on Davina's shoulder and gives her a little shake. "We *need* to make sure that our plan is solid. No mistakes, we can't afford it. Do you still have the cuff?"

Davina nods. "No one will find it."

"Good," I settle, breaking into their little argument. "Don't tell anyone where it is."

Davina's gaze falls back on me with a frown. We've been through a bunch of shit but nothing like this, and we've always had an answer.

It's just that I don't think we'll come up with something she'll like.

"Do you know of any magic that you have?" Nesrine asks both Dagen and I. "Anything you can do?"

"Nothing but being a warrior," Dagen answers. "I don't have anything out of the ordinary but keeping you girls at bay with your mind games. And even then, I don't know how I was able to do that. It's not something I can control."

"Same," I add. "Besides getting past the veil and Kali's

screams not affecting me that night when I saved Rohana and Davina, I don't have anything either."

"We'll take care of it," Atarah asserts, pulling Davina closer to her. "We just need you two to stay as far away as you can. Maybe sail away from the island together."

Dagen looks over at me. "Not a bad idea. Maybe it'll lessen her powers with us away from her."

"We can do that," I agree with a nod. "But we'll need a distraction, something to keep her busy while Dagen and I sneak back to my ship."

Kali motions at her bandaged shoulder. "I can tell her that I don't think my shoulder is healing properly. It'll only buy you a small amount of time though."

"We can sail out quickly," I vouch. "My men will be ready."

"Then it's settled for now," Atarah concurs. "Sail away as far as you can, and you can't come back until it's done." I nod, feeling Davina's regard back on me, begging me to look at her.

I can't.

I'm going to save her life for the last time.

CHAPTER THIRTY NINE
DAGEN

Doubt and unease fill my brain, hitting me over and over again, as Davina wraps her arm over my torso. She's been silent for a while, pondering over everything that happened tonight, surprisingly not arguing with the fact that Tobias and I are leaving in the morning.

I'm happy about that.

More than happy, I'm relieved that I don't have to fight with her about things that she already knows. That she's not naive enough to believe we can stay here.

A cold teardrop hits my skin, and I lean up, her head snuggled into the crook of my arm as she tightens her hold on me.

It breaks my soul to see her upset, that my strong little Siren has even a worry or concern about me. I can hold my own on a battlefield over men, but a sea witch, not something I think I can aid with.

Thing is, I don't want to leave her alone for her to fend for herself. I know that she has her sisters, but the concept of something happening to her has been twisting my gut since Atarah mentioned the idea of us heading out of here. I don't know how long we'll be gone. How far we'll have to travel to break some of Taysa's hold on us and, possibly, weaken her, but we have to try. There isn't anything else we can do.

"Blood," I mutter, brushing the top of her head with my fingers. "Look at me."

Weakly, she shakes her head, still burrowed into my side.

"I'm not going to get hurt."

"You don't know that," she murmurs. "She might know everything we're about to do."

I can't dispute her worries because I've thought the same thing. No one knows how powerful she is, what she's fully capable of, and the fact that she's still here sets me completely off ease.

"I'm worried about *you* getting hurt," I vow.

"I'm stronger than you."

I chuckle, letting my senses remember and feel how soft she is. How I'll miss this, her next to me, her sassy comments and the way my body reacts immediately to her closeness along with the sound of her voice filling my head with her words then finally being able to hear her out loud.

I've fallen too deep, never feeling this way about anyone before in my life. How I would burn the world down to keep her safe and sound on Merindah. But I'm metaphorically tied to not being able to do a thing at all except flee to protect her.

It's hard to swallow.

Difficult for me to accept and do, but I know we're limited with options, and it's all trial and error at this point.

"Will you miss me?" I ask.

"Absolutely not, Viking."

I smile. "Never thought I'd hear you lie, Blood."

"Never thought you'd leave," she counters.

Her words slam into my reality. It's as though I absorb them, and then they slay me all over again as the harsh authenticity of our situation is spoken about again.

"I don't want to," I utter. "I'd rather stay like this forever." Another exert of pressure along my ribs, her head burrowed into my chest, and I can't stand it anymore. "Blood."

She doesn't respond or move, remaining still and eerily

quiet. Pulling her over me, I lay her chest on top of mine so I can see her face.

Bloodshot eyes from crying, a stream of tears on both sides of her cheeks, and a soft sniffle peer back down at me.

"Don't remember me like this," she quakes. "Remember all the good things."

I wipe away a tear with the pad of my thumb. "Like the time you took my blade and ran it down the side of my face."

A broken chuckle emerges through her vocal cords, and she shakes her head. "Please, not that."

"It's the first moment I knew you were different. That you weren't like the others."

"Because I couldn't speak or go into the ocean, only difference."

A corner of my lips quirk. "Mhm, no, it was the defiance in your eyes."

"How about my interrogation skills?"

"You were horrible at it. You kept saving me from being tortured."

Her forehead creases. "You don't understand how ruthless my sisters can be."

"I got a taste," I allude, leaning up to get closer to her lips. "But it wasn't the kind I wanted at the time."

Pressing my lips to hers, she immediately opens her mouth to insert her tongue inside. I can feel the need in her kiss, the want of erasing the last couple of hours that decided we needed to separate from each other.

It wasn't going to be easy, fuck, it was going to be hard to be away from her. But I know without a doubt that I'll never forget a thing about her.

"I'll miss you too," she mutters along my lips. "So much."

"Be back before you know it." My hands roam down her back. "Just promise me you won't do anything stupid when you take the witch down."

"What classifies as that?" she jeers, peppering kisses on my right cheek.

My hands squeeze her ass while I thrust my hardening cock against her mound. "Dying, Blood. I'll need to fuck you immediately when I get back."

"Don't kill Tobias," she counters. "I *mean* it."

I let out a groan and look heavenward. "Do not mention *him* while we're together and my cock is begging to be inside you."

She pulls the mesh material covering her ass down her upper thighs. "Like this?"

A feral sound rumbles from my chest as I tug at the inconvenient cloth that's keeping me from doing just that.

"Yeah, like that," I state. "What are you going to do with it?"

She rakes some of her hair back with her fingers, still keeping her body weight on mine. "Pull your pants down and let's see."

I comply hurriedly with her request, letting my cock spring free and ready to let her take over. Like she has with my mind, my soul, and my—the realization hits me with such fervor that it has rendered me silent as it seeps into my entire body.

Is this what love feels like?

The panicked feeling of not knowing what's going to happen? The longing of wanting Davina at my side at all times? The torment of knowing that all of this might not work; our leaving, the fact that the girls could fail and be killed.

It sits uneasily on my chest, a twinge of anxiety trying to surface as I seek another way to keep her safe. I would do anything to make sure she lived through this. That when this was all said and done she will live another day and be the powerful, beautiful, and compassionate woman that she is.

I'm so deep within my thoughts that the moment Davina sits on my cock, a gruff exhale of air leaves my lips.

"Fuck," I groan as she rises up and sinks back down in languish movements. "You're going to kill me."

"Not my intention," she breathes, her palms landing on my chest. "I just want to get lost in you."

"I'm already there." I angle into her lips, searing this moment to memory. Praying to all the gods that we'll be able to come back here.

"Are you mine?" she respires, continuing her torture. The way her long hair cascades over her shoulders and the green eyes that swallow me whole, there's no doubt in my mind that I am.

"Completely and forever." She smiles at my submission, one I thought I'd never give to anyone, let alone my captor.

Laying a palm over my heart, she says, "I'll keep it safe."

I know she will, my heart will never beat the same without her in it.

My hands grip her hips as I thrust deeper, wanting to see lust fill her eyes. Her moans turn into soft groans as she pushes me toward my breaking point.

We stay silent, listening to the sounds we make, letting the feelings we're both weary of linger in the air as she comes moments later on me. Squeezing my cock with her tightness, I lose my shit when she bows down to kiss my neck with soft touches of her tongue, teasing and nudging at my flesh.

She doesn't remove herself from on top of me, more than likely loving the position of her having me underneath her. It doesn't matter to me, any arrangement of her body condensed with mine is what I want and need.

"No goodbyes," she finally says after a few moments. "We'll be back here."

I force a weak grin. "Absolutely, Blood. Just like this."

CHAPTER FORTY

Davina

I promised myself that I wouldn't run down the shoreline at Tobias and Dagen when they left the island.

That it would make it that much harder but also draw attention to Taysa while my sisters fabricated a story about Kali's shoulder bothering her and wanting to play a game of chess. The latter is a tradition we do with her, so it shouldn't throw her off to what is really happening.

My fear is that she'll sense the men leaving, and that will flag her suspicions and the outlet of the truths. The hold Taysa has on them explains everything that has transpired, and it's hard to accept let alone not rip her head off.

She betrayed us, and it hurts more because she raised us as well. Led us to believe she wanted to keep us safe when she had an ulterior motive the whole time.

Kali made me promise on our mother that I wouldn't slip into her room at night and murder her. It's also hard enough to keep Atarah and Brylee from calling her out after I agreed to it, becoming a mediator as well.

The only thing keeping us from making a move on Taysa is that we're still planning a method of attack. On what would be best to take her down the first time and not prolong it out with myself or one of my sisters getting hurt or killed.

Swimming in my lagoon, the warm water welcomes me. The sun illuminates the crystal clearness of the water, showing off the sandy bottom and my limbs. Feeling a sense of someone near, I glance over to see Isolde making her way in my direction.

She waves, a smile emitting off her oval face as a breeze picks up her pink, wavy hair. Stepping into the water, she swims over to me, casually taking her time through the aqua blue.

"Aren't you supposed to be inside?" I ask when she gets closer, her body floating aimlessly over the water.

"Figured one of us going missing wouldn't cause too much of an issue," she replies, twisting her body so that her frame is under the water.

"Did they leave yet?" I already know the answer to that question, it's not going to change. I just need it confirmed.

"Not exactly."

My brows furrow. "Did something happen?"

"Sort of."

"As *in*?" I snap, already on edge from the last day.

She hits me with a softness in her eyes. "We need to talk."

"Isolde," I warn. "I'm already on the verge of losing my mind. If you're about to tell me that Atarah and Brylee killed her or that you all let the sea witch go free to discover them leaving, I'd suggest you swim for the shore now."

Isolde looks heavenward. "It's none of the above, dear sister, but thanks for the threats."

"What happened then?"

"It's what I found." She takes an inhale of air before continuing, moving her arms around as though we're casually talking. "I was up all night researching aquatic and nordic witches because I don't know if she's both or one, so I read up on each. Since the boys are both linked to her, it doesn't matter how far they go, her power will never dwindle."

"So they have to stay?" My anxiety lifts a little at the both of them being near. Even though it's dangerous, my selfishness rejoices that I'll know where they are. That I could try to protect them against her and not wonder if they got lost at sea or that they were attacked by Hunters. A number of things could happen out there.

Isolde bows her head. "They have to stay."

"I mean, that's ideal, right? We can just keep them safe and stored away, maybe in the cove while we figure out what to do with—"

"There's more."

I nod repeatedly. "Okay, what else?"

"She's more powerful than us. Remember when we told you that Taysa screamed when you killed Edda?"

"Yes."

"I believe she was linked to her. She was in pain, weak for a few moments. Edda found us with no issue. I think Taysa guided her here."

"She has to have a weakness," I retort. "That just proves it. We can find it and—"

"She does—her sons." A numbness spreads over me as she stares at me expectedly.

"What are you saying?" I cautiously press.

Isolde bites the inside of her cheek, her blush-colored eyes glazing over in anguish. "They have to die."

"*Are you out of your ever-living mind?!*" I scream inside my head. I don't even notice I'm doing it, being like a second nature, but she flinches, catching every cut of my words.

Sluggishly, she shakes her head. "I wish I was, Davina. It's the *only* way."

"No," I shout.

"Davina, please, she'll hear you."

I step back in the water, wanting to be rid of my sister's opinion and the fact that I can't fathom either of them dying. I love them both, the idea of—

"We're not doing that," I fume. "*You* need to find another way."

"There isn't another one," Isolde settles. "I looked, the only shot we have is to take her power away from her. And maybe then we'll be able to—"

"*Stop.* I've heard enough of this." I make my way out of the lagoon, but a body I would recognize anywhere comes out of the garden and toward the tidal pond.

Dagen.

My eyes narrow at him as he comes closer, his expression soft and calm, setting my already wrecked nerves into overdrive.

They're trying to corner me into some foolish, rash decision, and I'm not going to stand for it.

I point at him. "Stay *right* there." He continues on, a white shirt exposing every inch and dip of his muscles while his long, wavy hair falls over his shoulders.

The sunlight hits him perfectly, a beautifully sculpted god. One that has stolen and broken down my defenses. Who made me feel alive again in a prison that I made for myself.

"I'll leave you two alone," Isolde utters as she brushes my shoulder to get back on land. "I won't be far."

Dagen's foot hits the water, and the ripples make a pattern along the surface. Each step in my direction rattles my hysteria.

"Blood," he says, his deep octave humming against my chest.

"You shouldn't be here. Where is Tobias?"

He jerks his head toward the castle. "Inside."

"But Taysa—"

"Is none the wiser," he continues. "She thinks I'm still going to steal the cuff from you."

I lower my head, looking at the reflection of his body off the water's surface. "Alright."

"We need to talk."

My eyes snap back up to him standing inches from me. "What?"

He reaches for me, but I flinch away, not wanting to be coddled right now.

"Your sister told you…"

"She's insane," I gripe. "All those mindless, useless facts floating around in her brain is making her crazy. I'll find a way."

I hate how no hope or facial expression of his offers any sort of support or agreement.

"Davina," he asserts.

"Don't call me by my real name at a time like this," I fume. "What do you want? No one is killing anyone."

"It's the only way." That sentence, it sounds so final. Like he's accepted this immediately, and that he's not giving another option a chance.

"You don't know that," I counter with narrowed brows.

"Might not, but we don't have time to keep searching. If she doesn't have the cuff soon, she'll know something is up." He takes a step toward me. "But the looming problem is that she'll still have Tobias and I. We are anchors of power for her, as long as we are still alive she remains potent and capable of killing you all."

"My father is a deity of a god," I retort. "She's just a witch."

"He's old and not here."

"He's still a *god* and *can* be."

"Davina."

"I'm *not* having anyone killed," I rebut through clenched teeth.

His hands grip my arms, and I don't pull away—I can't.

Everything about him calls to me. Even though I want to snap his neck in my head, I won't let his words sway me. Regardless of how my body reacts to him, how it sways in his direction, and all I want him to do is tell me that everything is going to be okay.

"I need you to listen," he asserts with a soft pressure to my flesh. "We need her power at the minimal, and you can't do that when Tobias and I are still alive." I try to pry myself away from him again. "*Without* us, she becomes weaker, and you might have a chance on your own. Your father is leagues away right now, and Nesrine is on her way to bring him back. But, like I said before, she's strong. She's a sea witch, how many of those are there?"

"None that I know of but—"

"You've given me more than anyone in this world, Blood. I will always be grateful for that. My only regret is that we never had more time. That we didn't come from the same place so that I could've met you sooner. So that I could've made you my wife. You'll never know how much I hold our memories near and dear to my heart."

"Dagen, you—"

"I'm not done," he proceeds, erasing all the space between us until our chests are touching. "With leadership comes great power and decisions, ones that you don't want to make. Ones that break you a little inside. After this, you will be fine, you *will* fight because that's who you are, and that's what I'm telling you to do. You will carry on, this will all be a distant memory but don't forget—"

I attempt to jerk out of his grasp for the third time, but he holds me still.

"You will always be that one for me," he whispers. "Nothing will ever compare to how much you mean to me."

Tears burn the back of my eyes as I peer up at him. His

blues glaze over in a watery enamel full of so much admiration and, dare I say, love that I feel like I'm choking in his hold. My body starts to tremble as I try to hold down the sob that threatens to free itself.

I won't survive this.

There would be no way that I'd be able to handle the death of my best friend and the man that I'm starting to fall for.

That I *am* in love with.

"Please," I whimper. "Don't do this to me."

"I'm doing it *for* you. And I don't regret this, it wasn't a hard decision to make. I regret nothing when it comes to you. Right down to everything that has happened, I would do it again in a heartbeat if it meant being able to spend this time with you."

"You don't know what you're saying," I sneer. "You want me to be *okay* with this?"

"I know you won't be, Blood," he consents. "But I want you to respect it."

"No, I *won't* respect it."

"You have to because it's going to happen. And you're going to do it." I'm out of his clutches and backing away from him.

"You must be the most ludicrous idiot I have *ever* met in my life," I shrill off a broken exhale. "You want *me* to kill you?" He nods. As though it'd be the most simplest thing to do. That it wouldn't matter that he'd assassinate everything that lives inside me.

"I'm not killing anyone," I snarl in a low menace tone. "I will not—" He's on me again, wrapping an arm around my waist and brushing a traitorous tear from my cheek.

Lowering his face, he breathes me in, closing his eyes to rest his forehead against mine. "Do you love me?"

I break down, my whole frame shaking in his hold as a fractured sob fleets from my lips.

I feel myself disconnect from my body. It can't handle the reality he's trying to lay out in front of me. My mind won't soak or accept it as being the only way for my sisters and I to make it out of this.

Dagen lifts me into the air and guides us deeper into the lagoon, stopping when the water reaches the top of his shoulders. I can't meet anything else but his eyes that bore into me with contentment and acceptance.

"Don't do this," I beg, wrapping my arms tighter around his neck. *"Please."*

He tries to smile but falls flat. "I have to, it's the only way to keep you alive, baby."

I open my mouth, but nothing aside from wrecked inhales and exhales make their way out. He hugs me, pressing a lingering kiss to my neck and moving up my jawline to my cheek. When he makes it to the corner of my lips, he pulls his head away to study my face.

"I love you," he decrees. "I love you more than anything in this universe. More than myself, more than life, more than any circumstances or outcome. You *are* my world, Blood. I will never forget you, even in eternal sleep, you'll always be my dream."

Claiming my mouth again, his lips give into everything that we both share.

The happy moments of us laying together in my bed.

The angry ones when I killed his men right in front of him.

The desired memories of bliss when he filled me and lavished my body with kisses and his mouth.

And now our last one that we'll ever spend together.

Lowering our bodies underneath the water, he continues to kiss me, gently and filled with every amount of love that he has for me. I feel it in every brush of our lips and every ounce of air I take from him.

He takes us deeper, not bothering to come up for air as he breaks away from me, opening his eyes to take a last look at me.

I'll never forget the glint in his blue eyes or the structure of his face. I'll never be able to erase how he made me feel and how much I wanted what he did.

A life of happiness and forever.

Pulling me back into him, our lips meet again, more shakily this time, and I know he's losing the air in his lungs. I'm aware of how he's fading from me the more I beg him to reconsider this with every caress of my mouth. He's dying in my midst, and he won't stop until he knows he's gone and I'm safe.

I break from the kiss, a loud wail breaking through the water as bubbles float toward the surface. Dagen's arms faintly pull me closer, his forehead resting into mine with his eyes still closed.

"Dagen," I beg. *"Please don't leave me."*

His lids open slightly, telling me that he has to for now. That one day we'll be together. That this isn't the end for us.

Another weak kiss, and a few seconds later, he's gone.

Everything is still, deathly quiet as his body starts to float toward the top of the lagoon, and I pull him up with me.

Emerging from the water, I yank him along as I swim to shore, where Isolde is waiting for me.

Helping me pull him to the dry land, his face has gone blue as I collapse beside him.

"Isolde," I wail, my hands curling to my mouth. "Oh my— what did I *do*?" Her arms wrap around me, holding me as my body violently shakes in heartache, shock, and grief.

My sister squeezes me to her side. "You saved us all."

CHAPTER FORTY ONE
Tobias

Davina is wrapped in a gray blanket, rocking back and forth in the short grass along the lagoon. Her red hair is still slightly damp, droplets of water falling to the ground as she mindlessly stares over the water.

Even though I can't see her face, I know that it's blank. That she looks beautiful as she ponders over what she had to do to save her kingdom and family.

That she hates herself.

I've known her for enough time to know that she'll carry it with her and that no one or anything will make her feel any different. The revelation of Dagen and I being brothers, the woman that is our mother, it'll never bring her world back on its axis.

I just hope she *tries* to live after this.

"You're going to need to find someone else to do it," Davina croons before I can utter a word. "I'm not doing it for you."

"Aw, now that's not very nice, Princess," I reply, trying to keep my tone light and airy. "I thought we were friends."

"Exactly." Her tone is ice, emotionless, something that sounds dead and empty inside. "You all had a conversation about this and didn't include me."

Because she would've said no. Had a royal fit about not having this happen, and as shady as it was, we had to ambush her about it.

What Dagen and I wanted was beyond the word selfish. Beyond the words "fucked up," but it was the only way we wanted to die—for the both of us. Not in a malicious and hateful way but because we both loved her, and it'd be the last thing we'd see before going off to Zeus knows where afterward.

I'm already on edge, as I stand off to the side, knowing that I only have a few more moments to breathe on this Earth. Only a few more minutes with the woman I'd give anything for—which I will. I'm starting to realize in swift thoughts that maybe this was what I was here for, to save her from my own mother. That I was supposed to be on that ship that day to protect Rohana, Kali, and her from my uncle's men.

"Maybe we were always supposed to be here," I tell her.

She shakes her head. "No, it's because of me that this all happened."

"You?" My brows furrow. "How?"

"If I hadn't gone to Coral Cove, you wouldn't be in my life. You wouldn't have needed to save my sisters and I."

"That would've been a boring life."

She peers over her shoulder at me. "I'm sure you'd be married by now with kids and—"

"No reminiscing on the what-ifs," I convey. "That's not what people do."

"They *do* it all the time." Returning her attention back to the lagoon, she tugs her legs underneath her and continues to stare.

"Davina," I utter. "I wouldn't change a thing. I'd still cut down that rope and free you."

"I would," she whispers. "I'd change *everything*."

"You know that I came up with this idea, right?" She twists her body to take me in, brows snapped together like I have literally gone off the deep end.

I did, with her.

And I'd fucking relive it again and again with the same outcome if I still got the many years of happiness that I spent with her.

"Why in the *hell* would you suggest this idea?" Her green eyes, now rimmed in red, glimmer in anger, and she may not forgive me, but I'd never forgive myself if she died because I didn't do everything I could to protect her.

Dagen didn't need convincing either, jumping right on board when Isolde told us everything. Being linked to Taysa, having her powers live within us and that no matter where we went as long as we were still alive, she'd be almost unstoppable. Triton was away, we didn't know how much time we had, and even then she may have something up her sleeve to stop him and the girls from killing her.

She'd have to or her whole plan of taking over under the sea while Dagen and I took the land and everything above the sea would be a waste of time. We all agreed that Taysa wasn't stupid and didn't lay out all her plans with Dagen and I. That there were still things we didn't know, and she wasn't about to lay all her cards on the table just yet.

Not until she knew Dagen and I would follow her. And the impression that we made with her in the dining room, we definitely weren't on board with her plans.

Dagen threatened to chop all her limbs off. I wanted to blow her up with the cannons on my ship. Both unrealistic as fuck and never going to happen.

"Deep down," I allude. "You know this is the only way."

Her jaw ticks. "It's *not* the only way. All of you didn't even give me a chance to figure out something else."

I hunch down to my knees, almost eye level with her. "I don't want to leave you, please believe that. But I think I was put in your life to keep you alive."

"Tobias," she says softly. "We can find another way."

"I don't think there is, to be honest."

"You don't understand what you're—" she breaks in a sob. "—what you're asking me to do. *Again.*"

My hand clasps under her chin. "I do know because I'd be like you right now if the tables were turned. I'd never be able to do it."

"But you're asking *me* to," she upbraids.

"Because you're stronger than me. And you have more at risk than I ever would." Her jaw trembles as she bows her head into her chest, wrapping the blanket tighter around her.

"I can't."

"Would you rather Atarah do it?"

Her head snaps up to me. "What?"

"She offered." Davina is on her feet, almost knocking me over as she makes her way toward the house.

Quickly, I get to mine, catching up to her and clasping her arm to turn her around. "I don't want to fight about this," I voice. "Just be here with me."

"My sister would do something so unimaginable and—"

"She hugged me before I came out here. Said I was an honorable man that would always be remembered."

"I don't care *what* she said," she leers. "I'm not—" She stops when I reach around my coat to pull out my revolver.

Her eyes widen as she takes a wobbly step back.

"I love you," I convey. "More than my own life. This will be the quickest way." She stares at it as though it has a million heads and it's about to snap at her. "Will you hold my hand?"

Her eyes float up to mine, glistening in unshed tears. She's trying her best to hold them back, to still be angry at me, but we are down the only path we were given to walk down.

This ends when Dagen and I are both dead and, since he is my brother—and I still don't care for him—I wouldn't be able not to follow behind him now.

"If you don't," I note. "His life would've been given for nothing because with my still being here, Taysa has me. I'm the other half, Princess. We have to follow through with it."

"How am I going to live without you?" she croons. "I can't pull—" I yank her to me, enclosing her in my arms and resting my cheek against the top of her head.

"You will," I tell her, feeling my heat rate heighten. "Because you'll live for the both of us. You'll kill the bitch and then name a kid after me."

Davina nestles her face into my chest, letting a violent sob sound into my shirt.

"I know you're scared. I am too."

She slowly looks up at me, tears streaming down her cheeks. "I don't want you to be."

"I just don't know what waits on the other side. If we'll be together again or—"

"We will." She nods profusely. "We have to be. My grandfather is a god, I'll make it happen."

I force a grin. "Okay, Princess."

I kiss her forehead, letting myself feel her skin against my lips for the last time. Breathing in the sea that I'll never sail on again and the crew that'll never know what happened to me.

"Be mindful of my uncle," I mutter against her skin. "I think he's about to sail this way for Sirens. And I have something to tell you."

"You kill Sirens to keep me safe," she replies. "I know."

I jerk my body a few spaces from her. "How?"

"There's been talk of a handsome pirate with wavy hair who sails on a ship with gold-rimmed cannons. Wasn't hard to figure out who that was."

"Why didn't you say something?"

"Because they've already been warned about going past the borders of Lacuna. That we couldn't protect them if they did. And it was...for the well-being of the kingdom that you did it to keep your uncle away."

"So you *do* understand how to keep the kingdom safe," I lightly jeer.

"Unfortunately." She squeezes me to her, resting her cheekbone on my chest and listening to me breathe.

"Taysa is gone," I voice. "She knows what...happened."

"I'm not ready to let go," Davina whispers. "You're everything to me."

My body starts to involuntarily shake at her words, the outcome of this starting to heighten my anxiety, and I am scared.

I'm terrified that I'll fall into a dark abyss and never see her again.

Kissing the top of her head, I say, "And you're more to me."

I pull her harder to me, giving myself a few more seconds, before breaking from her and placing the gun into her hands.

"Count," I order. "Right against the temple and don't miss." Her fingers wrap around the weapon, but she doesn't break her gaze from mine.

I might not make it before she pulls the trigger, my heart is thudding so hard in my chest that it's hard to breathe. Difficult to remain still when I know I won't be alive for another five minutes.

"Close your eyes," Davina says, grabbing my hand and holding it tightly. I do what she says, my exhales and inhales inconsistent. "Remember the time you said you couldn't stand me when I pushed you off your ship."

I nod but don't respond. I can't because my words will come out choked and broken, and I don't want to make this harder for her than I already know it is.

I'll miss her.

I'll miss her eyes and the quirk of her lips. I'll miss our

arguments and the way we promised never to leave each other mad.

I broke that rule when I discovered her with Dagen, but I'm here now, spending my last moment on this Earth with the woman who means the world to me.

"I was afraid if you would've kissed me that you would own a piece of me that I'd never get back," she continues then she sniffles and breaks into a sob. "But you did that anyway. I may have not shown it, but you were that person for me. You were my best friend and protector. You saved my life."

I bite my lower lip to keep from breaking down. To keep the small amount of courage that I have so that she doesn't back out of this.

"I love you, you know that? You were such a pain in my side, but I would never change meeting you. I wouldn't give it up for anything."

"I love you too," I whisper. "And—"

CHAPTER FORTY TWO

Davina

Forgiveness.

It's easier to give to someone else, giving them the responsibility to live with the consequences or fear of losing that said person.

Offering said word to something you've done—there's no running from yourself. It's constantly flowing through the mind, always something you have to live with while the silent torture starts to eat you alive.

That's already where I am.

I've fallen so deep in a hole of numbness that I can't fathom facing Taysa and fighting for her sons. I can't conjure enough energy to do anything other than feel the emptiness of losing both halves of my world.

The man I was in love with and the best friend who was more than a friend, a breathing mechanism to my life.

Living without them is indescribable, empty, and pure torment. It's almost as though it's not real. That I'm living in a nightmare that has lasted over the course of two days and I'm not waking up.

I'll never wake up from this.

The reality of going through every day for the rest of my life with this burden of taking both of their lives will forever haunt me.

Two men in one day.

Two humans who have won me over with their boorish and wild tendencies because that's just who they were. Men who lived for adventure and protecting what they had to.

Then they took on me and my sisters. Giving up their lives for the greater good, knowing they'd never be able to see it.

And even then, it was a risk.

Like Tobias said my father may not be able to take her down. To plan this whole ordeal without the confidence that she'd be able to win, Taysa was not a foolish woman who wouldn't have side plans set in place.

I mean, Dagen and Tobias were a perfect example of the small addendum to her plot to take the kingdom. Safely put in places for when she needed to use them, they'd be closely set right by my side.

She just didn't plan for them to take their own lives or that I would have the strength to even gauge in hurting them.

"You need to eat a little something, okay?" Rohana squeezes my hand that she's been holding for, I don't know how long, and waits for me to answer.

I don't.

Still staring at the shelf of books in various colored bindings, I notice how nothing is organized. That every story is mixed in with other ones, and I wonder how many of them have happy endings. How much trouble they had to go through to obtain it and if anyone in them has ever felt like me but been able to overcome it.

"She's in shock," I hear Isolde say to the room. "It was too much for her."

"I should've taken care of Tobias." It's then that my eyes snap from the bookshelf to land on Atarah. Her head is bowed into her chest, picking at her fingernails while softly bouncing her right foot on the floor.

I'm about to lash out at her with words. That I'd never

condone her touching either of them because I don't trust that she'd do it in the best way, but it's her vulnerability that stops me.

Atarah doesn't fidget. She doesn't pick at her nails because she's particular about them in the first place, and she'd never let any of us see her sweat.

The tone in her voice sounds small and defeated, guilty even. And it's then that I never considered how much of a toll it'd take on my sisters to ask and have me do what I have done to save them all.

Slowly, I bring my attention back to the bookcase, letting my eyes readjust to the books for a second time. Giving my mind a break so that I can try and think of something else. But I can feel the tension in my shoulders, the exhaustion coursing through my body, my gut hasn't stopped twisting, and it's not because I'm hungry. Looking at food would only make it worse.

All I want to do is wake up or go back to two days ago before everything came to light. To hold Dagen and Tobias close to my chest and never let them go.

I should've fought harder, refused their plan, and made up my own.

"Nothing has changed," Brylee announces as she enters my library. "Everything is secure and...quiet."

My sisters have been taking turns scouring the island and the perimeter of the water outside Merindah to make sure nothing was lurking outside our border. We're perfectly seated in the middle of the ocean where Taysa can attack from any direction at any given moment with Zeus knows what.

A hand touches my left shoulder, the smell of the sea and fresh flowers gives Brylee's identity away as she gives it a small squeeze. "Let's go get some air."

"Just let her rest," Rohana counters. "It's...it's just too much right now."

"It's too much being cooped up in this stuffy library," Brylee retorts. "And she looks pale."

"Do you want to?" Rohana mutters at my side.

"Why don't we just leave and give her some space?" Isolde offers, standing from one of the chairs at the small table I have along the wall. "We can come back to bother her later."

"We can't just leave her here locked up in a room by herself," Brylee argues. She leans over to look me in the face. "Doesn't that sound good, sweetie? We'll walk the beach, and we don't have to talk."

"Stop being pushy," Atarah snaps quietly, which is completely out of her element. The twins are usually the other way around. Atarah and her "I'm three minutes older" line that she always preaches to Brylee on why she's able to say whatever she wants. Brylee is the more comforting twin but obviously not today.

"When did you lose your pushiness?"

"When she had to—why don't you take another walk around the island a few times?" Atarah carps.

"Why don't *you* go take a walk around the island and burn off some of your attitude?"

Atarah stands. "How about we *both* go outside and I'll show you where I can—"

"I'll go outside," I chant, rising from the settee as the weight of all their eyes fall on me.

Making my way to the door, I don't wait for any of them to follow me. I'm actually hoping they don't, but my luck ran dry a long time ago, and now I don't deserve it.

I make my way down the short hall to the massive foyer, the same one Dagen followed me into when I let him out of his chains for the first time. When I shoved him across the room because he had a nag for touching me all the time and twirling me around like he had a right to.

Nudging the recollection away, I keep my head down, not wanting to look anywhere that held a piece of history of him. It wasn't as though I'd be able to live in my denial state for long because I had to give both of them a proper funeral. Make sure that they are laid to rest in peace because it was the last thing I'd be able to give them.

The moment my hand reaches for the sky blue door that leads outside, the floor starts to rumble. Freezing in place, I listen to the house start to creak and clatter with the belongings of the castle. The low roar of the ground outside announcing that something is wrong or coming.

Swinging the door open, I'm met with not a blue sky of clouds but green dusted with a dark overcast. My feet slowly move to meet the first step as I study the change of the weather. I've never seen or read anything like it in any of my books. It's strangely quiet, the waves barely making a sound along the shoreline as though the world froze.

The grains of sand jump off the beach at the progressive shaking of the ground while I take my first step onto the beach.

Casting my gaze over the ocean again, I see the start of a ripple forming. From the crest of the water, a set of octopus tentacles breach the skin of the gentle waves, reaching and curling in all directions.

But when the tint of green follows the rising purple limbs, my blood turns cold.

Taysa's eyes latch right onto me as the rest of her body appears from the water. But it wasn't the fragile-looking frame that she had days ago when I last saw her. It was curvy and voluptuous, perfectly molded to look twenty years younger than what her true age was.

Magic, it's the only explanation.

The red glint of a bottle swings in the air by one of the long limbs as Taysa strides toward the shore, confidence announced in every step she takes.

Each one crucifies me.

Reminds me of what she sacrificed, what I *took* away—from the both of us. I took her power while she took my life. My body was now a barren shell of depression and grief that would never fill with anything bright or luminous again.

That *she* took away from me.

"Davina." It's Atarah with a voice full of authoritative resonance. So different from moments ago when she wanted to coddle me and have everyone else leave me alone.

Her arm links with mine, offering the strength that I lack, as we both watch Taysa hit the sand. Dressed in all black, the shiny material clings to her body, getting kicked up by the wind that is increasing in speed.

"My girls," she bellows, still yards away. "I'm back."

Atarah keeps her gaze trained on her. *"Rohana is grabbing Tobias's gun,"* she states in my head. *"While Isolde is grabbing the Viking's blade. Both are going to tuck them behind your skirt."*

"Where are the rest of you?" Taysa asks, suddenly stopping when she sees it's only the two of us standing here to see her arrival. Her brow slowly peaks when neither of us speak, knowing that she's not welcome here, that she may have walked into a trap.

Regardless, she knows the goal—we want her dead.

"I'm here to make a deal," Taysa consults, still wafting around the bottle. I don't know what keeps pulling me to it, but it definitely means something. "Your freedom for Davina."

Atarah's body grows stiffer alongside mine, but she stays quiet.

"You have a night to think about it."

"We'll end this now," Atarah retorts back. *"Today."*

Taysa cocks her head to the side. "Don't be foolish, Atarah. You're the eldest, six sisters outweighs the one."

"And why would I do that?"

"Because you'll all die, my darling, and I actually do like you girls." Her dark eyes land on me. "But your sister stole something from me. My offspring died at her hands."

A mirthless laugh escapes my sister. "Then you might want to reevaluate your affection because I condoned it. Hell, I almost killed your youngest myself."

A hard twitch of her jaw and Taysa transforms back into herself, calm and collected.

"Mine would've been much worse though," Atarah continues, squeezing my arm against her ribs in a silent apology. "Davina was at least gracious."

The sound of my name triggers something within her head because her attention falls back on me, and it's filled with hatred and disdain.

"I kept those boys safe their whole lives," she snaps. "Tobias *saved* you."

"*Don't speak,*" Atarah voices. "*She's trying to spark your temper.*"

"You ungrateful little bitch," Taysa barks. "You *murdered* my sons."

Atarah raises her chin. "And they gladly gave their lives to save us."

"*I'm going to get sick,*" I utter to my sister, feeling the monotonous screw of my gut.

Just hearing Taysa say it out loud is sending me backward into the dark mindset of solitude. Where I'll never hear Tobias's jokes or lay in Dagen's arms again. The cruel reality sinking in again that I watched and did *nothing* when they both took their last breaths.

Because you needed to safeguard your sisters.

I hear my subconscious say it, over and over again, but it

does nothing to soothe away the disgust I feel toward myself.
It doesn't lift anything off my chest or take the weight that's
constantly pressing into my rib cage.

"*Hold on,*" Atarah mutters in my head. "*They'll be here soon.*"

She means our sisters, the ones I sacrificed everything for
—my happiness, my love, my whole entire life.

CHAPTER FORTY THREE

Davina

L ined up together, side by side, my five sisters and I face Taysa on the darkened beach. The sea is deathly calm, looking black from the inky-colored clouds overhead. Nesrine is still gone, on her way to retrieve our father, but I'm glad she isn't here.

One less to become injured or die, one less thing to have to worry about because right now I'm terrified.

I've given up more than I ever thought I'd have to in my lifetime. Made choices with my sisters full of curiosity and stories. Included a woman who was more than what I would've ever imagined with her mother-like tendencies and love that she casted toward us. Only for it all to be made up of lies and deceit, alluding me to do the unimaginable.

"If you hand over the cuff," Taysa states. "I'll show mercy on all of you."

"And what happens with Davina?" Atarah counters.

Those dark eyes shift to me and back to my sister. "The cuff will save her too."

"Don't believe you," Brylee sneers. "You're a lying old hag who's done enough to our family. The death of your sons lay at your hands."

"I was never going to harm them," she snaps. "You stupid little chits ruined *everything*." A crack of lightning follows her rant, making me jump in between Atarah and Kali.

"Stay calm," Atarah conveys. *"We're going to be okay."*

Oh, the naivety of her words does nothing to soothe me. We're in a load of trouble, and no amount of calmness is going to erase anything that is going to happen to us today.

The feel of metal and wood rub against my spine as Dagen's blade and Tobias's gun are slid under my skirt. Meant to at least hurt the sea witch for what she's done, but I don't think I can manage anything right now with my murky brain.

"We found that dark-haired woman Tobias brought in her room," Brylee states to all of us. *"With her throat slit."*

"Self-inflicted," Rohana adds in then glances at Taysa. *"Or self-made."*

"The cuff goes nowhere," Atarah orders. *"Where is it, Davina?"*

"I hid it in the forest, she'll never find it."

"We need to make a move," Brylee utters to all of us. *"Before she does something else."*

"What do you suggest?" Isolde asks. *"I have a feeling she didn't come alone."*

"I can bet she didn't," Kali pipes in. *"The sea being so calm feels like something lies not to far behind her."*

"One way to find out," I add. *"Someone needs to get closer."*

"And let me guess, that'd be you," Atarah snaps. *"You're the first person she's going to try and kill."*

"Exactly. Which is where the rest of you come into play."

Atarah squeezes my arm that she's still holding. *"No—"*

"She isn't wrong," Brylee cuts in. *"We need a distraction, she's it."*

"I swear to Zeus, you are all mad."

I start to pull myself out of Atarah's hold. *"I'm going to try."*

"Davina," Atarah warns. *"We don't have time to argue."*

"Then don't," Rohana breaks in. *"You have to trust her. You did with everything else."*

Atarah hesitates then drops her hold on me, letting me proceed to take a cautious step closer.

Taysa perks a brow, knowing that we can communicate to each other without anyone else none the wiser. That by my sisters letting me step forward when she wants nothing more than my head means that we have something outlined.

We don't.

Unless they do, which wouldn't surprise me after what transpired in the last few days. Seems like all the decision-making has been taken away and talked about amongst themselves.

Maybe I should've never been the one to make all of the decisions for the seven of us.

"You're not going to trick me nor are you going to win," Taysa seethes in my direction. "I'm utterly shocked that you'd turn against those boys. That you were so selfish as to kill both of them when they've done nothing but love you. I placed them in your care, knowing that out of all the girls, you would've loved them both." Her eyes constrict. "And then you *executed* them."

"It wasn't my idea," I retort. "It was theirs."

She scoffs at my fact and turns a darker shade of green. "They weren't suicidal. You're just a pretty little thing but nothing that would've—"

"I'm a *Siren*," I snap. "I can make them feel however I want them to feel."

"That wasn't something you were always good at, was it?" She jerks her head to my sisters behind me. "They're better at that than you are. You were just the curious, stupid one who always wanted to be where she wasn't allowed."

"And you were the slimy, old bitch that betrayed us, so who's better than who?"

A line appears between her black brows. "We'll see, won't we?"

My heart starts to quicken. "Guess we will but watch it," I warn, leaning a little to add to my pettiness. "We all know you're a tad weaker without the boys."

I wink, which makes the sea start to move more frantically. The waves begin to crash loudly against the shoreline while another jolt of lightning cracks through the sky.

"*Davina*," Atarah cautions. "*Watch the sea.*"

The moment she says it, is the instant I see it. Two heads emerge from the crest of tides followed by slick scales of gray that don't stop until they're high over Taysa's head. Sharp, pointed teeth and yellow bulging eyes gleam down at us, ready and waiting for their next command.

Giant eels.

On the left and right side of their master, their nostrils expanding to smell what lays before them, which are six snacks they want to cut in half with their deadly teeth.

"*Get back,*" Brylee demands.

But I don't.

Instead, I'm ready for the sea witch to beckon them to attack me so that my sisters can do something. For them to have the opportunity to do anything while I become the perfect bait and target.

However, we're going up against creatures that live under the sea, and using said element of water will be difficult to herd them with. The only things my sisters wield are rods covered in barnacles with sharp shelled tips, some with long, curved blades at the end while Atarah and Kali hold tridents just like our father.

Other than that, we're doomed.

Unless I can get one of them closer to the beach, I might be able to burn one.

"*I need them closer,*" I tell my sisters. "*I might be able to put a hole in one with my heat.*"

"*Can you do more than that?*" Isolde asks. "*Because they'll just turn around and bite you."*

"You were in flames when you killed Edda," Atarah states. *"Going to have to do that again, love."*

"I was?" I shrug inwardly because I don't remember. *"I'm going to have to get angry enough."*

"She linked Tobias and the Viking to herself, do I need to remind you of anything else that you did?"

Alright, so Atarah threw a low blow, which does make my jaw twitch and stomach knot at the same time, but I was the cause of their deaths and—

"If it wasn't for her, they'd be alive," Brylee adds.

"Okay, that's enough," I seethe. *"I got it."*

"Do you though?" Kali interjects. *"Seems like you've been too busy wallowing around the island feeling sorry for yourself to worry about the real reason why this is all happening."*

Slowly, I start to spin on my heels, finding all my sisters still standing where I left them, weapons in hand and waiting for Taysa's next move, but I'm putting holes in my sister's heads with my eyes.

"I said I got it," I gripe.

"Enough!" Taysa hollers from behind me. "It doesn't matter if I can't hear you, your plans will do nothing."

I lift my left hand in the air and summon her with my middle and index fingers. "Let's finish this then instead of *hearing* you talk about it."

Turning back around, everything remains the same— Taysa still stands there with a scowl and hatred in her eyes, the two giant eels wait impatiently for her to give her next decree, but it's Nesrine that didn't fit the picture the last time.

Set back a few yards from the eels and trident in hand, she positioned it horizontal to her right shoulder, eyes pinned on me and my direction.

I don't speak to her, nor do I keep my gaze on her except

for that split second before landing back on Taysa. If she's here, our father isn't far behind.

"Ready?" I taunt, feeling both Tobia's and Dagen's weapons brush my lower back.

A slow quirk of Taysa's lips spike up her face. "More than you'll ever know."

"*Throw it!*" Nesrine cocks her arm back, positions her elbow up, and launches the three-pronged harpoon at one of the eels.

A loud high-pitched shrill of pain echoes across the water as Nesrine dips underneath it to hide herself and her position from Taysa. The moment the sea witch turns to see what's happened, I'm reaching behind my back for Tobias's gun.

The handle itches in my palm, remembering the first time I held it. On why I possessed it in the first place. At the life I took to be in this spot, right here, defending my kingdom, my sisters, my father, and my home.

Staring down the barrel with both eyes open, I don't hesitate like I did the last time, I just pull the trigger. The heavy gun fires off my one shot of gunpowder that Tobias left behind and catches Taysa's left side. She flinches, hand going to the spot where I hit her, and that's when a lightning bolt hits the sand right in front of me.

Startled, I stumble back, catching myself before my butt hits the ground. My sisters flank my sides a moment later, pulling me back even though we need to move forward.

We need the water.

A shift of gray appears in my peripheral, and I shove my sisters back, as many as I can reach with my arms, while trying to find the head of the second eel. Its body wraps around the front and sides of us, which means it's behind us.

A wicked hiss vocalizes, and I don't bide any time, climbing over the body of the creature and straight in the direction of Taysa. The injured eel wails in agony back and forth, thrashing in the water, but she doesn't miss my movements.

Extending both her hands to her sides, she lifts them, making the air pick up in a frenzy. My feet dig into the grains of sand as I sprint toward her, the metal of Dagen's blade chafing my skin.

Another flash of light hits the turf at my right side, jolting me away from it as the smell of salt becomes richer in my lungs.

My vision stays locked on Taysa, determined and blood-hungry. I'm doing this for them, both of the men that gave up everything for me to be able to fight and not lose.

My body barrels into hers, but I don't knock her down. Instead, it was like she was waiting for me to touch her. Tentacles wrap around my waist and throat, lifting me off my feet as I land a foot to her gut before they extend the distance between us.

My hands go to the velvety skin, slipping right off them as I regain some sort of grasp.

"Your mother was fierce and feisty like you," Taysa alludes calmly. "Trusted too easily as well. You're the spitting image of her, that's why I brought you this." The red bottle appears in front of me as she cocks it from side to side. "You appeared there first but not before I took her powers and bottled them up in here."

I throw another leg in her direction but miss. "You're a backstabbing who—" The tentacles tighten around my windpipe, cutting me off.

"Not until I'm done with the story," Taysa tsks. "The cuffs would only come off once she was sucked of all her godly potency, but then *you* showed up."

"How did...Tobias get the other...cuff?"

"It goes to the closest bloodline of the person that killed

the god, which was him. I was long gone before you could even sense me near. And since then, I've let him keep it, not that he knew what it was, but I couldn't keep it in the sea. Your father would perceive it, and I couldn't be linked with it at the time. Then you had the other one locked away safely for when I was ready."

"You shouldn't have told them," I choke, clawing at the slippery limbs that hold me. "They were more fearless than you gave them credit for."

Taysa averts her eyes from me. "I know. I was so proud of them. " Black eyes fall back to me. "And then you took them."

The conviction is back, I can feel it right to my bones. And with both of us digging into the hollows of my soul, my heart cracks another fragment.

"Once I have the other cuff," Taysa imparts. "I'll have your mother's godly and paramount power."

"Going to have to find it first," I retort.

Another squeeze to my neck while another thick arm wraps around my middle.

"I would've let you marry him," she consents with a frown. "If it would've made Dagen happy and stay within our deal of ruling over the land and Vikings, I would've allowed it."

My hands go to the tentacle coiled around my stomach, feeling the meagerness of air making my lungs want to burst.

"I would've had to soak up all your power, but regardless, you'd still be alive along with your sisters and have both—" The dagger in my back is already in my hand and slicing into the tentacle gripping my neck.

A sudden intake of air fills my lungs as I slash downward, hitting the second arm wrapped around my body, and I'm immediately dropped to the sand.

Gasping for air, I coerce myself to get to the water. I haven't touched the sea since I got my voice back, and since the veil and its magic is now faded or gone, I should be able to go in without a problem.

Stumbling to the water, I'm tripped by a body part belonging to Taysa as I notice the waves being sucked back from the shore, seizing my gaze to the midsection of the sea.

A giant whirlpool forms, making a pit that is now hauling the wounded eel within its clutches as it tries to swim out of the strong currents.

Suddenly, bulky tentacles loop around my chest and under my breasts, hoisting me off the beach and into the air again, meeting Taysa's brows knitted together.

"Which one did you kill first?" she seethes inches from my face, her breath smelling like raw fish. "And how?"

I attempt to push the slick arm off me but to no avail as it tightens itself around my rib cage.

"Use your witchy powers," I carp. It only alludes more pressure against my bones, forcing air from my body from the pain that I need to breathe.

"Which *one*?" she snaps. "Those were my children."

"You obviously didn't care too—" Another squeeze as I keel over in pain.

"*Answer* me."

My eyes catch the dagger I dropped when I was discarded to the ground, remembering the time I ran it down Dagen's face to see how much he'd flinch behind his massive body and dark hair. How much man made up the facade when only defiance glinted in his eyes. His cocky attitude, the way he tried to taunt me as I watched blood seep from his flesh.

"*Enjoying yourself?*" he asked me.

At the time I was, yes, his blue eyes barely left me the moment I walked into that room. I felt the heaviness of them, the way they travelled up and down my body without abandon while I ignored it.

Tried to ignore it.

He got so deep underneath my skin that I wasn't able to pry him out nor would I ever want to now. The only thing I have left is that dagger and the painful, lovely memories that haunt me every second of every day.

"Dagen," I stifle, pulling my gaze back to her and shoving the next words from my lips. "I drowned him."

Her eyes gloss over in an opaque shade with fury and an inhuman glow as the tentacle squeezing me compresses more strain around my body.

I can't focus on anything else but the pain and lack of oxygen, coercing myself to peer back up at the ocean where Tobias and Dagen came to this island from. Watching the waves crash into each other, the eel now nowhere in sight, which makes me peer over my shoulder to find out where the other went to and how my sisters were faring.

I don't get to turn my head fully around because Taysa and I are propelled toward the sea by a collision of water from behind me. The element fills my nose while a hint of a burning sensation hits my skin the moment my body is fully emerged within it.

Breaking through the crest, I feel my body start to transform into my original being. My feet fuse together into my tail, the scales on my neck that help me breathe starts to develop, opening and closing at the air above the water.

The veil is just about gone, it's the only explanation of why I'm able to evolve back into what I was born to be.

Feeling the salt seep into my pores, the water immersing around me gives me confidence. I move my hands forward, playing with the water to see if it moves to where I want it to, and it does.

My powers are back, and Taysa is now at another inconvenience.

As Tobias would say, "She's in a heap of trouble."

But as Dagen would say, "She's fucked."

CHAPTER FORTY FOUR

Davina

A bulky hand clasps over my shoulder, yanking me backward into a hard chest. My heart fleets a few beats, recalling the same feeling. The muscles and the ocean blue eyes as I turn around to find my father towering over me with worry displayed all over his features.

He doesn't speak, just pulls me into the crook of his arm, gently pressing me into his bare chest as I breathe him in. Tears burn the back of my eyes, everything hitting me all at once again.

In the hold of my father, this would be the worst time for me to have another panic episode of loss and grief. I can only imagine the disappointment he must be feeling for the things I've done and kept from him. I would never want to lose his trust and respect—it means the world to me.

But so did the men that I kept and protected from him.

"You alright?" my father prods, still holding me into his frame.

I nod, relieved and thankful that Nesrine was able to find him. Without him I don't know if my sisters and I would have a chance.

I don't know why it didn't hit me that the whirlpool would be his idea. I've heard stories of him sucking down fleets of ships that have passed into our realm and not sparing a single person to get home to share the story.

"It's dead," I hear Nesrine inform, placing a wet hand onto my back.

"Help your sisters with the other one," my father orders. She doesn't answer, just places a cold metal object into my hands and, I assume, leaves.

Gripping the rod, I know it's the trident she used to take down the other eel, and I brush my thumb up and down the warm metal for more comfort.

"Where is she?" my father prods.

"We were both thrown into the sea," I convey.

Breaking away, my father stares down at me, his crown exhibiting the capacity of his being. The King of Lacuna, the son of Poseidon. "I'd tell you to stay back, but we both know that's not happening so be on your guard."

He moves a few feet away from me, lifting his golden trident and spinning it in the air. The water immediately moves, parting from itself right down to the bottom of the sea as it continues to widen at my father's command.

Together, we back up, as the water quickly dismantles itself until a moment later he halts.

"Taysa," he bellows, peering downward through the gap. I come to his side, seeing fish flopping on the wet ocean bottom until my eyes fall on the black figure glaring back at us.

"Triton," she answers back, tone laced in disgust. "I was wondering if you were going to show."

"Surrender yourself or die, your only two options."

A mirthless chuckle cackles upward. "You underestimate me, Your Majesty."

"I did," he confirms. "And now you'll pay the price."

"And so will you."

Instantly, my father is dragged underneath the depths of the water, leaving me alone to feel the gratification of Taysa's smirk.

"Daddy dearest won't be around much longer to save you, my love," she taunts. "Get ready for round two." The water collides back together, hiding her from me and sending a swell of water in my direction.

Raising my hand, I stop it under heavy strain, weak from not being able to exercise my powers of the sea for over the course of many years.

Using everything I can drain from within me, I shift the water underneath me, raising me toward the sky so I can have a better look at everything. Toward the shoreline is my sisters finishing off the other eel, struggling to get back to the water. It's inches from death as my sisters repeatedly stab the beast with their weapons.

Again on our home turf that was never a safe place to begin with.

Due to a veil that was never meant to protect us in the first place until Taysa was ready to sink her claws into all of us and use her sons against me. Ones she put in my life to care for and protect and vice versa.

Not only did she betray us but them, her own flesh and blood. The ones she made a promise to, as a mother, to always have their best interests at heart because that's what mothers were supposed to do. Put their children's needs before their own, give them love to help them grow and support to help them succeed and feel confident in this harsh world.

But she did none of that.

Instead, she sentenced them to death because it was the only way to make her lose some of the power that coursed through her veins that she planned on using against us.

And now they're dead by my hands.

By her design.

And I have to live with it for the rest of my life.

The blood that splattered on my face that was Tobias's.

Watching his lifeless body fall to the ground as a splintered wail broke through my lips at his death. How he told me he loved me and I was the only thing he didn't regret.

While I had to feel Dagen's lips pressed into mine as the air expired from his body while he clutched on to me as long as he could.

No one should ever have to experience what I had to—twice. Never have to see or feel the life leave the body of someone they love by their own demise to help the greater good.

The more I ponder back, the more I can feel the rage start to boil within my veins. The prickling anger that hits the back of my neck and propels down to my spine as I watch the giant creature attempting to slither back into the depths of the sea to hide.

My immediate thought is a wall of fire, blocking its entry into the water, and when my arms jerk ahead of me on their own accord, that's exactly what happens.

Through the trident in my right hand, a barricade of flames ignite, sending the monster cowering back from the heat. Then movement from my peripheral snaps my attention, and it's Taysa below me, a green mist floating around her body.

The glimmer of gold hits me next, my father standing feet from her as he thrust his weapon in her direction. She dodges it while the green aura wraps around his trident and attempts to yank it from his grasp. Thankfully, my father holds on to it, using the sea to collide into both sides of her body to make her let go.

Taking another glance to the beach to quickly count the bodies of my sister's, all six of them are now there—all moving around, appearing uninjured.

The sound of a loud explosion echoes underneath me, snatching my attention downward. My father is nowhere to be found, which sparks worry, but my fury overpowers any other emotion. It actually exceeds all my thoughts of movement because my arm is already cocked back and aimed at Taysa, thrusting the trident into any part of her body.

Before I even know if it hits her, my hands move to boost the witch upward with the sea so I can get a hold of her. She aligns with me in no time, the prongs of my weapon protruding through her gut before I yank it from her flesh. A pained shriek slips from her lips, which only increases the need to finish this.

Hand on her throat, I think back to Edda. The sudden urge and frenzy that overtook my body as I burned her alive, according to my sisters. The smell of burning flesh filling my nostrils as I stayed grounded and somewhat focused.

"You took away what was mine," I smolder in her face, feeling my palms heat. "You made me make decisions I should've never needed to make. Now I'll have to live with that for the rest of my life but you—" I return the favor of squeezing her throat. "—you'll get the easy way out. So you've won in some sort of way, and you'll die knowing that."

"I'm not done with—" I hear the singeing of her flesh as she yelps in pain, fingernails digging into my forearms. I can feel the pain, the slicing of my skin as she slides along it so I'll let go.

But it's too late.

I feel too much loss and pain, the enduring way I'll never be able to touch Tobias and Dagen ever again. How my life was always planned to end and be taken away by a woman who perceived to love us only to murder my mother and strategize to take away my father's kingdom.

"Not another word," I warn, looking into her brown eyes, which are no longer black. "I took away your power, I *butchered* it from you. You're not as strong as you used to be without them, are you? You felt your power slip away from you the moment I took each of their lives."

The familiar froth of tears hits my eyes, but I don't hold them back. Instead, I welcome them because it means that they still make *me* powerful.

"I'll *always* have them," I sneer. "They both loved me over you, and you, you foolish hag of a witch, will die knowing that too." She opens her dry lips to say something, but she doesn't get to express the weak words that she wants me to hear.

Instead, I shove her away from me, still on top of the water that arranges her vertical with me.

With every ounce of love, hatred, betrayal, and sorrow, I close my eyes and compel every emotion into Taysa. The burst of igniting flames sounds in front of me, followed by an ear-piercing scream.

Opening my eyes, Taysa is on fire, the water not putting any of it out as her whole body starts to char in front of me. The horrific smell of searing flesh smokes from her body and into my lungs, and I demand the process quicker, wanting to be ceased of her hollers and screams.

The moment she stops, is the minute I drop her back into the sea. My body feels drained of every last drop of energy that I possess, but I hold myself upward, raising my chin in silent triumph over killing the woman that murdered my heart and soul in one day.

And now I can bury Tobias and Dagen in the peace that I'll never have.

CHAPTER FORTY FIVE

Davina

I'm pulled into a million hugs from all different directions. Some hard and gripping, others soft with faint sobs that follow, but my father's is the most fierce of them all. Almost bowing my shoulders as he tightens his hold around my body.

I know that he's aware of everything that has transpired. The secrets I kept from him of Tobias, the trust I built with Dagen, and the love I felt for the both of them.

As well as the aftermath of what happened to keep us all together.

The sacrifices I made hit me all in different influxes, teeter-tottering myself side to side with what-ifs. But the end result of all of it wouldn't be something I could find myself wanting to give up, regardless of how it ended.

I just have to find a way to forgive myself.

"Everyone inside," our father orders, looping me around to his side and underneath his arm. "We have much to discuss."

We follow my sisters inside the castle and into the dining room, all of them silently taking a seat and waiting for my father to proceed with his banter. I sit to his right, as he pulls out a seat for me, and rests in the chair at the head of the table.

"Let me preface by stating how proud I am of each one of you," he asserts, back rod straight as he takes us all in. "At how you all handled yourselves during a situation that you've never had to face before. Then let me tell you how disappointed I am of you keeping things from me again."

Some of my sisters brustle uncomfortably in their seats while I keep my attention on the wooden table in front of me. I can't bare another emotion right now, let alone my father's displeasure of the lies and secrets I looped my sisters into.

"At this table there will be a pact made between us. As a family and the King of Lacuna, I demand to know anything that may shift the dynamic of this bloodline. I may not like what I hear, and maybe I haven't been the most open-minded and patient man when it comes to my daughters. I will work on that if I have all of your words that nothing will remain hidden between us from now on."

A soft chant of agreements fill the room, along with mine, as I hear the whining of the chair my father is seated in as he shifts his weight.

"Which brings me to my next order of business for you girls. Your grandfather has agreed to a few things, should you be in agreement to them, to keep you safe, happy, and above all for your loyalty."

"That's very generous," Atarah quips at the other side of the table to fill in the silence.

"It is, which is why I hope you all agree to them because he doesn't hand out things often to anyone." Clearing his throat, he continues, "He would like you to keep this island while he sets up his own veil of protection for you girls. No one but a Siren may enter nor get through the veil. If someone comes near it, it'd be like hitting a cliff of rocks. You all would be able to come and go as you please."

"That would be...wonderful, Father," Rohana replies, her voice slightly shaky.

"Anyone else think it's a good idea or are you rid of this place?"

"I'm in agreement," Kali interjects. "I'd like to still come here." I can feel her eyes on me, along with a few more pairs. They don't know if I want this place to be buried underneath the sea or protected, so they go with the only safe option, which is what I want.

If I can't have Dagen and Tobias, I want the place they had their last breath at, no matter how difficult or painstaking it'll be.

"I'll pass it along then," my father proceeds. "Which comes to the other offering from your grandfather, the men you sacrificed."

My eyes shoot up to him already looking over at me. He shows nothing, no hope or happiness, always hard to read at times when he was speaking of important matters about the kingdom or us in general.

"Both have implied devotion by giving up their lives freely to keep you all safe and give us a fighting chance to kill Taysa. You all get to choose which man you'd like him to bring back, which I'm going to assume lies in the hands of Davina."

My brows furrow as a tightening in my chest starts to form. "Choose?" It comes as a choke, a broken question that I can't believe he's asking me right now.

I can't pick someone to—

I shake my head violently. "No."

"No?" My father cocks his head to the side. "You don't want to pick—"

"*No.*" I clutch my hands together and try to compose myself in a soft tone. "I'm grateful, honestly I am. But I can't...there is no possible way…" I'm not able to finish my words because there is no one before the other.

I love Tobias and Dagen differently and entirely with every inch of my whole mind, soul, and heart. I'm not capable nor would I ever pick one over the other. I'd rather live without both of them. Not add on to my guilt by deciding who gets to live and stay dead.

"Are you sure?" my father presses. "Davina, this is a once in a lifetime—" I give him a curt nod.

"Yes, I'm sure."

His gaze stays on me a second longer before looking back at the table. "Does anyone else want to say anything about this?"

I follow his contemplation over my sisters, and it falls on Atarah, who is wearing a guilt-stricken look on her face. Her skin almost matches her hair and eyes with the blanched tone it's illuminating.

"Davina," she starts. "This was something I pushed to have happen. They agreed to it but—"

"I was the one who found it though," Isolde interjects. "I couldn't find another way at the time."

"I supported it," Brylee adds. "Because I wasn't going to give up any one of my sisters. I'm sorry, Davina."

I open my mouth, but Kali speaks beside me. "It's better to have one than none. You should pick."

"No," I repeat. "It's done."

"Do not let your stubbornness oversee this opportunity," Father professes. "If you need to think about it—" I'm on my feet, looking down at him while everyone stares at me with Zeus knows what kind of look in their eyes.

It's pointless, my decision isn't going to change.

"Please tell Grandfather that I am extremely grateful for his generosity in letting us keep the island. I love it here, I wouldn't want it to disappear. But as far as the pirate and the

Viking are concerned, I'll kindly decline the offer. Please send my wishes to him."

And with that, I push the chair back with the back of my knees, hearing the wood scrape against the tiles, and leave the room.

Leaving the only hope of seeing one of them again behind.

CHAPTER FORTY SIX

Davina

A school of yellow fish swim together in a flock within my vision, pulling me out of my deep thoughts of inner turmoil that I keep drawing to. It feels like an entire century has passed even though it's been less than two days that I killed Taysa, and today we're burying Tobias and Dagen.

For a pirate, normally a man that had passed away was shrouded in cloth and tied to two cannon balls. The thought of sea creatures eating away at his body made me vomit this morning, so we decided to keep him with Dagen and his traditions.

On a small ship that Sullivan and his men made, we'd send them both off to sea on it after lighting it on fire. It was reserved for men with high honor and, with them being brothers who just found out about each other, I thought them finding peace together might be nice too.

"Davina!" Through the ripples of the water, I hear Rohana's voice somewhere on the beach. Since the veil has fully dissipated, the ocean doesn't burn or irritate my skin anymore, so it has become my new hiding spot when I can't stand being on the island anymore and need space away.

Another holler of my name and I push myself from the ocean floor to peek through the calm waves. Rohana's lavender hair softly blows in the wind, and she cups her eyes against the sun in search for any sight of me, walking down the opposite side of the beach. A slow grin creeps up my lips at her innocence and sweetness that she's provided for me since everything happened. Last night, she wouldn't leave my side, sleeping on the side of the bed Dagen slept in when he was here. It keeps some of the memories but not all.

Blowing the surface of the water, Rohana stands about ten yards to the right of me and a few feet from the small wave that I just orchestrated to crash over her. The moment the cool water splashes over her frame, Rohana is already turning in my direction. Hair matted to her face, dark purple eyes in slits, and a frown trying to make me feel bad.

I do—a little.

But I miss how simple things used to be too. How all of us would spend time together on the beach teasing Atarah about how serious she always is, how Nesrine can't keep her eyes off any man that graces her presence, and how Isolde tries to practice on Sullivan and the other guards but gets scolded and shooed away from her prying.

Another century but it was only a few weeks ago, and two men changed our worlds but flipped mine upside down.

"Did it look like I was hot?" Rohana scolds, brushing back a glob of hair from her forehead. "Because I can assure you I was fine."

"Just trying to keep the sun out of your eyes," I jeer, stepping out of the water as my legs break apart from my tail.

"Thanks." She frowns down at her wet clothes and back up at me, just to watch the annoyance flee her eyes and fill with sadness. "It's time."

I bite the inside of my bottom lip and give her a nod, walking up the beach to the castle so that I can say my final goodbyes. My sisters have spent all morning picking flowers from the garden to decorate around their bodies but insisted I keep Tobias's gun and Dagen's dagger. Isolde agreed to shoot the arrow to light the ship on fire because I was afraid I'd miss.

I knew I'd miss because I won't be able to keep myself together.

Not seeing either of them since the day they took their last breath, I readied myself to see them one last time. Rohana informs me that everything is ready in the large study, where it was quaint and quiet, telling me to take my time as they wait for me outside.

Striding slowly through the large foyer, I turn to my right, focusing on each inhale and exhale.

I'm not sure I can do this.

I don't think I'm strong enough to see the both of them lying together knowing that I did what they wanted me to do. But also that I wouldn't be able to tell them that their sacrifice wasn't for nothing. The emptiness is too great, but to honor them both, I need to.

One last goodbye.

One last kiss to their foreheads.

One last conversation.

About to turn down the short hallway that Father uses when he's here, I slam into another body. Hands grip my arms so that I don't fall over, and when I glance up to tell whoever it is that I'm okay, my heart stops altogether.

"Hey Princess." Brown eyes gleam down at me, full of admiration and relief, as I blink twice to make sure I haven't fully lost my whole mind during the last minute I was left alone.

A heavy exhale leaves my lips. "Tobias?"

"Yeah, it's me." I jolt into the few inches between us and slam my chest into his, wrapping my arms around his waist as I cling to him for dear life.

His body is warm, feeling completely real and not made up in my head. His voice is that mellow tone that he has, always teasing and calm. And his face—

My head jerks to it, examining his temple where I hovered the gun over. "Oh my, your head."

I reach for it, not seeing any holes or blood, but Tobias clasps my hand and wraps his fingers around my palm. "I'm fine, I promise. Good as new."

"You're a ghost."

He smiles. "Not a ghost."

"I've read about this, you're back to haunt me because—"

"Davina, I'm not a blasted ghost." He raises his brows. "You're touching me, aren't you?"

"I think I was thrown in the water too hard," I deadpan.

His eyes narrow. "Would love to hear that story later but still not a ghost."

I squeeze his hand, feeling the rough calluses on the pads of his fingertips. "You're real."

"I'm real, Princess." I hug him again, tighter this time, as a sob that has been struggling to be released does. "Please don't cry."

"You don't even know," I choke out into his chest. "How...hard it was."

He brushes my hair with his hand. "I can only imagine."

"I missed you so much. I blamed myself for—"

"Hey." He pulls me from the warmth of his body and forces me to look up at him with a crook of his finger under my jaw. "I told you already. We both chose to do this. We both chose..." He stops, averting his eyes from me as he stares off into the foyer behind me.

He doesn't have to say it, I already know because I know my sisters and I know my father. I know that they'd pick Tobias over Dagen because he was the safer option, not that they didn't grow to like Dagen but because Tobias has been in my life far longer. He knew me and how much of a pain I was. That he'd always be here, no matter what.

But it still twists that vital organ with the realization that Dagen isn't here.

"I'm sorry," Tobias utters, releasing my jaw and tucking his chin into his chest. "I know it probably wasn't—"

"Don't you dare say it," I scold. Taking both of his hands in mine, I lace my fingers with his. "I would never choose him over you or vice versa. No offense, but I didn't pick either of you."

"That makes me feel better," he mutters.

"Tobias," I coo. "You can't begin to know how much I missed you. I am so happy to see you...it doesn't feel real."

"I think I know." He drags his head back to my eyes. "I missed you from the last moment I remember."

Another embrace with his fingers running up and down my back then a heavy exhale from his chest.

"You need to...I already got to say goodbye." I bow my head in response and pull from his grasp. "I want you to know that I'm okay with everything, Davina. I know you love me, but you love him too, and I'm good with having some of your love rather than nothing at all."

"You're too good to me," I whisper. "Way too—" The red bottle that Taysa was holding is pulled from his back pocket.

"Shut up, Princess, don't make my head bigger than it already is." He offers me the small jar. "Your sisters told me to ask if you wanted this to be buried with him."

I numbly take it and hold it to my chest. "What would you do?"

"I think it'd be a great way for them to get to know each other. Let them be in peace. I'll be waiting for you outside." He kisses my forehead before turning on his heels, leaving me to my own chaos brewing in my head.

My own panic that starts to spread through my whole body.

I still have to fully say goodbye to two people, I just didn't know I'd have to relive one.

CHAPTER FORTY SEVEN

Davina

The smell of leather and a flowery scent wafts around us together as I gaze down at Dagen's peaceful face. Laying on a bed of white sheets with yellow and purple petals surrounding his whole body, he looks like he's already in paradise. The sunlight beams through the windows as a warm breeze brushes some of his long hair into his face.

I push it back, feeling his dry skin and the softness of his mane. My palm skims down the stubble of his cheek, down to the beard he grew along his jawline. I remember the prickled tingle that hit the pads of my fingertips as I studied it. That I loved the roughness and dangerous look about him. It'd be the last time I'd get that feeling, throwing another gut-wrenching punch into my already empty gut.

Clasping my mother's jar tightly in my other hand, I rub the glass as though she might feel it. Possibly to gain some courage while standing here so I don't spend the whole time crying at his feet and begging him to come back.

"This is my mother, Kiherena," I tell him. "She would've loved you. Would have chuckled at your broodiness and how you liked to think you were so tough. She would've seen right through your softness and tried to coax it through, which she would've accomplished. It was hard not to be calm and tranquil with her around." A soft chuckle leaves my lips.

"I mean, I was a rowdy child, she got even myself to quiet down."

Silence answers me, threatening my self-control to weaken.

"I used your dagger," I continue to keep myself talking. "I sliced through some tentacles to get out of a bind with Taysa. You would've been proud, I held up my part of the bargain."

More eerie stillness.

"Two giant eels too, my sister and father took them down while I dealt with your—"

Super inappropriate to talk about his mother like that. I mean, Dagen knew what she was but still...

I clear my throat. "I had a ship built for you. It's not large, but I did an engraving in it. I studied how your clan wrote, all the different symbols and signs that you use, so I carved 'Blood' on the side. No one else is going to call me that, so I thought I'd use it one more time."

Squeezing the glass, I fight back my frustration and the burning sensation of tears.

"Um, my grandpapa said we could keep the island. I can go back and forth when I please, and he made up his own veil, this one won't be broken, of course, nothing but a Siren can get through it. I don't know how that would work because Tobias...he's here."

More quiet.

"That was the other thing. He wanted me to choose between...I didn't choose. It was ludicrous. How could I pick between the two of you? I shouldn't *have* to choose between the two of you because we should've never been here. You should be home with that ugly Edda and running your clan, *alive*."

I bite my lower lip, keeping wrecked sobs at bay.

"You should've never come here. Just stayed where you were at and told your father that he was mad. Dragons—" I scoff. "—who has ever seen a dragon? They're in books, Dagen, *books*. Who would sail so far for a stupid cuff that you know nothing about?"

I glance at his face, which remains neutral.

"You're going to say you don't question your father, well, maybe you should've," I snap. "Now I have to live with this. I have to relive that moment in the water over and over again and feel you leave me. I had to see the life leave your eyes and recall *everything*."

I don't stop the whimper that cracks through my chest nor the tremble that won't stop shaking my body. I need to get this all out so I can try my best to keep moving because I need to make sure I'm *here* for Tobias.

"I hate you," I wail. "But I love you at the same time. I don't know how to get through this, without you, I feel so lost. We should've never started anything, we knew—we knew deep down that it'd never work. And you died over it."

My body leans toward him, my palm planted on his bedside.

"I have to let you go today, and I don't think I'll ever be the same after this. I don't want to love you anymore, but I can't help it. You brought me to life in a way that I never knew was imaginable. You promised me with your eyes before you—" I gasp for air as I continue to seize and shake. "—your eyes. You said this wouldn't be the end, but it feels like it. It feels like I'll *never* see you again."

My palms start to sweat along the red glass that holds my mother's *whatever*, which does nothing for me because she's still dead. *He's* still dead, and the reminders hit me over and over again with no reprieve or mercy.

Straightening my spine, I study the bottle, not even my mother's presence makes herself known. The bottle holds nothing for me but another void.

"What good is it to be the granddaughter of a god if you

can't even have everything you want?" I propel the bottle against the far wall and hear it shatter into a thousand pieces.

Compelling myself to move, I lower my face to his and press a soft kiss to his lips.

"I love you, I didn't say it, but I do. Forever and always, I'm yours." One of my tears falls on his cheek, and I wipe it away. "Stay in peace, my Viking. I'll find you again one day," I whisper. "Just wait for me."

Every fragment of strength I have left moves my body toward the door. My forehead rests upon it when I get closer, painfully aware that this will be it.

Dagen and I will never be in the same room again.

We won't lie in bed together.

I won't hear his cocky mouth and the way his lips feel against my skin.

Goodbye sounds so final it doesn't sit right with us. I can't accept that this will forever be us, but for now, I have to consent to the reality.

I have Tobias.

Given another opportunity to spend more precious time with him while I promise to never take his being with me for granted. He's the only one that will be able to help me get through this.

My strength when I have none.

My hope when I'm forlorn.

And my faith that needs to forcefully be resolute.

My hand touches the brass doorknob, ready to brave through uncharted territory, when I pause at a sound outside the door, a soft shuffle. Backing from the door, I'm on guard still from the incident and fight with Taysa. I'm scared of any aftermath plans or anyone else that she may be linked with to finish her plan of power.

Tobias is outside.

Rushing back toward the door, I almost collapse to the

floor by the next sound. Something that is indescribable and unbelievable to my ears that I'm almost certain I've taken a turn for the worse.

"Blood." I suspend my breathing, repeating the same octave in my head.

Hesitantly, I begin to turn around, so beyond terrified that I'm hearing things I want to hear and still viewing the same sight I just did a moment ago. I built up a thin layer of courage to help me get through just today, I didn't need my subconscious breaking it down before I was out of the room.

Sluggishly pushing himself up, Dagen's eyes are open, fallen on me, and crystal clear blue. I recoil back, my spine hitting the wooden door as I take in his straining muscles to shift himself to sit. His lips that are outlined by his dark beard are wet by his tongue.

Ever since Rohana left me alone in the castle, I've seen *both* of them alive, and that's impossible.

I've seen them both take their last breaths.

Felt the emptiness fill my whole body.

Tobias and Dagen, they were ghosts or spirits back to haunt and torment me for my sins against them.

"Get your ass over here," he recites clear as day. "And kiss your man."

Slowly, I shake my head. "You're not real."

He perks a brow. "Are you already asking me to show you how real I feel inside you?"

"Dagen," I plead. "You're...*dead*." Looking down at himself to confirm that he isn't, he pulls his eyes back up to mine. "Apparently not."

My body begs to get closer, to feel him for myself and see if my skin collides with his or goes through it like mist. He watches me, intently and impatiently, as I expect the worst but hope for the best. My mind cautions me to be ready for my hope to fall flat while my heart implores that it's him.

My Viking.

His hand reaches out for me, locking around my wrist as my body settles in between his thick thighs.

Chest against chest.

Breaths mingled together, and that's all that I get to recognize before his lips are draped over mine, coaxing me to open wider so he can taste me. To possibly know that he's not dreaming either.

I oblige, his expert tongue making its way to mine, dancing and savoring. Making my body buzz with excitement, relief, and confusion.

"You're really here," he mutters against my lips. "You still taste the same."

"How are you here?" I feel him shrug as his arms wrap around my back.

"I don't fucking care as long as this is real."

Another lapse of his tongue along with mine and my mind starts to blur with everything but him.

His thick arms caging me closer. The stubble on his face that my thumb can't help but caress over and over again. The soft intakes of air that he takes in between kisses that heat the apex between my legs.

It feels real. I want it to be real, but my grandfather only gave my sisters and I one option of life.

Reluctantly, I break from him, staring into his lust-filled eyes that look back at me.

"What's the matter?"

I hold his gaze. "How are you here?"

"I don't know, what did you do?"

"I was saying goodbye," I reply. "Yelling mostly."

He cracks a smile. "Why doesn't that surprise me?" He presses a lingering kiss on my cheek and heads to my ear. "What else?"

"I got angry that you weren't responding to me." His

tongue licks the lobe of my ear, followed by his teeth, and I release a frustrated groan.

"What else, baby?"

"I told you that I loved you." His head jerks away like I just burned him.

"You said what?"

"I said that...I love you."

He gives my face a once-over before saying, "One more time."

"Dagen…"

His hold presses tighter, crushing me to his chest. "I want to hear you say it like it was the first time."

"I'm in love with you, you brainless Viking," I snap.

"Ah, yes," he mutters. "Just how I always imagined it." He presses a chaste kiss to my lips. "And so much fucking more."

His fervor heightens, more desperate and wanting, as he owns my mouth. Teasing me with his tongue as his hand squeezes my butt.

I flinch back, my fingers falling to his grueling kisses. "The bottle!"

"The what?" His brows fall together.

"The bottle my mother was kept in when she died."

"Kept in?"

I shake my head. "Well, no, it was her powers."

Dagen gapes at me, obviously lost. "Alright."

"Taysa said the missing cuff went to Tobias because he was the nearest bloodline to her when she murdered my mother. It contained the lock and key she needed to combine everything together. My mother's cuffs with her bottled-up power meant she'd have the power of a goddess."

He blinks at me.

"I threw the bottle against the wall because you couldn't answer me," I convey. "It held her power in it."

"And since I'm the closest...bloodline to Taysa who killed her, it went to me," he finishes.

"It brought you back," I quip with a smile. Dagen's face remains solemn. "What's wrong?"

"Where is Tobias?" My heart nearly floats in my chest at the mention of his brother. How he is actually concerned about him after a short time of knowing him and loathing him for most of it.

"He's outside waiting for you."

Dagen's eyes narrow. "He didn't follow through with the —" My hands fall to his chest.

"He did, he did. Just as gallant and as annoyingly as you did."

"Then how is he still—he's alive?"

"My grandpapa gave us the island and the option for us to choose a life of one of the men that gave up theirs to save his granddaughters."

"And dare I ask—"

"Ask me if I chose him and I'll kill you again," I leer.

"Yes, Blood," he consents with a smirk. "I'll ask him later then I suppose."

I kiss his nose. "He'll be happy to see you."

"Forgive me if I take my time seeing more of you," he retorts, leaning within the crook of my neck.

"We need to go tell everyone," I half-heartedly assert as he kisses the column of my neck then licks up the base of it.

"Later."

"But they're waiting for me to—" His teeth bite down gently into my flesh as he pushes himself off the bed and onto the floor.

"I'm waiting to be balls deep in you right now," he whispers, holding on to my waist for support. "And not even death can stop me this time, Blood."

"You're—"

"And I haven't tasted you in days," he retorts. "You wouldn't keep a man that was just dead from his wish, would you?"

I smile into his shoulder. "No, I guess not."

"Good, because my wish is marrying you today." I try to recoil from his body, but he keeps me where I stand as he compresses more kisses and his tongue into my neck. "Say yes."

I open my mouth, but he groans and thrusts his hard cock into my stomach.

"Say yes, Blood. You know you want me for the rest of your life."

"I want you for eternity," I reply, moving my face so that he has to peer down at me. "Because you know you can't die without me."

EPILOGUE
DAGEN

T*hree years later*

The sounds of screams and giggles loiter on the beach as I peer down the shoreline from the castle, watching Triton barely out of the water before each of my children are hanging off his arms. He visits every other day, Davina won't let them in the water on their own yet without one of us and, even after the years that have passed with Taysa, it's still badly burnt in her brain. She pokes me almost every morning to make sure I'm still real, that I'm still breathing, which leads to me *showing* her I'm still alive, still viable, still completely and utterly hers.

The day I asked her to marry me, she did. Tobias and Triton gave her away, which I use the term lightly. I still get threatened every time my brother comes to visit, still get a hard slam to the back of my shoulder from Triton as a subtle warning to keep his daughter happy every time he leaves. The glares have faded slightly, I'm starting to grow on him, especially since I've done nothing but make Davina and our triplets my priority.

"I'm taking them for a swim," Triton bellows, seeing me looking down at all of them trying to wrestle with him. "Tell my daughter that I have some guards with me to ease her mind. And stop teaching them your barbaric ways of hitting me in the back of the knees to take me down. And how to—" I extend a hand to get him to shut up.

"Got it," I reply. He sends me a glower, which I think turns into a slight smirk as he turns around, taking my two daughters and son into the ocean.

My daughters, Solandis and Dhara, are just like me—loud, bossy little beasts that want to fight all the time. Our son, Gathan, is just like Blood—mellow, patient to a point, and adventurous. Tobias demanded I name our son after him, that I owed him after he gave Davina away and decided not to fight me into a death match to see if I was worthy.

I would've kicked his fucking ass, but I didn't start that argument. Apparently, Tobias and I have the same mouth, pride, and need of being right.

"I told you that I was taking them around the island," Tobias carps from behind me, making my eyes already look heavenward. Since Davina and I had the kids, everyone wants them. Which isn't bad when I crave my alone time with my wife, but I'm always getting chastised by my brother or one of Davina's sisters. "Where are they?"

"Swimming with the King of Lacuna, do you want to argue with him about it?"

"No, I'd rather argue with you about it," he deadpans.

I peer over my shoulder at him as he stands alongside me. "When did you say you were leaving again?"

"Whenever I feel like it." He glances at me with innocent eyes the color of shit. "Are you trying to cut our brotherly love short?"

I scoff. "Don't get carried away."

"I was abandoned," he continues. "I have issues."

"If you use that line one more time…"

"You're going to hug me," Tobias lifts in an exaggerated tone.

I lift a brow. "Go ask Rohana."

Tobias's face falls, and his eyes cut into slits. "How quickly you can turn into an asshole."

"How already you were an idiot," I counter.

"That just added another week to my visit with you, Brother."

"Geezus fuck," I mutter, pushing myself off the banister. "I swear all you do is come here to bother me." I begin striding many, many feet away from him, to go find my wife and not hear how he denies having any sort of feelings for the lavender little Siren that has timidly had a fascination with him since I've been here.

I say she needs her head checked.

Davina wants to get involved and have another wedding.

I tell her to stay out of it.

She tells me to shut the hell up.

"It's the highlight of my visits," Tobias calls out after me as I turn the corner toward the library, where Davina spends most of her mornings reading.

Entering the room, she's laid out on her maroon chaise lounge, red hair all toppled above her as a book is placed in front of her face.

"Did one of the girls kill Gathan yet?" she asks behind her novel.

"Not yet, but I'm about to kill my brother," I convey, reaching for her book and tossing it aside. Her eyes widen as it falls off the lounge and onto the floor with a thud.

"Don't use your brutality on my only edition of—" I'm already pulling her to stand, wrapping my arm around her ass and lifting her into the air.

"I don't want to use my brute force on anything else other

than you," I mutter against her mouth, clasping onto her plush bottom lip.

Davina's legs wrap around my waist, tilting her head to take me deep with her tongue. My body hums while my cock pulsates in my pants, she can take me from irritated or calm to a lust-filled frenzy within a second. Everything about her screams to me, begs me to own and worship her, and I'll happily accommodate each and every time.

Her back hits one of her bookshelves, a sharp hiss leaving her lips as she bites down on mine.

"Taking your words to heart, huh, Viking?"

"Want me to go slower?" I retort into her emerald eyes.

She arches herself into me, her pussy brushing against my torso. "Think you can?"

"Fuck no." My lips are on hers again, demanding and teasing. Our bodies fused together like a puzzle, not complete without each other.

I live for this woman. I breathe, love, and adore her. I'd die for her again, not change a thing about how we came to where we are right now. Frustration and aggravation included.

"Did you tell my father about the new power you acquired?" she breathes into my mouth.

"I don't want to talk about your father right now of all times, Blood," I growl. "I'm trying to drive you mad with wanting me."

She presses another kiss to my lips. "I do want you." Another kiss. "All the time."

"Then let me—"

She pulls her head away. "But you have to tell him."

I huff like one of my children and fix her with an exasperated look. Since being brought back to life from the bottled-up powers of Davina's mother, I've adapted some forces of my own. Ones I've been having a hard time getting used to, if I'm being honest.

Fish annoyingly follow me around when I'm in the sea with the kids. I can sense trouble a league away, and my skin turns into armor when I feel threatened—that's the new one. The one that poor Tobias felt the hard way when he snuck up on me last week.

"I'll tell him later when he gets back with the kids," I tell her, leaning in to kiss her again.

"Promise?"

"Promise. Now let me make love to my wife." She nuzzles her head into the crook of my neck and grazes my skin with her lips.

"Your wife," she repeats. "I still love hearing that off your lips."

"I still love saying it."

"What else do you love about your wife?" She licks the column of my neck, and my cock strains to already be balls deep inside of her.

"I love when my wife doesn't tease me," I rebuff when I secretly love it. Not that I'd ever admit to that in my lifetime.

"What else?"

"I love when I'm so deep inside you that I don't know where I end and you begin."

She chuckles, her lips climbing up to my ear. "What else, Viking?"

"I love you, Blood. That's all there is to know."

The End

Coming up **Next** for the Sinister Fairytale Collection

THE SINISTER FAIRY TALES COLLECTION

LEGEND

M.R. LEAHY

Acknowledgements

First and foremost (and this might be vain as hell), to me. I never in a million years thought I'd be able to jump into left field and write fantasy. I never believed or imagined that I'd be able to build a world and characters that weren't either boring, didn't make sense or were just bleh.

So to me—*high five*.

To my boys—the late nights, the headphones in constantly, the need to stop me because you were hungry or wanted to tattle-tale on the other one—I love you. You might not understand it yet but all of this is for you.

To my other half—the support has been unreal. The random shaking of my head and you asking me what's wrong. When you ask me how it's going and I sigh in response. Thank you. Thank you for believing in me. Thank you for being my cheerleader. Thank you for just being you.

To my Bae—my other half, my venting session, my therapist and one of my biggest supporters—I couldn't do half of what I do without you. The phone calls and messages all day long. I am so honored and blessed to go on this ride with you that we call "the hustle". Thank you for believing in my art and knowing that I could do this. Siren wouldn't be what it is without you.

To my betas—those words though! The cuss words, the Facebook messages, the love for these characters, it means the absolute world to me. Thank you for taking the time to read my baby. Siren is unlike anything I've ever done and you went in with an open mind and helped tweak and shape the story. Thank you so much!

To my Athenas—my girls! I love you all so SO much. From our Savage Thursday posts to whatever else we go in there and do, I love the family we built. The excitement keeps me going. You're the gasoline to this hustle and I'm so grateful for each and every single one of you.

To my new readers, the ones whose never heard my name —Hey! I'm Hazel, nice to meet you. I hope you enjoyed this story and the retelling of The Little Mermaid. Ariel is one of my favorites since I was a little girl and I'm so happy that I got to give her a slight little tweak towards a dark and more "off the wall" retelling of the story. Thank you for taking the time to read it.

EVERYONE THANK YOU SO MUCH! IT MEANS THE WORLD TO ME. <3

Love,
  Hazel Grace xoxo

Hazel Grace Social Media

f ♥ ⊙ g BB a

Made in the USA
Monee, IL
01 July 2020

35352973R00203